KEEP Me Still

DELUXE EDITION INCLUDES THE NOVELLAS
LET YOU LEAVE and HOLD US CLOSE

Keep Me Still

Cover Design by Sarah Hansen of Okay Creations
Editor: Mickey Reed
Formatted by E.M. Tippetts Book Design

Published in the United States of America
First electronic publication: August 2013 by Caisey Quinn. (Special Edition)
Second electronic publication: November 2013 by Caisey Quinn (Deluxe Edition)

www.caiseyquinnwrites.com

LET You Leave

a novella

For Sommer

I'm in awe of you. Of your strength and your ability to handle a condition that would be more than most of us could bear. I consider myself fortunate to know you and beyond blessed to call you my niece.

I try not to live in the past. But sometimes the past lives in me.
-James Ford

I can feel them watching me. Warily. Wondering if something will happen that will cause me to snap like before. Some of the looks say they pity me, a few are intrigued, and the rest try to pretend I don't exist because they don't want to think about it. About how one second things can be perfectly normal and the next it can all be torn to shreds. Destroyed, ripped apart, and broken. Like me.

The hallway is crowded but no one bumps or brushes against me. An overstuffed backpack barely grazes me, and it's the closest I've come to physical contact in years. This time last year, the steady hum of voices and shouts would have caused me to crawl inside myself and hide, but I can handle it now. I work on my deep breathing like Dr. McCalla taught me and it helps.

Even though I've made it through the first two weeks of my senior year without a single incident, everyone still avoids me. No one wants to accept that they have no control whatsoever and tomorrow they could be walking down these halls just like me. Stared at like a ticking time bomb about to blow. Or ignored completely.

What they don't realize is I'm fine now. Mostly.

I raise my hand twice in Physics and Dr. Anders looks right through me both times. Even though I'm in the front row. Same thing happens with Mrs. Tatum in English. And Dr. Sands in Calc.

Maybe I should hold up a sign. I'M OKAY NOW FOR FUCK'S SAKE!

Then they couldn't ignore me. Whatever. I promised Aunt Kate I would try, and try I did. For two long and painful weeks. I'm over it. On Monday I'll sit in the back and sink down into myself like before. I'm invisible anyways.

~ **PAST TENSE:** Used to place an action or situation in the past. Or in my case, tense shit from the past that just won't go away. ~

CHAPTER One

Layla

"You're not really wearing that?" my aunt asks as I pull the dark hoodie over my jeans. "For God's sakes, Layla. It's eighty-five degrees outside."

I sigh and pull it back off, not really wanting to argue this early in the morning. And especially not with Aunt Kate. She's tried so hard to help me. She's been patient and supportive, and I know she spent a ton of money on designer clothes for my return to school. I'd get a job so I could pay her back but she'd just have to drive me to it. I know she wants me to be happy more than she wants money. Not much I can do for her in that department either.

Who knew trying to convince everyone you're normal could be so freaking exhausting?

"Fine," I tell her as I pull on a green short-sleeved plaid button-up over my black tank top instead. "Better?" I ask.

"Much," she says with a smile and hands me a cup of black coffee. "Maybe put some eye makeup on. You look a little tired."

"Thanks. You look fabulous today by the way, as usual," I call out to her back as she and her designer suit and perfect raven-colored up-do saunter down the hall. Leaning over to glance in the full-length mirror propped against my closet door, I see that she's right. I look tired. Probably because I haven't had a decent night's sleep since I was thirteen. I scrub a hand over my face and look around for some eyeliner.

Poor Aunt Kate. She just doesn't get it. It wouldn't matter if I spent all morning getting ready, putting on makeup, straightening my hair, and picking out the right outfit. I could probably strut down the hall in my underwear and it wouldn't make a difference. The image almost makes me giggle. And cringe. The last two weeks were hell. And here I was about to do it all over again. How did I get this far-gone?

CHAPTER *Two*

Landen

"It's just for a year," my mom says, like that makes it better.

"Yeah, just my senior year. No big, right?" I feel a little guilty smart-mouthing her when I know it isn't her fault. The sadness in her eyes keeps me from any further bitching I had planned. Taking the plate she hands me, I wrap it in newspaper before lowering into the nearly full box.

"Hope Springs is nice. It's gorgeous actually. You'll like it."

"Yeah, I'm sure I will," I mumble as I close up the box, folding the sides in to keep it closed without tape. "And if I don't, I can always drop out and become a professional mover."

"Landen," she sighs, putting the bowl she's holding down. My mom winces, and I lean over to hug her tiny frame. Lately she seems to be shrinking. At six feet, I'm average size for most guys, but she's barely five feet tall. I don't even hug her too tightly for fear I might break her. "Promise me, no more fighting when we get to Hope Springs. You're eighteen now and—"

"Have you eaten today?" I break in as I step out of the embrace, knowing she hasn't because all of the dishes are packed.

"I'm okay. Why, you hungry?" she asks as she writes "kitchen" on the brown box with a black Sharpie.

I just laugh because she knows I can always eat.

"I'll order a pizza." She reaches for the phone but we've already had it disconnected so I hand her my cell and smile as I lift a box to carry it outside.

"No mushrooms," is all I say as I step out of the kitchen.

Once I'm outside, I put the box of dishes into the back of the rental truck and look around. Mountains and a cool breeze greet me. I liked Colorado. More than Texas even.

Tuck and Danni will come by later and say goodbye and it will suck. They're the first real friends I've made since elementary school and leaving them blows. Even worse than leaving the guys on the soccer team.

Part of me wishes I could just load the crap in the truck, grab Mom, and go. Make a clean break. But thanks to the Internet, it doesn't really work like that. Fucking Facebook. Not that I haven't considered just going off the grid. But Danni would be pissed. And hurt. And I've hurt enough people for one lifetime.

"Dude, this fucking sucks," Tuck says, slapping a hand against the rental truck I'm leaning on.

"I know," is all I say. Danni is quiet, but I meet her gaze and I know she's holding back tears. She's not my girlfriend or anything, but we both know we were on the verge of…something. Lifeguarding at the pool all summer, we bonded. And so did our mouths. And a few other essential body parts.

"So what's the deal with this new place? Will you still play soccer or what?" Tuck kicks a boot against the tire of the truck.

"Don't worry, buddy. I won't cheat on you." I smirk and he fakes a punch at me. Danni rolls her eyes. "Yeah, the Colonel called, probably told them it was their civic duty to let me have a late tryout or something since we're moving because he got stationed there."

"I don't understand why you and your mom have to go," Danni says quietly. "Your dad's never even home but he totes you both around like luggage." She doesn't raise her voice but I can tell she's mad. Apparently so can Tuck because he takes a few steps back to give us some space and busies himself lighting a cigarette.

"Danni," I say, reaching out to hug her. "It's shitty, I know." Resting my chin on top of her head, I inhale her clean girly smell. Flowery shampoo and some kind of vanilla body spray I saw her putting on in the pool's locker room. Makes me want cookies. "My mom wants us to stay together, like a real family." I snort because we both know there's no such thing.

She looks up at me with big brown eyes and I can see the hurt in them. I know from a few of our late night chats that her dad walked out not long after she was born. "Yeah, I get that," she tells me, and I want to kick my own ass. *Nice, O'Brien. Just pour some salt in the fucking wound while you're at it.* "Call or text and let us know when you make it to Hickville."

I give her one last hug and Tuck salutes me. As they pull away in his old beater, I realize it doesn't really matter if I say goodbye to people or not. Shit hurts either way.

"Nice truck," someone shouts as I get out of the new Silverado my dad bought me. For my eighteenth birthday, he said, but we both knew it was a suck-it-up gift for my not giving him or Mom too much hell about this move. Or it's a warning to keep my mouth shut. With the Colonel I never know for sure.

"Thanks," I holler with a head nod in the direction of the voice.

A few female heads turn as I make my way into the generic school building, and I don't even bother to keep the smirk off my face. "Here we go again," I mutter to myself.

Finding the office wasn't too difficult since it was right inside the entrance. Now I've got the new kid special in my hand: a schedule and a map complete with locker number and combination.

"Hey, man. You Landen O'Brien?" a guy's voice greets me as I find my locker and fidget with the lock.

"Last I checked," I answer, wondering if this is an actual welcome or the typical there's-only-room-for-one-cocky-badass-in-this-school-so-watch-your-back greeting.

"Dwight Wilkins, but everyone calls me DW," the blond guy says, reaching out to shake my hand. I take it, giving it a firm shake before cramming my bag into my locker. "You're trying out for the soccer team today right?"

"Yeah, after school."

"Cool."

Jesus. Hope Springs must be a small town if this random dude knows my business already.

Apparently he isn't done. "I don't play with the grass fairies, man, but our football team just lost its kicker, and I've seen some YouTube videos of you scoring some badass Beckham goals." He shrugs. "So if you want to come play with the big boys, I can talk to coach."

For a moment I'm seriously confused. An insult, and not even an original one, tucked into a...what exactly? Compliment? Proposition? Whatever. It's too early for this shit.

"Yeah, man. I'll get back to you. When my fairy costume comes back from the cleaners." *You're welcome, Mom.* The old me would have just decked his ass on principle.

DW, or whatever his name is, laughs and grins widely. "Cool," he says. "Who you got first period?" he asks, nodding at my schedule.

"D-dub! You already harassing the new guy? What the hell, man?" A stocky dark-skinned kid comes up and claps me on the shoulder before I can answer. "Welcome to Hope Springs, soccer boy." I shrug out from under his grip. "Pay no attention to D-dub. He's just scoping out the competition," he says loud enough for the other guy to hear. "Miles Cameron, but everyone calls me Cam."

He holds out his hand. What's with this place? Nicknames and handshakes a requirement?

I shake it and adjust my bag on my shoulder. "Yeah, uh, it's been swell, and I appreciate the welcoming committee shit and all," I say to both of them. "But I'm gonna head on to class now. Later."

"Whoa, hold up," Cam says, coming up behind me. "Seriously, DW can be a real dick – that's what the D stands for actually." I almost laugh. "But he's cool, for real."

"Sure he is," I say, not believing him and not really caring.

"It's just the last new guy snagged his spot on the team and made a play for his girl, so he's trying to make sure you're not…" But I don't hear anything else he says. Because this girl—if she's real—just walked into the building and I can't stop staring.

Fuck me if this is "DW's girl" but I can't help myself. At every school in the past few years, I've ended up hooking up with some random who attached herself to me for whatever reason. It always just worked out that way and I never gave it much thought. Trish in Texas, Amy in Ohio, Lyndsie in Florida. None of them really mattered much until Danni in Colorado, but we were mostly just friends who happened to make out occasionally. I never actually *noticed* any of them until they forced me to. But this girl—this girl I cannot look away from.

"Who's that?" I ask, gesturing at the girl with hair a color I don't know how to name. From a distance it looks a normal shade of blonde, but the light coming in from the door behind her makes it look almost white and also like she's glowing. I know I'm staring but she doesn't seem to notice. In fact, she doesn't seem to notice anything as she makes her way towards us. Cam takes my schedule and points at a door to my left, but it can wait. "Seriously, who is that?" I ask again because I have to know.

"Who?" When he looks up, she's gone, disappeared into the classroom I'm about to go into, and I'm wondering if I imagined her.

CHAPTER Three

Layla

It's the third week of school and I'm wearing the outfit Aunt Kate wanted, but I'm done sitting in the front of the class and raising my hand and all that crap just so everyone can keep pretending I don't exist.

I sink down into a seat in the back near a window and stare out until I hear my name called for attendance. I raise my hand up and lower it quickly so I can go back to staring.

The window overlooks the courtyard below where we have lunch when it's nice out. It's sunny and the sky is a light shade of blue. Some kids are horsing around in the courtyard and I'm pretty sure they're freshmen. The irony isn't lost on me.

Pretty day, carefree people, sun shining. But it may as well be pouring rain in the middle of the night. Familiar black thoughts cloud my mind, and I wonder why I have to endure this torture. Why I survived. My mind wanders. Right back to the same place it always goes.

It's cold out. My mom pulls my red pea coat around my shoulders and makes sure it's buttoned. "I'm not a baby," I tell her, jerking out of her grasp. At thirteen I can button my own coat for Pete's sakes. I'm still a little pissy that my friend Tara couldn't come. My dad walks around our silver SUV and glares at us for a second before smiling.

"Can't even let me be a gentleman for one night," he huffs. I roll my eyes because he knows my mom isn't the type to sit around and wait for anyone to open her door.

"Sorry, hon," my mom says. I don't know if she's speaking to me or to him.

Snowflakes whirl a random dance around us, and my parents walk briskly down the deserted street, flanking me. When I was younger, we held hands and they would swing me. I used to think I was flying. The sidewalk is cracked and uneven, and a chain-link fence borders the side away from the street. For the first time I notice that downtown Atlanta is kind of ghetto.

"We should've parked in the garage," my mom mumbles under her breath. Our heads are down to keep the wind from blowing in our faces so I don't hear my dad's response. Every year we go see The Nutcracker at the Atlanta Civic Center, and every year my dad refuses to pay the twelve dollar fee to park in the garage by the arena. This year it's colder than usual, and my mom is annoyed but I think she's just grumbling because she likes to get a rise out of my dad.

"Where's the fun in that?" my dad asks, grabbing my hand and nodding at my mom over my head. She clasps my other hand.

"Oh no," I say, attempting to pull my hands out of theirs. "I'm not a baby anymore." I'm small for my age, but geez. I'm not a little kid. Why do I have to keep reminding them of this? They've been present for all thirteen of my birthdays.

They both squeeze tighter, and I give in and giggle as they pull me into the air.

Tires squeal to a stop on the road beside us and I'm put down roughly mid-swing. "Give me your wallet," a stocky man coming towards us in a black hooded jacket sneers at my father. My mom pulls me hard behind her so I can't see his face. Her fingers dig deep into my arms, and I'm not sure if I'm the one trembling or she is. My heart pounds so hard it's making me sick and my vision is blurring.

When a new student stands to introduce himself, I'm pulled from my thoughts. Because for some reason, the whole time he's talking about how his dad is in the Army and they move a lot, blah, blah, blah, the tall dark-haired guy is focused completely on one person in the room. Me.

When I get home, I see that Aunt Kate has left a note. She had to go into the office and there's lasagna in the fridge from last night's dinner. I tried to eat my lunch at school under the magnolia tree where I usually sit but I was kind of creeped out by the strangest sense that someone was watching me, so I'm starving.

New Guy staring at me in class obviously got to me more than I realized.

I do my homework while I eat and try to ignore the shadow of loneliness looming over me. Aunt Kate has made so many sacrifices for me—working from home, which probably cost her becoming a partner at her firm, paying for private tutors so I didn't have to go to school and risk having another public episode, and constantly taking off to attend all of my therapy sessions. Surely I can handle a few hours alone. I'm nearly eighteen years old for God's sakes. Next year I'll be at UGA or maybe Southern Cal if I'm lucky, and maybe then

I can escape the memories that haunt me. Leave the broken, damaged girl I've become behind.

I'll be fine. Just like I've been fine these last few months.

Smiling proudly to myself as I finish my homework and push up off the couch, I think about how far I've come. I even smiled at New Guy today at school. And I noticed how cute he was. He had a slight dimple in his left cheek when he smiled back.

Gathering my dishes, I walk towards the kitchen. And that's when it happens. A car on the street backfires and all my hard work is out the window.

The darkness comes first, and I am vaguely aware of the beautifully terrifying sound of glass shattering against the tile floor as I go down. I hope there won't be a bloody mess when Aunt Kate finds me.

"Layla? Jesus," I hear from somewhere far away. But I'm too far-gone to answer.

When I wake up, I'm in my bed feeling a little drained and whole lot out of it.

"Good morning, hon," Aunt Kate says. She leans over and checks something on my forehead.

"Another one?" I ask, though I already know the answer.

"Yeah, scared me to death," she says, lowering herself onto my bed. "You can stay home today."

"No," I answer, surprising us both as I throw the covers off. "I said I was going to get through this year and I meant it." If I couldn't make it through a year at Hope Springs High School, how the hell would I make it on my own in college?

I can see in her eyes that she wants to argue but she doesn't. "Okay," she says, standing to leave so I can get dressed. "Here." She hands me two white pills and a glass of water. "Oh hey. I picked up a really cute dress at a boutique downtown yesterday. It's hanging in your closet with the tags still on in case you don't like it."

"I'm sure I'll love it," I tell her as she steps out.

Just as I stand up and stretch, a pain shoots through my head and I feel the bandage with my hand. I should be used to this by now. Wincing, I make my way to the closet.

"Layla?" my aunt says, startling me as she pokes her head back in.

"Hm?" I find the maroon sweater dress and it is really cute.

"Your mom would be so sad to know that I'm letting you just 'get through' your life."

"I know." My head lowers at both the mention of my mother and the blatant, painful truth. "But it's the best I can do right now."

I've made it almost three full weeks into my senior year. Maybe I haven't made any friends like Aunt Kate wanted, but I'm doing just fine on my own. I'm busy congratulating myself on my brazen independence and fortitude as I grab my Physics and English books out of my locker to take home. I'm the only senior that has to ride the bus, but that's fine with me. I grab my iPod and earbuds for the ride, but just as I turn to leave, a large set of shoulders block my path.

"Excuse me," I say, angling around the guy who obviously didn't get the memo to avoid me.

"This is the weirdest school," he mutters to himself, causing me to look up. And up, because he's pretty freaking tall. Bright green eyes and a dimple smile down at me from under a mess of black hair. "Maybe you can tell me what's going on, because I feel like I'm in the Twilight Zone."

"What?" is all I can manage in reply.

"Look, I'm just going to say it because I'm new here and I have nothing to lose." He smiles again and his perfect white teeth practically gleam. Ah, yes. New Guy from English and History class. Now I remember. Cocky, athletic, and moves around a lot.

"Please, unburden yourself," I say, leaning against the locker and hugging my books to my chest, hoping he won't cause me to miss the bus.

"What the hell is going on in this place?" He looks around at students brushing by us on their way out. His expression says he finds them lacking. Maybe New Guy isn't so bad.

"Um, I'm not sure what you mean exactly." *Because I am the last person you should be asking. I have no idea what goes on around here, New Guy.*

I step aside to get around him again, but he tilts his head in this way that makes me feel bad for him.

"I don't really talk to many people, so I have no idea what's going on around here." There. Now that I've explained, I really need to get to my bus.

He lets me by but continues to follow. "School's over. What's the rush?"

"I have to catch the bus," I say, knowing I probably won't make it at this pace. He doesn't say anything else but walks beside me until we get outside. Just in time to see the last bus pull out. Great.

Aunt Kate's at the office today, and the last thing I want to do is call and make her leave work. I'm chewing on my lower lip and contemplating my options when New Guy speaks.

"Can I give you a ride?"

No.

"Yeah, um, that'd be great. It's not far," I tell him as I throw up a silent prayer that he's not secretly a murderer or something.

"You really shouldn't accept rides from strangers," he informs me with a frown. My stomach tenses in fear that he's mocking me. Retracting his offer. "Landen O'Brien," he says offering me his hand and a mischievous grin.

Something about the gesture and his expression has a smile lifting the corners of my mouth as I look up into his light green eyes. They're nearly crystal clear in the center but darker around the edges. "Layla Flaherty," I say, taking his huge warm hand in mine. I've only shaken hands with doctors so I'm unprepared for the tingling sensation that hits me.

Despite the overwhelming surge of electricity flowing through me from his touch, I'm oddly relaxed as we walk to his truck. I feel like I can breathe. He's new here. He doesn't know what happened to my parents or that everyone in school treats me like a pariah. Or why.

CHAPTER *Four*

Landen

Her southern drawl is so damn sexy it shoots straight from my ears to my dick. She needs help getting into the truck, and I am a gentleman, *of course*. But placing my hands on her waist to boost her in makes me realize how delicate she is. Fragile almost. And how much I don't want to let go. I'm never going to be able to figure this girl out. Her eyes gave me a firm no when I asked if she needed a ride but her mouth said yes. Mmm, her mouth is amazing. Watching her bite her lip in frustration nearly killed me.

The whole ride I'm tripping over my tongue, trying to find something clever to say. The normal Landen O'Brien act probably won't cut it with this girl since she obviously doesn't give two shits what anyone else thinks. By the time she points me to her street, I've relaxed a little but I'm getting lightheaded from trying to inhale her warm peach and honey scent. Rich and sweet and enticing as all hell. To make matters worse, she's wearing a dress that bares smooth, tan legs begging to be wrapped around me.

I shake my head to remove the inappropriate images assaulting my mind and clear my throat. "So you like classic rock?" I ask, hoping she does. She's barely said a word and I'm struggling to fill the silence. There's a bandage marring her forehead. I want to ask about it but it looks like she worked pretty hard on arranging her hair to cover it so I keep my mouth shut.

"I do," is all she says. But I sense she's smirking at me. "Why do you ask?"

"Uh, no reason." But there is a reason, kind of a lame one, and I think she knows what it is.

"You have it, don't you?" Her smile makes my heart rate speed up, and I'm nervous around a girl for the first time in my life.

"Have what?" I ask, still content to play dumb in case this is a sore subject. I'm probably like the millionth person to make the connection. I watch helplessly as she snatches my iPod off the dock in the dash. Shaking my head, I give her an apologetic grin when *Layla*, the rock version, comes through the speakers.

"Ah, and you have the ballad as well. Good for you." She's still smiling and it's doing something to me. Either it's because of me, or because of my iPod, whichever. I could seriously watch this girl smile forever. The thought kind of freaks me out but I shrug it off. When I pull into the driveway she says is hers, I want to think of a reason to keep her talking. And smiling. Like, maybe for the rest of her life. Because apparently this girl makes me lose my mind.

I'm tempted to walk her to her door and ask if I can drive her to and from school every day. But the coach told me I made the soccer team today so I know I won't always be able to drive her home.

"So, um, thanks for the ride," she tells me, unbuckling her seatbelt.

"No problem." For a second our eyes meet and it looks like she's about to say something else.

Again, I scramble to fill the quiet. "Um, hey, what happened?" Gently, my hand brushes her hair to the side, and I'm off balance just from the realization that she's letting me touch her.

"Oh, nothing. I'm clumsy," she says with a shrug, but her hands are shaking. I know I need to go, to back off. I can sense it. But there's something about her ocean-colored eyes that keeps me from looking away. Something's up. I know. I've had bandages and casts and injuries I couldn't tell anyone about either. But the tension is literally rolling off her so hard she's nearly vibrating. Subject change needed.

"You don't ever drive to school?" I ask, noticing there's no car in the carport.

"Don't have a car," she answers shortly, and then she looks away and pushes her door open before I can ask any more questions. As much as I want to beg her to stay in the truck a little longer, tell me more about her name, her favorite music, the bandage on her head, I can tell she's overwhelmed. So I let her leave.

She doesn't look back once. My eyes are glued to the image of her walking away from me. It doesn't make sense, but it bothers the hell out of me the whole way home.

As I turn onto my own street, I remember I was supposed to stay after school today for team workouts. I promised my dad I'd stop by the football field to try out for the open kicker position. Shit.

Mentally, I make up an excuse about feeling sick and leaving school early to tell the coaches when I see them tomorrow. But when I pull up and the Colonel's truck is in the driveway, I know I'm fucked.

CHAPTER *Five*

Layla

"You're home early," Aunt Kate says when she comes home a few minutes after me.

"Yeah. I, um, got a ride." *Please don't ask.*

"From?" she asks, sorting through the mail she brought in as she tries to look less interested than she really is.

"Landen O'Brien." And I can't help it. Saying his name makes me smile. It also fills me with a warmth I'm not expecting. I have a friend. Sort of.

At that my aunt drops the mail and stares at me. "Is he cute?" She's probably turning cartwheels in her mind at the possibility that I might stop being an antisocial loser after all. *Keep the dream alive, Aunt Kate.*

"No, he's got this messed up grill and he walks like a hunchback actually." Shuddering for emphasis, I bite my lip to keep from grinning.

"You're hilarious, Layla," she says with an eye roll.

"If I'm being honest, he's way better than cute," I say quietly, fully aware that my face is on fire. "And he's new so…" So he doesn't know what a complete freak show I am. But then, my aunt doesn't know how bad it is for me at school so I just keep the rest of that sentence to myself.

"Lay, I know you don't want to hear this, but if you do keep hanging out with him, you're going to have to tell him about—"

"It was a ride home. Relax."

But for the rest of the evening, I can't relax. All I can think about is Landen O'Brien's sweet smile and the way he blushed when I put on *Layla* in the truck. Maybe Aunt Kate was right. Maybe I can do more than just *get through.*

CHAPTER *Six*

Landen

"Here, put this on it," my mom says as she hands me a pack of frozen mixed vegetables for my jaw. Needless to say, when the Colonel called the Hope Springs High School athletics department to find out how my football tryout had gone and to get a game schedule, he was pretty pissed when the coach mentioned that I was a no-show.

"He just has high expectations for you, Landen. You know that," she reminds me. Making excuses for him has always been something she was good at. But her eyes don't meet mine. Believing her own excuses, however, she's not so good at.

After I'd run the five miles for my punishment, I was stupid enough to make a comment about how it was my life, and with the Colonel already pissed, he jacked my jaw in response. I should know better by now. And I'm big enough to take him. But I just really don't care anymore. And it would kill my mom to see us whaling on each other. So I suck it up like I've always done.

CHAPTER Seven

Layla

Landen's mouth feels so good on mine, I almost feel sorry for any girl who'll never get to kiss him. Almost. His hands are big and strong and warm on my hips, pulling me closer, as if that's possible. My body molds into him, and a fleeting thought races past. What if someone sees us?

I glance around the parking lot to see if anyone else has arrived but we're still alone.

Until a black Chevy Avalanche with tinted windows pulls up beside us. A man in a dark hooded sweatshirt jumps out and I recognize him but I don't know from where.

"Landen," I murmur against his lips but he's lost in our kissing. His tongue presses into my mouth when I open it and I can't breathe. "Landen. Landen, stop." I shove my hands against his chest but he doesn't budge. His hands wrap around me, clutching me closer, too close. The man's coming closer but I can't warn him.

"Landen!" I scream but it's too late. The gunshots ring out and his body goes limp in my arms.

"Landen!"

I wake up grasping my comforter. It's twisted and gripping me so tightly I can barely move to disentangle myself.

Well, that's a new twist on an old nightmare. Sweat soaks my T-shirt and I try to shake the images on the way to the shower. And now, for reasons that aren't his fault in any way, I don't want to see Landen O'Brien ever again.

Which is unfortunate, because as soon as I step outside, he's there. Waiting for me. Leaning up against his truck, looking like a magazine ad. Just like in my nightmare, I'm suddenly smothered and unable to breathe at the sight of him.

I've built walls around myself, carefully constructed them piece by painstaking piece to keep myself safe. Unseen, unaffected. And Landen's grinning at me with a smile that might as well be a sledgehammer. When he opens the truck door for me and our eyes meet, his intentions are clear. He wants to tear down those walls, send them crashing all around me. Doesn't he realize they'll bury me? Us?

"What are you doing here?" Part of me is relieved. I was starting to think I'd dreamed him. But the thought of dreams reminds me of my nightmare last night, and my stomach tightens as bile rises in my throat.

"Thought you might like a ride," he answers, smiling that tempting smile at me.

"This going to be a regular thing?" I ask out of curiosity as he helps me into the truck.

"Do you want it to be?" He arches an eyebrow and I can't help but smile back.

"If you do."

"I do," he says and his grin widens. "I think we're married now."

"You don't have to do this, you know. I can handle the bus."

He's still shaking his head when he gets in on his side. "Yeah, who doesn't love a bus full of obnoxious freshmen who don't shower after gym class?" He winks at me and my insides start to tingle. What is it about this guy? Why do I feel like he was sent here just for me?

"Actually I'm going to have soccer and football practice after school Monday through Thursday, but I can at least give you a ride *to* school and I can take you home on Fridays."

"You play both?" I didn't even know you could do that.

His jaw clenches, and it might be my imagination, but his knuckles are white on the steering wheel. "I play soccer but the football team needs a kicker so I'll be doing that too, probably."

Maybe he wasn't just sent here for me after all. "I think maybe I'd like to see you play. Both, I mean." I glance out the window so I don't have to see his face when he tells me I can sit with his girlfriend. Or so he won't see mine. He clears his throat and I turn back to him.

"Maybe some days you can stay after school and check out practice, maybe catch a few games? When I don't say anything, he hurries on. "I could drive you home afterwards."

"By the time games end I'm sure my Aunt Kate could come get me so you don't have to go out of your way."

"No, I meant, I *want* to take you home after. So you can give me the play-by-play on what you think of my skills," he says with a wink.

"Hmm, I'll think about it," I say, doing my best to keep my voice even though all I'm thinking about are the "skills" of his I've already dreamt of.

Chapter Eight

Landen

"Hey, Landen?" Layla asks me as we head into school. I can sense her literally shrinking back against the looks we're getting.

I fight the urge to put my arm around her. Barely. "Yeah?"

"What were you talking about yesterday when you said things were weird here?"

Oh yeah. *That.* My bombed pick up line. So glad she remembered. "Uh, well." I run a hand through my hair and decide to just lay it out there. "I thought I was going to have to fight someone just to talk to you. I mean, you're literally the prettiest girl I've ever seen in real life and I expected guys to be like, lined up. But you were always alone every time I saw you so…I've decided guys here must be blind and dumb." There, that didn't sound too bad. I watch her, waiting for her to tell me I don't have a chance.

She smiles this tiny little smile with only one side of her mouth turning up. Then she bites her lip and her grin widens, lighting up her entire face. And I can't breathe. No one has ever smiled at me like that. Like I'm the best thing that's ever happened to them.

"That's very sweet, minus the fighting part," she says finally and I exhale.

"Yeah, well, sweet's not something people usually call me, but from you I'll take it."

I watch her roll her eyes. "Gee thanks. And what do people usually call you?"

"It varies. But most of it's a little harsh for your ears."

The pouty expression she gives me makes it hard to think straight. "And what do you know about my ears?" she asks as we reach her locker.

"Hmm." I lean over and tuck her thick hair behind each so I can thoroughly inspect them. And also just to have an excuse to touch her. They're petite and adorable, just like I expected them to be. "Yep, just as I suspected. Way too delicate to hear some of the things I've been called," I say softly into her right ear. The shiver that runs up her spine shakes us both. For a second, I'm too stunned to speak. Just barely touching her and whispering in her ear made her shiver. Me—I made her shiver. And God help me, I want to do it again and again.

"Landen," she says softly, and I know I'm screwed. She's giving me that look, the goodbye look I've given girls time and time again.

"My bad," I say, pulling back. "Sorry I got all in your space. It won't happen again." She looks lost, and I want to punch myself for overstepping so soon and making her uncomfortable.

"It's not that, it's just—"

"It's okay. I get it." I take a full step back. But then she surprises the hell out of me. Right there in the crowded hall, she grabs my shirt and pulls me in close. Much closer than I was to her ears. I'm instantly drunk on the sweet scent of Layla Flaherty. Drowning in her wide ocean-colored eyes. It's a miracle I'm still upright.

"It's just, I don't really have friends here. I haven't had a friend in a long time. I like you, Landen. A lot. And I want to be friends."

I'm fucking ecstatic to be this close to her. But the friend word keeps cutting into me. I work hard to form a coherent thought while lost in the depths of her open vulnerable stare. "I want to be friends too, Layla. And I think I might like to be more than that. But if you're not interested—"

"I'm interested," she says, cutting me off as her eyes flash and burn into me. "But I might not be…ready for something like that."

"Then I'll just stick around until you are ready," I tell her with a grin. Her muscles visibly relax and I risk taking a step closer. "Patience has never been my greatest skill though, but I promise to give it my best shot."

"And what is your greatest skill?" She's backed up against her locker, and I want so badly to show her the answer to that question.

"I'll show you. When you're ready."

CHAPTER Nine

Layla

It takes me nearly all of first period to get my heart to beat normally again. Didn't help that Landen sat right behind me and his breath was tickling my neck. Whenever he's even remotely close to me, I seem to develop superpowers. My spidey senses kick in or something because I'm hyperaware of his every move. And constantly fighting the urge to grin like a crazed lunatic.

For the first time, someone sees me. And he's new, an outsider, and he thinks there's something wrong with everyone else instead of what I know deep down. There's something wrong with me.

I should tell him, like Aunt Kate said. Let him cut and run before it's too late. But I'm desperate. When he started to walk away from me today, I felt like I was drowning. So I reached out and grabbed him like the life preserver that he is. And he seemed to like it.

When I find him waiting under the magnolia tree where I normally have lunch, I can't help but smile. When he smiles back, my breath catches in my throat, and I think about his promise earlier. *I'll show you. When you're ready.*

"Okay if I have lunch with you?" he asks, and I notice his eyes look three shades brighter in the sun.

"Sure. Long as you don't mind your friends staring like you've lost your mind."

"What friends?" He looks honestly perplexed, like he didn't spend his first few days having lunch with the social elite of Hope Springs. Whatever. Never look a gift horse in the mouth and all that. I lower myself onto the grass across from him. "So, is your middle name Roxanne?" Landen asks after swallowing his first bite of pizza.

"Very funny."

"I was just curious," he says with a shrug. But the gleam in his eye tells me he was teasing. "I'll tell you mine if you tell me yours."

"Faith," I say softly. It was my mother's name, but there's no reason to pull this sweet, seemingly carefree guy down that dark alley of despair.

"Layla Faith Flaherty," he announces. "I like it."

"Glad you approve." I've almost finished my bagel when I realize he hasn't told me his middle name. "We had a deal," I remind him, and once again I'm treated to that adorable dimpled grin.

"It's Landen," he replies, and I know I've been tricked.

"So you go by your middle name then. What's your first?"

The thick knot in his neck bobs as he swallows his last bite of pizza. "Ah, a guy's gotta have some secrets. Plus, if I told you everything about me upfront, what reason would you have for hanging out with me tomorrow night?"

I almost choke on my water. "We're hanging out tomorrow?"

"Sure, that's what friends do, right?"

Heck if I know. "Okay, *friend*. And what is it we're doing tomorrow?"

"Grabbing dinner after practice? Maybe a milkshake too if you can guess my first name."

"And you've found my weakness," I say, clasping a hand to my chest as my heart threatens to pound straight out of it. We're joking around. I know that. I'm not completely mental. But my mind is asking a million questions a minute. *A date. He's asking me on a date...sort of. Or is he?*

"Milkshakes?"

I force myself to breathe normally. "Yeah. There's a place in town, Our Place. It has the best malted triple-thick chocolate shakes on the planet. And they give you the silver cup with the extra that won't fit in the glass and they have this marshmallow cream whipped topping…Okay, now I kind of want one."

"Layla, we've known each other for two days. Don't you think it's a little soon to have a *place*?"

I roll my eyes, surprised at how easily I'm able to joke around with him. Maybe all these years in social solitary haven't left me completely lame after all "That's cute. But no, it's actually called *Our Place*. An elderly couple owns it. They've been married for like fifty years and that's what it's always been called."

For the first time since we met, Landen looks a bit unsure of himself. "Um, so do you want to hang around after school tomorrow and watch practice or you want me to pick you up when I'm done?"

The lunch bell rings and I stand, grateful for an interruption so I can contemplate his offer. Okay, so I realize it's a simple question, and yet I don't know how to answer. If I stay after then it's casual, like we grabbed a bite to eat on the way home from school. But if he picks me up it's a date, right? I have zero experience with this type of situation whatsoever. Now would be an excellent time to have some girlfriends.

"Someone's overthinking things," he whispers in my ear as we head back inside.

I release the lip I didn't realize I was biting. "I think I'll just stay and watch you practice. That way I can break down my thoughts on your skills during dinner," I tell him as we round the corner into the crowded main hall.

His light chuckle warms me from the inside out. "Oh, I see. So I buy you food in exchange for criticism?"

"Precisely." Landen's smile is so wide it's infectious. I'm still smiling when he slides into the seat next to me in English. It's almost distracting enough that the negative thoughts I've lived with for so long don't attack, but as I sit waiting for Mrs. Tatum to begin the lecture, they do.

He sat at the popular table his first few days here. Laughed and joked with them. Hangs with Cam and the DW guy. Plays football and soccer with the same people who've basically blacklisted me. And there will be cheerleaders flocking to him any day now. If they haven't already. I'm fidgeting with my pen and chewing my lip off when Landen reaches over and stills my hand with his large warm one.

"There a pop quiz today or something?" he asks quietly. Mrs. Tatum begins speaking so I just shake my head.

Surely someone with a smile that genuine and an ability to calm me with his touch isn't plotting with the cool kids to hurt me. He doesn't seem like the type to ask me out on a fake date to humiliate me for the enjoyment of his peers. Though, the people he's been hanging out with so far would probably find that kind of thing utterly hilarious.

For the next hour I pretend to take notes as diligently as possible, but I can't stop thinking about the choice fate has seemingly thrown into my path.

Should I trust Landen O'Brien? Can I? Or will he just leave me behind, hurt and broken, like everyone else?

Sitting on the cold metal bleachers makes me wish I'd asked Landen to pick me up instead. I'm starting to regret my clothing choices. Last night when I told Aunt Kate I was staying after school and going to dinner with Landen, she made me try on ten different outfits, finally settling on a smoky gray lace-covered dress with my black knee-length riding boots. Fall is warm in Georgia, but once the sun begins to set, all bets are off.

After the impromptu fashion show, there was the Spanish Inquisition that left me wishing I were a guy. Surely Landen's parents didn't grill him about me like the torture I endured all through dinner.

Aunt Kate was excited and a bit wary. I could relate. Still can.

He comes off the field sweaty and winded. When his gleaming eyes meet mine, I smile, trying hard to ignore my lungs as they deflate. *Pull in oxygen, dang it.*

"Hey," he huffs out, clomping up the bleachers to where I'm still sitting. "I'm gonna grab a shower and change. You want to go sit in the truck and warm up?"

"Um, yeah, that'd be good," I say, and he reaches in his bag to retrieve his keys. Following him down the bleachers, I let myself admire his muscular frame. And his perfect backside. I can imagine how the muscles would ripple and shift if his shirt were off. How the sweat would bead and fall down those broad shoulders. My mouth goes dry just thinking about it. I'm actually pretty relieved to know that part of me exists. *Congratulations, Layla Flaherty! You're a normal teenage girl after all!*

"I won't be long," he says, his voice startling me from my ogling.

"O-Okay," I stammer, turning towards the parking lot as he jogs out of sight into the locker room. My back heats suddenly, and I know I'm the object of someone's murderous glare. I can hear my name being mumbled by a group of nearby cheerleaders. I think I hear Landen's too, but I keep walking.

As soon as I close the door and crank the truck, music fills the cab. It's the Red song that was playing this morning when we pulled into the school parking lot. *The Best is Yet to Come.* Seems like it actually might be. The intense scent of Landen's sharp, clean cologne surrounds me, seeps into me, and I can't get enough. The heat just intensifies it and I'm kind of hoping it'll linger on me so I can breathe him in even after he drops me off. This boy is making me weird. Or something closer to normal. I'm not sure.

I'm scrolling through his iPod, chuckling at the mass amounts of 80s music when he finally emerges from the locker room. Striding purposely towards his truck, towards me, he grins, and something that's been building inside of me releases, spreading through me with a slow and satisfying heat I want more of.

Something is happening to me, something I didn't even think I was capable of. I'm a little scared and a whole lot nervous. The tingling anticipation comes to an abrupt halt when Alexis Bledsoe, queen of Hope Springs High School herself, and a redhead whose name may or may not be Jena Becker join him. The two converge on him like vultures to a carcass and I watch helplessly as his grin fades.

They're saying something to him and he's listening but still walking. He nods politely and only stops when Jena reaches out and touches his arm. Heady feelings of jealousy possess me for a second but I shake them off. *Friends.* That's all we are. And even if we are more than that, he can talk to girls, let them touch his arm. I just wish it wouldn't be these particular girls. The ones who've spent so much time and energy hating me and aggressively recruiting for the Stay Away From Layla Flaherty committee.

It's none of my business so I force myself to go back to scrolling through his music. The names of his playlists almost make me laugh out loud. *Workin' Out. Makin' Out. Rockin' Out.*

I'm shaking my head when a click and a cool gust of air startle me. He gives me a tentative smile as he tosses his bag in the back of the cab and climbs into the driver's seat.

"Ready?" he asks, and his eyes are hooded and dark, like he knows he's asking if I'm ready for so much more than dinner.

Taking a deep breath, because he is and I think I am, I nod.

"Then off we go."

CHAPTER Ten

Landen

All through our first date we talk about soccer. And she doesn't once ask about the girls that accosted me outside the locker room while she watched from my truck. I'm waiting for it, but she never says a word. I should be glad that she's cool and not territorial like some girls but…I want her to be. And yes, I realize how fucked up that is.

I saw how her smile faltered and she lowered her gaze when they flanked me to tell me about some party at one of their houses this upcoming weekend. But she's carrying on like nothing happened so maybe I was imagining things.

"So there's a party tomorrow night, after the game," I inform her just before I take a huge bite of my cheeseburger. She smiles but her eyes go dim. "You want to check it out?"

"I'm not really a party kind of girl," she informs me with a look that says she barely managed to leave *dumbass* off the end of her sentence.

"Yeah, I mean, I can see that. But we're friends right? Friends do things together like grab dinner, watch movies, and go to parties."

Something that looks like anger tinged with hurt flashes across her face, and I quickly evaluate my previous statement.

"Sorry. Didn't mean to be a condescending dick." This girl apparently has no friends, for whatever crazy ass reason, and I just told her in a special ed teacher voice what friends are supposed to do together. *Smooth, O'Brien. Don't make plans for second date.*

My apology falls flat and I really am sorry so I reach across the table to stop her hands from fidgeting.

"Hey. Seriously, I didn't mean it like that." She's staring at our touching hands like they might catch fire any moment. "Tell you what, I'll tell you my real first name *and* I'll buy you that milkshake."

Her lips curl sweetly upward and I'm at a loss for words. That look, the one that says I've made her day, made her life, stops all mental function. When everyone looks at you like they're sizing you up to see what they can get from you or they're trying to contain the sheer disgust and disappointment the mere sight of you causes, you start to avoid people's direct gazes altogether. Until a girl you didn't know existed two weeks ago looks at you like you're the only reason she's had to smile in her entire life.

"Landen?" Shit. She's been talking and I missed it.

"Yeah?" No use pretending I have the slightest clue what we're talking about.

"Chocolate, with extra cherries," she says and I'm staring at her mouth. *Pull it together, man.*

"Right, got it." I drag myself out of our booth and walk to the counter. Sliding onto a stool next to an old-timer, I order Layla's shake and wait. Glancing back at her, I notice she's not looking at me but at the man next to me. Turning, I notice he's hunched over, slowly counting out change on the counter with unsteady hands. His jacket could use a wash and he probably hasn't shaved or bathed since the nineties.

Wow, I did not see this coming. The fact that there are homeless people in perfect little Hope Springs blows my mind. Before I have time to second-guess it, I pull a twenty from my wallet and signal a waitress.

A tired-looking but attractive brunette about my mom's age saunters over. "Your shake'll be ready in just a sec."

"Yeah, thanks. I'm gonna take care of his too," I tell her with a nod at the man next to me. "He needs another coffee, a slice of that pecan pie, and uh, um, a double cheeseburger."

"That okay with you, Clyde?" the waitress says to the man. The tension in my chest releases when I realize he's a regular. Not that it makes him any less homeless but at least he has somewhere to go where he's welcome. That must be nice.

"Make it to go," he sneers and then turns his watery glare to my face. "You feelin' good about yourself now, kid?" Shit, he's mad.

"Listen, mister, I'm trying to impress a girl here. So if you could just play along, let me be a Good Samaritan this once, I'll let you buy mine next time."

"Hell. What are you? Six foot, six two? I doubt I could afford you, boy." He grunts but his weathered mouth is attempting a grin.

I laugh and offer my hand. "Landen O'Brien, sir."

"Clyde Riley," he says, clamping his trembling hand into mine surprisingly firmly. "You new around here?"

"Yes, sir. My father is a Colonel in the Army. We just moved here from Colorado."

"No shit? I served back in my day. Took a bullet to the shoulder and couldn't shoot anymore so they kicked my ass out. Honorable discharge, they called it. I'll give you one guess how honorable it was. Takes a lot of dedication to be a Colonel."

I bite my tongue so I don't say anything disrespectful about the Colonel. Nodding, I take the shake and extra cup of cherries the waitress brings to the counter.

"Pleasure to meet you, Mr. Riley," I say, and he clasps me on the shoulder.

"Gonna take a lot more than that to impress the looker you're with."

I laugh. "Yes, sir. I'm gathering that," I tell him before returning to my date.

I make her guess my first name before I hand the shake over. She takes a drink and I am so gone. Lost. Her smile, the little sigh she lets out, the way her eyes light up. All of it. I'm broken down and rebuilt. And nothing will ever be the same again.

CHAPTER Eleven

Layla

Our first date involves milkshakes, my favorite, so I'm smiling at him more than I normally do at anyone. Probably more than I've smiled in my entire life.

"How about I give you a hint and let you guess?" Landen asks as he lowers himself into our booth, carefully holding the frosty glass my shake is in, the silver cup with the extra, and a small, clear container of bright red maraschino cherries.

"Oh-kay," I answer slowly, unsure as to what exactly he's referring to. I'm still reeling from watching him buy dinner for Clyde. And talking to him like they were old friends. Respectful. Genuine.

Somehow, Landen O'Brien is becoming precious to me. I may have zero relationship experience but I'm pretty sure it's not supposed to happen this fast.

On a napkin in the middle of the table, he's using my extra cherries to make a letter. It's an R.

"Ralph?" I guess.

He shakes his head so I keep at it.

"Remy, Rudolph, Rusty?"

His brow creases and he stares at me. "Seriously? How many guys do you know named Rudolph?"

I smile and continue. "Rick? Roger?"

He shakes his head and adds a Y.

"Ryan?" I pop a cherry into my mouth.

"Your prize, pretty lady," he says, handing me my shake finally. Taking a hard swallow of the frozen chocolaty goodness, I close my eyes and barely stifle the shiver from the cold.

"Your name is really Ryan O'Brien?" God, parents are so weird sometimes. Not that I would really know, but why would they give him such a rhyme-y name?

"Ryan was my mom's maiden name and she's an only child. Her parents passed away right before I was born. I guess it was her way of making sure her family name was carried on in some way or something."

Oh. Well. That makes perfect sense. "So why do you go by Landen?"

"Because my parents were smart enough to know a rhyming name might be grounds for an ass-kicking, or at least a few teasing jingles. And we move a lot. Figured it'd be ammunition for picking on the new kid."

"I kind of like it. Sounds like a weatherman or something."

Landen laughs, and the deep timbre combined with the icy cold of my shake have chillbumps prickling my skin.

"Well, I'm pretty shitty at science so a degree in meteorology is probably out."

"Ah, that's too bad. What a waste of a perfectly catchy name. Sportscaster maybe?"

He laughs again and I'm quickly becoming addicted to the sound. And to the companionship. It's intense in a nerve-rackingly electrified way and yet relaxing in a comfortable way I can't understand. We barely know each other and yet…I don't have time to finish my thought because Landen reaches over and swipes some whip cream from the corner of my mouth. His finger is so hot it leaves a burning trail in its wake.

"Sportscaster is a possibility," he says quietly, and I'm too busy reeling from the memory of him touching my lips to say anything. "So, Layla Flaherty, what are your future career aspirations?"

"Um, Lawyer maybe, like a child advocate one," I answer. "Or special education teacher or counselor of some sort."

"Ah. Quite a list you got there. Any idea what college you'll go to?"

"UGA is a possibility. It's where my parents went and where my Aunt Kate graduated from law school. She teaches a night class there. But I'm also thinking of going somewhere as far from Hope Springs as possible. Like maybe California." *Please don't ask why.*

"Nice. UGA is a good school, decent football and soccer teams."

"You planning to play sports in college?" It seemed like a perfectly normal question, or at least I thought it did. And I wanted to get the focus off of me. But Landen's eyes go dark and his mouth draws inward.

"Guess so, if I get a scholarship."

He's stopped meeting my gaze and I'm confused. "Soccer or football?" I ask, hoping not to upset him further.

"Soccer if it's up to me. Football if you ask my dad." His look gets even darker and I feel like I've hurt him somehow. Reaching across the table, I put my hand on his. He jolts upright and his eyes brighten.

"Sorry, I didn't mean to pry," I say, holding his stare.

He exhales loudly and relaxes under my hand. "It's not a big deal. I just want to play soccer somewhere, maybe even overseas. Maybe I'll follow you to Cali." He pauses to wink at me before continuing. "But the Colonel has dreams of West Point. Playing football and learning military strategy. Because that's what it takes to be a man." His voice goes all deep and loud at the end and I know he's mocking his dad. He rolls his eyes but they're still strained.

"There are worse things than having a dad who wants the best for you," I say softly.

An emotion I don't recognize flashes in his eyes and he raises an eyebrow but doesn't say anything. *We both have secrets*, I think to myself. *Wonder if they'll bind us together or tear us apart?*

A week after our date that might not have been a date, the morning announcements start off like normal. Lunch menu, volleyball, football, and soccer scores. I'm only paying attention to see if they mention the six goals Landen scored last night.

Watching him play is like watching a hurricane. He's an unstoppable force of barely contained energy tearing down the field. And seeing him after, sweaty, breathing hard, eyes bright, and an adorably self-assured smile spreading across his face…I can barely think straight around him as it is, but after soccer games I feel like he might just grab me and run away caveman style. And the terrifying part is, I would probably let him. Happily.

Football games are a whole other story. He's controlled, stiff, and almost unfeeling before, during, and after. He's good, and he's made some amazing field goals, but he's like a robot version of himself. I asked once why he even bothered with football when it was so clear he loved soccer so much more and he looked so angry I wished I hadn't brought it up.

"My dad is the reason I play football," is all he said, and that was the end of that. Something is definitely up with him and his dad, but I figure if he wants to talk about it, he'll tell me. It's certainly not like I can hassle anyone for trying to keep secrets.

My name on the announcements tugs me out of my contemplation about Landen and his dad.

"What did they say?" I twist around to ask him.

"You're supposed to report to the practice field after school," he whispers.

"Why in God's name would I have to—" but I don't get to finish because Mr. Baxter nails me with a glare as he begins taking attendance.

The day seems to drag on as I contemplate why in the world I'd have to go to the practice field after school. I've never played a sport or been in the band or anything that would've necessitated my spending time on the practice field. The only reason I even know where to find it is because we run on the track around it during P.E.

Landen tells me after sixth period that he has to check out early but that he'll be back in time for practice if I want to stay and catch a ride home with him.

After school I grab my stuff and head to the practice field where the soccer team is warming up. The football players are on the actual field, and I'm not sure which one Landen will be on first. He usually just gets a few kicking drills in and then heads over for soccer, but today I see him standing around with the guys on the practice field. As I'm looking around for anyone who might have needed me here for whatever reason, his eyes meet mine and my face begins to tingle as if I've been stung by something.

The shy smile teasing his lips tells me it's him. Somehow he bribed someone to get it on the announcements. The whole soccer team turns and each of them holds up a sign. It takes me two tries to focus and read the message.

Layla Flaherty, will you go to Homecoming with me? Pretty please, with a cherry on top?

Landen's the only one without a sign. He strolls past them, coming to a halt just in front of where I'm standing, blushing and dying.

"In case you need a little more incentive," he says, holding out a Styrofoam cup I recognize from Our Place.

"Chocolate?" I ask.

"With extra cherries," he adds, smirking because he's so proud of himself. But I can see the wariness in his eyes. And once I take the shake from him, his hands seem at a loss for something to do.

I take a long swallow of my drink and it's the best milkshake I've ever had. My face has gone completely numb and my knees are weak, but I'm enjoying watching him squirm. He's an exceptionally confident guy, I'm pretty sure his ego can sweat it out a few more seconds.

"Layla?" he asks, tilting his head in that way that makes me want to kiss him in front of the whole soccer team.

My mouth curves into a wide grin and I nod slowly, because of course the answer is yes. And every cell in my body is alive with panic. Because I couldn't have said no if I'd wanted to. And also, because I'm falling a little bit in love with Landen O'Brien.

Chapter Twelve

Landen

The sight of Layla in a deep purple strapless dress and black fuck-me heels makes my mouth go dry. And dammit, I do not want to take this girl to Homecoming. I don't want to take her anyplace where other guys can see her.

She sashays down the stairs and I'm struck dumb by how different she looks from the first time I saw her. Her chin is tilted up and her shoulders are back like she knows she could make me come just by looking at me the right way. I don't know where that girl went that hid behind her hair and tried to disappear into herself but I don't exactly miss her. But now everyone's going to see what I saw all along. And I have a seriously shitty feeling that the fight I braced myself for when I first saw her is coming after all.

"You look..." I don't finish because there aren't words for how she looks. Now I can see why that Shakespeare dude made up some of his own. Her smile is like a club to my kneecaps, and I'm grinning like an idiot.

"Let's go outside," Layla's aunt demands, ushering us out the door so she can take enough pictures to wallpaper the entire house. She pulls Layla aside for a moment, and it looks like they're arguing so I turn away. Before I have time to wonder what the deal is, she's back to snapping away.

And I hope she's not using zoom because some inappropriate things are happening in my black dress pants. And I'm the bravest son of a bitch alive when Layla leans close to me for each new pose. My fingers skim her bare shoulders, the zipper of her dress, and as I help her into my truck, I chance a hand on her backside just to see where she'll draw the line. I must've done something right in a past life because she doesn't. Though her cheeks are a little pinker than before when I join her in the cab of my truck.

"Bad news," I say with a shake of my head. "School burned down. They're holding the dance at a local hotel. I got us a room."

For a split-second her eyebrows twitch and I can see the *is he serious* in them. But my grin gives it away and she slaps my arm.

"You're an idiot," she tells me with a laugh.

"Yeah, but I'm your idiot," I say without thinking. Her potent peaches and warm honey scent has me intoxicated and unable to control myself or my mouth. To hell with it. It's not like she doesn't know. Like everyone doesn't know.

"Are you?" Her eyes widen. Okay, maybe everyone doesn't know.

"Layla, seriously? What, you think I skip school to buy milkshakes for just anybody?" I clear my throat because this is going way heavy sooner than I'd planned.

She's biting her lip and it's making it hard to concentrate on my driving.

"If you want to make it safely to the dance, please stop doing anything that draws attention to that perfect mouth of yours." There, now it's out there. If she didn't know how I felt before, she sure as hell does now.

Her face is full-on blood-red now, and it turns me on even more knowing that I put that color there. But I am so wrong if I think for one second I'm in control. Layla scoots over, close enough that her side touches mine, and rests her head on my shoulder. She sighs into my ear and I have to stifle a shiver of my own.

"Just so you know," she says, "I don't *accept* milkshakes from just anybody."

I force my throat to swallow as I kiss the top of her head. Yeah, I knew that. And the weight of what she's really saying presses down on me. I'll be her first everything. Date, boyfriend, kiss, and however far she'll let me go. I don't think I've ever been anyone's first anything before. God, please don't let me fuck it up.

Before I've even finished my silent plea, the Colonel's face flashes in my mind. Of course I'll fuck it up—that's all I'm capable of.

CHAPTER *Thirteen*

Layla

Being invisible was safe and I took it for granted. I see that now as Landen and I enter the gym.

Being seen is dangerous. As the eyes of nearly two hundred students watch us walk onto the dance floor, I kind of want to go back. Because I know what they're all thinking. Why her? Why would the hot new guy, star of both the football and soccer teams, want anything to do with her? I feel like sending a mass text to all of them. *Heck if I know. Text me back if you figure it out.*

But Landen doesn't acknowledge any of them. He just pulls me onto the dance floor and wraps his arms around me like we own the place. Either he's rhythmically challenged or he just doesn't care, but regardless of the song playing, we sway slowly back and forth, pressed against each other like no one else is even there. Under the crisp coolness of his cologne on his shirt, I can smell *him*. Landen smells like fall. Like a warm breeze just before dusk that sends leaves floating free. Breathing in so hard I'm lightheaded, I pull him even closer.

A low noise halfway between a growl and a groan escapes his throat, causing my body to warm to a dangerous degree. My stomach plunges, like I'm leaning over the edge of a giant black hole and I just looked down.

Jason Mraz sings about not giving up as I clutch Landen's neck a little tighter. *Kiss me*, I think forcefully at him, tilting my chin up to let him know I'm ready now.

For a second I think he's going to. His face lowers and his hooded stare meets mine. But then he steps back, straightening and pulling away.

His voice is so sharp it startles me. "I'm gonna grab a drink. You want something?"

Um, yeah, I want something. *You.* "Sure. Punch or Coke or whatever's over there." I slink off the dance floor behind him, wondering what in the world just happened. Is he just seriously parched or what?

Lingering on the edge of the dance floor, I watch as he gets two cups of punch and heads back towards me. He's barely a foot away from the table when Jena Becker steps directly in his path. Give the chick a point for persistence. Her short red one-shouldered dress is two sizes too small but she's curvy enough to pull it off. She places a perfectly manicured hand on Landen's arm and I feel like a flabby slug compared to her.

I can't hear them over the blaring Ke$ha song that just came on but I can tell she's flirting her ass off. Landen's nodding a lot but he's focusing more on his punch than the half-naked girl next to him. I can't help but be a tad pleased about his obvious discomfort.

He finally says something and she sneers in response before stomping off. I'm almost worried about her breaking an ankle the way she's punishing those stilettos. Almost.

When Landen finally makes his way back to me, he looks apologetic and maybe a little confused at my stupid grin. "Let me guess? There's a party after," I offer, knowing that's what Alexis and Jena are always hounding him about. Why girls want a guy to get drunk and molest them is beyond me. If the guy doesn't make an effort sober, anything he does under the influence probably doesn't mean much.

"Uh, yeah," Landen stammers, and for the first time he looks at me like maybe he wants to go. A lump threatens to form in my throat and I'm almost relieved that he didn't kiss me and that we're still "just friends." Even if it is just friends complete with air quotes included because we both know it's more than that. But at least I can give him a chance to back out before any major lines are crossed.

"Well I don't know what she was so angry about. You can drop me off and swing by the party after, right?"

There. Take your out if you want it.

But it's hurt and confusion that settle onto Landen's features. I sip my punch and pretend not to notice.

"Yeah, I could. Or I could tell her to give it a goddamn rest already because my girlfriend isn't really a party kind of girl." His words linger in the air and mine don't come right away. "Hope that's okay because that's what I said." Landen shrugs but I know he's waiting, leaning over that gaping canyon just like I did earlier.

So I grab his hand and jump. "It's a shame you tell Jena Becker how you feel before you bother telling the aforementioned girlfriend."

Landen turns, his expression open and hopeful. "What I told Jena was wishful thinking. What I'm asking you now is if you're interested in the position. The pay sucks but the benefits are decent."

"Hmm." I bite my lip before taking another drink of my syrupy sweet punch. And then I inhale deeply to gather all of my courage. "I think I'm going to need further explanation of these *benefits* you speak of."

Landen flinches with shock and I stare at him straight in the eye, still hoping to convey my thoughts telepathically. *I'm ready.*

"This was fun but I'd like to discuss my benefits package privately," I tell him. Truthfully, I can feel the angry glares of Jena and her friends as they huddle nearby. And I want the kiss he owes me from earlier, but not in front of anyone. It's ours and I'm not sharing.

Chapter Fourteen

Landen

We dance for over an hour, and it takes all the self-control I have not to throw her over my shoulder and sprint to my truck when Layla says she's ready to go.

As it is, I'm walking pretty damn brisk-like and practically dragging her behind me. She's giggling so I think she's okay with it.

The double metal doors are all that stand between me and heaven. That is until Cam, DW, and Brent Becker cut us off.

"What the fuck did you say to my sister?" the very angry center for the Hope Springs varsity football team demands. *Aw hell.*

"I told her I wasn't interested and that I have a girlfriend, obviously." I nod back towards Layla, who's damn near cowering behind me. I will not fight in front of this girl. *I will not fight in front of this girl.* It becomes my mantra and I cling to it as I focus on controlling my breathing. But Brent's all bowed up and I can tell Cam and DW know what's coming. They came to try and stop him but neither one will do much more than try.

"Listen, I don't want my sister dating the faggot-ass kicker. But if she likes you, you'd be lucky for her to give you the time of day."

I. Will. Not. Fight. In. Front. Of. This. Girl.

My fists clench and I take a deep breath. "You're right, but lucky for you, the faggot-ass kicker is taken."

Brent's jaw ticks a few times and I know he's itching to punch me. *Feeling's mutual, buddy.* But Cam and DW pull him back, and he whirls around and punches the metal doors instead. The impact rattles my bones and I'm thankful that it wasn't my face that took the brunt of the blow. Not that I haven't taken much worse.

I don't know if there is a glitch in the space-time continuum or what the hell happens but time literally slows. A gust of outside air flies in as Brent storms out, and I turn to tell Layla we'll go out a different way so dude doesn't get the impression I'm following him, looking for a fight. But she isn't behind me. Or rather, she isn't *standing* behind me.

"Layla?" I scream, dropping hard to my knees. She's on her back on the floor, tremors rocking her body, turning into full-on convulsions. And I'm fucking helpless and panicking. Her eyes roll back in her head and I grab her to me.

"Call a goddamn ambulance, 911, or what the fuck ever," I scream at DW and Cam but I don't wait to see who pulls out their cell phone first. Something warm and wet leaks onto the floor around her. I want to cuss the universe but I know that won't help her. I've never seen anything like this in my life. Never been so scared. Even when my dad wrestled me down and kicked and hit me until I blacked out. And I was only ten then. Up until now it was the worst thing that had ever happened to me. It's not even a close second to this.

"Shh," I whisper in her ear, trying to drown out the sound of Cam calling it in. "It's okay, baby. You're okay, Layla." *Because you have to be. I need you to be, dammit.* "I'm here. You're safe. It's okay. I got you," I keep murmuring over and over in her ear until finally she goes still.

We're surrounded by teachers and chaperones and students, and I know now this is what they were talking about with the Freaky Flaherty shit. And I want to burn the motherfucking gym down Carrie style knowing this has happened before and they made fun of her for it. If I weren't here, who would be holding her? Or would she just be a spectacle for them to gawk at?

The Colonel's voice answers me. *If you weren't here, this wouldn't be happening at all.*

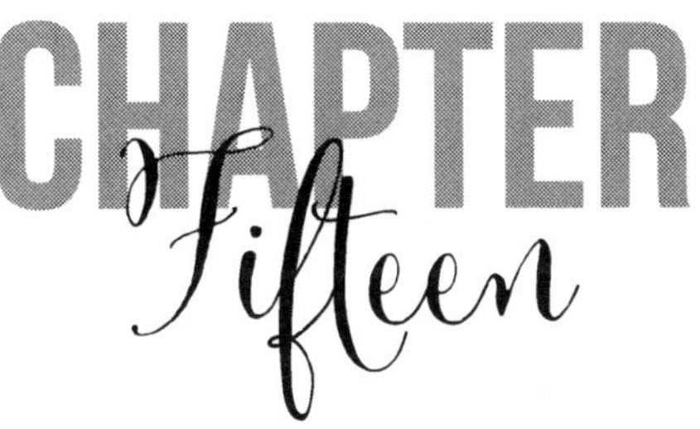

Chapter Fifteen

Layla

I wake up in a gown I don't have any recollection of putting on under a thin blanket and the nauseating glow of fluorescents. Great.

The back of my head hurts like someone took a hammer to it, so I ease off the pillow. Aunt Kate stands and crosses the room, looking tired and ten years older than she is.

"No," is all I say when I see Landen dozing in a chair next to me.

"You're okay, Layla. It was a bad one, but you're fine."

"It's okay, baby. You're okay, Layla. I'm here. You're safe. It's okay. I got you," I hear in my head even though Aunt Kate isn't talking.

"Oh my God," I groan, burying my face in my hands. It happened again, in front of everyone just like freshman year. Even worse, it happened in front of *him.* Tears burn in my eyes but I choke them back. Shame shoves my head down and I wish Landen wasn't here so I could cry in peace.

"You're awake," he says groggily. The clock across from me is blurry but judging from the placement of the hands, I'm pretty sure it's a little after midnight. I'm hooked up to an IV but I know from previous experience it's just to keep me hydrated. A heart monitor is clamped on my finger and the machine beeps steadily. Guess it's not programmed to recognize when a heart is breaking.

"I didn't want you to know," I whisper, and Aunt Kate nods and gives me a weak smile as she backs out of the room.

"Layla," Landen says, standing and coming closer. "I already knew. Alexis Whatsherface told me my first week here."

His words are supposed to comfort me. I can tell by his expression, but they ruin everything. Well, they ruin whatever was left after my spectacularly humiliating meltdown.

"Landen," I croak out, wishing I had some water. "Please go." I close my eyes because I'm drained and exhausted and don't have the strength to handle the hurt on his face.

It all makes sense now. Understanding dawns on me, the pieces of the puzzle snapping together so loudly it's a wonder I don't have another episode. That's *why me* out of all the girls he could've chosen. Same reason he bought old Clyde dinner at Our Place. Landen's a bleeding heart looking for charity cases to rescue.

"Layla, what did I—"

"I'll call the nurse and have you removed. Go." My energy is fading fast and I'm running out of strength to hold back my tears of weakness, of defeat. I tried to hide from what I was and I lost. It found me. I don't know what I was thinking. I am what I am. Can't hide it forever.

Landen doesn't move. He just stares at me open-mouthed and wide-eyed. I clamp my fingers down on the red call button and a beep echoes overhead.

"Do you need something?" a woman's voice echoes through the speaker, and I almost break down right then. Yes, I need a different life. One where my parents don't get gunned down in front of me, one where I don't have seizures that cause me to spaz out and piss myself in front of the whole freaking school. And lastly—listen close, universe—one where the boy I'm falling in love with doesn't date me out of pity.

"I'm going," he mumbles, ambling away from me like I've kicked him. "Call me when you feel better, okay?"

I force myself to nod, even though I know I won't. "Can I have some water please?" I ask into the air once he's gone.

I hang on until the nurse brings the water. "Thank you," I say, wanting to tell her to send my Aunt Kate home too. But I don't. And I don't even take a drink of the water she brought because I'm at war fighting off my tears as soon as she's out the door.

CHAPTER Sixteen

Landen

She woke up in the hospital and the first thing she did was kick me out. If she didn't look so weak and exhausted, I would've put up more of a fight. But it was clear, for whatever reason, the only thing she wanted when she finally woke up was for me to get the hell away from her.

I storm out of the hospital in a blind rage. I need to find Brent Becker. Or pray the Colonel's home and go there and piss him off good. I need to hit. To be hit. To kick and fight and hurt and be hurt. I need the kind of pain that makes sense. The kind that cuts and bruises and breaks bones. Not this fucking internal shit that twists and aches and makes me insane. And helpless. If this night has a theme, it's 'Landen O'Brien is a worthless, helpless piece of shit that ruins everything.' Maybe that's the theme of my life.

Somehow, through my rage-filled haze, I make it to the party at the Alexis chick's house hoping Becker's here. I barely paid attention when they gave me directions at the dance, but it's not hard to find with the dozens of cars parked out front. Leaving my truck parked sideways on the lawn, I make my way inside. Some guys are arguing in the doorway. A few others are playing quarters at a poker table, and several couples are practically fucking on the couches. But I couldn't give a shit about any of them.

A thrill runs through me at the thought of Becker hitting me as hard as he did those doors because I'm a twisted motherfucker like that. Maybe he'll really mess me up and I can get put in the same room as Layla. She can't kick me out if I'm in traction.

"Becker?" I roar when I can't find the lardass son of a bitch. Jena steps out of the kitchen instead. Wrong Becker. I tell her so.

She kind of looks like she's been crying but I couldn't care less. "Where's Brent?" I ask, and she shakes her head.

"He didn't do it on purpose, Landen. It's not his fault." She's pleading but I don't care.

"You need to go," Alexis says as she comes closer. "Let me or DW or someone drive you home." She presses against me, placing a hand on my chest.

"Get the fuck away from me, you stupid bitch," I say and instantly I regret it. And not just because she recoils like I've slapped her. I don't talk to women that way—any women. And I'd kick the shit out of any guy who did.

But before I have time to apologize, Brent Becker comes out of a bathroom with his hands up. But not in the way I want.

"Chill, O'Brien. My bad, okay? I didn't know that would happen. I don't even know that girl."

"That girl," I begin through gritted teeth, charging him like a bull with rabies, "is in the fucking hospital right now because you had to act like a fucking—"

"I punched a door, man. Usually people don't fall out just because someone punches a door."

"And you wanted to punch me. You should have. Here's your chance."

I watch as he contemplates this. *Do it already.*

He doesn't. He lowers his hands. *Fuck.*

Guess I'll have to try harder. "I'm sorry, Alexis. What I said was rude. The stupid part, I mean. The bitch part was well-deserved." Surely he'll hit me now. But apparently he doesn't care as much about Alexis as his sister I guess. So I turn my focus back to him. "And I'm sorry I didn't want to take your slutty sister to Homecoming."

That does it. He hits me so hard I see spots. I swing once, grazing him as he dodges me, but on the second swing I connect. He shoves me backwards until I fall and hear the satisfying sound of glass breaking. I roll us away from the shards, hitting and kicking for all I'm worth. Which, truthfully, isn't a whole hell of a lot.

All around us squeals and screams and shouts ring out as everyone realizes there's an all out brawl taking place in the middle of the room. Becker lands a right to my jaw and it clicks. I clutch the collar of his polo and pull his head to mine. Hard. "Agh," he moans in pain from the unexpected headbutt. I see stars but I'm thinking clearly for the first time.

Damn. This isn't going to help Layla. This is only going to help me. But I'm too far-gone to stop now. Oh well. Hindsight and all that shit I guess.

I slug Becker twice more and try to get up but our legs are tangled so crashing back down I go.

He slams my head against the hardwood floor twice before someone pulls him off me.

I'm yanked swiftly to my feet and wrapped from behind by someone towing me towards the door.

"Dude, you okay? That's a lot of fucking blood." Cam releases me roughly once we reach my truck.

"I'm fine." I spit the blood out of my mouth and wipe it with the back of my shirtsleeve.

"I don't know what the hell is wrong with you, man, but remind me not to get on your bad side."

"You're already on it," I inform him.

"Yeah? Well that sucks because I actually like you. Even though you are obviously majorly fucked up. Guess you and Freaky Flaherty deserve each other."

Well, so much for going home.

When they finally pull me off of Cam, we're both bloody and spent. And I'm under arrest.

CHAPTER Seventeen

Layla

"Layla, sweetie?" I open my eyes to see my aunt standing over me. Her hair is a mess, which is so unlike her it's startling.

I'm so grateful to be home in my own bed instead of in that hospital that I never want to get up. I was discharged early this morning and I've already slept through lunch. I should probably eat something but the thought of food sends a wave of nausea rolling hard and fast over me. "I'm getting up," I tell her, using all my might to swing my legs over the edge of the bed. The room tilts slightly and I take as many slow, deep breaths as I can manage.

"Um, you might want to stay put a sec," she says, lowering herself on the mattress next to me.

"What's going on?" I know they ran a ton of tests at the hospital like they always do, but surely I don't have life-threatening results back this quickly.

"It's Landen," she answers quietly, stroking my hair.

"Oh God." I can already hear the rest of her statement. *He's been in an accident, he's paralyzed, he's dead. He was gunned down by muggers when he left the hospital.* I shrink into myself and try to steel my nerves for whatever's coming.

"He's been arrested."

Well. That's…unexpected.

"Arrested?" My mind conjures images of what I've seen on *Cops*. Him cuffed and being shoved into a police car. My sweet, hurt Landen whose heart I shattered into a million pieces last night. Because mine was.

"Apparently he had an…altercation with the boy from the dance. And then a different boy who was trying to break it up."

"Where is he now?" I ask, picturing him alone in a filthy jail cell, trapped behind bars.

"His parents picked him up. But I have a friend who works as a bailiff and does some corrections stuff, and he said Landen's dad was livid, almost to a point where he had to be restrained himself."

Guilt washes over me, and a cold, hard lump constricts my airway. If I'd just sucked it up and let him stay at the hospital last night, none of this would've happened. I must look as awful as I feel because Aunt Kate scoots closer. Her next words don't make any sense.

"Lay, does Landen ever talk much about his dad?"

"Um, no," I answer, scanning my mind for anything Landen has said about his dad. "Just that he's a Colonel in the Army and pretty much forces him to play football. He never comes to any of Landen's soccer games, but that might be because he has to work."

I've been to every one of Landen's games. I've met his mom, a petite, attractive woman with dark hair like her son, but his dad is never there. I've only seen Colonel O'Brien at the few home football games I've been to. But Landen didn't introduce us. I squeeze my eyes shut, as if that's going to help me think. It kind of does.

"I don't think they get along too well. Landen tenses up every time he's mentioned."

"Hmm." Aunt Kate uses her gaze to put distance between us and my empty stomach twists tightly.

"Why? What's going on?"

"Oh, nothing. Just curious about their situation." She strokes my hair once more and stands, smoothing her pale blue oxford button-up. "Listen, I've made you some oatmeal and toast, and there's juice in the fridge. Get some rest and we'll see how you're feeling tomorrow. I think school is out for this week."

"No," I say, forcing my weak body to stand. "I'm going to school tomorrow. If I start doing this, letting this keep me from school, you know what will happen. It's happened before."

"Layla, I know you're upset. And I'm sorry, truly I am. But school really isn't an option or even a priority right now. We have an appointment with a specialist tomorrow morning and some lab tests on Tuesday. And honestly..." Aunt Kate bites her lip. Whatever else she has to say, she's not too excited about. That makes two of us.

She takes a deep breath and speaks in a rush. "I'd like you and Landen to take a breather. You've been hanging out a lot and you're both going through some things you need to deal with before going any further with your relationship or friendship or whatever you kids are calling it these days." Her smile is forced and I can't even muster an attempt at one in return.

"I don't think that's an issue. Pretty sure whatever it was is over." Not that being Landen O'Brien's latest charity case didn't have its perks.

"Well, then, I'm sorry about that too. He seems like a nice enough boy, though this violent streak that apparently runs in the family isn't exactly something I find endearing."

Violent streak? My mind can't even reconcile the sweet boy who stood up for me and *saw* me when no one else did with a violent version. My vision swims from the strain of trying. "I'll come down later," I tell her, curling back into my covers. Maybe I can just sleep this whole mess away.

But as soon as I sink down into the depths of unconsciousness, he's there. Bloody and bruised. Broken. And alone. Like me.

"Layla, he's here. *Again,*" my aunt Kate says through my bedroom door.

He's been stopping by the house every day since Homecoming. I want to see him, want to ask if everything is okay with him and his dad. But he knew. The whole time. While I was convinced he just liked me for me—that he just noticed me all on his own and was interested—he was pretending. Because he knew about my seizures and wanted to rescue me from the big bad bullies of Hope Springs High School to make himself feel better or whatever. Well, I'm not interested in being rescued. I've survived more than Landen O'Brien could even imagine, and if he thinks being ignored at school because of my freakouts is more than I can handle then he—

"Layla, for God's sakes. He's just going to keep coming back." Okay, now even Aunt Kate is annoyed with my knight in shining armor.

I crawl out of bed and open the door. My knight is actually wearing sweaty soccer practice clothes but he still looks pretty damn good.

It's Thursday, and I haven't been back to school since the dance, but he's been coming by at the same time every day without fail. Aunt Kate has been diligently sending him away at my request, but I guess she's tired of being my personal security.

I don't even greet him. I just open the door and retreat back to the safety of my bed. But he follows. Lowering himself onto the mattress, he looks at me with these puppy-dog eyes, and I'm flustered. His face is still mildly bruised from his encounter with Becker, and I do kind of feel sorry for him. His wounded expression breaks my heart a little.

"What? Just say it, Landen."

"Why wouldn't you see me? Or answer my texts or phone calls at least?"

"Because," I force out. "Because you knew, and you acted like you didn't and…" *And I am a fricking idiot who thought maybe you were just genuinely interested in me.*

"Okay," he says slowly, angling his shoulders towards me. "So I knew. So I asked about you when I first moved here and Alexis Bledsoe spouted some shit about you having seizures. So?"

"So…wait, why did you ask about me?"

"What? What do you mean why?" Landen shakes his head, and I have the strangest urge to run my fingers through his thick, dark hair.

"Um, why as in why did you ask Alexis Bledsoe, or anyone for that matter, about me?"

He rubs his neck and glances around my room. "I already told you. I wanted to talk to you. You were always alone, like you didn't want anyone bothering you and I didn't want to be the new guy hassling the queen of the school."

I snort and then I remember I'm still in my PJ pants and a tank top. Dear God, I'm not wearing a bra.

Pulling my covers up to my chin, I drink in the boy who saw me when no one else did. "But why?" I whisper forcefully. "Why me?"

"Jesus, Layla. What do you want from me?" He tenses, and I can tell he wants to get up and yell. He's all hyped up from soccer practice and trapped in my pristine room with my Aunt Kate probably listening right outside the door. "You walked in that first day and I…fuck, I don't know. You had this, like, glow about you and I couldn't take my eyes off you. I expected to see you running the school, looking down your nose at the pieces of shit not worthy of breathing the same air as you, shaking your ass on the football field, and being followed around by an asshole boyfriend who regularly beat the hell out of any guy who so much as looked at you. None of which would have deterred me, by the way. I was prepared to deal with whatever. And then none of that turned out to be accurate. So I thought maybe we'd get to know each other and hook up until I moved again or graduation or whatever. But the more we hung out, the more I wanted…more than that."

Neither of us says anything because, well, there doesn't seem to be anything to say. I want to kiss this beautiful boy—man—Landen. But I'm not ready for that and I'm not sure what would happen if I tried. And I haven't brushed my teeth yet. Tears prick my eyes because I'm not a charity case. And he did just notice me and wanted to get to know me. And I've made a mess of everything. Because I've never done this before and I have no idea what I'm doing.

"Because I have seizures and you wanted to save me damsel-in-distress style?" I ask, just to make sure.

"Because you are beautiful and kind and I love…being with you."

"Landen—" I start, but he's not done.

"Friends tell each other stuff, Layla. And I was hoping, as we got closer, you'd fill me in on the details about your seizures. I didn't rely on anything Alexis or anyone else said because honestly, I couldn't give a shit what they think."

Friends. Seven letters. I'm beautiful and he wants to get to know me better. But we're just friends. Seven letters have never been more confusing. And he's not done.

"But that was the most terrifying thing I have ever experienced, and if there's something I could've done to prevent it, like rip Brent Becker's arms from his body so he couldn't hit that door, then I want to know."

"There's nothing you could've done," I tell him. My voice is so low I'm not sure he hears me, but he scoots closer on the bed so I'm pretty sure he does. The raw hurt in his eyes compels me to keep talking. To tell him everything. Taking a deep breath, I close my eyes so I don't have to watch his face while I reveal my painful secrets.

"I was thirteen. We were on our way to see The Nutcracker—we went every Christmas." Swallowing hard, I gather all the strength I have to tell him what I've only discussed with licensed professionals. Relaxing my grip on my comforter, I let it drop because I might as well be naked. I open my eyes and find him staring intently at me. As much as I want to squeeze mine shut, I hold his gaze.

"My parents were teasing me, trying to swing me in the air like they did when I was little, and I was irritated. Because I was a *teenager*." I roll my eyes at the innocent girl whose biggest problem in life was parents who babied her.

"We were walking to the Atlanta Civic Center Complex from a parking lot a few blocks away because my dad refused to pay to park closer. My mom was annoyed about having to walk so far in heels in the cold. Everything was so…*normal*. And then there were tires screeching, and a guy jumped out of a huge black truck. It was dark so I couldn't see him clearly. My mom shoved me behind her, to shield me I guess, though I had no clue what was going on at the time."

The throat choking sobs are coming and it's getting harder to breathe. Landen waits patiently as I pull myself together so I can finish. He wants to reach out and touch me. I can tell by the way his hands twitch in his lap, but he doesn't and I'm kind of glad. A hug or even an arm around would shatter me right now.

"The guy yelled at my dad to give him his wallet. From behind them I could see my dad scrambling to empty his pockets but his wallet was in his jacket pocket and when he went to get it…I guess the guy thought he had a gun or something because he shot at us. Four times." I flinch because I can still hear it. *Bang. Bang. Bang. Bang.* I can still smell it. Burning.

"And then he jumped back in the truck and left. He didn't even take my dad's wallet."

My eyes unglaze as I finish and I'm back in my room with Landen instead of on the side of the road in Atlanta. He's dropped his head into his hands and is attempting to pull his hair out from the looks of it.

"But you weren't hurt at all?" he asks, finally raising his head so his bloodshot eyes can meet mine. "Physically, I mean."

"There's a scar under my hair, just above my left ear where a bullet grazed me." Without thinking, I reach up and touch it gingerly, not that it still hurts or anything. It's just a reminder. Everything can change. Everyone can leave.

"Jesus," Landen hisses through his teeth. "And the seizures?"

I shrug, because I've gotten through the worst of it. "Started soon after. My mom…fell back on me and I hit my head pretty hard. I was practically unconscious when they found us. I had a severe concussion and was later diagnosed with seizure-inducing PTSD."

"Are they random or is it loud noises that cause them?"

"Um, both I guess. I've had a few that came on for no reason at all, but most of them have been triggered by loud banging noises. Freshman year I was new here and someone's chemistry project randomly exploded. I seized out in the lab in front of everyone. I was humiliated and just really messed up over the whole thing. Aunt Kate let me be home-schooled for a long time. I came back this year hoping to start over. But no one has forgotten. They've all pretty much avoided me ever since."

"Brent Becker is a dead man," he says evenly.

"It's not his fault. It's no one's fault, Landen. This is just…my life." I watch as he takes a deep breath. He's aged ten years from this conversation alone.

"Did they catch the guy at least?"

I shake my head. "No. The cops said it might've been some type of gang initiation or something. But no one was ever arrested."

"I'm sorry, Layla. God. I'm so sorry."

I don't know what to say so I just shrug.

"But the seizures, is there nothing they can do? Medicine, or surgery, or something?"

"I've tried several medicines. Some worked okay but they made me feel dead inside, which for a while was a nice change. But Aunt Kate didn't like the zombified version of me so I mostly just take a migraine medicine that doubles as a seizure suppressant. I'm usually okay unless I get anxious or a loud noise catches me off guard. I get regular EEGs to make sure my brain activity is normal and all that."

"Thank you," Landen says softly and I'm confused.

"Thank you for what?" For getting EEGs?

"For telling me. For trusting me." His hand slides over my comforter and finds mine and I feel safe. For the first time in forever.

He has this look in his eye. For a second, I'm positive he's going to kiss me. Then he leans in and places his lips to my forehead. Time stands still the moment his mouth touches me. I don't even think my heart beats. That single point of contact changes something between us. When he pulls back, I'm struggling to remind myself to breathe.

"It's what friends do, right?" I force out a laugh to break the tension. But his darkening gaze presses deeply into mine.

"No idea. We're a hell of a lot more than friends, Layla Flaherty."

Chapter Eighteen

Landen

Her aunt is kind of hovery and overprotective, I'm learning. At first I thought it was because of her medical condition, but after a month of dating, I'm pretty sure it's because she's realized I'm a walking, talking erection.

They're coming over for Thanksgiving, Layla and her helicopter aunt, and I'm stressed out for a couple of reasons. Layla knows my dad and I don't get along. But she has no idea what an understatement that is. Here I am, always giving her shit about friends telling each other stuff, and I have one hell of a secret myself.

When the doorbell rings, my heart pounds, forcing blood to rush so hard through me I can hear it in my ears. Christ I need to relax.

I clench and unclench my hands a few times as I walk to the front door. *Everything will be fine. Just keep your mouth shut and don't provoke him.*

Right. The Colonel's been drinking and watching football all day. I could breathe wrong and provoke him. No idea why my mom thought this was a good idea.

When I open the door to see Layla on the other side of it, she takes my breath away. You'd think I'd get used to that face. That smile. Those eyes that light up every time she sees me. You'd be wrong.

"Hey, babe." I give her a hug and her aunt raises an eyebrow so I back off.

"Happy Thanksgiving," Layla says softly. "We brought pie."

I grin and take the two pies they're carrying as they follow me into the kitchen. My mom makes a big fuss over Layla's dark red sweater dress type deal, and they talk about food while I set the table.

When my mom calls for my dad to join us, I drop the carving knife I've been holding. We're just sitting down when he walks in. The air becomes thicker, and without thinking, I reach over and put my hand on Layla's bare knee. Somehow this calms me. I glance over to see if it's okay and she's biting her lip. Damn, I want to bite that lip. Okay, maybe it doesn't calm me exactly but it does distract me from the many ways in which the Colonel could ruin this dinner.

She puts her hand on top of mine and I nearly choke on my drink. I clear my throat before I speak. "Colonel, um, Dad, this is Layla Flaherty and her aunt, Katherine."

"Kate," Layla's aunt corrects me. She reaches to shake his hand but he ignores her, taking a drink of the dark liquid in his glass and eying my girlfriend in a way that makes me want to tackle his old ass to the fucking ground. Kate's eyes narrow and I see from the corner of my eye that she's sizing him up. Probably figuring out all my secrets and plotting the easiest exit route for her and Layla.

"This the reason you missed those two field goals last week?" His voice is gruffer than usual, his words slow and falling over each other. Great. He's drunk. Not that he's full of sunshine when he's sober, but drinking brings out a darkness in him that I don't want close enough to cast a shadow anywhere near Layla.

"No, sir," I answer evenly, hoping he'll let it drop.

My mom, ever the peacekeeper, jumps up to fix his plate. "Sit. Relax," she tells him. He does, but his eyes don't leave the girl next to me. She's rigid under my hand until I give her a little squeeze. A forced smile pulls at her lips and again, I want to kiss that mouth so badly. Want to lose myself in the taste of her. The feel of her.

"Maybe if you spent more time practicing and less time gawking at Blondie, you'd have made those. Field goals win games. Or lose them, in your case."

I take my hand off Layla's knee so I don't crush it. "We were down by two touchdowns, sir. I don't think two field goals would have made much difference."

Layla's focusing on her plate—not touching it, just staring at it. Probably wishing she could disappear. Suddenly, without any change in her demeanor, a hand lands on my thigh. Despite the tension in the room nearly choking us both to death, my dick twitches at her touch.

"You watch your mouth, you hear me? Two field goals can be everything. If you took football seriously, there'd be scouts coming to see you." The Colonel goes on about monumental games where field goals made all the difference. He might even refer to me as soccer fag once or twice. But my sole focus is on the small warm hand on my inner thigh.

She's rubbing in a slow circle, applying pressure now and again—probably when she thinks what the Colonel says is affecting me. My mom and Kate are trying to make small talk but even their words are barely registering.

"Are you even listening? Goddammit. Can't even show some respect for five fucking minutes. How the hell are you going to make it at West Point?"

His fist hits the table and Layla flinches. Son of a bitch.

"Don't do that," I say evenly. Her hand leaves me and I'm untethered. No longer attached to Earth by anything that matters.

The Colonel's red-rimmed eyes bulge. "What did you say to me?"

"Jack," my mom breaks in. "Why don't you go back down to the den and I'll bring you some pie?"

He ignores her. As usual. "You were man enough to backtalk to me once. Do it again. What'd you say?"

Adrenaline has me breathing so hard I can see my own chest heaving. "I said, don't fucking do that. Don't hit things or slam things around Layla. She has a condition. Noises like that can—"

"It's fine," Layla says quietly from beside me. "I'm okay." Her hand returns, and I realize there will be immediate consequences for my actions. It all makes sense. This is why my mom invited them. She thought he'd behave around company. But when the Colonel stands, I know she was wrong. And so does she.

So does Layla's aunt apparently. "I think we're going to clear out of here and let you all have some privacy." She stands and jerks her head not-so-subtly towards the living room. We both look at Layla, waiting to see what she'll decide. She'll run straight out the door and never look back if she has any sense.

"That's enough, you two," my mom says in the sternest voice she's capable of.

"Like hell it is. Just because he's got his little piece of ass here, he thinks he can—"

"Excuse me?" Kate lurches at the same time I do.

"Apologize," I command. This is it. It's been coming forever. It's almost a relief. Today's the day I hit back. I just wish she didn't have to be here to see it.

"I don't know what she's done to you or if she's just convinced you that your dick is bigger than it actually is. But you're on very thin ice." He's standing now, leaning towards me, staring me down, with both hands gripping the table. Probably so he doesn't break my neck in front of so many witnesses. I've never understood why he hates me so much. I've just accepted that he does.

"We're going, Layla. *Now*," Kate announces. She reaches for Layla and I have no idea what happens next. Everything goes bright white and blinding pain collides with my face.

It takes me a second to get my bearings. Motherfucker. He sucker-punched me when I looked away.

When I can see again, I see her. Tears filling her eyes as her aunt pulls her towards the door.

"I'm sorry," is all I can say, but the ringing in my ears keeps me from hearing my own words.

CHAPTER Nineteen

Layla

He hit him. His own father hit him so hard his head turned to the side.

I reach a hand up to my own face because I can feel his pain as if it were my own. This is why he doesn't talk about him. Why he tenses up at any mention of his dad, of football, or anything related to either. It makes so much sense I feel like a self-centered moron for not catching on sooner. I was so consumed by protecting my own secrets I never bothered trying to figure out his.

Aunt Kate drags me out of the kitchen, but when we get to the front door, I can't leave. I can't just walk out on the boy who kept me still, who whispered in my ear that I was safe, who calmed me when no one else could or cared to.

"Give me a few minutes? Please?" I beg as she walks out the front door, pulling her keys from her purse. "At least let me say goodbye and make sure he's okay."

She huffs out a breath. "Five minutes."

I can't believe he's been living like this. I need to see him, need to hold him and tell him it's okay. Even though it obviously isn't. I need to do…something.

"Ten. Please? You saw…"

She closes her eyes. And then she looks up for a second before answering. "Tell him he can come stay at the house if he needs to. At least until his dad sobers up."

I nod, grateful she's not making a fuss. "Okay. I will. Thank you."

I shut the door quietly behind her before turning to head back into the room of doom even though my every instinct is shouting at me not to.

It's as if the house has become attuned to the tension. That or Landen and his dad carry it between them like an invisible aura that permeates everything it touches. Each step I take towards the kitchen pulls me into thicker, heavier airspace. My heart pounds forcefully against my chest as I turn the corner back into the violent atmosphere I just escaped. Or was dragged from.

Landen's mom is at the refrigerator, eyes closed as she wrings a green plaid dishtowel in her hands. Her lips move in a silent prayer and I want to scream at her to do something.

The boy I've only seen this worked up after soccer games stands with his bright green eyes blazing and his chest expanding noticeably with each breath. Glancing down I can see that his fists are clenched.

The Colonel is leaning almost lazily on the counter for support but as I come around to the side I can see the sneer on his face. They're in some type of standoff. Waiting for the other one to make a move so all hell can break loose. Each daring the other to start something that will end in bloodshed. I want to scream and cry all at once. Mostly I want to bash Landen's asshole of a dad over the head with the heaviest object I can find.

No one has so much as glanced in my direction. I can practically taste the adrenaline and testosterone surging through the room. Around me, into me.

"Hit me again," Landen says so low I almost don't hear over the blood rushing in my head. "Like you mean it this time. Hit me while I'm looking instead of when my head is turned." His voice is lethal, laced with pure hatred but something else too. A sadness maybe. Confusion. Or hurt.

His own father. My mind is struggling to comprehend the very idea that any man wouldn't be bursting with pride at having a son like Landen.

"Landen," I whisper. My voice barely carries itself to him. His head turns and his eyes widen at the sight of me standing there. If his dad uses this opportunity to catch him off guard again, so help me, I don't know what I'll do.

The Colonel lets out a noise, it might be a word, under his breath but I can't make it out.

"Maybe you boys should go to your separate corners. You're scaring poor Layla to death." His mom forces a smile and huffs out a breath as if it's all in good fun. Before anyone has time to do anything, the Colonel turns and staggers around Landen and walks out the back door. I flinch when it slams but I was expecting it so it doesn't cause any tremors to come.

But Landen's rage flares anyways. "The next time he slams something or does anything to cause Layla to so much as blink too much, I'm fucking killing him," he says to his mom before turning towards me.

Our gazes collide as he comes towards me. The heat in his sends fire scorching through my veins. I want to grab him, kiss him. Tell him this isn't his fault. That there's something majorly messed up with his dad. I want to beg him to come home with me and never come back to this awful place again. The place where he should be safe and loved and isn't.

My hands ache to touch him but the force field created by his residual hostility holds me back. "I'm going downstairs," is all he says before he walks out, leaving me alone in a sea of awkwardness with his mom.

Looking at her, I know she can probably see the questions in my eyes. She doesn't meet mine as she speaks. "He's not a bad man, just… stressed. He'll go out to the shed and blow off steam. Landen's probably downstairs in the den doing the same. They'll be over it by tomorrow." She lifts her shoulder slightly and rolls her eyes. "Men." She offers me an apologetic smile but her eyes hold the truth. I don't smile back. I know what she's doing. Trying to make light of something very dark.

How long has she been doing that? My stomach plummets at the thought of a little boy with messy dark hair and tear-filled green eyes being kicked around like a junkyard dog.

"Okay," I choke out over the lump that's formed in my throat. "Thank you for dinner. I'm going to go down and say goodbye."

"Door's down the hall on your left," is all she says.

When I find the door on the left, I think his mom must be mistaken. Or I chose the wrong one. It's pitch black and I'm gripping the handrail to get down the stairs without falling and breaking my neck. "Landen?" I whisper into the darkness.

"Over here. Take five steps and make a right. Put your hands out." His voice is thick and low. Wounded. Angry. I do as I'm told until I feel a well-worn leather couch beneath my hands.

I reach until I feel him and lower myself onto the seat beside him. Minutes pass and neither of us says a word. Until I can't take it anymore. "That happen a lot?"

"Depends on what you mean by a lot."

"Jesus, Landen. That's not okay. He *hit* you." I find his arm and wrap mine around it, leaning over into him. I don't know how to comfort him, how to make it better. But God I want to so badly.

"It happens," is all he says. His voice is raw and broken and it sends a painful sensation crashing over me. Peels away my skin and leaves my nerves exposed.

I want to climb on top of him. Kiss him, devour him. Fix him. Make it better, like he does for me. I take a few deep breaths and turn towards him. I can't see it, but I know that muscle in his jaw is probably flexing. Know his fists are clenched.

"I'm so sorry." I reach up and place my arms around his neck, pulling him to me, yanking him into a hug he may not want but I need.

He snorts out a small laugh. "You're sorry? What the hell, Layla? Don't apologize because my dad was a drunken asshole and disrespected you. That just makes it worse. I should've made the bastard spit teeth."

"No, you shouldn't have. He's drunk, like you said. No amount of hitting will fix that."

"Might be worth a shot," he grumbles and pulls back. I open my mouth to protest but he lays his head in my lap and lets out a sigh.

I rake my fingers through his hair for several minutes. "Does it hurt?" I ask, lowering my hand and tracing lightly over his jaw. It's too dark to see if it's bruised but I can feel that it's swollen. My tears catch in my throat. Crying won't help him. Plus I never cry in front of anyone. Haven't since I was a kid.

"Not too bad. I can take it."

"You shouldn't have to," I answer, my voice barely above a whisper. I wipe the few tears that escape onto my cheeks.

"Neither should you. Not from him or anyone. Listen, that shit at school, the way everyone—"

"Shh." I shake my head, even though I know he can't see. "I can handle it."

"Say the word and I'll set every single one of them fucking straight. I've already warned Cam and DW. If you so much as hear anyone whisper Freaky Flaher—"

"Landen. Enough. I'm fine. It doesn't bother me anymore. Not since…" *Not since you came. Since you saw me.* "Since you."

For a full minute he's silent and completely still. I'm almost afraid I've shocked him into a coma. And then something warm and unexpected presses against my inner thigh. Holy Lord. Landen just kissed me on the leg. He's never even kissed my mouth. I want him to. I want him to so badly I can't stand it. It's all I can do not to grab him and drag his face to mine. But with the tension from tonight's dramatic events and the mention of the way things are for me at school…our pain is out in the open instead of buried where we normally keep it. And it's leaking out into the room and suffocating me.

Part of me doesn't want him to kiss me for the first time right now because I don't want the memory tainted by how much we're both hurting. And part of me doesn't want him to because in this moment, with his secrets right on the surface, I'd give him anything. Everything. If he kissed me right now, it wouldn't stop there.

And we both know I'm not ready for that.

My breath hitches as he places another kiss on my thigh, higher this time. His right hand inches up my dress, gently caressing my leg as he goes.

A steady pulse begins somewhere inside of me and lands at the juncture between my thighs, just below his head.

"Landen," I breathe.

His lips tickle my flesh as he speaks. "Tell me to stop and I'll stop."

My mouth forms the word but doesn't say it. The sound of my own breathing fills my ears. His lips are parted this time when they come into contact with my inner thigh and I can feel the wetness of his tongue coming closer to my panties. A small whimpery sound escapes my throat and he grips me harder, his hand coming closer to touching me in a place I've never been touched.

This is not smart. We should definitely stop. Except…it feels like he needs this. Needs me. A distraction. Something good to come out of being blindsided by an angry drunk that's supposed to love him. Protect him. Instead of being the one he needs protection from.

And I'm aching for him to touch me. All reason is fleeing the room leaving nothing in the space we occupy other than want. Need.

His fingers graze the edge of my panties as he places another gentle open-mouthed kiss on my inner thigh. And another. He's waiting for permission. He won't push any further without it.

I let my hands twist in his hair and try to think straight.

I've never been kissed and I'm about to let him put his fingers inside me. Or go down on me. Or both. Whatever he's about to do, I'm about to let him. I've heard girls talking about it in the locker room and on the bus. I know what it is. I live in the world. It just never sounded all that appealing until right this moment.

"You can touch me," I say softly into the darkness.

"Layla," he groans, pulling his hand back a few inches.

"I want you to." It's true. I'm ready. Ready for all of it. As long as it's with him. I trust him. I'm high from the realization. Or maybe from his hands and mouth touching me in between my legs. Both probably.

"Layla, your aunt's ready to go," his mom calls from the top of the stairs.

I nearly have a heart attack right that second.

The intimacy between us snaps, slapping us both back to reality. Landen sits up so fast he nearly headbutts me. "Oh God. I'm sorry. I shouldn't have…I don't know what I was—"

"It's fine. Stop." I grab his hand and squeeze as I stand up and smooth my dress down over my thighs. "I have to go. I'll call you later." My legs tremble beneath me as I try to make my way around the couch through the darkness.

"I think that's supposed to be my line." There's a hint of laughter in his voice and it makes me smile. This Thanksgiving wasn't such a bust after all.

"Very funny."

He stands and starts to walk to the stairs beside me. "I'll walk you out."

As much as I don't want to leave him, I don't want him to have another run-in with his dad even more. "Stay. I'm a big girl. I can find my own way out."

"I'm not afraid of him." The evenness of his tone makes me sad. He's really not afraid. He's completely accepted the fact that his own flesh and blood could jack his jaw just for the heck of it at any time.

Placing a hand on his chest, I press him back towards the couch. "I know you're not. But I think we've both had enough excitement for one night. Don't you?"

He sits and I can feel his head at my waist. "Maybe."

I run my fingers through his hair one last time. "Happy Thanksgiving, Landen."

He snorts out loud. "Right."

"Hey. Don't do that. I got to see you. Normally holidays are Stove Top from the microwave or pizza in front of the television. We don't go too crazy since it's just the two of us. But I got to see you, so it's good. I'm happy."

"You are?" There's an emotion thickening his voice that I don't have a name for.

"Not that your dad is such a jerk, but that I got to be with you. Yes."

"That helps," he says so low I almost don't hear.

"Hey, my aunt said you could come to the house and stay for a while. If you want." My eyes are finally adjusting, and I can see that he's leaning back into the couch with his head tilted back.

"I can't leave my mom. If I'm not here when's he's…I just can't leave her."

His words wrench something loose inside of me. Landen the protector. Mine and his mom's. I can't kiss him goodbye on the mouth because if I do I'll never leave and Aunt Kate will have to come drag me out. But I can't just walk out either. Not after everything that's happened.

Leaning over from behind him, I slide my arms down his chest and press my mouth to his abused jaw in a whisper of a kiss. I let my lips graze the side of his face from his jawline to his temple before placing a lingering kiss on his forehead.

I don't know how exactly, but somehow I know it's enough.

Three weeks later, neither of us has mentioned the events of Thanksgiving. But things are different. Easier somehow. The high school marching band goes by, playing our school fight song. Landen's arms wrap me from behind, and I'm dizzy from inhaling his cologne and clean soap smell. His full lips barely graze the side of my neck, just above my scarf, and my knees go weak. He's getting braver. Probably because I never stop him. I press my backside closer against him, relishing the closeness.

"Easy," he mumbles into my ear, the deep soft cadence of his voice sending a shockwave of pleasure vibrating through my core.

"I'm really not," I say, twisting around so I can grin at him.

"Tell me about it," he grumbles, squeezing me tighter around the waist.

I giggle as I turn back to watch the parade. Landen O'Brien has turned me into a girl that giggles. Wonders never cease. It's cold out, colder than usual this time of year, but in Landen's arms I'm warm. Safe. The safest I've felt since my parents held my hands moments before a stranger took them from me.

I'm so grateful for him in this moment that I barely stifle a shudder at the thought of how I almost lost him. Almost didn't let him in. I tried to push him away after Homecoming. But he wouldn't be pushed. He showed up every day to drive me to school. Stalked me to every doctor's appointment. Okay, maybe not stalked, but showed up and refused to leave my side. Pestered me to death in class, until I couldn't avoid him anymore. And then his own dark secret came out on Thanksgiving, and much to many a cheerleader's dismay, I was his and he was mine.

I see the darkness in him, and the light, and I want it all. And tonight I'm going to tell him. That I love him and I'm ready. I want him to be my first kiss, and maybe when we're both ready—or when I'm ready because I'm pretty sure he was ready like *yesterday*—the first man I sleep with.

I've almost had two seizures since Homecoming. One when two sophomores got into a fight next to my locker and one of them banged his head on a metal door beside me. And another time when they shot off fireworks I wasn't expecting after our last home football game. Both times Landen was there, wrapping his arms around me like they are now and whispering in my ear.

"You're okay. I've got you. You're safe."

Both times he kept me still. The tremors came and went but no full-blown seizures like before. Even the doctors can't explain it in medical terms. But they think my PTSD stems from being afraid of what was about to happen to me, from feeling unsafe and alone. Landen is my cure. I snuggle closer to him, and a satisfied yet pained groan escapes his throat.

My stomach is tied in knots of anticipation at the thought of Landen's mouth on mine, his tongue inside of me. I'm nervous and a little scared. Scared of crossing a line I'll never be able to come back from. Scared it will change things. He's my best friend—heck, my only friend if I'm being honest—and I can't imagine my life without him.

But right now, with his body pressed against mine and his breath on my neck, I can't imagine anything that would ever separate us.

He knows about my parents, my seizures, and I know about his dad. Something about knowing each other's darkest, ugliest truths has made us even closer than any kiss ever could.

And we're both going to UGA next year—together. Staring at his hands, I wish we didn't have gloves on so I could feel his skin now. But I know I will later. A little shiver passes through me and he leans down and murmurs into my ear again.

"Cold?"

His voice has my insides turning to molten lava and I can't speak so I just shake my head no. He holds me tighter anyways and I'm glad. His grip is the only thing keeping me anchored to Earth. Otherwise I'd probably float off into outer space from being so full of lightness for the first time in so long.

If we weren't pressed up against each other so tightly, I might not have felt the shift in his stature when his shoulders went stiff.

"Fuck me," he mutters under his breath, and I almost say "maybe one day," just to see his reaction. But his eyes are tight when I turn in his arms and his mouth is set in a grim line. It's an expression I've only seen him wear around his asshole of a dad so I search the crowd for the Colonel.

But I don't see him. The parade is ending and the crowd thins around us as we turn to leave.

"Landen." I tug on his gloved hand so he'll slow down, but he's like a man possessed. When a couple about our age appears in front of us, he squeezes my hand so hard it hurts.

"O'Brien, long time no see, man," a shaggy-haired guy says, reaching out a hand. I hear Landen suck in a breath just before the dark-haired, dark-eyed girl with him launches herself at Landen and kisses him square on the mouth. His hand drops mine and I'm lost in an undertow of confusion and pain. It's a chaste kiss but it slams into me like a punch to my gut. Because it was mine. The kiss she just stole. *He's* mine. Or so I thought.

"Your mom called our mom and said you guys were moving back so we decided it was time for a road trip and came to help you pack," the girl says, smiling up at my…Landen.

It's too much to process at once and my head swims. Who is this girl? And he's moving? Back? Back where?

"Layla," Landen says, grabbing my hand and pulling me forward into the little group. "This is Tuck and Danni Anderson, friends of mine from Colorado." Maybe I imagine it, wishful thinking and all that, but it seems like he puts special emphasis on *friends.* "Guys, this is Layla Flaherty," he tells them while I stand open-mouthed, trying to think straight.

Colorado then. He's moving back to Colorado and he didn't even bother to tell me.

"Hi," I say quietly, waiting for more of an explanation.

"I was going to tell you, tonight, about…everything," Landen says, directing his words solely at me. But I can't make my tongue work to formulate a response.

"Aw hell," the Tuck guy says, running a hand through his hair. "We'll meet you back at the hotel, man. Let you guys talk." He shoots Landen an apologetic look and says that it's nice to meet me. I parrot his words because my brain's not able to come up with any of my own.

Danni runs her eyes over Landen and her mouth forms a tiny smile. "Sorry to accost you like that. Just thought it'd be a nice surprise." If she's looking for confirmation, Landen doesn't offer any. Just nods and says that he'll see them later.

Once we're alone in the cab of his truck, it comes on slow, gradually getting louder until the ringing in my ears drowns out everything else. But I'm not about to seize out. No, this is much worse. I'm about to do the one thing I haven't allowed myself to do in front of anyone since my parents were killed. I'm about to cry.

CHAPTER Twenty

Landen

"It's not what you think," I tell her in the cab of my truck after Danni and Tuck appeared out of nowhere and ruined my life.

"Okay," she says softly and I don't miss the tremor in her voice. She's fighting to keep her eyes dry, swallowing hard and waiting for me to explain. I take a deep breath and give it my best shot.

"My mom is leaving my dad. He's a bastard, as you well know. And she's had enough. 'Bout fucking time right?" Air escapes my lungs in a snorted huff, but she doesn't speak so I keep talking. "She's going back to Colorado. Day after tomorrow. She had a job there and they want her back. She wants me to go with her, and Layla, honestly, I don't want to. But my dad went pretty ballistic when she dropped the bomb. It's not like I have a ton of options here." Yanking my gloves off, I reach out to touch her. She flinches back so I rake my hands through my hair instead.

"When were you going to tell me?" she asks without looking at me. She's staring at her hands and she's that girl again. The one she was when I first got here, pulling into herself, throwing up walls. Back then they were brick; now they're steel, double reinforced, impenetrable.

"Tonight. I wanted you to enjoy the parade. Then I was going to take you home and tell you and your aunt about my situation. Because this isn't the end, babe. You know that, right? I want to talk with Kate about you coming to visit and maybe making the trip to meet halfway."

"You know I don't drive, Landen," is all she says, and her voice is so empty I'm dying. It's far, fuck, I realize that. But what I feel for this girl isn't geographical. I've had that before. *So long, see ya, it was fun.* It's all I've ever had. Until now. This isn't that. And we've already both committed to UGA in the fall. As soon as my mom told me what was going on, I started looking for jobs I could get and apartments I could live in this summer so I could move back as early as possible.

But she's acting like I just said I'm moving to the moon. And won't be back. Ever.

"That's what planes are for," I say, begging her to smile with my eyes.

"You should probably head on to the hotel so you can pack." The chill in her voice leaves me cold. No. Fuck this.

"Layla." Her name is a plea on my lips, and I'm reaching out to grasp her face. I've waited—God knows I've waited—for her to be ready, but she needs to know how I feel and she needs to know now. Leaning closer, I breathe in her sweet scent, licking my lips in anticipation. But she jerks out of my grasp and scoots away from me.

"I'm ready to go home now."

"No, dammit. Tell me what to do. You want me to stay? I'll stay. I'll sleep in my truck in the goddamn school parking lot." Without my permission, my hands slam into the steering wheel. She flinches next to me and I feel like an asshole—like my dad. "This isn't my choice," I tell her, knowing I sound like a dick. But I'm out of ideas.

I watch as the silent figure of a girl next to me chews her bottom lip. It's not fair—she's pissed and hurt. I get it. But she's punishing me for something I have no control over. Sort of. I'm eighteen. I've thought of refusing to go and trying to find a place of my own, getting a job. But what kind of time would I have for her then? None. And what if I lost my job, or my grades dropped and they rescinded my scholarship? She can't see it now, but I do have plans of a future with her, and I'm still protecting those plans with everything I'm worth.

Until she sets them on fire and scatters the ashes out the window.

"It's fine, Landen. I overreacted. Friends can live in different states—that's what the Internet's for, right?" She waves a hand in front of her, batting my heart out of the way. "But I'm tired, so I'd like to go home please."

She forces her lips to smile, but I can see the pain in her eyes, as hard as she tries to hide it. We're back there again, where we hide things from each other and pretend we don't care. *Friends.* Fantastic.

When I pull into her driveway, my mind is flooded with irrational thoughts. I'll tell her I love her, throw myself on the lawn and refuse to go, propose. Shit. Something. But she's still stiff and non-responsive. Barely offering me half-hearted smiles and nods as I tell her about the scene at my house earlier today when my mom lost her shit and finally stood up for herself. For me. She's not even listening. If I followed through on any of my crazy ideas, she'd probably just step over my body and go inside.

Maybe I misread *everything*. Maybe she really just needed me as a friend and that's all it was. Is. Rusted razor blades skinning me alive would feel better than this. But no matter what happens tonight, or tomorrow, or whenever, I promise myself I will always be a friend to this girl if that's what she wants. If she'll have me.

I turn the key in the ignition to turn the truck off, but it's not necessary. Layla leans over, giving me one last whiff of her and a peck on the cheek. She whispers, "Have a safe trip. I'll miss you." And then she's out of my reach.

So long, see ya, it was fun.

What the hell? She's out of the truck and at her door before I can form a complete thought.

I get out and cross the lawn just as she shuts the door behind her. She didn't even look back.

Raising my hand to knock, I hear her aunt's voice from the other side. "Layla? Jesus, what's wrong?"

And then I hear it. Oh God. The sobbing sounds almost like an animal. An injured one. She held it in the whole way home but I broke her. I broke the girl I'd worked so hard to help. She didn't cry when everyone at school treated her like a leper. Didn't shed a single tear when she told me about her parents. And yet her cheeks were damp the night she saw my dad hit me and she's falling apart right this second. *Because of me.* Weakened by the realization that all I cause her is pain, I sit on her front steps with my head in my hands like a fucking lunatic. Because I can't fix it this time. I won't be around to pick up the pieces of her heart. Because I'm leaving. Like always.

Because you fuck everything up. When will you stop being so goddamn selfish? The Colonel's message finally comes through loud and clear.

I'm loading the U-Haul in the hotel parking lot with Tuck when my phone buzzes in my pocket. Mom said the Colonel is having them shut off and we'll get new ones as soon as we can afford it, but apparently mine still works. I've been planning all night what to say to Layla, how to make things right before I leave. Trying to figure out my options in case she asks me not to. Because if she so much as hints that she wants me to stay, that she needs me to, then I'm staying. But when I look at the screen and read the two words she's sent in response to all my pathetic begging and pleading messages, there's nothing left to say.

Goodbye Landen.

I can practically see her reaching up to touch her scar. Her permanent reminder of what I tried so hard to convince her wasn't true. Only to turn around and prove that it is. *Everyone can leave.*

I stare at her message. I know what it is. It's closure for her. The kind she'll never have with her parents. I would've stayed, figured something out if she needed me. She doesn't. So she's letting me leave.

KEEP
Me Still

For Landen

You have such a bright future ahead of you. You've already proven your strength at just a few days old. I'm so glad you came into our lives. I'm in love with you already.

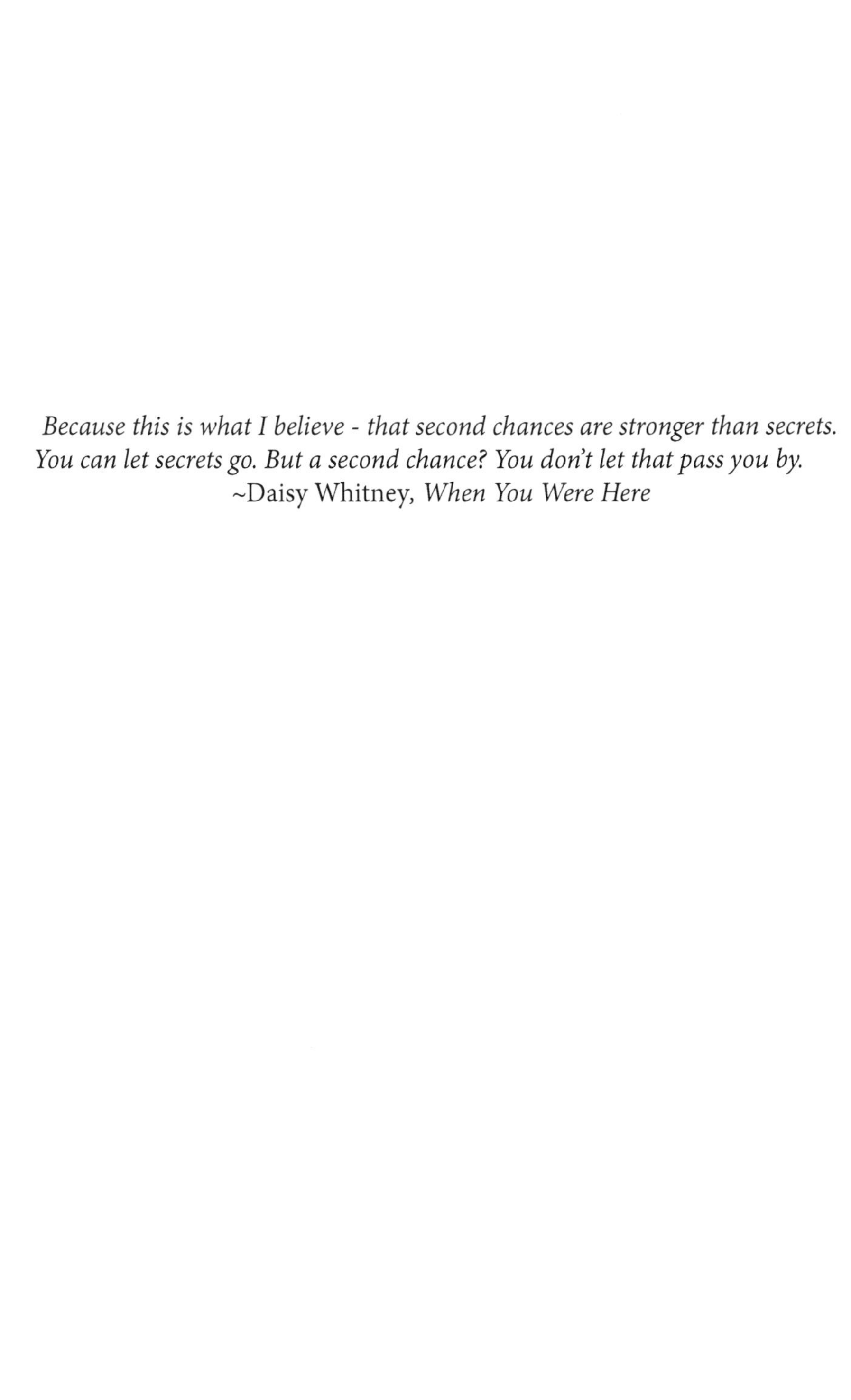

Because this is what I believe - that second chances are stronger than secrets. You can let secrets go. But a second chance? You don't let that pass you by.
~Daisy Whitney, *When You Were Here*

It's cold out. My mom pulls my red pea coat around my shoulders and makes sure it's buttoned. "I'm not a baby," I tell her, jerking out of her grasp. At thirteen, I can button my own coat for Pete's sakes. I'm still a little pissy that my friend Tara couldn't come. My dad walks around our silver SUV and glares at us for a second before smiling.

"Can't even let me be a gentleman for one night," he huffs. I roll my eyes because he knows my mom isn't the type to sit around and wait for anyone to open her door.

"Sorry, hon," my mom says. I don't know if she's speaking to me or to him. Snowflakes whirl a random dance around us, and my parents walk briskly down the deserted street, flanking me. When I was younger, we held hands and they would swing me. I used to think I was flying. The sidewalk is cracked and uneven and a chain-link fence borders the side away from the street. For the first time I notice that downtown Atlanta is kind of ghetto.

"We should've parked in the garage," my mom mumbles under her breath. Our heads are down to keep the wind from blowing in our faces so I don't hear my dad's response. Every year we go see The Nutcracker at the Atlanta Civic Center, and every year my dad refuses to pay the twelve-dollar fee to park in the garage by the arena. This year it's colder than usual, and my mom is annoyed but I think she's just grumbling because she likes to get a rise out of my dad.

"Where's the fun in that?" my dad asks, grabbing my hand and nodding at my mom over my head.

"Oh no," I say, attempting to pull my hands out of theirs. "I'm not a baby anymore." I'm small for my age, but geez. I'm not a little kid. Why do I have to keep reminding them of this? They've been present for all thirteen of my birthdays.

They both squeeze tighter, and I give in and giggle as they pull me into the air.

Tires squeal to a stop on the road beside us, and I'm put down roughly mid-swing. "Give me your wallet," a stocky man coming towards us in a black hooded jacket sneers at my father. My mom pulls me hard behind her so I can't see his face. Her fingers dig deep into my arms, and I'm not sure if I'm the one trembling or she is. My heart pounds so hard it's making me sick, and my vision is blurring.

The gunshots wake me and I'm sitting upright in bed. For a second, I think I'm in a hospital room. There's another bed next to mine but it's empty. Shit, where am I?

Sweat beads down my back and I breathe deep, in through my nose and out through my mouth like Dr. McCalla taught me. College—I'm in college. Not in Georgia, but in California. In my dorm room. And thank God my roommate isn't here to see my early morning freak out.

Maybe I can still pass as normal. For now at least.

~**PRESENT TENSE**: Used to locate a situation or event in present time. Or a tense situation you thought you had put behind you that turns out to be much more current than you realized.~

CHAPTER One

Layla

The sprawling campus of Southern California State University, or SoCal as the locals call it, is crowded as my roommate, Corin Connelly, and I make our way to Freshmen Orientation. Several people move in random directions ahead of us wheeling large luggage carts.

"Wow, how glad are you that we moved in early right now?" Corin asks, her red curls blowing in her face as she turns towards me.

"Extremely." Though I'm managing. A year ago I couldn't have stood this—the chaos, the crowd, the noise.

Corin is from New York, and even after a week of living together, she still hasn't told me exactly why she picked a college so far from home. Not that I really disclosed much either.

I did mention that if I hadn't gotten out of my tiny hometown of Hope Springs, Georgia, my head would have exploded. I just didn't explain that it was literally a possibility. And I left out the gory details involving Landen O'Brien and the brutal beating he'd given my heart. I'd been planning to go to UGA until…well, until he left.

Now, I'm all alone on the other side of the country. Starting over. Finally.

I'm trying my best to live each day to the fullest. The word they keep using after every EEG and test they've run the past six months follows me around, orbiting my every thought. *Inoperable.*

I've said it so many times to myself that it's lost all meaning.

What Corin doesn't know—what no one in California knows, thank goodness—is that I barely got through high school due to a seizure disorder.

Because I'm especially defective, my particular disorder was one no doctor could explain until recently, when they discovered that my seizures aren't strictly from my Post-Traumatic Stress Disorder, the result of seeing my parents murdered in front of me five years ago, like we originally thought. Apparently God wanted to cover His bets when it came to making my life as difficult as possible. So I also have a decent-sized subdural hematoma pressing on my brain as well. Possibly from the fall I took when my mother fell on me after being shot. A souvenir of sorts of the worst day of my entire existence.

No matter how you look at it, I should not be alive. And yet…here I am. My Aunt Kate raised me after my parents' death. She's also the only other person on Earth who knows about the late-breaking brain injury news. I have every intention of keeping it that way.

Inoperable.

"We've got some time," Corin says, interrupting my thoughts. "Want to run in here and grab a coffee and chill for a few? Maybe let the crowd thin out a bit?"

"Sure," I answer, amazed and grateful that she's already noticed my discomfort in large crowds. I can't even imagine how she would've handled the way I used to be. I'm so much better now that it's as if I'm a different person. And it's mostly because of him. *Landen.* Thinking his name causes me to flinch internally—I don't even want to know what saying it out loud would be like. But it's been over eight months since I've had to. Maybe I'll never have to again. The thought sends an odd sensation of relief tinged with sadness coursing through me.

As we browse through the bookstore, a girl sitting alone in a plush armchair and staring out the front window catches my attention. Her clothes are black, her hair dark and ran through with purple streaks. With my blond hair and pink oxford button-up over a jean skirt, we look nothing alike. But there's something about her, about the way she's sitting and staring—like a casual observer in her own life—that has me fighting off memories of my senior year of high school. A year I've tried so hard to forget.

Corin's voice pulls my attention from the girl—but not my eyes. I can't look away. "So according to Elyse, it's like totally obvious when freshmen sit in front of the lecture hall."

Elyse is our RA and she's been filling Corin's head with this type of vital knowledge since we moved in. Not a day goes by that my roommate doesn't dump some Elyse-infused wisdom on me.

"And don't be early to class or write down everything the professors say." She points a finger at me. "Oh, and don't dress up or wear a lot of makeup either." Corin goes on, and I'm craning my neck but I've lost sight of the girl in the window. "Layla, are you even listening to me?"

"Mmhm. Show up late, sit in the back, dress like a slob, don't take notes. Got it."

She blows out a frustrated breath. "I'm serious. If it's obvious we're freshmen, we won't get invited to any of the good parties. And if we do, it'll just be by guys who think we're stupid and going to give it up."

"I solemnly swear that I will dress for comfort and sit in the back with you. Happily." I'll have no trouble blending in like she wants because I've done it before. Sat in the back and tried to disappear. I was good at it, too. Or so I thought.

Soon we've made it to the front of the line, and I've forced myself to stop scanning the place for the girl who I think might be my kindred spirit, if there is such a thing. I order an iced mocha and pay while Corin orders her ginormous caramel macchiato next to me. I make a mental note to remember what she likes for when we're cramming like maniacs and it's my turn for a caffeine run.

I smile at her profile, so proud of myself for finally getting here. For clawing my way out of the darkness that shadowed my past and making it to where I always wanted to be. On my own—not a burden on Aunt Kate or Landen or anyone. My life is finally some semblance of normal. Again, the familiar guilty tug pulls because I couldn't have gotten here without him. Without the one person who hurt me almost as much as the man who murdered my parents.

As we turn to leave, I glance at the now empty chair by the window and wish I'd said something to her. Let her know that someone saw her, noticed that she existed. Mattered. Because that's what he did for me.

But I don't have time to regret not speaking for long, because when Corin and I step out of the store, a black truck full of guys drives past. One of them whistles, probably at my supermodel of a roommate, and my world pitches hard right.

"Hey, you okay?" Corin asks, coming closer to me.

I take a deep breath and the panic subsides. *Don't do this. Not now, not here.*

"Yeah, I'm good. I probably should've eaten more this morning." Smiling as wide as I can get my face to manage, I force the memory of a boy with a very similar truck out of my head.

"Okay. Holy shit, those guys were hot," Corin announces, changing the subject as she practically skips ahead of me on our way to the stadium. "I love college already."

"Maybe you should have gotten decaf," I answer, willing my mouth to keep grinning as I try to shake off my memories of that truck. Maybe I should just tell her everything so I don't have to exhaust myself forcing smiles and reminding my lungs to breathe every time something like this happens. Or maybe I should grow up already and stop letting every single thing on Earth remind me of the boy who broke my heart.

Part of me just wants to tell her everything, get it all out. My condition, what my last test results indicated, and even about *him*. But another part of me still can't trust another person with my heart for fear they'll shatter it all over hell like he did.

CHAPTER *Two*

Landen

Dorms for athletes are nicer than the ones for regular freshmen. Thank fuck because if I had to cram in some tiny closet with a dude I barely knew, well, one of us probably wouldn't make it out alive.

As I carry my crap in, I notice that I'm in one of two adjoining quad rooms that share a bathroom. Four shower stalls, sinks, and toilets are all that separate me and my roommates from four other guys on the university soccer team. Could probably throw a hell of a party in there, get some serious steamed-up action going in those showers with whatever girls are willing. Not that I've felt much like partying this past year.

I already know most of these guys from summer workouts so we don't waste time with introductions. We just pick out our beds and unload our shit. Lucas Taite and a few older guys from the team tell us the best places to party on and around campus as we finish up.

"We're getting introduced at freshmen orientation in a few hours so you fuckers need to get a move on," Ben Blackburn sneers. He's from Scotland so it comes out more like "fookers." He's the fullback and the biggest dude on the team. But he's only an inch or two taller than me. Not that I'm comparing. He's also a complete dumbass and how the hell he's made it to his junior year of college is beyond me.

"And don't forget, ladies, you have to clean the field house and spit-shine the locker rooms," he adds, probably because he gets off on hassling the eight of us who are freshmen. For now I'm letting it go because I don't want to get kicked off the team. It'd give my dad a hard-on if I fuck this up. *Soccer is a pussy sport,* he informed me each time I chose to play it instead of football. I grit my teeth and dump my comforter and sheets onto my bed so we can head to the field house.

"Chill, man," Skylar Martin says under his breath as he does the same. "It's just for a year, and then we'll be the ones giving the orders." He says something else but I don't hear it. Because what he just said reminds me of a time I've shoved, kicked, and fucking wrestled out of my memory.

"It's just for a year or two, Landen," my mom would say each time we moved. Right, a year or two. Long enough to make a few friends so it would hurt like hell when we had to leave again, but not long enough to ever be missed. Same shit, different town. Not that my stupid little kid feelings mattered compared to the Colonel's oh-so-important highly classified position. I learned the hard way what complaining about moving so much got me. Stitches. A cast. Compliments of dear old dad. By the time I entered high school, I learned to keep my mouth shut. I also learned not to bother forming any kind of attachments to anyone. And I was doing a pretty damn good job. Until we moved to Hope Springs. Until I met *her*.

"O'Brien, you good to drive?" Skylar asks as we load into my truck. He's watching me with a weird look in his eyes. As if I weren't one hundred percent there. Shit, I must've been spacing out again.

"Yeah. I am. It's not like we'd all fit in your P.O.S. anyways." Once we're all in, I back out into the street and head towards the field house to clean up before orientation. Skylar, Austin, and Michael are crammed into the extended cab of my truck while the guys rooming in the quad attached to ours are piled in the back. Not sure if that's legal in California, not sure I give a fuck either.

"Dude. It kind of smells like a girl in here. You hiding a chick in the floorboard?" Skylar asks, looking around, probably for an air freshener or something.

Fuck me. I knew I should've gotten rid of it. There's a bottle of lotion in the center console that belonged to her. Because I'm slightly addicted to the sweet peaches and cream scent of Layla Flaherty. It lives on. Just like the image of her perfect face that's seared into my mind.

I nod to the console and he laughs. "Nice. Jerkin' lotion in the truck. I hear ya, buddy."

"Belonged to a girl I dated," I practically grunt at Skylar, praying he'll shut the hell up about it.

"Was she hot? Cause I'm getting a semi just from the smell."

I go to punch him lightly, but if his flinch is any indication, I failed. I don't like him talking about her. Just the thought of him—or anyone—thinking about Layla like that, with a half hard dick, is enough to make me see red.

He holds his hands up and looks at me like I'm nuts. Probably because I am. “My bad, dude. I didn’t realize.” I want to ask him what he didn’t realize, but at the same time I don’t want to know.

He doesn’t hit me back, but pain thumps me hard in the chest, because hell yeah she was hot. Better than hot. Amazingly breathtakingly, fucking gorgeous. So much so that the first time I saw her I was pretty sure I was going to have to fight some guy, or maybe several guys, just to talk to her. Shocked the hell out of me that not only was she always alone, but that everyone at Hope Springs High School avoided the shit out of her. The most beautiful girl on the damn planet and she was isolated in her own little world day after day.

Freaky Flaherty. That’s what I overheard some of the other girls call her. I heard them because they said it loudly. On purpose. One thing I learned from moving around so much was that at small town schools, girls had a habit of waging wars on one another with a military precision that would’ve made the Colonel proud. I half-expected her to be one of them. But Layla had been a target, blacklisted her freshman year by girls with less than half her beauty and none of her class. My sweet girl, an angel who never hurt anyone, was so used to being ignored and avoided that she had a really hard time letting me in. By the time I convinced her I was worthy, it was time to move again. So all I proved to her was what she knew all along. Everyone can leave.

Chapter Three

Layla

"Oh we are so doing this," Corin informs me as we reach the stadium. There's a dozen flyers covering the concrete kiosks surrounding the entrance, so I have no clue which one she's gushing over. If it's sorority rushing or some crap like that, she's on her own. Dropping my nearly empty cup in a trashcan, I step closer to see which flyer she's talking about.

She pulls one off and hands it to me. "I did this in high school and one of the floats I worked on was in the Macy's parade. Seriously, it's so much fun. We have to sign up."

I skim the purple and gold writing on the poster promising *Fun*! *Free food*! *And a chance to express ourselves creatively and meet our peers*! if we sign up to decorate floats for Homecoming. Oh joy. But Corin is practically twitching with excitement, and this was the whole point of coming here. Leaving the old me, the one who never would've decorated a float for Homecoming, behind. "Okay. Sounds good to me." I hand her the flyer back, watching as she shoves it into her huge purse.

"I never went to any dances back in New York. Did you go to Homecoming? I bet you were like Homecoming queen or some shit, weren't you?" she asks as we continue walking towards the Grecian-style arena.

"Far from it," I tell her, once again trying not to think about that year. That night especially. The way Landen looked when he picked me up. So handsome in his tux that he took my breath away. The way his full mouth quirked up in a nervous smile when I told him I was ready to go—ready to be his. The pain in his eyes when I woke up in the hospital and kicked him out because I was humiliated. Of all the nights my stupid seizures could have ruined, they ruined Homecoming the most. "I went to Homecoming but left…early." Via ambulance.

"You know, I never thought I'd be jealous of a cheerleader," Corin says as we make our way to some open seats in the arena.

"And you are now because…?" I glance down the field at the overly bronzed girls standing at attention with smiles plastered on their made-up faces.

"Because *day-um*, they've got a nice view." She nods, and I can see cheerleaders surrounding groups of athletes with flags labeling their different sports. Soccer and football are together. *Wonder which one he ended up playing?* I force myself to look away.

"Definitely didn't have you pegged as a football groupie," I say, nudging her as we sit.

"Oh, I'm not. Emo boys are way hotter. But there's something about all that blind aggression. Muscles and sweat and testosterone. Yum." Corin fans herself with one of the programs we were given detailing the agenda for orientation.

I can't help but laugh. "Down, girl."

She kicks her feet up on the seat in front of her. "So what's your type, Georgia? Jock? Emo? Nerd? I bet you're really into super smart guys, huh?"

"Eh." I shrug, praying she'll drop it. But we live together. Probably going to have to throw her a bone. "I dated an athlete once."

"Really?" She leans back and looks at me like she's trying to picture me with a football player on my arm. "Yeah, I can see that."

"Didn't last long. I pushed him away and he…left." Damn you, throat lump of tears to come. I swallow hard and focus on the program in my hand like there's going to be a test on it.

"Hey, I get it. You're kind of…closed off. I can totally see you pushing some hottie away. But aren't athletes supposed to have like superhuman endurance or something?"

Oh, he had some endurance all right. Enough endurance to turn down all the girls who threw themselves at him the minute he moved to town. Enough to wait for me to be ready to let him in. Enough to enlist the help of the entire varsity soccer team at Hope Springs High School to hold up signs asking the school freak-show to Homecoming. *Pretty please, with cherries on top.*

"Think they're actually going to make us sing?" I shrug and point out the corny lyrics to the alma mater, hoping to change the subject. But in my head all I can think about is how much time I wasted pushing Landen O'Brien away. And how much it hurt when he finally left.

The marching band is warming up, and the President of the University is making her way to the podium. A few other official looking people surround her, and I'm tempted to take a picture with my phone even though Corin would probably make fun of me.

But this is it—the start of my new life. The one I am going to live, loud and full and without regret. Because that's all I have in my past. Pain, shame, and soul-stinging regret.

I'm done with that now. As soon as this orientation ends, I'm moving on. Letting go of the anger at the man who killed my parents and the pain of missing them. While I'm at it, it's time to move past the bone deep ache that paralyzes me every time I think of Landen O'Brien tricking me into trusting him so he could bail.

But when the marching band clatters into song, I'm shivering despite how warm it is in the stadium. Because I'm not in the stadium anymore. I'm at home, standing on Main Street, watching a Christmas parade. With a boy who's about to break my heart into so many pieces that I'll never be able to put it back together again. Not that it was in such great shape to begin with.

CHAPTER *Four*

Landen

"We've still got nearly an hour before orientation," Skylar informs us, checking his watch as we finish up at the field house. "Let's run by that diner we passed and grab a shake or something."

"No," I say before I can stop myself. I just want to get in my damn truck and avoid this conversation altogether.

"Yo, O'Brien, you cuttin' weight or something? No shakes and now you're a speed walker?" Austin calls out after me.

I sigh and turn to face them before climbing into my own personal peach-scented hell. "If you guys really want to go, we can. But I don't want to hear any of you bitching at workouts tonight when you're puking your asses off."

"Dude, you got something against shakes?" Skylar says, finally reaching the truck. Some girls walk by and he's momentarily distracted. Guy has the attention span of a fucking goldfish.

"Naw, just ready to get to the stadium and get this shit over with." But I'm lying. Truth is, if I never see another chocolate shake again, it'll be too soon. Because I don't just see a milkshake. I see her.

Eyes closed, luscious lips curved into a satisfied grin, little pink tongue swiping that whipped cream from the corner of her mouth. And that smile. That damn dream-invading smile, the one that will probably haunt me for the rest of my life. The one that changed everything. That changed me.

I stay in the truck while the rest of them go in the diner, pretending I have pertinent shit to attend to on my phone. Once they're out of sight, I lean my head back on the seat and close my eyes. I never even got to kiss her. If I'd known just how short our time together was going to be, I would've kissed her every day. Every hour.

The truck door opens and I sit up straight. "Dammit," Skylar mumbles as he dribbles some of his shake down his team polo, snapping me out of my memories of the girl I shouldn't be thinking about in the first place. Must've zoned out while they were in the diner.

"Nice," Austin jeers, laughing and pointing. "In t-minus thirty minutes we're going to be introduced to the whole freshman class and goalie here has cookies-n-cream shake splattered down the front of his shirt. Smooth, man."

"Don't spill that shit in my truck. I mean it," I warn him. "Or you will pay for a full detail or detail it yourself, motherfucker." Not that I'd really follow through on the threat. Because then I would lose it, her sweet scent. As much as it tortures me, it's all I have left to remind me. Even though the memories sting, it's a pain as familiar and unwelcome as the pain my father caused. Terrifying. But necessary. A heroin addiction would probably be healthier.

My phone buzzes in my console and I know it's one of three people. Tuck, Danni, or my mom. Texting to see how it's going, to check up on me or whatever. I don't bother looking at it, though, because I'm distracted. A redhead and a girl with hair like Layla's are walking into the stadium as I pull into the parking lot. I nearly slam into a concrete kiosk I'm so distracted.

"You been drinking?" Skylar asks, bracing his hand on the dash.

"Not today," I tell him as I whip into an empty parking space. The lot's pretty full. It's going to be a hike to the stadium but I probably need the fresh air to clear my head anyhow. Because I might be hallucinating.

All eight of us head toward the stadium, searching for the gate number we've been told to enter.

"It's B8, dumbfuck," Michael argues with Dean, who swears it's C8 we're supposed to be looking for.

"Oh shit, I forgot about this," Skylar says, tearing a flyer off the nearest kiosk. "You know we have to decorate a team float for Homecoming? Coach said the shit is mandatory."

"No way," Michael says, snatching the flyer to look it over. "Ah, there's free pizza at least."

"Wow, fatass. Way to find the silver lining," Austin says, smacking Mike in the arm. The two wrestle around for a few minutes but I keep walking. Homecoming. Of all the time I spent with Layla Flaherty, Homecoming was the most fucked up night of all. Either that or Thanksgiving, but I'm pretty sure Homecoming wins.

If I'd known what she'd been through, known that she'd witnessed her parents being gunned down in a random mugging as a kid and was plagued by seizure-inducing Post Traumatic Stress Disorder, I would've ripped Brent Becker's arms from his body before I let him punch that door. But I didn't know. Not all the details anyways. Before I could blink, she was convulsing on the floor and I was screaming for someone to call 911. *Freaky Flaherty,* they called her. When I saw what caused them to nickname her this, I wanted to burn the gym down Carrie-style. Small town bastards.

But when I wrapped my arms around her and her seizing stopped, I felt like King of the damn world. Because I was stupid enough to think maybe someone needed me.

I lose sight of the girl with hair like Layla's once we enter the stadium. It's barely controlled chaos in here. We find the seats marked Soccer and sit while some official looking people in suits set up a podium and fool around with sound equipment.

Testing the limits of my neck, I glance up into the stands, hoping to find that girl again, and kind of hoping not to. Part of the deal is that I don't make myself obvious. Scrolling through messages on my phone, I see a text from my mom. She just recently learned to text, and boy does she make use of this knowledge.

The cheerleaders are lining up next to our seats, and several guys lean around me to stare. Jesus. It's like they've never seen women in skirts before or something. But yeah, I do a quick once-over just for the hell of it. And so no one calls me a fag. Not that I don't love the Colonel's favorite nickname for me, but after I left Georgia and moved back to Colorado, I took a lot of shit. Because I didn't hook up with Danni—or anyone for that matter. Because I couldn't get a blonde from Georgia out of my head. Or my heart.

And every time someone called me that, it reminded me of that piece of shit Becker and him calling me that just before he caused Layla's seizure. And then I see her face, looking horrified in that hospital bed. Embarrassed, ashamed, and mostly like she can't stand the sight of me. I'm terrified of seeing that look on her face again. Maybe she and the Colonel could start a club.

"Dude, you look like you're thinking about murdering someone. Care to share?" Skylar asks, finally peeling his eyes from a busty brunette with pompoms standing next to us.

"Nah, I'm fine." It's a lie I'm used to telling.

They announce the football team first. Cocky pricks.

Skylar and Austin are arguing back and forth about who's going to bang which cheerleader and punching each other over me when they disagree. I almost miss it when they call my name.

Standing quickly, I offer a small wave at the crowd and sit back down. But my neck is hot and I feel someone watching me, even after they move on to introducing the Lacrosse team. And Crew. And even the cheerleaders. Leaning back in my metal folding chair, I glance all around, scanning the stands for whoever's stare is burning a hole into my back.

Random faces blur together and I'm unable to distinguish any one person concentrating on me specifically. Maybe I'm just tired. Or paranoid. It's been a long damn week.

After all the athletes have been introduced, a few more people yammer on about what an exciting time this is, how the university is part of our family now, and they're here for us if we need anything. Unless we get caught with booze or drugs. Then we're the fuck outta here and they wash their hands of us. Yeah, sounds about like the concept of family I'm familiar with.

They're wrapping up the speeches and we stand to sing the lame-ass alma mater. Like any of us know the words. A gentle vibration in my pocket tells me I have a new message and I pull out my phone.

Party tonite @ Blackburn's. Bring beer. And girls.

It's from Lucas Taite, and I glance around to see Skylar, Austin, and a few other guys glancing at their phones. First night—impressive. The ink's probably still wet on the Collegiate Athlete Code of Conduct I signed in Coach's office this morning.

Good thing I brought my fake I.D. The girls might be a little harder to obtain, but I'm sure Skylar will be on top of that. Literally, I bet.

I turn to tell him he's on chick duty when that feeling of being watched pummels me again. It's so intense that I can tell which direction it's coming from. Up and to my right. The marching band is filing out, but in between the tubas and drums I see her. The girl staring at me like she's seen a ghost. And not one she's particularly fond of.

She looks slightly different than the girl in my memory. Her skin is a darker shade of golden and her hair is a little lighter, like she's been at the beach. But it's her. I can feel it with everything I am. I want to call out, ask her to wait for me while I climb the bleachers like a maniac to get to her. But the horrified expression she wears keeps me still and silent for a full minute. She's done waiting for me. She said everything she had to say with her last text message nearly nine months ago. **Goodbye Landen.**

CHAPTER *Five*

Layla

"Can we go?" I say to Corin, standing abruptly, because I'm getting out of here whether she comes or not. I can barely hear my own voice over the drums, or maybe that's the sound of my heart pounding in my ears. I know in my head I'm here, in college, not in Hope Springs. But the memory is so vivid I might as well be right back in Georgia, watching my world fall apart at a Christmas parade.

"Landen!" the dark-eyed, dark-haired girl squeals as she throws herself into his arms.

"Huh?" Corin asks, having just started to get up to sing the alma mater with the rest of the stadium.

"I need to go, *now*." The stadium spins around me and staying upright is a struggle. *Focus, Layla. Don't do this here. Let it go.* But my mind isn't cooperating.

The dark-haired girl kisses him, right on the mouth, right in front of me. But that didn't hurt as much as the words that came after.

Your mom said you guys were moving back to Colorado. So we came to help you pack.

All through the parade, I'd been tingling with anticipation. It was the night I was going to tell Landen I was ready—ready to be more than friends. I was going to kiss him, let him be my very first kiss, my first boyfriend, my first everything. And he was hiding a secret girlfriend back in Colorado the whole time. One he was about to move back to in a matter of days, a fact he hadn't even bothered to mention to me.

"Danni," he informed me with a panicked smile. *"Friend of mine from Colorado."* Apparently, in Colorado, *friends* kiss each other on the mouth.

Corin lifts her designer knock-off bag and the bright purple *Welcome to SoCal* bags we've been given from the floor and slings them over her shoulder.

"Sure, let's go. You all right?"

"I'm fine. Just not feeling so well." Because my past has just caught up with me. He's here. It's really him. I saw him when we first sat down but only from the side and I was sure I was imagining things. *Maybe that guy just looks like him, sits like him, runs his hands through his hair like him.* There wasn't a roster in the programs we were given so I had to wait until they called his name. *Number thirteen, striker, Landen O'Brien from Colorado Springs, Colorado.* He's not *from* anywhere, I thought to myself before my brain had time to catch up with my heart.

This was supposed to be the beginning of a new life. My new life. The one where I start over, where no one knows that broken girl from Hope Springs, Georgia, or what she's been through. And he's here. At my dream school. Sending all my painful high school memories flooding back, threatening to drown me. He wouldn't have even applied to SoCal if it weren't for me. I knew he probably wouldn't go to UGA after everything that happened. But why *here*? I've seen him with my own two eyes and it's still not real.

"Um, Layla, was that fine piece of soccer hotness just calling your name?" Corin asks as we exit the stadium. *Was he?* Oh God. He saw me too then.

"Huh? No, I doubt it." But I pick up the pace and she side-eyes me so hard I'm breaking down under the intensity. "Maybe."

"And you're running like your panties just caught fire because…?"

"Because," I say, trying my darnedest to swallow even though my mouth is the Sahara. "Because I do not want to see him."

Or do I? Dang it! I do not want to *want to* see him.

"Listen, speedy, you're gonna have to slow down a little. These boots ain't made for sprintin'," my roommate informs me.

I sigh in frustration and slow the slightest bit. "I kind of know him, or I used to, a long time ago."

"Uh huh. Looked like he was pretty interested in a reunion."

"Yeah, well, I'm not," I snap. My teeth clench, and immediately I regret pulling this bitch-move on Corin because she seems nice enough. And let's face it, I'm not exactly in a position to turn down a friend. And we have to live together for at least a year. But every thought associated with him hurts. What we were, what we never got the chance to be. How much I missed him. *Still miss him.* The image of that girl, *Danni,* he called her, leaping into his arms and kissing him when I was supposed to be the one doing that. Just before he told me he was leaving, finishing out his senior year back in Colorado because his mom was leaving his dad and needed him to go with her. He forced his way into my life just to leave when I already had more than enough abandonment issues to send a therapist's triplets to college. Ivy league.

Fricking Landen O'Brien and his uncanny ability to interrupt my regularly scheduled life.

Corin doesn't say anything else when we get back to the dorm, but when I collapse on my bed, she sits across from me on hers. She's completely still and her probing hazel eyes are wide as she waits for me to carve out my heart and show it to her. I fidget with my plum-colored comforter, tracing the random pattern with a finger. I figure I'll just wait her out. But moments later, when I look up, she's still there. Still waiting. And it's not like she has anywhere to be or like I can get away from her. This roommate thing is going to take some getting used to. At least Aunt Kate had a demanding job to deal with.

"He was just a friend," I breathe out, relenting and making a mental note to suggest she major in criminal justice so she can make good use of her impressive interrogation skills. Just the look on her face has me wanting to spill my guts.

"But..."

"But it had the potential to be more. A lot more. And then he moved away." I shrug. There. Easy peasy. Doesn't sound so bad. "And now he's here."

She leans forward, propping her elbows on her knees. "Layla, I have eyes. You were trembling with...rage or fear or something. Did he *hurt* you?"

It takes me a second to realize she means like in a sexual assault kind of way. "No," I shake my head, but my heart is cussing me for a liar. Demanding that I not reduce what it went through. "Not like you mean, but yeah. Um, I thought it was more than it was...more than friendship. Turns out he had a girlfriend in Colorado, where he was from. And he went back to her and that was that."

And I deleted every text and voicemail he left afterwards because I couldn't stand the pain.

"What a dick," Corin proclaims, and with three words she's the best friend I've ever had.

I can't help but laugh at the outrage on her face. "There's maybe a little more to it than that. But I don't even know all the details for certain, and it's exhausting to think about. I just can't believe he's *here*."

"Oh shit. Do you think he might be stalking you or something?" Her eyes widen almost impossibly. "Should we tell someone?"

Sighing, I glance up at the ceiling. "Um no, I don't think so. I think he might have failed to apply to any other schools besides this one and UGA, where we were supposed to go together so..."

"So here you are, both of you." She grins, an impish little smirk sneaking across her face, and I don't like where this is going. "It's like fate or something."

"No." I cut her off with a shake of my head. "Not fate." Or maybe it is. Fate and I have never been friends.

"Fine. I don't really believe in any of that anyway. But at the very least maybe you guys could talk, and he could explain why he went back with that other girl—"

"No."

"Okay, well, it's kind of a small campus and—"

"Corin."

"Okay, okay," she says, holding her hands up in submission. "But can I ask one more question?"

Huffing out a breath, I lean back into the white and silver pillows on my bed. "If you must."

"Did he, I mean…is he *the one*?"

"The one what?"

"You know, the one. The one who took your v-card."

"Oh my God, no. I'm still carrying that particular card, thank you very much." I roll my eyes up to the ceiling, wondering if that would still be true if Landen had stayed. If I'd never met Danni.

She mercifully ignores the fact that I'm probably the only virgin on campus. "Well, was he like your first kiss or something? Cause I gotta tell you, the way you ran out of there…"

She doesn't say anything else and neither do I. The silence stretches out long and awkward between us.

Corin is from New York. She's got tattoos all up her back. I saw them when she was changing for bed last night. And I saw the economy-sized box of condoms she had in her dresser when we unpacked. Now there's a girl who's lived. She is most likely not a virgin. And I'm about to tell her I've never even been kissed. She's kind of high-strung—I'm almost worried she'll die of shock and that I should keep this to myself for her safety.

"Layla?" My eyes are closed, and I'm wondering if I can pretend I've dozed off. I feel drained enough to make it a reality. "Layla Flaherty, roommate of mine, at the very least you are going to give me some juicy details about making out with that beautiful hunk of man meat."

I swallow hard and give my head a small shake. "Can't."

"You guys never even kissed? Seriously?" I don't have to look over to know her thin, perfectly arched eyebrows are ascending into her hairline about now. "Wow. But he looked so—"

"I've never been kissed. By him or anyone." There you go—commence freak out.

Corin doesn't disappoint. She jumps up, slamming her head into a shelf above her bed, knocking several pictures down. I glance over to see her rubbing her head and glaring at the shelf like it attacked her. And then she's looking at me like I just told her I was raised by little green one-eyed men on planet Cyclops. "You're like a…"

Loser?

"Unicorn," Corin finishes, catching me off guard.

"What?"

"Layla, holy hell. You're eighteen, gorgeous, and no guy has ever kissed you? It's not even…I mean, it doesn't even make logical sense. Especially since classes haven't even started and a ridiculously hot guy looked more than ready to climb over an entire marching band to get to you."

Her words force my mind to picture him. He's even more beautiful than I remembered. And Good Lord. That look he had in those hypnotic green eyes of his. Hungry. Determined. It sends me crashing back down to reality, and I kind of want to disappear into my bed or grab my laptop and get online to find out if it's too late to transfer to UGA.

I must look as close to losing it as I actually am because Corin sighs and stands up. "I am going to leave you be—for now. But tonight, there will be parties. We will be at these parties. You will be getting kissed at said parties if it's the last thing I do." With that announcement, she turns to head out into the common room but I stop her.

"Hey, um, thanks for leaving with me. I know I was kind of intense." *And intensely bitchy.*

She offers me a sympathetic smile. "No problem. That's what friends do," she says easily just before she slides the door closed so I can have some privacy. Good thing, because I'm pulled down into a painful memory I can't escape even if I want to.

"That's what friends do," he said, holding me in his arms after I told him what had happened to my parents. "They tell each other stuff. They keep each other still when no one else can. They show up at the hospital with flowers."

"Friends." I choke back a sob.

"Always," he promises with a squeeze. My heart slows in my chest, because for the first time in my seventeen years, I want more. I want Landen to be so much more than just my friend.

I doze off drowning in memories.

"I'm all done in the bathroom if you want to shower," Corin tells me when I emerge bleary-eyed from our room hours later.

I stumble into the tiny common area that barely holds a flat screen television, the futon Aunt Kate bought us, and a desk that was here when we moved in. "Is that a hint?" My clothes are rumpled and my makeup is probably smeared all over my face.

"Um, actually it's a direct order, but I thought I should phrase it nicely since we've only been living together a short time."

"Gee, thanks."

"Layla, the goal is to get boys to want to kiss you. Though you could go as you are and pretend to be wasted and I'd probably have to fight them off you."

I snort. "You're hilarious."

"There's a party within walking distance of campus. We're going. A cute boy is going to kiss you before the night is over. Here." Corin throws a scrap of fabric at me that I think is supposed to be a dress. But mostly it's a sheer crimson sleeveless shirt.

I eye it cautiously. "I thought you wanted me to get kissed. Not raped."

"Ugh, this is going to be harder than I thought." She rolls her eyes. "Wear tights under it, if you must."

Oh, I must. And a sweater over it while I'm at it.

A half-hour later, I'm showered and Corin is fighting me on the sweater. I give in and wear her nearly see-through shirt-dress with black leggings and flats. The dress I can handle I suppose, but the stilettos she wants me to wear are out of the question.

After I've finished with my hair and makeup, I stand next to her in the full-length mirror on her closet door.

Corin's legs are bare under a tiny white lace skirt. Her black leather jacket matches her clunky knee boots, and she looks like something out of a magazine with her smoky eyes and red lips.

"I doubt many guys will notice me with you around," I say, nudging her to let her know I'm okay with this. More than okay really. Getting noticed will never be my thing.

"Layla, I don't know what you see when you look in the mirror, but I was just thinking that you look like the girl every guy wants to take home to Mom. And I look like the slut he hooks up with behind your back."

"You don't look slutty, Corin." Well, not really. Racy is a better word. I shake my head. "You look like a friggin' supermodel. The only reason a guy might even talk to me tonight is to get your number. Makes me wonder what the person in charge of assigning roommates was thinking."

"They were thinking that you needed me," she says, nudging me back. I force a grin but my stomach tightens. I needed someone else once before too, and that ended in my already battered heart being nearly decimated. "And hey, I was thinking—"

"Oh no. She's *thinking* again."

"Shut up. Seriously, I am all for getting you kissed tonight because honestly, you don't know true bliss until someone has made the world spin around you. Made you dizzy and tingly with a deep, hot as hell kiss that goes on and on until you don't care if you ever get to breathe again." She sighs and tilts her head in my direction. "But I can be kind of pushy, in case you haven't noticed. If you don't want to do this, say the word and I'll drop it."

Her words already have the room threatening to spin on me. Because one face is burning to life behind my eyes. "No, um, I mean, I'm in. It's time. It's way past time I think."

"Hells yeah." Corin's triumphant grin has me rolling my eyes, but inside I'm a twisty aching mess. Because the only boy I can imagine kissing me until he steals my breath is the one I've vowed never to let that close to me again. Which is why I have to get myself out there and kiss someone else. Immediately.

I give my too-short dress one last tug. "I'm ready. Let's go."

CHAPTER Six

Landen

"I think a case of Natty will be enough?" Skylar asks once we enter the Stop-N-Shop right off campus.

"For me," I say as we reach the beer coolers. "But what are the rest of you fuckers going to drink?"

Truth is, I probably won't drink at all. I can barely remember my time in Colorado for how hard I tried to drink Layla Flaherty out of my mind. Danni and her brother Tucker dragged my ass out of the darkness like soldiers might pull a wounded brother from battle. If they hadn't, I don't know where I'd be right now. Probably not in college. Not so close to her. Again.

Skylar yanks a case from the cooler and the familiar temptation pulls at me. Maybe I *should* just get wasted so I can stop thinking about that look on her face. All the looks. The trusting smile from our first date, the longing in her eyes at Homecoming while she waited for me to man up and make a move, the humiliation that broke across her face when she woke up in the hospital, the way her eyes dimmed when she learned I was leaving, the way she shut down completely before I left. And the worst one of all. The panicked anguish displayed so clearly on her face when she saw me in the arena today. Because she doesn't want me here.

On second thought, I'm going to be getting trashed after all. Beer's not going to cut it though.

"Hey, man, you know if there's a liquor store nearby?" I ask the clerk as he rings us up. The kind of pain losing Layla Flaherty inflicts on a man cannot be soothed with beer. You have to douse it in gasoline, burn it out, retch it up, and let it bang against your skull for days afterwards, just for a distraction. Knowing the whole time that it'll be back before you have a second to miss it.

"Down on Fifth next to Big Jim's Pawn," the old man grumbles. He flicks my ID back at me and I have a feeling he knows it's a fake but doesn't really give a shit.

"Thanks," I say with a nod as he hands me my change.

Fifth is damn near in the ghetto. California is like that, I'm learning. One minute you're cruising by mansions and stores you can't even afford to park at, but two wrong turns later you're in a town they only mention in rap songs.

"Dude, liquor?" Skylar asks as we search for the store.

"It's necessary," I inform him.

"Have anything to do with that girl blowing you off at orientation earlier?" He's too observant for his own damn good.

"Something like that," I say, licking my lips in anticipation of the burn as the liquor store appears on my left.

I've already broken the neck on the bottle of Johnnie Walker when we get to Blackburn's. The condo is a two-story with a balcony and people are spilling out every which way. The darkness I'm carrying begs me to go back to the dorm and drink alone until I pass out but I'm already here. And Skylar is super pumped about kicking Blackburn's and Taite's asses at beer pong. I've let enough people down for one lifetime. So I stay. For now at least.

Bass from a song I can't name off the top of my buzzed head throbs out into the street, pushing against us as we make our way through the crowd.

The kitchen is narrow and several girls brush intentionally against me as I clear a spot for Skylar to put the case down. I clutch my bottle of Johnnie tight because I'm not sharing.

Skylar is busy texting some chick he knows from high school about bringing her hot roommates to meet up with us. I lean against the counter next to a couple too busy inhaling each other's faces to notice me.

The alcohol puts up a hazy wall around me, separating me from the commotion I'm supposed to be a part of. This isn't me. I don't really want this. I want her. My Georgia peach, as Skylar has already started calling her, though he doesn't know the half of it. Pizza and a movie on my couch with her in my arms would be heaven compared to this—this fake life I couldn't give a shit about. Class, practice, games, and parties full of faceless randoms that can't hold a candle to her. It's going to be a long four years if I have to keep this up.

Yeah, I'm out of here. "Hey, man, you okay if I take off?"

Skylar glances up from his phone. "Aw hell, dude. Kelsie's roommate is all excited to meet you. What's the problem, man? You need a hug?" He slips his phone in his pocket and comes at me with arms open wide and his lips puckered. "Come to Papa."

"Get the hell away from me, dickslice," I say, shoving him backward.

He frowns at me. "Come on, O'Brien. Don't be a pussy. So some chick blew you off. There's probably a dozen or so here who'd probably be happy to blow you off in a way that doesn't make you all pouty."

"Fuck you," I say before putting a deeper dent in my bottle.

"What's going on, ladies?" Ben Blackburn booms, swiping Johnnie from my hands and taking a swig before handing it back. The kitchen is closing in on me and my vision is slightly blurred.

"I've killed guys bigger than you for less," I damn near growl at him, but he laughs. Maybe I'm losing my edge.

"Don't piss him off. He's already trying to bail," Skylar tells him as a few other guys from the team cram into the obscenely overcrowded kitchen.

"Afraid we'll kick your ass at beer pong?" Blackburn challenges, backing up to lean against the fridge.

"Yeah, shit keeps me up at night." I take another mouthful of liquid courage from my bottle and contemplate slamming my fist into his chin for no other reason than he'd hit me back and the pain would be a welcome distraction.

"Let's get Taite and do this," Skylar says, stepping between us.

"Taite's working something right now. Probably best to leave him be. Besides, I can handle you girls all by myself."

"I'll be on Blackburn's team," Dean speaks up. I hadn't even seen him come in. Whatever. I amble into the living room behind them.

But as we set up the plastic cups on our side of the sticky table, I get a clear shot of exactly what Lucas Taite is "working." And I see red. Literally. And it's not just the label on my bottle. It's the color of her dress. And her perfect lips.

Before Skylar or anyone else can stop me, I'm around the table, over a couch, and pressing Taite against the wall with my forearm.

"Jesus, O'Brien. What the fuck?" He tries to snarl at me but I've caught him off guard. If I press any harder, I'll probably snap his windpipe. My senses are heightened and I can hear his every breath. Or maybe that's her breath. Or mine.

"There are a hundred other girls here. Find one." My voice comes out low and lethal, so much like my father's I almost don't recognize it as my own. The image of his hand skimming slowly down Layla's bare arm unleashed an uncontrollable rage inside of me. The way he was leaning into her, watching her mouth as she smiled up at him. My forearm is practically vibrating with the need to hurt him. No, my entire body is, like I've been plugged into an electric wall socket. Fuck, I'm losing it.

"I'll have you kicked off the team for this," he says evenly, barely loud enough to be heard over the blood rushing in my ears.

"How about I break your goddamn legs and then neither of us will play?"

"Taite, you good?" Blackburn calls from behind me. I almost flinch at the thought of a beer bottle shattering over my head.

"Yeah," he says, straightening as I pull back and let him up off the wall. His eyes stay on mine, and I hope he sees the threat in them. It's valid.

"I'd get some air if I were you," he says under his breath, and I have to admit, it's not a bad idea. Because if I look at her right now, I don't know what will happen to any of us. So I grab my bottle off the Ping-Pong table and storm out the nearest door without looking back.

Dropping down onto some concrete steps off the back porch, I take a drink and try to clear my head. Not that Johnnie really helps with that much. A minute hasn't even passed when I feel someone behind me. Probably Blackburn about to jump me or something. I take another drink and wait for the blow but it doesn't come. A high-pitched female voice does though.

"So you don't want her but no one else can have her either? Is that it?" The shrill, shrieking redhead is unfamiliar to me, but boy is she pissed. I twist around to face her, realizing it's probably not a good thing that I'm sitting and she's standing above me.

"Don't believe I've had the pleasure of making your acquaintance," I slur at her. "Who the fuck are you exactly?"

"I'm Layla's roommate. And I know exactly who the fuck *you* are. You're that *guy*. The one who tossed her aside for some chick in Colorado and then showed up here to ruin her life."

Jesus, whoever she is, she has her sights set on pounding the shit out of my heart. And the girl has impeccable aim.

"Corin," Layla says softly, coming up behind her. Her voice slams me back into high school. I force myself to fight off the onslaught of memories and focus. I'm here now. In the present. We're both different, and I can't do a thing about any of the pain I caused either of us in the past. But I want to. I want to apologize my ass off and beg for her forgiveness. Damn. It's kind of a shitty time to be trashed.

"I'm sorry," I say, doing my best not to slur the words. I try to look her in the eyes, but there's two of her. The one from my memories and the one actually standing here. They blur together and then back apart and I blink in an attempt to focus on the girl standing before me now.

Her roommate pulls at her arm, but she keeps her gaze on me. At least, I think it's on me. "Don't, Layla. Don't let him apologize. Walk away. Because what happened in there was bullshit and you know it."

Damn, Ginger is really amped up. Maybe even more than me. But I'm glad to see that Layla has someone protecting her, like I should've done.

"I'm okay," she says, touching the other girl's arm. "I'll come back inside in a minute."

She turns the full force of her bright ocean-colored eyes on me, and suddenly I'm the one who needs protecting. Because I want to grovel at her feet. I want to beg her to give me another chance, to forget everything that happened and start over. Or pick up where we left off before it all went to hell. I want to blurt out that I love her and I miss her and I haven't stopped loving her or missing her since the day I left Hope Springs.

I need a do-over dammit. And I need it to start right the fuck now.

CHAPTER Seven

Layla

He's still angry, but the outside air seems to be diluting his rage enough. There's something wild and desperate in his eyes that scares me a little. I walk to the edge of the back porch and lower myself onto the steps next to him. My heart forgets how to beat for a second and ends up all out of rhythm.

His black Henley is snug and unbuttoned at the top. I'm not ready to look at his face yet so I focus on the small gray buttons. "Landen," I say, both loving and hating the feel of his name on my tongue. I'm a little dizzy from the shots I did with the Luke guy and Corin. I'm probably getting even more intoxicated from Landen's whiskey-drenched breath.

"Layla," he says, his voice rough and raked over, making my head swim. The memory of what we were before, what we almost were, hits me hard enough to knock the wind out of me. High school was yesterday. And it was a lifetime ago. And I'm lost, trying to remember how to talk to him and breathe at the same time.

I take a few calming breaths in an attempt to compose myself. "You gonna show up every time a guy makes a move on me?" I take the bottle he's staring at and pull it to my lips. Smells about as enticing as nail polish remover mixed with paint thinner, but I take a drink anyways, using my tongue to catch the trickle that escapes onto my lips. My esophagus immediately bursts into flames and I close my eyes, temporarily blinded by the pain.

When I open them Landen's darkened stare meets mine, and it's a wonder my flesh doesn't melt under the intensity. I remember his eyes being a much lighter shade of green.

"Depends," he says, and I have to scramble through my memory to figure out what question he's answering as I hand him back his bottle. "You gonna make out with all my teammates?"

Ouch. My body reacts first, struggling to stand, to put some distance between us. But he reaches out a hand, gripping my thigh, and I'm frozen to the concrete. Words form in my mind but don't make it to my mouth. *I've never made out with anyone. Why are you here? Why didn't you ever kiss me? How's Danni?*

"That was a shitty thing to say. I'm sorry." His hand relaxes but doesn't leave my leg.

"Maybe we don't have to do this to each other," I suggest, unable to look at him. "Maybe we can just leave it."

He stiffens. "Please don't say you want to be friends, because honestly, I'd rather you break this bottle over my head and use it to slice me open."

"Jesus, Landen. I wasn't going to say that. I was going to say we can be civil, we can live and let live. We're both adults now—it doesn't have to be like…like it was in there."

"That what you want?" he asks, round, warm eyes pleading into mine.

"Mmhm," I murmur, because what can I say? *No, I want you. I want you to have kissed me back then, to have loved me like I loved you, to love me still. To keep me still like you used to.* Yeah, no.

"You're different," he announces suddenly, his voice clear and devoid of the intimate intensity that's been singeing between us for the past few minutes.

I shrug. "People change."

"The Layla I used to know wasn't much of a party girl." He's smirking at me, and my skin prickles in annoyance.

"The Landen I knew wouldn't have pinned a teammate against a wall for no good reason."

"Oh I had a reason," he mumbles, and I'm beyond irritated at his arrogance. "He was touching you."

Anger flares within me. "Oh, no! Some guy finally saw me as more than a charity case, so you had to sweep in and fix it? A member of the male species saw me as more than a friend, and you're pissed because I'm supposed to wait until you sort out all your women and figure out what you want from me? I'll pass."

"All my women? What the fu—"

"Tell *Danni* hello for me," I say, finally standing and bracing myself to walk away. For good. "And feel free to leave me alone from here on out."

"Dammit, Layla," he shouts. Shattering glass rings out across the small yard as the bottle he's thrown connects with the wooden fence. Whirling around, I meet his panicked stare, but I'm okay. The darkness doesn't come, because the medicine is working. For now. But he's an asshole for doing it and we both know it.

"Nice." The acidic pain and disbelief leak into my voice. It hitches but I don't care.

"God, I'm sorry," he slurs. "Layla, please…I'm so fucking sorry." He runs a hand through his hair and struggles to stand. Looking at him, I can see he's damaged. Broken like I was when we first met this time last year. And he helped me, pulled me out of the darkness. A part of me is grateful and wants to reach out and pull him up now. Return the favor. But I'm still hurting. Seeing him still hurts. Bad. And it's a hell of a lot more likely that he'll just pull me down with him if I try.

Chapter Eight

Landen

She walked away. Just like before. Didn't even bother with a goodbye this time.

And I deserved it. It's for the best, I tell myself the next day at practice. Layla Flaherty has the power to ruin me. To turn me into the worst version of myself. I finally cut all ties with the Colonel, so I'll be damned if I give anyone that kind of power over me again. Not even her.

"Hey, about last night. My bad, man," I say to Taite while we line up for sprinting drills. "I know her, and we have a bit of unfinished history." My pride tastes like shit going down, but dude could make my life a living hell if he really wanted to. And I was out of line. He didn't know I knew her, and who the fuck am I anyways? She's obviously over it, whatever it was.

"It's cool, O'Brien. But maybe next time you could just casually bring it to my attention if I'm scamming on your girl?" He grins and I feel like an even bigger dick because Taite's not Blackburn. He's actually a decent guy.

"I'll do that," I say as I move up in line. But I won't. Not really. Because she wasn't really ever mine. And it's time to let her go.

Let her go. Let her go. Let her go. I'm repeating it in my head like a lifeline as I run myself into the ground after practice. If I'm exhausted, I can't lie awake thinking about her. About how much stronger she is now. The irony isn't lost on me. Once upon a time, she was an island, and I pulled her to shore. And now I'm all fucked up and lost in the dark, and she's the one holding the damn flashlight.

But why should she save me?

"Not that I'm not enjoying this five-mile sprint after practicing my ass off, but you about done yet?" Skylar's keeping pace with me but his gray practice shirt is drenched. "Because I'm damn sure done."

I'm not. Not until I run her out of my system. Or at least my need for her. "You can go back to the dorm if you want. Bake some cookies or some shit."

"Fuck you, dude. Seriously. You need to get laid something fierce."

I pant for breath but force myself to go faster. "You volunteering?"

"Naw, but I'll take an ad out in the school paper if you want. Uptight motherfucker, needs a release, preferably of the vagina kind."

Laughing makes my side pinch so I slow to a stop and put my hands up on top of my head.

"Your Georgia peach not giving it up or what?" Skylar presses, leaning over to clutch his knees.

I don't say anything, but he's in dangerous territory, so I level his ass with a glare. Taite didn't know any better, but Skylar does. Maybe not all the details but the gist.

He doesn't take the hint. "If you love something, sometimes you just gotta set it free, or some bullshit."

"I can hardly believe you don't have a girlfriend," I tell him.

"Yeah, well, your girl's redheaded friend was pretty damn fine looking. Hook a brother up."

"She's not my girl." Not anymore anyways. Damn, my side is stinging.

"So I noticed, and by the way, your pussy lips are showing. You gonna do anything about it or what?"

What can I do? I almost ask him out loud. But the answer's so damn obvious I could trip over it. Letting her go is not the direction I should be headed.

"I got Red's number last night," Skylar continues, pulling me from my revelation. "I could call and see if they want to hit a club or two with us tonight. And while I'm nailing Red, you and Peaches could knit some sweaters together or something. Maybe a nice little satchel for her to put your balls in."

Fuck it. The worst that can happen is she can say no. "Yeah, you do that. And maybe don't mention to Red that you plan to "nail" her. She seems pretty lethal. Probably mess you up pretty good if she heard you say that."

"Don't worry about my game, O'Brien. I got this." He's grinning like it's a sure thing, but that girl was ferocious as fuck, like a rabid dog that eats balls for breakfast. I have a feeling she'll chew Skylar's cocky ass up and spit him out. Oh well. Not my problem. I have my own shit to worry about.

CHAPTER Nine

Layla

"What's this?" I ask my roommate as she strolls in and sets two bags on my bed. One is plastic and from Target and the other is small and brown.

"My surefire remedy for a broken heart," Corin says, nodding at them.

I'm still in bed, unwashed and waterlogged from tears I should've kept to myself. I sit up and peek in the plastic bag. A half pint of Ben & Jerry's Half Baked, a box of Kleenex, and a tube of shimmery coral-colored lip gloss. I check the paper bag. A few sample size bottles of liquor stare back at me.

"I don't get it." And how did she buy liquor? Something tells me Corin gets around pesky things like rules and laws regarding the proper ID required to purchase alcohol.

"Oh! I almost forgot the most important part." She turns, grabs a CD from her collection, and pops it in the player on the nightstand. "Don't worry. I'll load this on your iPod later."

"What is it?" A woman's voice fills the room, and I swear to whatever higher power is listening, it's my pain personified.

Corin hands me a slim case with a gorgeous and tatted up woman on the cover. Christina Perri, *Lovestrong*, it says. Never heard of it but this woman is singing to my wounded soul like she's experienced the exact kinds of loss I have. I make a mental note to like her on Facebook and add her to my Spotify playlist.

"You have exactly fifty-eight minutes and fifty-four seconds to wallow in your self-pity. Eat the ice cream, cry if you need to, use the Kleenex." She pauses and hands me a spoon so I do as I'm told. "And then, when the music stops, you are going to shower. Then we're going to get ready to go out. Pour yourself a drink." She stands and retrieves the little liquor bottles from the bag. "Put on some lipstick." I pull out the lip gloss and she nods with approval. "And pull yourself together."

I can't help but grin. "Wow. You come up with that yourself?"

"No, Elizabeth Taylor did. But it works. Trust me." With that, Corin leaves me alone with my pain and goody bags.

And it kind of does work. By the time the CD ends, I feel like a human being again. Though songs four and five on the disc slayed me all over again and I almost ran out of tissues. I take a shower and call my Aunt Kate afterwards because I've been avoiding telling her about Landen for long enough.

"I'm sorry it's difficult Layla, but you've survived worse," she reminds me once I've finished with the sordid details.

"I know. I just…didn't expect to see him here."

Aunt Kate clears her throat. "But isn't it kind of nice to have someone you know there? I have to admit, I'm having a hard time with you being all the way across the country."

I sigh and bite my thumbnail. "I don't know. Seeing him wasn't easy. I don't know if we can just be friends. Maybe I'm being stupid," I admit, because maybe I am overreacting. Maybe it's a good thing that he's here.

"Layla, you are the exact opposite of stupid. Not to mention the kindest, most forgiving girl I've ever known. I'd like to take credit for it except your mom was always the good-hearted one. Hence why she was the counselor and I'm the bitchy lawyer."

"You're not bitchy," I tell her with a laugh. Except I've seen her in court and she is pretty ruthless actually. "Just good at your job."

"I just want you to be happy…happy and safe," she adds quietly.

"I know, and you're right. I can play nice with Landen. He means well." I think.

"I know you can. You're not only sweet and kind but you're strong, probably the strongest girl I'll ever have the pleasure of knowing."

"Thanks, Aunt Kate. Love you."

"Love you, too, Lay. Miss you."

Her faith in me is enough to help me put on the strapless black dress Corin persuaded me to buy at a trendy boutique downtown. I slip on the heels I wore to Homecoming, and memories threaten to suffocate me. The girl Landen turned down to go with me to the dance had a brother—a big one who wasn't too happy that his little sister got her feelings hurt. He argued with Landen at the dance then punched the metal doors open to leave the gym. Down I went like the London Bridge.

The feel of Landen holding me in his arms, keeping me still when no one else could, starts to drag me back into that black hole of hopelessness. Corin pours me a shot of something that smells like melted caramel just in time.

"He's in love with you," she says from behind me and I almost jab my eye out with the mascara brush. "You know that, right?"

I turn to her as a huff of disagreement leaves my throat. "No, he's not."

"He almost broke that guy's neck for *talking* to you, Layla. Maybe it wasn't the healthiest display of affection, but there was an awful lot of pent-up emotion in that boy."

I shake my head. "Can we just not talk about him tonight?" For the sake of my already fragile mental well-being. "I need a break."

"Sure, no talking about him. Promise." But she doesn't look at me as she says it.

We go downstairs and take a cab to some club called Shortie's because neither of us wants to walk a million miles and risk breaking an ankle. Plus we may slightly resemble hookers in our club clothes. A remix of Titanium is throbbing and pulsing through the club as Corin drags me onto the dance floor.

I've never danced like this in public, but her energy is contagious, and I'm shaking everything I have for all I'm worth while we scream the lyrics at each other. One day I'll tell her what this song means to me, what I survived. But for now I'm focusing on letting loose and having a good time. My parents would want that for me. Though they might not have been be too excited about the underage drinking.

"I owe you," I shout over the music. A demon of vengeance sent me Landen O'Brien, but an angel of mercy sent me Corin.

"Hold that thought," she shouts back.

"What?"

"Please don't hate me." She bites her lip and I'm completely confused.

"What?"

Corin grabs my shoulders and spins me around. And either it's the mother of all coincidences or my roommate is a traitor. Because Landen is sitting at a table on the edge of the dance floor with another guy. And they're watching us. Closely.

"What the hell, Cor—"

"Layla, chill a sec. Just list—"

But my eyes are stinging and I'm plowing through bodies to get as far away from all of them as possible. Is it too much to ask for me just to be happy? But my heart's an even bigger traitor than my roommate. *You want him here. You're glad he's here.*

When I come out on the other side of the dance floor, I'm at the bar so I give it a try.

"Can I get a shot of tequila please?" I'm still buzzed from the shots Corin and I downed in our room, but the Landen O'Brien surprise attack special kind of killed my warm, fuzzy tingles. And I want them back, dang it.

The guy doesn't even ask for ID or check to see if I have an under twenty-one hand stamp. And I do. But the shot appears and I'm going for it.

"I'll have what she's having. Make it a double," a deep voice that still sends spasms of pleasure and panic surging through me says from behind me. "I always wanted to say that. *Make it a double*," he murmurs in my ear and my knees threaten to give. He places a gentle hand on my lower back.

"Well now you have," I snap. Somehow the hurt, loss, and feelings of utter frustration I've come to associate with him add up to my being royally pissed off. I've got all this nervous energy and no place to put it.

"Wanna do a body shot?" he asks, and I turn to see if he's completely lost his mind.

"With you?"

"Hell yeah with me. Why, you interested in a replay of last night? Want to see me lose my shit again?"

I blink at him. "Not particularly."

He leans in closer, his breath fanning my face and drawing my attention to his mouth. "So what are you interested in, Layla Flaherty? Because I'm lost trying to figure you out."

I'm interested in moving on. The words linger on my tongue but they're not entirely true.

"So you've resorted to stalking me?" He shrugs and I go on. Saying what I shouldn't say because I'm too weak to hold it all in when he's this close. "I should say closure, right? So we can both move on. But since I've had a shitty day and I've been drinking, I'm just going to say what I really want."

"Which is?"

Jesus he looks good in the deep green T-shirt that brings out his eyes and hugs his broad shoulders perfectly. I let him sweat it out while I run my tongue over my hand, sprinkle it with salt, and then lick it off. Thank God Corin taught me how to shoot tequila so I don't make an ass of myself. He shifts his weight as I down my shot, but when I reach for the lime wedge I sat on the bar, it's gone.

"Looking for this?" he says, holding my lime just out of reach. Ugh, my mouth is fighting the urge to pucker but it's a losing battle. Corin said lemons would be better but I hate lemons.

"Landen!"

"Tell me what you want first."

"No," I say, making a grab for the lime but missing. Damn, he's tall.

He cocks a brow. "Why not? Scared?"

"You're the one who should be scared," I say, trying to sound fierce like

Corin but failing miserably.

"Oh, I was scared at first. Seeing you." He looks down at me, breaking through my defenses with the determined power of his glare. "But I'm done with that now. Now I'm doing what I want. I just need to make sure it's what you want, too."

"I *want* my lime wedge. Give it to me."

"Oh, I will." Landen snakes an arm around my waist and pulls me against him. "Open up."

I swallow hard, and for a second I consider refusing. But I want that lime. And I want this man even more. Who knows if we'll ever be this daring with each other again? So I open my mouth and he slips the lime in. And I suck it. Hard.

Heat pools between my legs, and I rub my thighs together to try and calm myself, but it doesn't work. This isn't a feeling I'm used to. It's been a very long time since he had this effect on me. Maybe I used to think about him this way before, once upon a time, but that was a different girl. One who wanted love and marriage and all that Happily Ever After nonsense.

When my last EEG results came back abnormal right after he moved back to Colorado, I decided that girl could forget it. And him. And now I'm looking up into Landen's perfect face, and I want something else. I want a physical connection. That kiss he owes me and then some. It might break us both, but I'm done being the girl who cries and hurts and longs. I want to be the girl who gets what she wants. For once. And the universe is not my friend when it comes to giving me what I want.

So I'm going to take it.

CHAPTER Ten

Landen

I don't know what's changed in the past twenty-four hours, but Layla's "live and let live" approach seems to have lost its appeal. We're taking shots of tequila and she's looking at me like she wants to bite me. After seeing her dancing in that tight-ass dress, I'm in.

Funny thing is, I had a completely different plan for tonight. When Skylar mentioned meeting up with them at a club earlier, I was dead set on flirting with some other girl in front of her so she could get a taste of her own medicine. I didn't want to hurt her or anything, but I wanted to make her at least admit that she was jealous. That she had some kind of feelings for me other than that *friend* bullshit she was trying to sell me.

And then we walked in, and she was writhing against the music, her bare skin an array of colors under the flashing strobe lights, and I went so hard I had to sit down. Immediately.

Skylar and I were in the middle of giving each other shit about which one of us was more pathetic for coming here when Corin spun Layla around to face me. And damn, my erection died a painful death. She looked pissed. Super pissed actually, and I hated myself for ruining her night. I know what she's been through, know better than anyone how hard it is for her to let go and have a good time. And I'd kind of hoped she might be happy to see me, but I'm a dumbshit apparently because she took off and disappeared into the crowd. Because I get off on punishment, I took off after her.

"If my being here is keeping you from enjoying yourself, I can go," I tell her once we've ordered our second round of shots.

"Why would you say that?" She was laughing about my tequila face, but my words narrow her eyes and she's still. I'm sitting on a barstool with her standing between my legs and my body is very aware of how well that dress hugs curves I don't remember her having. Curves I want to get to know intimately in the very near future.

"You were tearing it up on the dance floor when I got here and now you're not." I shrug like I don't need confirmation that she wants me here like I need my next breath.

"I'm having fun here. Why, you wanna dance or something?" Her tone is light, but her eyes are still guarded.

Or something. We're testing each other. Still putting on a show, when all I want to do is unravel her, peel away the pain, and get back to that level of comfort we had when she would fall asleep in my arms watching movies.

"I want to watch you dance."

"Hmm…guess you should dance with me then. I mean, that'd be the best possible view." She looks up at me through her eyelashes. "Unless you want me to dance with someone else."

Like hell. The mere thought has me ready to attack a faceless stranger for daring to touch her. "Lead the way and I'll follow."

The dance floor is crowded, and she's still my Layla in a lot of ways, so she parks us on the periphery of all the other grinding couples. A slower song comes on and she's moving tentatively around me, nothing like the sexy shimmy she was doing with Corin. I wrap my arms around her and pull her close to me so she can feel how turned on she makes me, and it seems to give her courage. And I have just thoroughly fucked myself because she's pressed against my dick and I'm bulging so hard it hurts.

My mouth grazes her bare shoulder and she shivers. I'm about to press my lips to her exposed neck because God help me, I have to, when Corin and Skylar spin into us and Layla pulls away—just enough that she's out of reach of my mouth. She glances shyly up at me, like they just caught us going at it or something, and I see that girl I knew a year ago. A million questions launch themselves in my brain but I'm ignoring those fuckers with all my might. This isn't about questions and answers and clearing up what went wrong. I want her to have a good time, and I want her to be able to have a good time with me without all this shit between us. More importantly, I want *her*.

So I huff and puff and barely resist the urge to piss a circle around her every time another guy checks her out. We dance, and it's fun. And hot as hell. Until her roommate pulls me aside when Layla's talking to Skylar and tells me in no uncertain terms how many people she knows in New York who would be happy to puree my balls for the right price.

"Got it," I tell her with a nod. "Balls gone."

She glares at my answering grin, but I can't be angry with anyone who obviously cares so much about the same girl I care about. There's something about Layla that has everyone wanting to protect her. She's tougher than when I first met her, bolder, but that vulnerability is still there, and it still sends testosterone coursing through me at dangerously high levels. I can't take it anymore. I have to know the answer to at least one of my questions.

Leaning down so I don't have to shout over the music, I let my lips graze her earlobe. "Can we get some air?"

She nods and we head towards the door. The outside air smacks me in the face, but it's a welcome change from the damp heat of the club that had Layla's intoxicating scent threatening to drown me. There's something else coming off her, something warm and sweet, and once again, I'm barely controlling the impulse to lick her. Damn, there are *a lot* of places I'd like to lick her.

She's leaning against the brick wall of the club and inhaling the fresh air as desperately as I am.

I clear my throat. "So Skylar's really into your roommate." *Or, he wants to get into your roommate.* Same difference for him I guess.

"Yeah, I can see that."

"You having a good time?"

"I am. Are you?" Her shoulders stiffen and mine sag because we always come back to this. Plagued by this fear that we don't feel the same way about each other looming over us.

"You *know* I am," I tell her, stepping closer to remind her of how close we were a few minutes ago and how well she could feel what a good time I was having. "Can I ask you something? Maybe more than one something?"

She eyes me warily, like I'm either about to propose or tell her this was all a big joke. "If you must."

Wow, we've been here before. The first time we ever talked. For half a second I'm that cautious guy again, afraid of offending or disappointing. But that guy struck the fuck out with this girl once already, so I'm done with him. "What is it about me that still has you all tensed up and pissed off? Because I didn't come here to hurt you, not to this club and not to SoCal."

So quickly I almost miss it, her walls come down, the ones she always puts up when I get too close. Her beautiful eyes open so wide I almost lose myself in the endless blue-green pools. But then she recovers, blinking and clearing her throat. Her defensive stance relaxes a little more and she sighs. "I keep telling myself I'm putting the past behind me, you know? Moving forward and all that. But sometimes when I see you, or you look at me a certain way, I'm right back there. Left behind in Hope Springs and..." She looks away briefly and I want to grab her, kiss her until any pain I ever caused disappears into the night. "Hurt. I was hurt. And angry. Here you had this other girl waiting for you, and I felt like a complete idiot when I found out."

My head swims in confusion. "Whoa, what other girl?"

She glares at me for a full minute before answering. "*Danni*," she spits out.

Danni? "Jesus, Layla, *that's* what you were so pissed about?" I snort out a laugh and she pins me with a fiery look as full of anger as I've ever seen her. "Her?"

"Don't laugh at me, O'Brien. You were the first boy I ever liked that way, and I had all these plans of telling you after the Christmas parade, of letting you be my first kiss, and maybe more, and you and your friends dropped this… bomb on me. Bomb after bomb actually, and it sucked. Bad." Her eyes flash, reflecting the pain I caused and didn't stick around to heal. That damn parade. The one that ended with Danni and Tuck surprise attacking us and blurting out in front of Layla what I hadn't yet told her.

"It wasn't like that, *Flaherty*. Danni and I—" My words make her flinch. I reach out but she steps back, pressing herself up against the building to get as far from me as possible. "Layla, please listen. I was crazy into you. I just knew it was new for you and I wanted to take it slow. Which, by the way, wasn't easy for me. And yeah, a relationship like that was new for me too, if I'm being honest. But Danni wasn't even an old girlfriend. She was just my best friend's sister and a girl who had a habit of being openly affectionate, and not just with me. She and Tuck know about my dad so they check in on me from time to time, but that's it. Maybe she and I had a little fling the summer before but it was nothing like what you and I had." *Have*.

I watch her bite her bottom lip, a storm swirling in her eyes as she contemplates my confession. "Well, you shouldn't have let her kiss you like that when we were…whatever we were. And I shouldn't have heard that you were moving back to Colorado from her."

My chest tightens from the sting of the pain in her voice. "Agreed, on both accounts. I'm sorry." Leaning into her space as far as I can without touching her, I lower my voice. "Forgive me?"

"I'll think about it." She's smiling. And I can breathe again. "And now I get to ask a question."

"Fair enough. Have to admit, knowing you were jealous is a pretty big turn on." I shove my hands in my pockets so I don't reach out and grab her to me like a fucking animal.

"Why are you at this college?"

My thoughts struggle to catch up to the abrupt subject change. "Um, to get a degree of higher learning and play soccer?" It's a question instead of an answer and she doesn't miss it.

"Are you asking me if that's why?"

"I'm asking in hopes you'll accept that answer instead of the real one."

"Why?"

"So things don't get weird." *And you don't run away screaming. Or hit me. Or hate me.* Truth is, I can never tell her the real reason I'm here.

"Can things get weirder than this?" she asks, stepping a little closer.

I hope to hell things can get weirder. I hope they can get downright awkward and uncomfortable, like maybe as she searches for her underwear on my bedroom floor later tonight.

Taking a deep breath, I give her the best answer I can. "I'm here because I couldn't go to UGA after what happened. You blew me off and I was hurt too. I didn't want to see you on campus, on the arm of some guy I might accidentally murder with my bare hands." Kind of like I almost did Taite.

She cocks her head. "How's that working out for you?"

"Not well." I laugh uneasily. "Okay, my turn."

She folds her arms, as if she's trying to hold her secrets in, and I'm starting to like this game. A few girls giggling loudly behind me stumble past us into the club, and Layla smirks and raises an eyebrow at them. I'm pretty sure one of them checked me out. I wasn't playing around earlier. Her blatant jealousy has my dick throbbing. But the answer to my next question will probably function to solve that problem.

"So lay it on me. Who ended up being your first kiss?" *Please be someone I don't know.* I only had two friends, if you could call them that, in Hope Springs—Cam and DW. If it was one of them, I'll be using my next long weekend to drive to Georgia and kick some ass.

Layla shakes her head, and for a second I think she's just refusing, holding out on me. "We should probably get back in there before Corin sends a search party."

"Whoa. I answered your question. All of them actually. So let me have it. I promise not to go looking for him." I'm a dick, because that's not entirely true and deep down I'm kind of hoping whoever it was sucked at it.

But then her cheeks go pink and hope runs wildfire rampant in my chest. She shakes her head again, biting her lip as her eyes say the one thing I want to hear. She's never been kissed. My eyes zero in on her perfect untouched mouth. I reach out, using my thumb to pull her full bottom lip from between her teeth. "No one?"

She shrugs and I force myself to pull my hand from her mouth. She's back to wearing that same tentative, guarded expression, and I'm feeling the screwed up combination of sheer joy at the fact that her mouth is still unclaimed and a significant degree of guilt for all the dirty thoughts I've been having for a girl who's never even kissed a guy. Well, that part's easy enough to fix.

"Don't go running on me now, Layla Flaherty," I say, giving into the urge to pull her to me. She feels so damn good in my hands, soft and firm at the same time. "Not yet."

"Landen," she breathes, placing her delicate hands on my chest but not making an effort to push. Or maybe I'm too full of myself to feel if she pushes. "Stop. We're in public."

Uh, yeah. And I was grinding all up on her ass in *public* a few minutes ago, but this is making her uncomfortable? Glancing around, I see a break between the club and the next building over so I pull her into it. "This better?"

"Um." She's breathing harder, and the space between the two brick buildings is so tight her chest is pressing against mine.

"Tell me what you want," I demand, pulling her two wrists into one of my hands. I lift them above her head so I can feel her body on mine without our hands in the way.

"I want…" She pauses to swallow, and I don't know why I need her to ask for it…but I do. I need to know that this is what she wants. That I'm the one she wants. "I want to have fun, to stop worrying and feeling guilty all the time just for being alive."

Okay, well that wasn't exactly the response I was hoping for, but beggars can't be choosers. "And how should we go about making that happen? Specifically," I clarify, letting my lips rest just a few inches from hers. I can feel her breath on my mouth. "Tell me what I can do to help."

Her little pink tongue swipes her lips, coming so close to my own I can practically taste her, and I nearly come undone right then and there. "You should kiss me."

I move in closer, but only a tiny bit. "And why would I do that?"

Her voice is so low I have to lean in to hear her clearly. "Because you want to. Because I've been waiting for a very long time. Because you can."

Her words fill me with heat and need. I want so much more than to kiss her. But I'm not going to get greedy here and risk losing her all over again. My plan to make her jealous earlier was just a ploy to get her to admit she still wants me because I still want her. I'm pretty positive I'll always want her. So now this has to be the best damn kiss two people ever shared in the history of kissing because I need her to want it again and again.

Tension builds in my chest at the thought of finally kissing Layla Flaherty, and I'm a little afraid of screwing up her first kiss. But I owe it to her. It should've happened a long time ago.

"Someone's overthinking things," she whispers against my lips, and I twitch with anticipation and nostalgia.

It's the exact phrase I used to use on her when she'd go off in her head. She remembers. Dammit, I'm losing control. I tighten my grip on her wrists and run my nose down her cheek. I place a soft kiss on her earlobe and feel her body sag forward as her legs buckle beneath her.

Using my other arm to hold her around the waist and keep her vertical, I whisper, "Here? Is this where you want me to kiss you?"

Her breath comes in quick gasps, and she shakes her head no. So I let my lips skim the side of her face and holy hell, she even tastes like peaches. And I should definitely not be thinking about tasting her, but a torrent of images unleashes itself. I know I'm gripping her too hard, but she doesn't complain.

I press myself against her and place a chaste kiss on her cheek. "Here?" I ask, doing my best to feign innocence.

"Uh uh," she groans, and I brush my face against hers until our lips are touching.

"Here?"

"Yes, please," she says against my mouth, and I try to take it slow, I really do. But when her lips part, opening her to me, I'm done being gentle.

My tongue sweeps inside, desperate for hers. She's tentative at first. Barely skimming her own tongue against mine with sweet little licks. But I press harder and she matches me. Layla lets her teeth graze my lower lip and I groan. I can't even concentrate on memorizing each sweet touch of her perfect mouth because the knowledge that I'm the first, the only man to ever have her this way, has me mindless and infuckingsane with need. She's mine goddammit, and the primal urge to shout it from the rooftops is almost impossible to resist. I release her wrists so I don't bruise or break them and she wraps her arms around my neck, raking her hands into my hair. Keeping my hand out from under her short dress is an exercise in torture. My body aches for release, but this is her first kiss, for fuck's sake. We have to stop here. For now.

"You did not just give her the very first kiss of her life in an alley," Corin's voice rings out from beside us. "Although, it looked pretty hot, so I might allow it."

Growling low enough so only Layla can hear, I pull my mouth from hers, taking a moment to appreciate her flushed face and swollen lips. Her eyes are glazed over, and I'm hoping it's a result of my lip-locking skills and not the alcohol. I drop one more kiss on her pouty lips, unable to resist, before turning to face her roommate. "Jesus, Ginger. You have fan-fucking-tastic timing. Anyone ever tell you that?"

"Anyone ever tell you the definition of romance? Here's a hint. It doesn't include dirty alleys downtown. And for the record, the last guy who called me Ginger hasn't been seen or heard from in months." Her deadpan tone makes me wonder if she's serious.

Skylar appears behind her, and they both look hot and tired and ready to go. Judging from my roommate's rumpled clothing, he's been doing some intense grinding of his own. I smirk and pull Layla from the alley. *Our alley.* Deal with it, Ginger. And even better? Layla doesn't let go of my hand on the cab ride back to the dorm.

So for tonight at least, I'm the luckiest bastard alive.

CHAPTER Eleven

Layla

It's all I can do not to pull Landen from the cab and drag him back to my dorm room. The magic of tonight is already fading and the thought of losing him again has me on edge. If I ever start to forget that he can disappear at a moment's notice, I touch the scar above my left ear to remind myself. It's my permanent reality check. The one I need to remind me of the truth. Everything can change. Everyone can leave.

Corin was right. Kissing Landen, being kissed by Landen, changed me. The tension I've clung to for so long it became a part of me just lifted into the sky, and I didn't care if I never pulled in another breath for as long as I lived. The world spun faster, and I think I left the ground for a few seconds while Landen explored my mouth. My whole body trembled, but not in the terrifying way like I'm used to. More like humming with the steady buzz of being alive.

Why do people need to do drugs when kissing feels like this?

"Hey, about what Ginger said," Landen begins as he walks me to the front door of Campbell Hall. "She's right. That probably wasn't the best place I could have done that. I should have—"

"Landen," I break in, placing a finger on his lips to stop the rest of his sentence. "It was perfect."

He swallows and nods at me but I can tell there's something else he wants to say. Dread settles over me, effectively cutting off my endorphin overload.

"Hey, um, Corin and Skylar seem to be hitting it off." I'm trying to change the subject to dispel the awkwardness that's shoved its way in between us. Landen clears his throat and glances over to where I'm looking. Corin is standing with her arms folded, watching Skylar tell her something that apparently requires a lot of frantic gesturing with his hands. "Wonder what that's all about."

"He thought he was going to get lucky tonight," Landen says with a smirk. He pulls his gaze from our roommates back to me and grins wickedly. "Guess we're both going home disappointed."

He's joking, Layla. Right, I know that. But he probably is disappointed. I'd never kissed a guy before. It wasn't as if I knew what the hell I was doing. And if he'd hooked up with any other girl tonight instead of wasting his time on me, he'd probably be getting a lot more than a goodnight hug. *But he didn't.*

I pull myself out from inside of my head and take a moment to appreciate how beautiful he is. Not that I haven't memorized his face and then subsequently tried to forget it once already. But as I let my eyes cling to every inch of him, drinking in his full mouth and square jaw before covering his thick, muscular neck, he stills, almost like he's doing the same thing to me. Thoughts I have no clue how to deal with intertwine in my mind. *What would it be like to run my tongue over the masculine knot in his throat? To feel his stubbled jaw on my neck, on my bare breasts? In between my thighs?*

"Good Lord," I whisper at my thoughts, barely stifling a shiver.

"Kissing me is similar to a religious experience, or so I've been told." Gleaming green eyes meet mine as he teases me.

"I was just realizing how…" *Much I want you to kiss me again.* "Late it is."

"Yeah." He groans and the throaty depth of it touches me all the way to my core. "And we have practice tomorrow and workouts tomorrow night. And because they obviously hate freshmen here, we have that ass early class Monday morning."

Oh yeah, Intro to University Academics or something. Ugh, I'd forgotten. "Corin and I will probably take turns going to that one. We can always share notes if you, um, need to sleep in sometimes, because of soccer or whatever."

"Yeah, the hangovers and late night orgies with cheerleaders will probably take their toll and I'll end up failing Intro to Not Screwing Up College."

My eyes narrow at his words because it's been nearly a year since I knew him and I can't tell if he's serious. But then the corner of his mouth turns up and I have an overwhelming impulse to slap him. "Cute. Well, maybe while you're busy with your cheerleaders, I'll see if Luke feels like hanging out."

Now it's Landen's eyes that narrow and I'm the one grinning. "I think you're underestimating how much Lucas Taite values the use of his legs."

"And I think you're underestimating what a good kisser I am." I lift my chin in defiance, daring him to argue. I was going for playful, but his glare is lethal. "Maybe he'd risk it."

"I've never underestimated anything about you, Layla. No reason I would start now that I know from experience." His fierce tone weakens my knees and tightens the muscles in my stomach. "And I'm sure as hell not sharing."

"I was just kidding," I say softly, hoping he'll return to his smiling, eye-twinkling self.

He's still staring at me intently, but he looks less ready to murder someone. "Me too, babe," he says lightly, prompting me to release the breath I didn't even realize I was holding. "Cheerleaders have never been my thing. I prefer girls on the gymnastics team—much more flexible."

Now that he's calmed down a notch, I smack him in the chest. But he catches my wrist and uses it to pull me into the danger zone where I am his to do what he wants with. Landen and my lungs are not friends. This close to him they deflate and I'm gasping for breath in a pathetic attempt to refill them. I'm about to curse myself for being so weak until my eyes find his. He's just as lost as I am. We don't know how to do this with each other. We didn't get this far before. High school was a slow burn, a lit fuse taking its sweet time. This time we've hung out once and we're already sorting through the debris from the explosion. We're standing over that gaping canyon again. This time it's Landen who jumps first.

"None of them even rate compared to you."

Relief floods me, and I couldn't keep the smile from spreading across my face if I tried. "I don't even have anyone to compare you to."

"Guess I've cornered the market where kissing is concerned, huh?"

"Something like that." Kissing and everything else.

"You kids about done here?" Corin says, pulling me from Landen-land.

Landen sighs. "Seriously, Ginger, your timing is impeccable. Can I get you a collar with bells or something so I can hear you coming next time?"

"Behave yourself," I whisper, but I can't help but grin.

He lets me step back, and I feel the effort it takes. His expression relaxes visibly, and I wonder if maybe letting me go is easier. Letting him go would definitely be easier. Smarter. Cut and run before one or both of us gets hurt. But I really don't want to. Because I am a fool of the lowest form, one who repeats the same mistakes. With a smile on her face.

CHAPTER *Twelve*

Landen

I *give* Ginger all sorts of hell about interrupting us, but honestly, I'm only mildly pissed and mostly grateful. Because Layla has the power to crack me open and leave me bloody on the sidewalk. This close to her, my thoughts hang out way too close to my lips.

"So we have an inter-squad scrimmage Tuesday night if you ladies want to come," Skylar tells the girls as we drop them at the door.

"We'll see," Ginger says, playing coy. I raise a brow to smirk at my roommate, hoping to convey my thoughts to him. *So much for getting lucky. I feel ya, buddy.*

"Hey," I say, pulling Layla a few feet from the other two. "Ginger was right about one thing. I owe you some romance. Milkshakes after the game Tuesday night?"

Her delicate lips, still swollen from my kiss, work so hard not to curve into one of her breathtaking grins. *Say yes.* "We'll see," she murmurs, following her roommate's lead.

So she wants to play hard to get? That's fine. I can chase her as hard as she wants. Leaning down, I whisper into her ear, "Extra cherries if you're a good girl."

There's no containing the shiver that pulls her body closer to me. "Hmm, what does being a good girl entail exactly?"

"Cheering loudly for me and not at all for anyone else." Especially Lucas motherfucking Taite.

"I think I can manage that. What about Skylar? Can I cheer for Skylar?"

Laughing, I nod. "Yeah, he's the goalie. But I think he's already landed his own personal cheerleader." Layla follows my gaze to my roommate—who is getting a lingering hug from hers.

"This door's locked after hours," Ginger tells us, breaking from Skylar and heading our way. "We have to go in the side entrance. Layla, do you have your card with you?"

"Yeah," Layla answers, and we head around to the side of their building. I don't really like how isolated it is, and I make a mental note to make sure she always gets back in time to use the main entrance if I'm not with her. Or maybe I can just make sure I'm always with her. Yeah, I like that idea better.

Just as I pick up my jaw from the ground after watching Layla fish her student ID access card from her bra—which is pale pink, by the way—a group of guys slamming out of the metal door make her efforts unnecessary. Fuck, I didn't realize she was in a co-ed dorm.

Instinctively, I press myself to her, wrapping my arms around her. "It's okay. You're okay," I start murmuring directly into her ear. But she's not trembling. Not even a little. And all three of them are looking at me like I'm nuts. Looking down, I can tell, even in the dark, how red her face is. And I'm confused. "Are you okay? You didn't—"

"I'm fine," she says sharply, extracting herself swiftly from my grasp. "They didn't even run into me."

Run into her? Damn right they didn't or they'd be flat on their asses. I'm flipping my shit like a little girl because the ear-shattering clang of that door should've sent her straight to the ground. But it didn't. Is she cured? What else have I missed?

I stare at her, waiting for an explanation, but she just nods towards our roommates. Oh, she doesn't want them to know. Dumb jock finally gets it. But she and Ginger *live* together. And Ginger knew exactly who I was at that party. So she told her about me, but not about the seizures? I'd be flattered if I wasn't so pissed.

"Layla," I say, wrapping my fingers around her upper arm. "You need to tell your roommate about—"

"No." She presses her lips together tightly and shoots me a death glare. "Goodnight, Landen."

I have officially made it weird. But I don't care. Even if she is better, Ginger needs to know in case Layla has a random relapse or something. I know from experience—that's some shit a person needs to be prepared for. Or warned about at least. "Layla," I demand, and now the girls are glaring at me like I'm Asshole of the Year. Skylar pulls my arm away from Layla and presses his weight against me, forcing me to take a step back. "You have to tell her."

Layla lifts her chin, her eyes flashing at me. "I don't *have* to do anything. *Goodnight, Landen*. Skylar."

"Go home, soccer boys," Ginger says, winking at Skylar and shooting an annoyed look at me.

"She has to tell her," I say to the air once they've gone.

"Tell her what, dude? You sure know how to kill the mood, by the way," my roommate informs me. No kidding. "What's your fucking deal?"

I force my body to relax, even though I'm still in fight mode. "Yeah, you weren't getting any tonight anyways."

"Not with you cock-blocking all over the place with your little freak out. They might've invited us in if you hadn't lost your mind back there. What's your problem?"

I should tell him. So he can tell Ginger. Shit, Corin. Her name is Corin. I have to stop messing with her because I need her on my side when it comes to Layla. But it's not my secret to tell. I can't betray her like that. Even if it is for her own good, which it is. "Um, Layla has a condition. Not one I'm at liberty to discuss. But her roommate should know."

"Ah." He sags against the wall. "You want me to say something to her?"

"I don't know." I kick a rock off the path as I start walking across campus to our dorm. Of course Layla's dorm would be as far from mine as possible. She's always made me work for it.

Skylar follows me. "Okay, well, what *do* you know?"

"That I probably just pissed her off."

"Yeah, I think that's a definite possibility. Think they'll come Tuesday?" Skylar snorts at his own comment. "I mean, Corin's definitely going to *come* Tuesday."

"Oh yeah? Because your *hugs* induce mind-blowing orgasms or what?"

Skylar shoulder-butts me. Hard. "Hey, man. Don't underestimate a guy who doesn't make a move right away. Girls like for you to play hard to get, hold out on them until they're begging for it."

Yeah right. Or you screw it up and miss your chance altogether. Been there, done that.

Chapter Thirteen

Layla

I should be pissed. The right thing to do here is bitch Corin out for setting me up in a precarious situation with a boy I'm supposed to be staying away from.

And yet…

I'm still high from the memory of his mouth on mine. My body still tingles from the heat of his hands. Everything's changed. But in a way, it hasn't. Because I'm terrified he's going to tell Corin—and God knows how many guys on the soccer team—about my seizures. And when he does, I might as well be right back in Hope Springs.

"So what was his deal back there?" Corin avoids my stare as we walk into our room. She sits on the futon and starts pulling off her boots, earrings, and assorted bracelets. "What do you need to tell me?"

Red lights flash behind my eyes. Immediate subject change needed.

"Corin, who cares about his deal? What the hell was that about tonight?"

"Don't pretend to be mad," she says while rolling her eyes and pulling her hair into a messy knot on top of her head. "I saw you two in that alley. That was hot. Seriously. And I'm not sure he's playing with a full deck, but it was about damn time someone made a move."

Busted. *Contort face into mask of frustration—quick.* "You promised me before we left there'd be no talking about Landen O'Brien tonight."

"Yes, I did. And I kept that promise. I didn't hear anyone *talking* about him tonight. Until now."

I stay in the common area of our room contemplating this while she steps into the bedroom to put on pajamas. She's right. Damn. "Okay, so you found a loophole. But I call B.S. because you know what I mean."

Sighing so loudly I hear it from the other room, she slams a drawer shut. “Fine, I’m sorry about the sneak attack. But we were already planning to go out, and Skylar texted and asked if we wanted to meet up. I didn’t even say that we did. I just casually mentioned where we were going. It’s a free campus, Layla. They can go out wherever they please.”

“I realize this. I just didn’t know you were going to be slipping intel to the enemy.”

I can hear her laughing as I brush my teeth in our tiny bathroom. “If that’s how you treat an enemy, God help any boy you consider an ally. In fact, you still look a little dazed and turned on. Please don’t try to make out with me tonight. I’ve already had my share of sexually confused partners—I’m sticking with straight boys only from here on out.”

“Okay,” I say, pointing my foamy toothbrush at her. “We are definitely coming back to that.”

She cackles loudly, and I can’t help but feel like the least experienced person on the planet. “Seriously, Layla, he’s got some issues, like probably some major ones that are going to make anything with him difficult…but can you imagine turning away now and just forgetting about that kiss? ‘Cause I gotta say, I’m having trouble forgetting about it and I was just a casual observer.”

“See, now *you* wanna make out with *me*, don’t you?” I rinse and spit and go into the bedroom to change. When I’m done I plop down next to her on the futon.

“Stop changing the subject.”

“He just…he just makes me so…ugh!”

She waggles her eyebrows at me. “Horny?”

I shudder. “Oh my God, never say that word to me again. I hate that word. It’s so crude and not even a halfway decent way to describe what Landen O’Brien does to me.”

“Mmhm.” She leans back and lets her eyes scan over me. “You can clutch your pearls all you want, Georgia. But that boy twists you all up, and I don’t think kissing’s gonna get the job done.”

“Whatever. You basically said he was nuts. Now we share one kiss and I’m supposed to do him?”

Her forehead wrinkles as she contemplates this. “Ah, no, you’re probably right. Maybe hold off on that. But sometimes we have to let things happen to us, you know? Even uncontrollable things that might turn from bliss to shit before we can rein it in. Because that’s *living*. Things have to happen, you have to go on scary adventures, follow your heart, and let it lead you down dark alleys that may dead end in a pit of despair. Otherwise you’re just *existing*, and who the hell wants to settle for that?”

Is that what I’ve been doing? Her words spin around me in the tiny room, taunting me, smothering me. “But…”

"But nothing. You need to decide if you're ready for this, 'cause it's coming. He's here, and I saw the look on his face, in his eyes, every time I interrupted you tonight. There's a storm brewing between the two of you. Either hang on, let it pick you up, and risk letting it beat your heart to hell and back before setting you back down or you can batten down the hatch and tell him to leave you the fuck alone. And if he hurts you, I'll be here to put a hit out on him with a few simple texts and a photo. But you have to know it's a possibility. Which, judging from the condition you were in earlier…you do."

Corin's voice is filled with emotion. There's an experience behind the pain she's warning me about, and I want to ask her to tell me about it. But I'm hoping she will when she's ready. Her warning hangs in the air between us, and I'm trying desperately to weigh the pros and cons of giving Landen a second chance in my head. But all I can see is his face. All I can hear is his voice. And the thought of never again feeling his warm touch sending trails of liquid fire down my skin has me cringing inside.

I suck in a lungful of air and look up at her. "What if I don't know what I want yet?"

"Then you need to tell him to back off till you figure it out. Good luck with that." She snorts, and I smile at the thought of him watching me dance tonight. He was right—I am different. But it's a good different, and it's because of him. He should be the one to reap the benefits of all his hard work. "And hey, whatever he was wanting you to tell me so bad…you can. I know it may not seem like it after tonight, but you can trust me." Corin's normally clear voice is soft and clouded with emotion.

"I know," I answer back just as quietly.

"*Boys*," she sighs out, raising her voice back to its normal decibel. "Can't live with 'em, can't tie 'em to your bed and use them as you see fit." She shakes her head in mock exasperation. "Damn societal norms." I can't help but laugh, but when I sober up a little, she puts on a straight face. "Maybe just take it one day at a time. Like, what do you want right now?"

I stretch and yawn, feeling my neck and back shift with a satisfying pop before I answer. "Right now, I want to eat those double-stuffed Oreos you're hoarding behind your makeup bag and watch *Pitch Perfect* until I pass out on this futon."

Corin's laughter is like bells chiming, and I notice for the first time that she has a few freckles across her nose. Maybe that's why she wears so much makeup. But they're cute, and I bet Skylar Martin would agree. Hm, another complication. If my roommate dates his roommate and teammate, could I really rid myself of Landen anyways? Do I even want to?

Before I have time to answer myself, Corin jumps up to grab the Oreos and the movie and my phone buzzes on my desk. "Can you grab that while you're up please?" I ask, pulling the patched quilt Aunt Kate gave me up over my lower half and getting comfy against the pillows. Corin drops the Oreos in my lap and I rip back the plastic. "Why do they even bother to make regular Oreos when there's double stuffed?"

"You have one new message," my roommate says in her automated voicemail voice, ignoring my question as she hands me my phone.

Had a great time 2nite. Sleep might not come so easy if you're mad at me…

My heart speeds up and my face goes all tingly. *Batten down the hatch!*

But I can't.

Hmm, poor baby. Hate to think of you tossing and turning all night. I've barely hit send when my hand vibrates.

You could come over and read me a bedtime story.

Oh dear Lord. **Not sure how your roommates would feel about that.**

He mentioned earlier that he and Skylar share an apartment-style set up with two other guys and that the four of them share a bathroom with another quad. I wonder if female athletes have the same set up. No way in hell eight girls could share a bathroom. Boys are weird.

They'd deal. We can be quiet.

What am I going to do with this boy? **Have you lost your mind?**

A few minutes go by with no response, and I wonder if I've been too much of a prude. He knows I don't know how to do this sexy texting stuff. I don't know how to do anything sexy really. And for the first time, this makes me sad. I want to be sexy, want him to want me like I want him. Because he has sexy down to a damn science.

"Layla, we watching a movie or what?" Corin asks, raising an eyebrow at the ridiculous parade of emotions marching across my face as she leans towards the television.

"Um, yeah, I—"

My phone buzzes again, interrupting my response, and I look down.

Yep, I looked everywhere. Guess I lost it. Keep an eye out and let me know if it turns up around you? I'm pretty sure that's where it was the last time I saw it.

"Layla, pause or play?" she asks, as the Treble Makers take the stage on the screen.

What am I going to do with you? I send back.

Hopefully some things we can't mention in public. I nearly jolt off the futon at his words.

"Layla?" Corin demands.

"Play! Hit play!" Jesus.

CHAPTER Fourteen

Landen

Her aunt has been holding out on me. And I'm not going to be able to focus on anything until I get some answers.

We have practice Sunday at noon, so I call her as we walk to the stadium, making sure to trail behind my teammates far enough to be out of hearing range.

"Landen? Is she okay?" Kate's worried voice greets me.

"She's fine. She's more than fine actually. Which is why I'm calling."

"Oh-kay," she says slowly, and I can hear her typing stop. It's only nine a.m. in Georgia, but I know she's probably already put in a day's work.

"The other day I, uh, *someone* threw a glass bottle against a fence and last night some guys came out of a metal door hard enough to rip the damn thing off the hinges. And she was *fine.*" I was a mess, however, though there's no need to mention that.

Her typing resumes. "That's a good thing. It means the Topiramax is working. So why do you sound all wound up?"

"Because I didn't realize she was better when we made this arrangement," I whisper angrily into my phone. That is to say, I didn't realize that she wouldn't need me after all.

Layla's aunt sighs loudly. "It's not failsafe. A car could backfire on her way to class, triggering an episode. Or there could be a shooting on campus, God forbid. That's the problem. I'm a million miles away and there's no guarantee that she's cured. Her test results are indicative of far worse problems than her PTSD. So in a way, the seizures saved her life, because we might not have known about the hematoma otherwise."

"Right, I get it. It's just, I'm not sure how she'd feel about this. And if she wants me out of her life at any point, I'll have to respect that." Even if it kills me.

She sighs again. "We've been through this. If it weren't for you, she'd be at UGA right now and I could be the one keeping an eye on her. But after you left, well…you know. And she decided to move across the damn country. And since she wouldn't let me come with her, I *need* you there. *She* needs you there, even if she doesn't know it."

"Um, she might be coming around somewhat. But if she finds out that we talked, that I turned down playing pro soccer in Ecuador to come here and babysit her, I have a feeling there will be hell to pay—for me and you both." And I don't have the luxury of being a permanent fixture in her life. I can be disposed of. "What do we do then?"

"Look, you're the one who hassled me every other day after you left about status updates. You're the one who swore you just wanted what was best for her. If things have changed, then just say so. Go back to Colorado or play soccer overseas or whatever and I'll figure something out. I can contact someone at the university and have them notified of her condition." She takes a deep breath, and I can practically hear her debating about telling me whatever comes next. "If something does happen, I'd feel a hell of a lot better knowing you're there with her, at least until I can get there. But I get it. You have your own life, and it's been a while since you've seen each other. Things change, people change. If you want to back out, then do it. No hard feelings."

Yeah right. And she's got a point. Several actually. When Layla blew me off via text message, I damn near lost my mind and drove straight back to Georgia every damn day. But my mom needed me and Layla wanted nothing to do with me. So I resorted to calling her aunt at work pretty much every day until she started giving me updates on how Layla was doing. What meds she was on, if she'd had any more seizures, how they were treating her at school.

Not that I was all that worried about the last one, since I'd threatened Cam and DW until I was blue in the face before leaving, and both guys swore to look out for her and to keep the girls from giving her shit. Not that they really had since Homecoming. Whether they felt sorry for Layla after seeing how bad it was or just didn't want me to blow the fuck up on them wasn't clear. Or important. So long as they treated her with the kindness and respect she deserved.

I lean down and pretend to tie my shoe to put off going into practice with the others. "I don't want out. I just don't want her to find out about this and hate me." Just when she's finally starting to let me in. *Again.*

"Okay, first of all, I see no reason she would need to find out. And secondly, I don't think she could ever hate you. Would she be mad? Well…yeah. But hate you? I don't even think she's capable of that. Plus, she's a smart girl. Angry as she'd be, eventually she would see sense and know that this was done with her best interest at heart." Her voice stays steady but I can tell the woman is trying to convince herself of the shit she's shoveling onto me. "Just be discreet, Landen, and everything will be fine."

"I hope you're right." *But I suspect you're dead-ass wrong.*

"I'm not gonna lie. Yesterday kicked my ass," Skylar tells me Monday morning. Stretching until my hands damn near smack the doorframe, I realize I'm pretty fucking sore too. And texting Layla till after midnight probably wasn't the smartest move.

"Probably didn't help that we went to practice slightly hungover," I point out.

"Yeah, I'm thinking that was a dumbass move, not that I wouldn't do Saturday night over again."

Ditto, my friend. "Speaking of which, did Corin mention if they were coming to the scrimmage tomorrow night?"

"Nah, she's playing hard to get. But twenty bucks says they show up."

Today, Skylar and I are going to Intro to Getting Your Ass Up Early in the Fucking Morning while Austin and Dean and the others sleep in. But tomorrow, I'm not getting out of bed until noon. Especially since we need to be rested for our scrimmage against the upperclassmen. Remembering the thrill of Layla watching me play soccer has my adrenaline surging full force, and I'm wide awake even before we stop at the coffee shop on campus.

Skylar's texting while we wait in line. Whether it's the girl he knows from high school, Corin, or some other chick he's managed to run some game on in the few days we've been here, I have no idea. But he's grinning like an idiot so it's definitely one of the above.

When he orders two coffees, I know it was most likely Corin. And if Corin's coming to class, then Layla probably won't be there since she mentioned that they were planning to switch off. But knowing Layla, she won't miss the first day of class for anything, so I order an iced mocha in addition to my black coffee.

"Dude, you are so pussy whipped," Skylar tells me as we walk to class.

"Oh yeah? I'm not the only one carrying two coffees."

"Yes, that's because I'm trying to get laid. You, on the other hand, are chasing one you've already had when there's at least ten thousand other fine-ass girls around."

I clear my throat without looking at him and take swig of my steaming, bitter coffee.

"Oh, no. *No way.* You lost your shit on Taite over a piece of ass you haven't even tapped? Whoa, that's like a whole new level of pussy whipped. It's like…

shit, it's like you're titty-whipped or something. Please tell me you've at least rounded the bases."

I glance over at him, irritated at how well he's putting the pieces together. "How old are you man? Cause I'm having flashbacks of the junior high locker room."

He snorts. "Yeah, okay. I'm just saying, you're ruining the freshmen experience, my friend."

"Says the guy who said my pussy lips were showing and I needed to make a move."

I watch as he shakes his head in a you're-a-complete-dumbass way. "Yeah, a move to hit it one more time so everyone would know that shit was yours and then back the hell off. Not to get all bleary-eyed and follow her around like a damn stalker."

So much for being discreet. Running my hand through my hair, I try not to sound as panicked as I feel when I ask, "Do I really seem like her stalker?" Her words from Saturday night come back to me. *So you've resorted to stalking me?*

"Let's recap, shall we? You shouted her name across the whole freshmen class at orientation and tried to run her down, went balls-to-the-wall *psycho* on Taite for *talking* to her at a party, showed up at a club you knew she'd be at, molested her in an alley, and reacted like a lunatic when some guys *almost* ran into her. Now you're taking her a coffee on the first day of a class that, once again, every freshman enrolled will be at."

Son of a bitch. So much for discreet. "Well, it sounds bad when you say it all together like that. Here, you take this one too and be the damn gentleman."

Skylar looks awkward carrying three coffees, but there's no way I can ask for hers back now. I just need to take a step back. Be friendly, but not overly interested because, like her aunt said, she's a smart girl. If I don't back the hell off at least a little, she's going to know something's up.

Walking into Hilton Hall Auditorium, I groan at the crowd. She won't like this. But then I remember how she handled the club. She's doing better. And I have got to take it down a notch if even Skylar thinks my behavior is excessive.

Maybe I won't even sit near her, and I'm definitely not going to bring up the scrimmage tomorrow or shakes afterward again. If she comes with Ginger to see Skylar then that's cool, and if she doesn't, that's okay too. I'm psyching myself up to give her some space when Skylar turns down an aisle and I see her and Ginger—fuck, *Corin*—already sitting. And all my plans to chill out are shit. Because she's wearing these short-ass shorts and her long tan legs are crossed in front of her. On the foot propped in the air dangles a flip-flop that matches her snug pink T-shirt. She's jiggling her leg just enough so I know she's uncomfortable in the crowd—and just enough to drive me insane with want.

My pulse ramps up as we say good morning, and they thank Skylar for the coffee. Layla leans around my roommate, making a special point of saying good morning to me. She licks the whipped cream from her bottom lip, and I can't help but remember the soft, sweet feel of her mouth on mine.

I nod at her like I'm too tired to chat and drop myself into the seat next to Skylar.

The lecture starts and I'm congratulating myself on keeping my eyes off her legs and her pretty little pink painted toes, for the most part anyway, when my phone buzzes in my back pocket. I didn't even realize I was sitting on the damn thing.

It's a text from Skylar. **You are so screwed. Maybe after tomorrow night's scrimmage you and legs can go ring shopping.**

I don't bother with a response but I jab my elbow hard into his ribs.

"Damn, dude," he hisses at me.

"Keep your eyes off of her fucking legs," I hiss back. Both Layla and Corin lean forward to see what the hell is going on with us.

And I see it. The look on her face that tells me she's hurt that I'm not sitting by her, and that I didn't say good morning. And my one goal in life has been not to cause her anymore pain. As soon as our gazes cross paths she turns her head abruptly and focuses intently on the heavyset brunette lady conducting a lecture that may or may not be on time management. Who can concentrate with so much of Layla's skin exposed? I wish it were winter so she would put on some damn pants and maybe even a sweater.

I've got to figure out a way to back off without hurting her. Because if things go as far as I want them to, and she finds out what the hell I'm really doing here, I will have forfeited any chance I had of her being mine. Ever again. And dammit, now that it's even a remote possibility, the thought of not having her is razor blades raking me raw. *Just slow your roll, O'Brien.*

A voice I've contained for so long pushes through my internal struggle. My father's voice. *Why did you ever think you could do this? You will screw this up and ruin you both. Just like before.*

CHAPTER *Fifteen*

Layla

Something's up. Landen ignores me all through freshmen seminar, and when I ask him about his class schedule, he mutters something vague about not having it with him.

Corin's watching us both like a hawk so I pretend I'm not affected by his lack of interest. Because I'm pretty sure he's pretending, too. I felt his gaze more than once during the lecture, and his neck muscles are straining visibly. He's working awfully hard to ignore me and I have no idea why.

Though I have my suspicions. Several girls stop their conversations to check him out as we exit the building. I'm not an idiot—he's kind of a catch. If you like tall, muscular, dark, and broody. Which, who am I kidding, I obviously do. But whatever. If he wants to play this little game, I'm in.

"Skylar, seriously, thanks for the caffeine," I say, slowing so I'm closer to him than Landen. "Our AC went out last night and we were like, nearly naked and still sweating. I barely got a wink of sleep. Did you ever cool off, Corin?"

"Hell no, and we are definitely going to get a fan today." If she's onto my reason for mentioning the sauna that was our room last night, she doesn't seem to care. Skylar's eyes are bulging nearly out of his head, and I try not to be too concerned that he's picturing me and Corin half naked. And possibly in bed together.

"Almost took you up on your offer to come sleep in your room," I say sweetly to Landen, nudging him gently with my shoulder.

"Yeah, we had workouts and I passed out right after I texted you," he says without looking at me, making a big show of nodding at a girl coming towards us in a yellow tank top and tiny jean skirt. She gives him a sly flirty smile and I almost expect her to run into his arms and kiss him like his *friend* did once before. But I shake it off and she walks right on past, giving Skylar the exact same smile. *Slut.*

Ugh, I suck for thinking that. What is this boy doing to me?

"Hey, O'Brien, can we borrow your truck?" Corin asks, catching us all off guard.

"What?" He looks at her like she just asked him to donate a kidney. "I mean, what for? And how'd you know I have a truck?"

She nods towards Skylar because it's obvious how she knows. "So we can go buy a fan, *hello*. The Campus Transport goes to the shopping center where Target is, but can you see me and Georgia here lugging a huge-ass fan onto the bus? Come on, we'll be careful with your baby."

Landen rubs the back of his neck and looks at Skylar, who shrugs. "I have English now and then we have practice and conditioning from noon till three. I can take you after." So much for not knowing his schedule.

"You don't trust us?" Corin pouts.

Landen rolls his eyes.

"We'll all go, grab some dinner, and maybe watch a movie or something," Skylar chimes in, glancing at Corin to check her response.

And in a quirky little twist, I realize she's making an effort to avoid him. I have no idea what's going on with everyone today, but I would like to go get a fan and spend some time with Landen away from campus so I can figure out what his deal is.

"Sounds great," I say with a smile. At the very least, maybe Skylar and I can be pathetic together.

"Why are you avoiding Skylar?" I ask Corin once the guys have branched off away from us. She and I have Psych 101 together, so at least I can get answers from her.

"What do you mean?" She twists a curl around her finger but doesn't look at me.

"I'm just trying to figure out why Skylar and I, who barely know each other, were maintaining most of the conversation this morning, while you and Landen tried to pretend we didn't exist."

Huffing out a huge breath, she lets go of her hair and shifts her bag on her shoulder. Her face is scrunching, and I almost want to tell her she doesn't have to explain anything to me. When she speaks, her voice is low as if she thinks someone nearby is eavesdropping. "Layla, you and I are pretty much opposites in every way. You're a virgin and back in the day, I was…not. Like, pretty much any guy who looked at me twice got lucky. I was a sure thing, you know?"

No, I didn't know. Shame practically radiated off her. "Oh," was all I could manage.

"Sorry for the TMI, but I'm past that now. I've been through a lot of shit—shit no one should ever have to go through alone. And coming here, I told myself I wouldn't just jump in bed with the first guy who paid attention to me. Because I can tell you, a one-night stand is not, in fact, the start of a healthy relationship. So I'm closed for business…indefinitely."

She seems embarrassed and a little lost, not a look I'm used to seeing on her, so I link my arm through hers and lean in close. "You're closed for business and I'm trying to get laid. Who'd have guessed?"

Corin cracks up, and several people turn to look as we file into Baker Hall.

"Seriously, Corin, I think that's awesome. You do what you have to do for you, okay? And if Skylar pressures you, I'll find that hitman app on my phone and have him taken out." I wink and she smiles.

"I'm afraid once he knows he'll blow me off, and he's kind of fun to hang with. Guess I'm not ready to send him running for the hills yet."

"Can I ask a question?" I ask, lowering myself into the seat next to her.

"Shoot."

"If you're celibate, why all the condoms?"

She smiles a sad smile that makes me feel helpless. "A gift from my mom, in case I fall off the wagon, or mattress I guess. She doesn't have a whole lot of faith in me."

"I have faith in you, Corin," I tell her. As the lecture begins and we open up our blank notebooks to copy words from the PowerPoint presentation a balding man is giving, I can't help but wonder if Landen and Corin aren't all that different. But then I remember his nod at that girl on the sidewalk this morning. A heated wave of insecurity seeps into my skin. Maybe he isn't turning over a leaf. Maybe he's still sleeping with anyone he wants to. Maybe he just doesn't want to with me.

CHAPTER Sixteen

Landen

"Corin totally ignored me this morning. I am definitely hitting the showers before we pick them up."

Smirking at him, I let out a small noise of disagreement. "Maybe she's not impressed with your mad skills. Maybe a shower won't even help."

"Uh huh, says the guy falling over himself to get to a girl who is never going to give it up."

Skylar and I give each other shit all the way back to the dorm after practice. I need to go for a run, exhaust myself so I won't have any energy left for lusting after the girl I'm supposed to be playing it cool with. But they're waiting, and if I want to shower, there's not really time.

Lazy piece of shit, my father's voice says in my head. And dammit, I've at least got to get a short run in. I tell Skylar so and he looks at me like I'm insane. Which I am.

An hour later, we pick up the girls and they climb into the backseat of the truck cab. Neither of them say much, and Skylar fills the silence talking about practice and what a dickwad Blackburn is. Twice I catch Layla's stare in my rearview, but she's blocking me out, and I'm not sure what has her so guarded. No, that's not true. I was a dick this morning, and now I'm getting a taste of my own medicine. Fair enough.

Target is kind of crowded for a Monday night, but I guess a lot of freshmen are without AC and probably some other shit they should've brought. Corin and Layla debate on what type of fan to get for fifteen minutes before Skylar gets frustrated and grabs an oscillating floor fan from the shelf.

As we leave the store, rain starts misting from the sky while Skylar and Corin argue about whether we should get Mexican food or run by the diner closer to campus where she's planning to put in a job application, leaving me and Layla straggling behind.

"You still want me to come tomorrow or what?" Layla demands, breaking the silence.

"If you want."

She aims a pointed look dead at me. "I asked what you wanted."

"I mean, I'm sure you have studying and better stuff to do than come watch a scrimmage. It's not like it's a real game or anything."

"Okay," is all she says. I don't know if she means "Okay, I'll come" or "Okay, I have better things to do." What I *do* know is that watching her putting up the walls I worked so hard to tear down sucks. Bad. There has to be a way to balance keeping an eye on her for her aunt, getting close enough to have a chance at making her mine, and never letting her find out exactly how I wound up here. I sure as fuck wish I could figure it out.

The rain pelts us with the fury of ten hells as we reach the truck. Damn, I don't have bed cover to keep the fan dry. Probably not a great idea to shove it in the back with the girls, but there's really not any other option, and we're all getting soaked while trying to figure out what to do with it.

"I'll run back in the store and buy a tarp," Skylar says just before making a mad dash through the parking lot. The girls climb in the back, and I'm grateful Corin didn't go with him. I need the buffer before I just start spilling my guts to Layla and ruin everything.

The two of them are talking quietly; heads leaned together like girls do when sharing secrets. Or when talking about what a dick you are while you're a foot away. I climb in the truck and arrange the huge box on the passenger seat.

"Everything okay?" I ask, twisting around to look at them.

Wearing matching masks of innocence, they turn to me, wide-eyed. "Everything's great," Corin says sharply. "We're going to the diner so I can get an application and Layla can get a milkshake. Skylar can get over it."

"Okay," I say with a shrug. Layla and her milkshakes. I smile at the thought, and I cringe slightly because watching her pleasure over her chocolate shake with extra cherries is going to be hell on my dick. A three-hour practice and a three-mile run did nothing to quench my need for her. I glance in the rearview and there's a mischievous heat in her eyes, like she can read my thoughts. Skylar's right. I am so screwed.

My overly observant roommate pulls the door open, interrupting my thoughts, and grabs the fan. I get out to help him wrap it in the blue tarp he just bought. Once we've wrangled that bastard into the bed and gotten back into the truck, the rain eases up. I pull out of the parking lot and look both ways as I get back on the main road that takes us back to campus.

Up ahead I can see the gridlock, and I rack my brain as I press the brakes to try and think if there's a back road to the diner. Skylar's from here, so I ask him if there's another way we can go.

Before the words are even all the way out of my mouth, the clouds let out and sheets of water pound down on us. The poor fan is probably destroyed, tarp or no tarp. Or at least the box will be.

"Damn," Skylar says under his breath. "I'm thinking you could take Langston over to—"

But he doesn't get to finish because the squeal of tires drowns him out. The sickening crunch of metal comes at the exact moment of impact. Layla's scream matches Skylar's "Fuck!" and I slam the truck in park and bail over the seat, nearly tackling Corin in my attempt to get my arms around Layla. She's trembling hard and I know what's coming. And that she's going to be humiliated. Because this was her chance to start over and it's ruined. Ruined because of me.

"You're okay. It's okay. I've got you. You're safe," I say into her ear, rocking her gently. Raking my eyes over every inch of her to make sure she is, in fact, okay, I realize that it's me who's not okay. I love her and I need her and I need to be there for her as much as I need to breathe air to live. Also, I'm bleeding.

A few minutes later, her trembling subsides as tears slick down her face and onto me. I hear sirens. Skylar has a small gash on his forehead and Corin is rubbing her neck but they're okay. I glance out the back window and see a tan Suburban jammed into the back of my truck. But I don't care. We're okay. Layla is in my arms and she's safe.

"You need to get back in the driver's seat," Corin says softly, "before the cops think something majorly shady is going on."

She's right, but I can't let Layla go. I look down into her moist blue eyes, pulled in by her need for me, and I can't move. I don't want to. They can think what they want.

"Fuck it," Skylar says, sliding over into the driver's seat.

Without another word, Corin climbs over the center console and buckles herself into the passenger seat, leaving me and Layla alone in the back.

"I'm sorry, baby. I'm so sorry," I tell her, and her eyes grow even wider in her pale face. And I am sorry. For leaving her last year, for not trying harder to tell her how I felt, and for being here under false pretenses that she doesn't know about.

"Not your fault," she murmurs, tucking herself closer to me.

I can feel her breath on my neck, and this is so not the time, but I lower my lips to her forehead and then to her wet cheeks before placing them against hers. When she moves her mouth firmly against mine, I realize I've been fooling myself if I think the only reason I'm here is because her aunt asked me to keep an eye on her.

I'm here because I needed a second chance. She gave me one this past weekend, and I screwed it up by being a first-class asshole this morning. And now I need a third chance. I hope to hell there's not a limit on the number of chances this girl is willing to give me. Because I am a fucking idiot. And I'm going to screw up. A lot.

CHAPTER Seventeen

Layla

The police officer raps on the driver's side window and I flinch. For one dark and terrible moment, I'm back there. My life trickling out onto the concrete. Sirens and flashing lights. A man in uniform leaning over me and saying, "*She's okay—she's alive.*"

But I kind of wasn't. Or at least I wished I wasn't. And then I never figured out how to come back to life afterwards. Not really.

Landen holds me and rocks me and pulls me out of the darkness. Like he did at Homecoming. Like he did when two sophomores got into a fight next to my locker and again when fireworks went off unexpectedly after a football game and I nearly seized out in front of the whole school. He holds me and keeps me still. Like he always has.

I'm cold, abnormally cold, and I know if he lets go I'm going to go into shock. I thought I was past needing him, needing anyone. But as he holds me and grazes his lips across my forehead, mumbling over and over that it's okay and I'm okay…I know I'm not. I am the opposite of okay because I need him. I need him so badly and he's already left me once. I reach a hand up to touch the scar I got the day my parents were killed, but his grip is too tight for me to reach.

After giving the police our IDs for the accident report, the overeager medics make us all go to the university medical center and get checked out. Skylar gets a whopping two stiches in his forehead. Corin and I leave with matching pain pill prescriptions for whiplash.

Landen was actually injured the worst. He has a huge cut on his forearm that took eleven stitches. Plus a steering wheel-shaped bruise already forming on his chest since the rear impact didn't set off the airbag. But he never once complains. The whole time we're getting seen he never goes out of arm's reach, even though the resident checking us out tried to make him get an x-ray without me. Stubborn ass that he is, he refused. I'm going to feel horrible if he has a broken arm or something.

Since Landen's truck was towed to a local body repair shop, and the ambulances drove us to the hospital, we have to take a cab back to the dorms.

"Well, this was a hell of a first day," Skylar says as we get out at mine and Corin's dorm.

I smile at his joke, but I'm panicking. If, no, *when* Landen leaves, I don't know how I'm going to face Corin and explain my not-so-little freak out. I'm so tired and hollow it's as if the entire universe is pressing down on me. Landen's the only thing keeping me vertical right now.

I slip my hand into his and he squeezes tight.

"Corin, would it be okay if, um, Landen stayed in our room tonight?" Before she answers, I realize I should've checked with him first. His body tenses at my words and I feel stupid for assuming. "I mean, if you don't mind," I say to him.

"It's cool with me," Corin answers before Landen can respond. "But don't athletes have to check in or something at curfew?"

"Yeah we do," Skylar informs us. "But I can call Dean or Mike and tell them what happened."

"Do that," Landen says, squeezing my hand again and pulling me closer. And the bone chilling cold that settled into me dissipates, replaced by warmth radiating directly from his touch.

Because he felt me shivering, Landen insists I take a hot shower when we get into our room. Even though the AC still isn't working and none of us thought to salvage the fan. As I step out of the steam-filled bathroom in my robe, I can tell they were talking about me by how quickly they fall silent. Landen and Skylar are sitting on the futon, and Corin's in the desk chair. Her face is flushed, but it's nothing compared to the raging inferno in Landen's bloodshot eyes.

"Guess the freak's out of the bag," I mutter, crossing into the bedroom to put on pajamas. I grab a gray T-shirt and matching pink and gray shorts and slam the dresser drawer. Why can't I just be normal? Maybe I should just let go of any hope I had left of having a normal life. Tears pinch my eyes, and I kind of wish I hadn't asked Landen to stay so he wouldn't have to see me like this.

"Hey." Landen's deep voice, heavy with exhaustion, startles me. I flinch as he slides the partition between rooms shut behind him.

"Hey," I answer, avoiding his stare.

"Please don't be mad. I didn't tell them everything. Just that you have a condition and that what happened in the truck could've been a lot worse. Corin really needs to know, Layla. She's your roommate for God's sakes."

"I'm not mad at you," I tell him, and surprisingly, it's the truth. "I just wish I didn't have to be like this." My voice breaks at the end and Landen crosses the room to put his arms around me.

"You are perfect. You're the strongest person I know," he says to the top of my head.

"How can you say that?" I ask as the tears begin to fall "I'm damaged, defective, like there's a glitch in my brain or my wiring or something." The tears fall faster, and I'm angry, but not at him, not really. "You should be with someone normal, someone who doesn't fall apart at loud noises, screeching tires, and cars backfiring."

"Layla," he tries to break in but I've broken the dam and I can't stop the pain from flowing out of me and onto him.

"Do you have any idea what it feels like to come to in a room full of people staring at you in horror and have no idea what kind of humiliating spectacle you just made of yourself? How shame slams into you as you realize you're thirteen, or fourteen, or hell, seventeen years old and you just pissed yourself for everyone to see? It takes everything I have to walk down the street, to enter a crowded room, and not run out because I know it could happen at any moment and I can't really control it."

"Stop. Listen to me. Tonight was my fault. Do you understand that? I was trying to find a side street to avoid traffic and I was distracted and—"

"No, Landen." I shake my head. "No. It was pouring rain, and it was a freaking fender bender. Any other human being would've been fine."

"I don't want any other human being. I want you." His eyes are full with heat and blazing into mine as he backs me up against the wall between the beds.

"Why?" I choke out over my stupid, shameful sobs. "Why in the world would you want me?"

He tilts his head, looking at me as if I've asked a ridiculous question as he takes a step closer. "Why in the world *wouldn't* I want you? Jesus, Layla. I've always wanted you, since that first day. Not a minute has passed since the first time I laid eyes on you that I haven't wanted you. Needed you. I will always want you. Even if I screw this up so badly you stop wanting me back." His name escapes my lips just as he covers my mouth with his.

The need in his kiss shatters me. Breaks me apart and puts me back together again all at once. Pulling him to me and pushing myself at him, I taste my tears on his lips. When his mouth leaves mine, I cry out, but his breath is warm on my neck as he opens my bathrobe. A spasm rocks my body into him and he groans, sending heat flooding through me. His flaming dark eyes take in my exposed body, and I drop the pajamas I was holding onto my bed. His fingertips skim the bare skin of my arms, raising chillbumps all over my body.

"I never should've left," he whispers, dropping to his knees and throwing my world off its axis. "Why did you let me leave?"

"I thought—" When his lips sear the sensitive skin on my stomach, my head falls back against the wall. "*Oh, God.*"

"What? You thought what? Tell me," he murmurs against my hipbone. My whole body is racked with a steady trembling that, under any other circumstance, would be terrifying. "I can't think straight with you doing that," I choke out, and he stills. I plow my fingers through his hair. The softness tickles between my fingers. "I didn't mean for you to stop."

Landen's throaty laugh vibrates against my lower stomach and he trails hot wet kisses north until he's standing upright. "Layla," he says simply, as if I'm not melting into a puddle on the floor, weak with want.

"Landen," I huff out, pulling my robe closed. "Never figured you for a tease."

Arching an eyebrow, he grins wickedly at me, and I'm nervous he's going to throw me on the bed right this second. But he just leans down and kisses me on the forehead. "I think we should let our roommates have this room, separate beds and all. You and I can continue you this later—once they're asleep."

Oh no. Dread and guilt hit the pit of my stomach simultaneously. Corin's celibate. I didn't even think about how Skylar staying here might be uncomfortable for her. "Good idea," I tell him as I drop my robe, giving him one more glimpse of my naked body before changing quickly into my previously discarded jammies.

"Jesus, Layla. You're really testing my self-control here."

I smirk at him. "Aren't athletes supposed to be all about control?" I throw my robe back over my clothes since Skylar's out in the common room.

"I'll show you control," he mutters, taking a step towards me and yanking me to him using the string from my robe. He backs me up to the wall once more and plunges his tongue into my mouth until I'm panting for breath and clinging to him for more.

He pulls back, grinning when I moan in protest. Holding my hand, Landen slides the partition into the wall and pulls me into the other room where Corin and Skylar are sitting and talking in the same spots where we left them. My face warms instantly. The walls aren't that thick and the partition is even thinner. They probably heard everything, or at least the highlights.

Corin's eyes are lined with exhaustion but wide with concern. "You okay?" she asks.

I nod, even though I'm not. I'm dizzy and weak and my insides are on fire.

"Hey, um, so I have a buddy with a studio apartment nearby and he's out of town. This has been a shitty night for all of us so Corin and me were thinking maybe we'd go crash there. It'll give you guys some time to talk in private."

The Skylar I've come to know typically would've given Landen a big obnoxious wink, but right now he seems to genuinely comprehend that something intense is going on. As much as I want to be alone with Landen, I know how much Corin's celibacy means to her, and I don't want her compromising that for me.

Landen is nodding but I put my hand on his chest. "No, it's fine. We can sleep out here and Skylar can have my bed."

"No offense," Corin breaks in, "but as much as we enjoyed that little interlude, uh, we're going." She stands, grabbing her purse, and Skylar pulls himself up off the futon. "Besides, it's too damn hot in here and Skylar's friend has working AC." She looks right at me when she says *hot* and I know she's not just referring to the temperature.

"Okay…but can I talk to you for a sec, um…in the hall?" I try to convey silently to her with my eyes that spending the night alone with a boy is not the best way to remain celibate.

"Layla, I know what you're going to say. And it's fine. I have it handled. Promise." She hugs me and whispers, "But be careful. You know where the condoms are," in my ear before she and Skylar turn to leave.

"Um, you be *careful* too," I say, and then I'm alone with him. Alone in nothing more than an extended bedroom, with the boy who has the power to destroy me. Again.

CHAPTER Eighteen

Landen

The universe is a bitch. A bitch who I must've screwed and forgot to call the next day. Because the exact moment that Layla let me pull open her robe, and I knew she was giving herself to me completely, was the exact moment I developed a conscience.

I couldn't do that without telling her the truth. But once I tell her the truth, she's going to be understandably pissed. And done with me. So much for balance.

After Skylar and Corin leave, we're alone and things are careening downhill from hot to awkward at an alarming speed. It's probably for the best, though my dick would definitely disagree. I lower myself onto the futon where she's sitting, staring at the door.

"You okay? If you really want them to stay, I'll call Skylar and tell him to get his ass back here."

"No, I, um…" She pauses to clear her throat and I look around the room. It's very Layla. Deep purple everywhere and throw pillows all over the place, much like her room back home. Well, her home. I don't think I've ever actually had a home.

"I'm worried about Corin," she says softly, staring down at her hands. I lean back and watch her fidget for a moment. Delicate fingers twisting in her lap, full bottom lip pulled tight between her teeth.

"Not to be a jerk, but your roommate seems like the kind of girl who can handle herself. In fact, maybe I should be worried about Skylar." It's a joke and I expect her to laugh but she flinches back and glares her ass off at me.

"What the hell is that supposed to mean?"

"I didn't mean anything bad. She seems like a tough chick, that's all." I grin. "She's instilled fear in my cold, dead heart on more than one occasion. And I was raised by a man who was specially trained by high-ranking government officials in how to instill fear."

"Oh. I thought you meant that she seemed slutty or something." Her cheeks flush and she offers me a small smile.

Yeah, okay, that too. But I'm not stupid enough to say it out loud. I shrug. "No, but I'm not a big fan of that term anyways. Girls can like sex and do what they want without me trying to label them for it. In fact, uh, before you, those were my favorite types of girls."

No. Dammit. Words, come back. Why did I say that? Oh yeah, because I'm being honest and trying to make triple sure I don't get laid tonight. Got it.

"Oh really?" Layla says with a grin, but she pulls her knees up to her chest, and I know I'm ruining everything. I know because I'm doing it on purpose.

"Yeah, I mean, what's wrong with a girl who knows what she's doing? And who doesn't have a ton of expectations? I always knew it was only a matter of time until I moved again, so why bother with anything with potential? You see where that got us."

"It got us here," she says so low I almost don't hear her. "Is here so awful for you?"

No. Yes. Fuck. I need to punch something. To go for a run until I don't have energy to think or feel or give a shit. I almost laugh at the irony. I cut my father out of my life after the divorce but I can't cut him out of my head. Without him around to punish me, I punish myself.

"You weren't too happy to see me at orientation. Or at the club." I shrug like her turning away from me didn't cut me deep a hundred times over.

"It was a surprise, that's all."

"And not a good one, right? Because of that night, because I left."

She sighs and twirls the tie-string on her robe. "Because I was *confused*, Landen. My feelings for you have always been overwhelming and new and… scary." She whispers the last word and I'm hit with so many emotions I can't respond right away. The very same emotions I've learned to shove down so far they never show.

"Why?"

Her adorable little nose scrunches. "Why what?"

"Why are you scared?" I ask her, brushing her still slightly damp hair back behind her ear. Like I don't know. Like I'm not two heartbeats from running out of here to keep us from doing what we both know we're going to do. That's why I tried to put the breaks on. We need to talk, hash out the truth before going any further. But I'm selfish, like the Colonel says. So I stay put.

"Honestly? You know how it was for me in Hope Springs. I was isolated, ignored, and frankly, I was managing because part of it was my fault. I liked them giving me space at first, and by the time I wanted to reach out…it was too late. I was getting through, but that's all I was doing—just *getting through* my life, going through the motions on autopilot." A sadness that tightens my chest, making it impossible to swallow, washes over her face. "And then you showed up. And you saw *me*. You thought there was something wrong with them, and even after you learned about the five-piece set of emotional baggage I was carrying, you still wanted to be my friend. And more. And you made me feel things again. Things I hadn't felt since before my parents died. And things I'd never felt period."

"And then I left," I mutter, disgusted at myself all over again.

She huffs out a breath and finally releases the string she's been twisting. "You did what you had to do. I see that now. How would you have felt if you'd sent your mom back to Colorado alone? And, God forbid, how would you and the Colonel have lived together? One of you wouldn't have made it out alive."

She's more right than she knows, but now's not the time. She's scooched herself closer to me on the futon, and her robe has fallen open. Under her small gray T-shirt I can see the outline of her breasts and it's distracting as hell. Not to mention the tiny plaid shorts that barely cover her smooth thighs. Aw hell, now my voice is cracking and shaking the same way hers did. "I wanted to come back. I had plans for us to meet up halfway and maybe go on Spring Break together but…"

"But I shut you out," she finishes for me. "Because I was hurt. And there was some other stuff going on, medical stuff that just…had me starting back at square one. Back to going through the motions. And if I let you back in I would've had to feel. And I really didn't want to feel anything."

And there it is. My opening. The words that should prompt me to tell her why I'm here, not that that's even the exact reason anymore…but still. She deserves to know.

"Speaking of the medical stuff, Layla, there's something—"

"Shh, Landen." She cuts me off with my name on her breath and then, even more effectively, her actions. Pulling up on her knees to lean into me, she wraps her arms around my shoulders and hitches a leg over my lap. She's straddling me, sinking her clear aquamarine eyes into mine, and I can't even remember what I was going to say or why.

"Layla," I groan, placing my hands on her hips.

"I'm ready to feel now," she whispers. She grinds herself against me and I fall down into the endless pit of emotion I've been edging around since I left her. Head first.

CHAPTER Nineteen

Layla

I didn't know if he planned to hash out our messy past all night, but I didn't want to talk anymore. Especially not about my medical issues. So I climbed onto his lap and covered his mouth with mine.

Judging from his instant reaction beneath me, I'm obviously not too bad at this. Though he made it clear he's been with more experienced girls. Some animalistic instinct in me has the urge to show him I'm better than them. That I can be the best he's ever been with and all he'll ever need. Even if I'm not so convinced it's true.

Pressing my hips down on him feels so good that I moan embarrassingly loudly. It doesn't seem to do anything but make his mouth that much more eager to invade mine. His thick, warm tongue lashes against mine and I graze my teeth against it, making it his turn to moan.

Finally.

All the pent-up hurt and wounded frustration seep out of my body, loosening the obsessive death grip I've had on control for the past five years. This isn't just my chance to start over like I thought—it's *our* chance. Fate brought us back together, and now I'm ready for the kind of relationship he needs. My muscles relax around him as he pulls my robe off of me. I'm just about to yank my shirt over my head when he stands, still clutching me to him in mid-air.

"Um, Landen," I mumble against his mouth as I tighten my legs around his waist.

"Bed," is all he says as he carries me back into the bedroom.

I expect him to lay me down on my bed but he sets me down on my feet in between the two beds.

"Where were we?" he mumbles more to himself than me. Oh, right. Before.

Sucking in all the courage I possess, I curl my fingers around the hem at the bottom of my T-shirt and lift.

My heart pounds so hard he can probably see it throbbing out of my chest now that I'm topless. I expect my body to betray me, to start trembling like a nervous animal, but I'm steady. Because it's Landen. Landen—who brought me milkshakes. Who risked humiliating himself by enlisting the help of the entire soccer team to ask Freaky Flaherty to Homecoming. Who let me hold him in my arms after the Colonel hit him on Thanksgiving. The boy who saw me at my worst and kept me still.

He kneels to slide my shorts down and sucks in a breath when he remembers I'm not wearing panties. I step out of them and realize that it's Landen who's trembling now. My head falls back again as he resumes his slow, torturous path of warm, wet kisses between my hipbones. Liquid fire burns between my legs, and I'm getting twitchy as I wait for him to touch me where I'm throbbing.

Looking down, I see my erect nipples above his thick, dark head of hair. Pulling my fingers through it, I clench tightly, almost unable to take any more. His nose dips into my belly button and I moan out loud.

Landen looks up at me. Pure unadulterated desire radiates from his stare, and the little girl in me is self-conscious about playing grown up with someone who's done this before. But I'm ready. I'll be past ready if he doesn't hurry up. And why is he still wearing all of those clothes? Random thoughts race all around inside of me but I just want. I want so bad it's painful. I didn't know it would throb and ache like this.

"Layla," he growls, grabbing my backside with both hands.

I squeal in surprise, and he pushes me almost roughly onto the bed. He pulls his hands out from under me and uses them to spread my thighs open. *Oh my goodness. This is going to kill me, rip me apart, and send the pieces of me flying around the room. Or burn me alive and send my ashy remains scattering in the wind.*

"Landen." His name on my lips is a plea for him to stop, to give me a second to breathe, to think, but when he looks up for permission, I nod.

So slowly that I'm gripping the comforter for dear life, he runs his burning tongue up my inner left thigh. And then my right one. I can barely speak over the whimper that escapes my throat. "Landen. *Please.*"

"Since you said please," he says, his deep voice vibrating against the most sensitive part of me.

I'm struggling not to clamp my legs shut just for the friction. Wet heat scorches my tender flesh as he opens me with his tongue. As much as I want to watch, my eyes squeeze shut as I completely lose my grip on reality. One hand in his hair and one hand full of comforter, I fight the urge to scream with everything I have. This is a dorm after all, and as Corin and Skylar pointed out, the walls aren't all that thick.

Landen's mouth licks and sucks and kisses me, alternating between slow and frantic as I barely restrain my hips from grinding myself against his face. I'm wet, not just from his mouth, but from my own moisture. And I've never been so high, but I need him inside, filling my hollow ache.

"I want you," I barely manage to get out.

Another groan into my open, slick folds and I almost lose it completely. But that small spot inside of me is still throbbing for him. Pulsing desperately and pulling me inward until it's all I can think about.

"I know, baby," he says, spreading my thighs even farther. "And you're gonna have me."

"Y-You, you promise?" I'm falling over, hanging on by the tips of my fingernails, raking them down his head and neck.

"Promise," he says, pulling his head back just long enough to press a finger inside of me. The pressure is painful until he reaches that throbbing ache inside. His tongue strokes my clit as he presses in deeper and it's too much to take at once.

"Oh. *Oh, Landen. Fuck.*" I don't know who this woman is with the throaty sex voice, but I'm glad to know she exists. I don't even curse out loud. Apparently she does.

"Say fuck again," he growls into me.

"Fuck, fuck, fuck," I pant slowly as he pushes his thick finger in and out of me at the same pace. "Fuck me, please, Landen. Pretty please with a cherry on top." *My cherry*, I almost add.

"No, Layla. I'm not going to fuck you," he says softly, and my raging orgasm almost comes to an abrupt halt.

"What?" I struggle to catch my breath. He pauses to press his finger deep once more, bowing my body off the bed. A desperate moan escapes me, and I glare at him. "W-Why not?"

"Because I'm going to taste you with my mouth, worship every inch of you with my tongue, and open you with my fingers until you come. And then I'm going to make love to you like I've wanted to do since I first watched you drink that damn milkshake at Our Place. Slow and deep like you need it, like your first time should be. After that, if you're not too sore and you still want it, then, and *only* then, will I fuck you. Understand?"

Oh my holy hell. Thank you, universe. Thank you, demon of vengeance, who brought this pain upon me in the form of Landen O'Brien. More please.

"Yes," I breathe, writhing and shivering as he pulls my orgasm from me with his fingers.

"Yes to what?"

"Yes to…all of that," I say as he sucks all of me into his mouth, and then I'm spinning, swirling away from him, from my body on this bed, unable to care if the whole dorm hears my cries.

When I come back down to earth, he's watching me with hungry eyes. "I could watch you come forever."

My sex voice woman is missing in action, still floating in outer space somewhere, so I bury my face into the nearest pillow.

"Look at me," Landen orders, and dang, he's demanding about this stuff, I'm realizing. Kind of a control freak. I already knew that about him, but I had no idea he'd be all giving commands and making me say what I want in bed.

Or that it would get me so hot.

I move the pillow and look at him, overheating instantly at the sight of his mouth and the memory of what he just did with it. I can't help but wonder how people do these intimate things to each other and then go on with life business as usual. Pass the salt and all that.

"You are the most dangerous kind of beautiful," he says, brushing my messy hair away from my face.

I can only imagine what a wreck I look like after that, but with the way he smiles at me, he must actually think I am beautiful right now. I lean in and kiss his mouth. I can taste myself on his lips. It's kind of strange and kind of a turn on. I pull at his lower lip with my teeth and he groans.

His voice is raspy against my mouth. "You even taste like peaches, sweet like I knew you would be."

"What do you taste like, Landen?" I ask, as my sex voice woman comes back to me. "And more importantly, what's with all the clothes?"

"You gonna do something about it?" he challenges, rolling on his back and resting the arm that isn't wrapped around me above his head.

"I'm going to try," I answer, sitting up to straddle him like before. I undo the button fly on his jeans, concentrating all my efforts on it even though I can feel him watching me. Once I'm done, I slide down, pulling his jeans with me. He helps by kicking them off so I don't have to move off the bed.

"Shirt," I say, figuring maybe it's time I give some orders of my own. He arches an eyebrow at the command but props up on one elbow and reaches behind his head to lift his shirt slowly off. Suddenly I'm lightheaded.

This isn't the first time I've seen him with his shirt off—I used to watch soccer practice when they played shirts and skins and all that, but having him down to his snug boxer briefs in my bed is another animal entirely.

I lick my lips, thankful there's still moisture left in my body, and inch his black underwear down starting at the waistband.

When his thick, corded erection springs out of the fabric, I gasp out loud.

"That is not going to fit inside of me," I blurt out, mindless with panic.

A wide self-congratulatory smile spreads across his face as he winks at me. "It will, I promise. Gonna be a tight fit though." He shrugs like this is a good thing.

"Holy fuck," I breathe, shaking my head because I know how tight I was clenched around his *finger*.

"You can touch me," he says, his voice tense. "Go ahead."

Sliding my hand around him, I feel every vein in Landen's dick as I stroke the velvet smoothness of his flesh. Again, silly girl me giggles in my head. *Oh my goodness, I'm holding Landen's penis!* But sexy, grown-up woman me pulls her bottom lip between her teeth, glances at his face, and is thrilled to see that his smirk is gone. He's watching me with a lust-fueled intensity that has my entire body overheating.

Lowering my mouth to him, I reach out with my tongue and lick, smiling when I feel him go rigid under me. Surely this can't be that hard. But knowing it's my first time and not his threatens to splash a cold wave of insecurity over me. The new competitive Layla pushes through, and I remember how good his mouth felt on me. I want to make him feel that good.

Even better, if that's possible.

I pull my lips tight around my teeth and let my tongue massage the sensitive ridge on the underside of him as I sink him into my mouth. Using one of my hands to wrap my hair and hold it out of the way, I let the other one skim slowly up and down his inner thigh, softly raking my nails into his warm skin.

I'm probably glowing bright crimson with the heat filling me, but I don't care. I don't care about much right at the moment. He's always in control, always coming to my rescue. This time I want to watch *him* lose himself because of *me*. I lick every inch of him, flicking my tongue up and down and around in circles before drawing him as deep as I can handle into my wet mouth.

"Fuck, Layla," he grunts out.

A shiver of pleasure thrills through me. Now I know why he wanted to hear me say it so badly. "We will baby," I say, sitting up and imitating his assured patience even though a sharp, needy ache has begun swirling inside of me.

"Damn right we will," he growls, sitting up as he grabs me with both arms and flips us so I'm on my back under him. A small yelp escapes my lips and I smile at him.

"Landen," I breathe, arching my back as he smiles back at me and begins to place gentle kisses on my throat.

I want to say his name again and again, let it linger in my mouth. In the tiny space between us. But when his mouth finds my breast and he begins the same worshipful process on my nipples that he performed on my clit earlier, I'm unable to recall my own name, much less his. Noises are coming out of me. I hear them, but I can't control them.

I can feel his hard length rubbing steadily against me, and I can't take this anymore. I need him inside of me to fill my hollow ache, press against my pulsing muscles, and push me over the edge.

"Underwear," I say, even though I'm not exactly in an ideal position to be giving orders.

"Yes, ma'am," he mumbles into the dip between my breasts. After he yanks his underwear the rest of the way off, he leans down and picks up his jeans. At first I'm confused, but when he pulls out his black leather wallet, I know what he's looking for. And this is the tricky part. Because he might say no.

I sit up and put my hand on the one he has reaching into his wallet. "I just want to feel you, only you, with nothing between us."

His eyes go so wide that it's probably painful. "But babe—"

"I know, okay? I paid attention in health class. But I'm on the pill. Aunt Kate insisted, and....I trust you."

"Layla," he whispers, seeming lost.

"Please? Just the first time," I beg.

"I've never done it without a condom," he tells me, making me want it that much more.

He's thinking it over and I decide just to leave it up to him. He knows what I want, but I'll take whatever he decides to give me. I pull my hand away and lie back on the pillows, waiting.

I watch as my lost boy swallows hard and puts his wallet on the nightstand. "Just this once."

I notice that he's unsteady, and for once, I'm not. His hands press into the pillow on either side of my head as he braces himself above me. "Okay," I whisper.

"It's going to hurt at first. I'm sorry. I'll be careful with you," he promises. His eyes meet mine and I see the panic in them. The steady throb inside of me pulses more intently, and I'm not exactly sure I want him to be careful with me.

Reaching up, I put both of my hands on his upper arms, feeling the steady quiver in them. "It's okay. You're okay. I've got you. You're safe, I promise."

He smiles, looking down at me from under those thick, dark lashes, and the quivering subsides. "Guess it's your turn to keep me still," he says, and I want to laugh. Or cry. Or both. Three very dangerous words threaten from behind my teeth but I hold them in. We'll deal with that later. For now, he's mine and I'm his.

And that's all that matters.

Reaching my hands up higher and placing them on either side of his face I stare into his eyes until reality shifts and we're connected on a level that surpasses the physical realm. "I want to keep you always."

He nods without breaking eye contact and something passes between us that bonds us even more than our bodies are about to.

"Oh God," I moan as his thick, swollen head parts my folded flesh, stroking up and down from cleft to center and I almost lose it.

"You're so wet, baby. That should help ease the pain, I promise."

I can't speak so I nod. I trust him.

A guttural sound tears from his lips as he presses slowly into me. *Oh my dear Lord in Heaven.* It hurts, worse than I expected. I'm consumed by the pressure of him, pinching and tearing into me. A pained whimper from low in my stomach pushes past my lips, and Landen freezes above me.

"I'm okay," I try to assure him but I'm not really. His eyes blaze down into mine, but he doesn't move. Something's wrong. "Landen? I'm okay. Really. Please don't stop."

"Say you want me," he says, ferocity changing his voice to one I don't recognize.

I clench, desperately trying to cling to him as he starts to pull out of me, and I'm torn, in more ways than one. It hurt, but now that he's been inside of me…I can't stand the feeling of him not being inside of me. "I want you," I tell him, need thickening my own voice.

"Say you want me here, Layla. Say you're glad that I'm here." It's a plea and a command, and I don't know where he's going with this.

I'm turned on and scared at the same time. Why is he angry all of a sudden? Reaching up to touch his face once more as I wrap my legs around him, I do as he says. "I want you here, Landen. I'm glad you're here." *I love you.*

And then I kiss him, needy for his mouth in so many ways. He groans again as he slides himself all the way back into me. I'm raw and aching, but when the tip of him hits that spot in me, every tense muscle in my body softens around him.

"Landen," I whimper, his name straining out of me as I lift my hips until our hipbones chafe against each other. "Yes, please, *oh God*, yes."

Harder. I'm ready for it harder, faster, but I'm not sure how to tell him, so I deepen our kiss, hoping he'll get the message. I'm sweating and so is he, our damp bodies sliding against each other, and I wish this could go on forever. But I'm not going to last that long. My insides grip him so tightly it's a struggle for him to move inside me.

"Baby, I need you to come for me, okay?" he pleads as he pulls back from my mouth. "It will last longer next time, I swear."

I whimper because I'm there, now, and it's so much more intense with him inside of me. My back is arcing off the bed so hard I'd be afraid my spine was going to snap if I could think straight. My fingers dig into his muscular shoulders, probably hurting him, but he doesn't complain.

"Come in me, Landen," I say because I want to feel him pour himself into my pulsating walls—I want him to be a part of me even after this is over. It's reckless and insane, and if my last EEG hadn't said what it did I would never do something so impulsive, but who knows what our relationship will be like after this.

"Layla—"

"Please. I-I *need* it."

He doesn't answer as his neck veins bulge and he squeezes me so tightly it's painful but in the best kind of way. I'm flung over the edge into bliss-filled rapture, shuddering and shivering on my way into and out of the darkness. He thrusts into me once more, and I feel it. Searing and filling the inside of me in scorching bursts.

The sensation sets off a series of aftershocks and I'm clenching and tightening around him, rhythmically pulling him in deeper as he comes.

"Look at me," I say softly, wanting him to open his eyes so we can have this shared memory. "Please."

His previously green eyes are so dark with his dilated pupils that they're practically black as he releases everything he has into me. "You're mine, Layla," he whispers when he finishes and eases down on top of me, never once breaking our eye contact. "You're mine."

I nod because he's right. Partially. I am his. Until my secrets ruin both of us. "I know," I whisper back, wishing I could promise to be his forever.

Chapter Twenty

Landen

Layla's body should be sculpted and displayed in a museum somewhere.

She's dozing in and out, lying on her stomach next to me with her slender arms tucked under her and a peaceful smile on her lips. Her dark comforter is pulled up to her waist but not far enough that I can't see the perfect curve where her back dips and rises at the top of her divine ass. I held her for a while afterward, but we were both burning up, so she rolled away from me.

It was her first time and she seems content, happy even. Hell, she's practically in a coma, so I'm feeling pretty good about myself. But as much as I enjoyed releasing myself inside of her, I'm all jittery and wound up with emotion. Like I'm the one who just gave up my virginity. In a way, I guess I did.

I've had sex before. Layla knows that. But what I didn't tell her was that I'd never actually made love to anyone. Never done anything more than screw whatever random girl I was dating at the time, and not really even all that well, because I never gave a shit before. It's been over a year since I've slept with anyone. There's been no one else since I met Layla, so it's a wonder I lasted as long as I did.

And I damn sure never went in without a condom on. Ever.

Just the memory of sinking into Layla's tightness, the perfect fit of her warm, wet opening around my dick, is enough to make me hard all over again. And looking into her eyes, her voice pleading with me to come inside of her, I was so gone—beyond reason, beyond sense. So totally and completely bound to this girl. And what's worse, I'm goddamn *thrilled* about it. And terrified, because I have to tell her how I ended up here and why. I should've already told her. Maybe it's too late now.

I let go of the breath I've been holding, hoping it will take some of the tension in my chest with it. No such luck.

"Was it okay for you?" Layla's sleepy voice asks, tearing me from my thoughts.

"Is that a serious question?" I turn over on my side to face her. "Because pizza is okay. Hell, perfectly cooked steak is okay. That was…that was not even in the same universe as *okay*."

Her smug little grin calms my nerves and eases the tension from before, though it tightens some other vital parts of me. "Mm."

"Was it okay for you?" I ask, running my hand gently down her arm and hoping she's not too sore.

"Mmhm," she murmurs. "Milkshakes are okay, Landen, and I love milkshakes, but that was…that was extra cherries and chocolate syrup and warm caramel and—"

My laughter cuts her off, and three words I've been dying to tell her catch in my throat. But until she knows the truth, I can't burden her with that. Before I lose myself in thoughts of the many ways I can royally fuck this up, she leans forward and presses her mouth to mine.

"Is it normal that I already want to do it again?" she asks against my lips.

"Who the hell cares about normal?" I reach out, pulling her still naked body onto mine.

"What if I can never get enough?" she asks just before she slips her moist tongue into my mouth.

"Hmm," I groan against her lips. "I'm sure we could work something out. I'm not going anywhere." *I won't leave you like before, swear to God.*

My words must be enough to reassure her because her eyes flash with mischief and she grins. "Won't they miss you at the scrimmage tomorrow?"

"Nah, I'll be too drained to play anyways."

She growls a ferocious little sound from her chest, probably the sexiest sound I'll ever hear, and pulls herself up onto me. "But I was planning to come tomorrow," she pouts, thrusting out her swollen lower lip and looking down at me like she's an expert in seduction. Maybe she is. Maybe some people are just born with these abilities, and they don't come from experience.

"Oh, you will come tomorrow. And the next day, and the next day." Sitting up, I pull her to me and kiss her until my head swims from lack of oxygen.

"Landen," she says softly, pulling back and using a finger to trace the round bruise forming on my chest from our accident.

"It's okay. My arm hurts worse than that, to be honest." Thank God they put a bandage over the stitches, or I would've probably already pulled those fuckers out by now.

"Will you really be okay for tomorrow?" The concern filling her eyes sends my heart thudding against my chest.

"I will be…if you don't kill me, that is."

Concern turns to something darker and more dangerous as she slides herself over my erection. Condom, we have *got* to use a condom. But as she brushes her slick, folded flesh up the length of me, I don't care if she wants to get pregnant, get married, move to the ass end of Georgia, and do this every day for the rest of her life. Whatever she wants, I will give it to her.

Forever if she'll let me.

"I should get going so you can get some rest," I tell her as the sun beats in through the window.

She grunts her disapproval, too weak from what we've been doing to each other to formulate words, so I don't make a move to leave. But we both have class in a few hours, and I have practice at noon, followed by a team meal before the scrimmage. I know Dean and the others are going to the Intro class, but she and I both have classes right after, so it's not like we can sleep in much.

Though I would if she wanted to. Knowing her, she won't want to miss class, even for this. I lean over, grab my phone from my jeans, and set an alarm. Her grip tightens on my chest. "Relax, I'm staying."

"I know you are," she murmurs.

I chuckle, kissing her on top of her head. Fuck, this girl makes me *chuckle*. Skylar is going to give me so much hell. "Just need to set an alarm, babe."

And I should sleep, I really fucking should. But I can't stop staring at her. Running my hands through her silky hair and down her smooth back as she drifts to sleep in my arms. Because she's mine now. So utterly and completely mine. Even though I'm an undeserving bastard.

I've parted her, broken her, filled her, and stared into her eyes as she came. Surges of pleasure and possessiveness have me hot and tense, so I push the covers away and let the image of her naked body burn itself into my retinas until I pass out.

CHAPTER Twenty-One

Layla

"Dang girl, did you guys get *any* sleep?" Corin asks as I walk into our room after class.

"Mmm, a little." This must be what it feels like to be a zombie.

"Well, you have the glow of someone who just got spectacularly laid, but the dark rings under your eyes say you could use a nap," she informs me.

There's nothing I can do to stop the grin that sneaks onto my face.

"Yeah, like I said, must've been good," she says.

Part of me wants to rehash every detail just to remind myself it really happened. But I can't even imagine speaking the words out loud to describe what Landen and I spent the night doing to each other. "It was," is all I say.

She shakes her head and grins back at me. "I'm glad your first time was nice for you."

"Me too. It *so* was." As was my second and third time. I'm still all warm and tingly when I remember the position I put her in last night. "Oh God, Corin. I'm such a crap friend. I felt so horrible about sending you off alone with Skylar knowing…what I know."

She rolls her eyes and gestures for me to sit next to her on the futon. I notice that *Pitch Perfect* is paused on the screen, and I laugh. She made so much fun of me for being obsessed with it, and now she's addicted too.

Synchronized lady dancing to a Mariah Carey chart-topper is not lame!

"It was fine. We talked, and he was…understanding," she tells me with a sly little smile that says there's more to the story.

"Wait. You *told* him?"

"Yeah. I mean, he wasn't like super excited about it, but like I said, we talked. We kind of bonded, I guess you could say."

"Traumatic experiences will do that to you," I mutter.

She shrugs. "Yeah, um, we didn't bond quite like you and Landen obviously did."

My face warms, and I take a deep breath before settling into the cushions. "It was kind of…a long time coming, you know? I mean, I pushed him out of my mind for so long that it just seemed natural to push him away. But…"

"But he won't be pushed," she finishes for me.

I nod, grateful that she understands. "Do you think I'm crazy?" I'm worried my changes of heart can't be counted on one hand since Corin met me.

"Who the hell am I to judge you?" she asks with a sad smile, the one that hints at shame in her past. Maybe we have more in common than I initially thought. She's wrong—we're not opposites. At least, not completely.

"It just seems dangerous, and kind of scary, and so unlike me. But I'm tired of being afraid, you know?" I shrug, but my own words stab me in all my weakest places. "I want him, and life is short."

"Uh, yeah, and he obviously wants you too. But he might be able to resist you tonight if you show up to the game looking like a corpse."

She's right. I need sleep. It's still a few hours until the scrimmage. After casting a longing glance at Anna Kendrick on the screen, I struggle to my feet. "Wake me up in an hour?"

"How about two hours?" Corin suggests.

"Yeah, okay. Sleep is my friend."

Collapsing onto my bed, I grab my phone so I can set an alarm in case she falls asleep, too. I am not the only one who appears to have been up all night. When I unlock the screen, there's a text.

Can't stop thinking about tonight.

Heat sparks in my center, flowing outward until the darkened room is nearly glowing.

Me either. It's been so long since I've seen you play. I'll see you at the arena.

His response takes a few seconds so I go ahead and set my alarm.

Yeah, that too. Rest up. Might be a long night.

Oh Lord, help me, this boy. And I'm wet just thinking about him, but I'm sore too, so hopefully he's not completely serious. Definitely going to get some rest just in case.

Landen

We're lining up to be announced individually when I catch sight of Layla and Corin coming down the bleachers out of the corner of my eye. My girl is carrying a humungous Coke and stepping carefully down the metal steps, looking even more radiant than ever. Thoroughly fucked looks so damn good on her. It's a struggle for me to remain still.

Even from far away, she feels me watching and turns to look. Grinning like an idiot, I wink and nod at her, warming at the way she grins back. I can tell even from here that she's blushing. Looking for the entire world like she knows something secret and special about me. Because she does. She knows what my mouth feels like between her legs, how my dick fits perfectly inside of her, and what flashes in my eyes as I come…inside of her.

For a second my knees threaten to go weak beneath me, but a sharp elbow in my side rips me out of my fantasy. "What the piss, man?" I hiss at Skylar as the booming voice on the PA system begins announcing our names and positions. I won't give him the satisfaction of rubbing my side to ease the sting, but I'm getting his ass back later.

"You were having a wet dream so I thought I should wake you."

After the scrimmage ends, Corin and Layla wait for us outside of the field house. I'm feeling pretty damn good, because even though I didn't outscore Taite, he only beat me by one goal. It's a hell of a lot better than I've been able to do in practice, so I'll take it.

Corin is smiling at Skylar like they have a secret, though he admitted they didn't sleep together. Now I'm kind of wondering what they did do, especially when he puts an arm around her like it's the most natural thing in the universe. I don't think I've ever seen him be affectionate with a girl unless he was trying to get her number to schedule a hook up.

"Landen, you want to explain what this is all about?" Layla barks, yanking my attention to her, not that it wasn't headed there anyways.

"What is it, babe?" I ask, leaning down to kiss her on the mouth. Because I fucking can.

But her lips are barely responsive, and she's holding a copy of the soccer media guide like it's a dead animal. She thrusts it at me and I read the page containing my picture.

Perhaps Southern California State's greatest acquisition this season is Landen O'Brien, who turned down offers from several professional teams to walk on as the team's second string striker.

More shit about me moving around a lot because of my dad, and so on. Oh hell. "Yeah, it's my bio." I shrug like it's no big deal. "I didn't write it. The media chick did after she talked to my mom."

"Ryan Landen O'Brien, you better start explaining yourself right now," she demands, glaring at me with everything she's worth.

"We're gonna give you two a minute," Corin says, pulling Skylar away.

As Skylar passes me, he leans in and whistles low. "Guess the honeymoon's over, huh?"

I wait until they're out of earshot and adjust my bag so it blocks their view. "I was going to tell you." Except I was hoping I wouldn't have to.

"Tell me what?" she says, leaning away from me in a way that causes me actual physical pain. "That you turned down God knows how many scholarships and a chance at your freaking dream to *walk on* at SoCal?"

Yeah, it sounds kind of nuts. Because it is.

I rub my eyes like I have a headache, but really I'm just stalling for time and trying to think. Maybe I should just lay it all out there, Layla's Aunt Kate be damned. But then the devil on my shoulder whispers, "Tell her just enough."

Stepping close enough to smell her sweet scent, I inhale sharply and gather the courage and breath I need to explain. "Don't be mad, okay?"

Layla doesn't move or blink or do anything to indicate if she'll be mad or not so I go on.

"I had already turned down a bunch of scholarships, planning to go pro with a team out of Ecuador. Then I found out you were moving out here on your own, and I was…worried. And I wanted another chance. So I called and tried to go back on turning them down, but they'd already given the scholarship to someone else. So I came as a walk on." I shrug like it's not a big deal at all, like it doesn't tell her exactly how crazy-stalker-ass in love I am with her. "In the spring I'll get another formal try out, and next year I'll be on scholarship. I get some assistance because of my dad's military service, so my tuition is covered. I worked a lot in Colorado and saved up. I can pay for the dorm, fees, and books until summer semester." She's biting her lip and tears are welling up in her eyes faster than I can figure out how to make them stop. "Layla," I say softly.

"So it wasn't fate after all then," she says quietly, looking down at the program as I hand it back to her. "It was planned."

"Hell yeah it was fate," I tell her, reaching out to lift her chin and look into her eyes, hoping to keep those damn tears from falling. "It was fate that my dad got moved to Hope Springs and you were there, like you were waiting for me. It was probably even because of fate that you missed the bus and needed a ride that first day. Or maybe that was my fault. And it was damn sure fate that made you see me as someone worthy of your time and attention, because I can't imagine what the hell else it could possibly be."

A smile curves her full lips and I exhale in relief. Jesus. Disaster fucking averted. For now, anyways. "The last two weren't fate, Landen," she tells me, coming closer and letting me wrap an arm around her. "The last two were all you."

She lifts up on her tiptoes and gives me a gentle brush of a kiss that leaves me hungry for more. I deepen it, sliding my tongue against her teeth until she lets me in. Dropping my bag, I wrap both arms around her and kiss her long and hard.

Whistles and catcalls ring out around us as the rest of the team comes out of the locker room, but I couldn't give a shit. Let the jealous bastards look. But Layla pulls back and grins sheepishly up at me, her cheeks going pink. Her swollen lips and glazed eyes have me wanting to grab her up and run Superman-style to her dorm, but we have plans to hit the diner with Skylar and Corin. And I promised my girl a milkshake.

So I huff out my disappointment, pick up my bag, and offer her my arm as we walk towards our roommates. "Ready for that milkshake?"

"I'm not going to be able to hold my food down if you two are going to be eye-fucking each other all through dinner," Skylar says before she can reply.

"Sucks for you," I tell him with a shrug. Layla giggles softly beside me. We're following Skylar and Corin down University Avenue towards the diner when Layla tenses beside me. My body is so attuned to hers that I almost grab her, anticipating the spasms, but glancing over I can see that she's trying to look casual. She's staring straight ahead. Her shoulders are stiff and her mouth's trying to turn down in that way it does just before she starts chewing her lip off.

"What's wrong?" I whisper into her ear.

A tiny shiver pushes through her, and I grin because I love that I've always had that effect on her. "W-What if I'd been awful to you when we saw each other again? What if I'd just shut you out, like before? What if you gave it all up for nothing?"

But she hadn't. "That's why I came. You could shut me out from across the country, but good luck shutting me out when we live in the same zip code."

I expect her to laugh, but she stops walking and turns to face me as soon as we reach the diner. Round, stormy eyes wide with concern look up at me… and I nearly fall in. "But you gave up your dream. Why would you give up your dream of playing overseas to come here and risk me being a total bitch?"

"Hey," I say sharply, nodding at Skylar to go on in without us. "Don't ever say that about my girl. My girl could never be a bitch to anyone."

"Landen, I'm serious," she says, growing impatient with my stalling techniques.

"Shit, Layla, what do you want me to say? I missed you. I wanted another chance, and I took a risk. Because that's what you do when you care about someone." I shrug like she isn't the first person besides my mom I've ever cared about. "I couldn't let things end the way they did. I needed you to know how I felt, and I knew once time passed and we both got over how things went down, there would still be that…that, *thing* between us. Those feelings. We weren't ready to be what we needed to be for each other in high school, or the universe wasn't ready for it. But universe be damned, because I'm done fighting the way I feel about you."

"And how do you feel about me?" she asks, shifting her weight from one foot to the other, which draws my attention to her legs sheathed in tight denim.

"Hmm, how do I feel," I murmur, remembering those smooth bare legs wrapped around my waist as I sank myself into her luscious heat.

"Landen!"

Smiling, I look up and pin her with my predatory glare. "I feel like I could buy you milkshakes forever and ever if it will make you happy. A lifetime supply, on me."

The correct response would be for her to laugh, to nudge me and say she might take me up on my offer. But Layla's never done what I expect. She winces like I've said something hurtful. Then she swallows hard and forces a smile onto her face. "Corin and Skylar are waiting."

"Whoa. Let them wait. Tell me what the hell is wrong."

"Nothing," she whispers, and I can hear the effort it takes her voice to leap over the lump in her throat.

"Tell me," I say, making a grab for her arm as she turns away from me to go in the diner.

"Wait, I have another question," she announces suddenly.

My neck nearly snaps at the abrupt change of pace. "Okay, how about you answer mine and I'll answer yours?"

"It was nothing. I'm fine. Just a nice thing you said, that's all." She waves her hand, and I want to call her on the bullshit, but I'm kind of curious to know her other question.

"Whatever you say. What's your question?"

She eyes me. "How did you know I wasn't going to UGA? That I was coming to SoCal?"

And there it is. That other damn shoe. The one I've been expecting to drop since she let me kiss her in the alley. This is it. The opening to tell her everything. And I should man up and do it, I really fucking should. But maybe the Colonel was right.

Maybe I am just too damn selfish.

Chapter Twenty-Three

Layla

"It's called the Internet, babe. And the magic of texting. Cam and DW kept me up to date on what was going on with everyone," Landen says as we walk into the diner. The milkshakes are okay here, thick and sweet but not as rich and chocolatey as Our Place, the diner back home where Landen took me on our first date.

I'm still trying to process the fact that, even though we hadn't even spoken to each other in over eight months, Landen gave up his dream of going pro to come here and try and get me to give him another chance. He took a risk, he said. I've never taken a risk of that magnitude, so I'm having trouble understanding why he would do that.

When our cheese fries and shakes arrive, Corin is laughing hysterically at something Skylar said, drawing my attention to him. He's cute. Maybe if he weren't sitting so close to a perfect specimen like Landen, a girl might even call him hot with his perfect smile and dark curly hair. But he might as well have "player" stamped on his forehead. Corin seems to know this already, so I don't comment. Not like I'm an expert anyways.

But our waitress is a petite brunette and her tiny white uniform is a size too small. I don't miss Skylar noticing, but Corin pays no attention. Just as I'm about to kick the goalie under the table for being a rude jerk to my roommate, Landen nudges me. "What?" I murmur, tilting my head towards him as I watch Skylar memorizing every detail of the waitress's ass.

"He's doing it on purpose," Landen says, barely loud enough for me to hear. "To make her jealous."

I blink. "Seriously?"

At that Landen laughs, and Corin and Skylar both look up at us. "What's so funny?" Skylar barely manages to peel his eyes from the waitress to ask.

"Layla's getting upset because you're working so hard to get Corin's attention."

"Nice, man. 'Preciate it," Skylar snarls before shoving a handful of cheese fries into his mouth. "Fucker," he mumbles through his full mouth.

Corin rolls her eyes and shakes her head, but she's blushing a little. *Blushing.* Corin. It's like we've entered an alternate universe.

"Well I hardly think undressing the waitress with your eyes is the way to get Corin's attention," I huff, still annoyed.

"It's okay. I can get her number for you, if you'd like," Corin offers with her *I know a secret* grin.

And now I feel like an idiot for getting upset on her behalf. If she knows what Skylar's doing and doesn't care, then there's no reason I should be all worked up about it. I can't figure out what kind of game they're playing, but I'm glad things aren't as complicated with Landen and me. Well, they weren't until I found out five minutes ago that he came here just to be with me. I should probably be cracking under the pressure or something, but somehow I'm not.

His presence next to me in the booth keeps me from fidgeting, and I can't help but lean into his warmth. Glancing up, I watch as he takes a drink of his shake. The way his throat muscles work to pull it down makes my stomach tighten. I look away for fear I might not be able to keep my hands to myself if I don't.

When I drop a fry on my shirt and reach down to get it, I feel his eyes on me. Slowly, I lift it to my mouth. "Corin, did you take notes in Intro this morning? I need to get them from you."

"Yeah," she tells me, still smiling from whatever Skylar just grumbled about her getting the waitress's number for him. "It was all about how to study for comprehensive exams. Probably nothing you don't already know."

I nod and take a drink of my shake. Corin's eyes flicker to my right, and I know she's noticing Landen watching me. Honestly, I'm a little bit scared to look. Without turning, I slide my hand in between his thighs and give the denim a little squeeze. Muscles tense beneath my hand, and I carry on with Corin as if I don't notice.

"Was it that same lady lecturing again today?"

Corin shakes her head. "Some dude with a comb-over. I think they get guest speakers or something."

Skylar smirks at what I can only imagine is a pained expression on Landen's face as I rub my thumb in slow circles on his inner thigh. Just being able to touch him has me drunk with power. "I mean, what professor wants to show up ass early and tell all of us how not to screw up and fail out? They probably draw straws every night to see which loser has to come show us how to sharpen our pencils."

I laugh at his comment and so does Corin, but Landen is silent beside me.

That is until Skylar and Corin start arguing over the necessity of bacon on a cheeseburger and whether the correct term is syllabi or syllabuses, and whatever the heck else they're going on about, and I feel his breath on my neck. I lift a cherry to my mouth and clean the whipped cream off with my tongue before eating it.

"I know what you're doing," he says, his voice soft and deep, laced with the hint of a threat. "Just be ready to get what you give, sweet girl."

My hand freezes on his leg, and now I'm the one tensing up. I turn my head and smile into his eyes. "That a promise?"

"It is," he tells me, taking a drink of his shake without breaking eye contact. "You about done?" His head tilts towards my half-empty glass.

I glance at my unfinished drink. "I am now."

Skylar clears his throat and I jump, causing Corin to giggle out loud.

"Can she get a to-go cup?" Landen asks the passing waitress without acknowledging our company. There's a man slumped over in the booth across from us, and I try not to stare as the waitress refills his coffee.

"Sure thing, handsome," the waitress replies with a wink. I look to see if Landen notices but he doesn't. Skylar looks a little miffed though.

Corin smiles at me while I try to figure out a way to be alone with Landen without ditching her. "Skylar's got study hall for athletes at the library, so I think I'm going to join him. My Calc class is a bitch, and the professor speaks zero English, so I'm going to see if there's a tutor available to meet with me."

I'm just about to ask if she's sure it's okay, but Skylar gets out of the booth and drops a twenty on the table. Their bill couldn't have been more than ten or twelve bucks, but he doesn't seem to care. He's too busy watching Corin slide out after him. His hungry gaze says the double bacon cheeseburger he just inhaled didn't help his craving for Corin. She stands up and takes his hand willingly.

Celibate or not, *something* is going on with those two.

"Kind of late for a study session, isn't it?" Landen asks, arching a brow at his roommate.

Skylar glares but doesn't respond.

"Corin, you can stay out as late as you need to. I'll go to Intro tomorrow and get the notes." I'm only hit with a tiny twinge of guilt since I know she's smart enough to realize this is a mutually beneficial arrangement.

"Fuck Intro," Skylar declares, nearly scaring the waitress to death as she hands us our checks and me my to go cup. She makes a point to smile at

Landen, and I notice extra numbers scrawled onto the ticket she hands him. "Dean and Mike can go the rest of this week. We'll take next week. This every other day shit is for the birds."

"Agreed," Landen says, adding a few bills to Skylar's twenty and leaving the slip of paper with the waitress's number on the table.

Maybe the big tip will ease the sting of rejection.

"Hey, can I get a ride to the body shop this weekend? My truck should be fixed, and I need to run downtown to pick it up or the bastards are going to start charging me for leaving it parked there."

While the boys work out the logistics of retrieving Landen's truck, I turn to Corin. "Hey, run to the ladies room with me?" I ask, hoping she'll agree without a big fuss. She nods and we tell the guys we'll meet them outside.

Once I've used my herculean strength to open the fifty-pound bathroom door and we're safely inside, I whirl on my roommate. "Please be honest with me. I'm not an idiot, and I highly doubt the boys have mandatory study block right after a scrimmage. Where are y'all really going?"

"I love when you say y'all, Georgia."

I glare at her until she answers my question.

"Geez, Lay, relax. It's not mandatory. It's just a blocked off time where the athletes get to use the Arts and Humanities library and it's closed to everyone else. Tutors are available and they give free help. I mentioned I was going to get a job to pay for a tutor since I'm probably going to bomb Calc, and Skylar invited me along—says I can say I'm on the girls' soccer team and the tutors don't really check to verify."

Corin holds her hands out as if to prove she's telling the truth. As if clenching your hands closed means you're lying or something. I chew my lip and study her face, looking for any traces of bullcrap. "There's an assignment due tomorrow that might as well be in Japanese. Actually, that's the only language my professor speaks and unfortunately I don't." She shrugs and I ease up on the inquisition.

"Sorry to get all in your face, but I don't want to be *that* roommate."

"Um, okay. What roommate? Far as I know, you're the only one I got." Corin turns to the mirrors beside us and does a quick check of her makeup.

"The one always running you off so I can be alone with my boyfriend." Wow. Saying it out loud makes me feel really stupid. Boyfriend actually seems kind of minimal a term compared to what Landen really is to me, but I don't have the mental energy to figure all that out right this second.

"You're not, trust me," Corin assures me with a shake of her head. "If you were, I'd totally tell you to get a room. I really do need help with my homework, and if I can scam a free tutor…then hell yeah. Who knows? Maybe hanging with Skylar will be beneficial after all."

"Yeah, looked like y'all were negotiating some benefits earlier."

Again, Corin blushes and it throws me off.

I'm not sure what to think. "Seriously, you can tell me to mind my own business, but what's the deal with you two?"

She grins at her reflection before turning to me. "If I knew, I would tell you. But honestly, I have no idea. He knows he's not going to get a hook up from me, so I don't really know what his deal is. I've told him I'm not playing, that I'm serious about not sleeping together. No matter how much I like him, that I'm not going to change my mind." Corin pauses to fish a dark tube of shimmery lip gloss from her purse, and I wait while she puts some on. "If he's pursuing me because I'm a challenge, then he's an idiot who's wasting his time. But if I can get help with Calc and a place to hang occasionally so you and Landen can have some privacy, then I don't see the harm." She shrugs. "His friend's studio apartment was pretty bad-ass, by the way, so everybody wins."

"Well, everybody except Skylar." I snort and shake my head. "I mean, all you can do is be up front with him I guess. But Corin, be careful. He doesn't strike me as the type of guy who gets turned down a lot." Or probably ever.

She gives me an impish grin, and I have a feeling she knows this. "Deal. And hey, if you ever don't want to be alone with Landen, you can, like, signal me or something, and I'll just refuse to leave the room."

Now it's my turn to grin, earning me an eye roll from my roommate. "Um, actually—"

"Yeah, that's what I figured."

Chapter Twenty-Four

Landen

"Corin's celibate. You know that right?" I ask Skylar as the girls head to the restroom. I know I'm an ass for repeating something Layla told me in confidence, but if I can help Skylar avoid a painfully awkward situation, then I probably should. He definitely had my back when I needed to skip curfew last night. On top of that, he figured out a way to give Layla and me some privacy, so I kind of owe him.

Though I haven't forgotten the jab to the ribs before the game.

"Yeah, man. I know she's *trying* to be at least," he says, glancing at the check he took off the table with the waitress's number on it.

"Layla says she is, like actually is. As in, not *trying* shit."

"I realize this," he tells me, folding the check and pocketing the ticket.

"So what the hell are you doing?"

"Chill, O'Brien. Look, if you want to give me advice about defending the goal, knock yourself out man. For real—you're a striker and a pretty decent one, so I'm all ears. But as far as girls are concerned? You were here five minutes, hooked up with your high school sweetheart, and now you might as well be handcuffed to her ass. So you can keep all that lovey advice and shit to yourself. Let me worry about my off-field game."

"Please tell me you at least see the irony of the situation?" Grinning, I watch as Layla and Corin come out of the bathroom, both smiling. Layla's smile, the one she's been using since last night, is kryptonite to my knees.

"No, but I'm sure you'll tell me, you pussy-whipped bast—"

I cut him off before the girls reach us. "You're the *goalie,* dude, and yet the first girl you try to score with is totally blocking *you.*"

"You're a dick."

"So I've been told."

"You guys ready?" Layla asks as she comes closer.

Her eyes widen, and I know she senses the tension between Skylar and me. I smile and wink, letting her know everything's fine. Just dumb guy bullshit. Nothing to see here.

"You guys go ahead. I'll be out in a sec," I tell them.

Layla tilts her head, but I just nod for her to go on out with the other two. So she does.

Layla's quiet after Skylar and Corin leave us alone, heading towards the library. The campus is peaceful as we walk to her dorm and it's kind of nice, so I don't make pointless small talk. I'm too in my head to really form any coherent sentences anyhow. Part of me wants to be a gentleman, kiss her goodnight at her door, and go on back to my own room.

My dick is not a fan of that particular part of me.

As her building comes into view, I decide I'll leave it up to her. I'll kiss her goodnight, and if she invites me in, I'll go—obviously. But I won't keep forcing my way into her life. One day, I will have to tell her about the situation with her Aunt Kate and what she did to get me here.

But today is not that day. New plan is to get her to the point where she knows one hundred percent that she wants me in her life before I drop that nuclear missile on our relationship. Then if she pushes me away, at least I know I gave it my best shot.

Layla turns to face me, and I'm such a goner. Who the fuck am I kidding? If she pushes me away, I will come back. As many times as it takes. Because there's no way in hell I'm letting this girl slip through my fingers—again. Ever.

"You paid that man's bill, didn't you?" she asks, turning abruptly on me.

"Huh?" I'm playing dumb because I don't want her to think I'm putting on a Good Samaritan act to get into her pants…though I would probably be willing to try that if I got desperate.

She pins me down with her stare. "The homeless man across from us at the diner. I know you noticed him. You stayed behind to pay for his meal, didn't you?"

I clear my throat, deciding I might as well be honest about everything I can. "I might have." And I might've given him an extra twenty as well. "Or maybe I stayed behind to save the waitress's number in my phone. She wrote it on the check, you know."

For a split second, the wounded look that crosses Layla's face has me hating myself. But then her lips curve up just a little and her eyes go soft. "Like on our first date, when you paid for Ol' Clyde's pie, and he told you that you'd have to do a lot better than that to impress me."

God, I'd nearly forgotten that part of our date.

Ol' Clyde was Hope Springs' resident homeless guy. A Vietnam vet with a hell of a temper who frequented Our Place, Layla's favorite diner. My dad was a son of a bitch and all, but he made it clear that anyone who'd served his country deserved respect, no matter how he'd ended up. It had scored me some major points with my date, though I hadn't even realized she was paying attention.

"Are you coming up?" she asks so low I barely hear her. She pulls her ID card from her purse as I come back from the memory. The questions in her eyes are a lot more complex than the one on her lips. Her mouth says, *Come upstairs and be with me if you want.* Her eyes are asking questions I'm a little nervous about answering out loud. *Do you want me? Do you love me? Is this going to be a regular thing?*

Yes, hell yes, and dear God I hope so.

"If you want me to, then I am."

"I want you to," she says easily, sending my heart hammering into my throat.

My mind travels back over the past few hours. Layla coming down the bleachers, cheering my name for everyone to hear, yelling at me about giving up my chance to play pro, drinking that damn milkshake slow enough to kill me.

I follow her up the stairs and my knees bitch at me about not icing them after the game. But the rest of me is practically sprinting past Layla in anticipation of spreading her naked body out on the bed and burying myself so deep inside of her I can't fucking see straight.

I've barely closed the door behind me when she reaches for me. My heart rate ramps up several notches as I inhale her sweet peach and now sweet whipped cream scent. It's a dangerous combo, and over her blonde head I'm eyeing that futon to determine if it's big enough for me to make love to her on it how I want to.

"I love watching you play, Landen," she breathes against my lips.

Grinning like a maniac, I lower my head so she can get some leverage on my mouth without standing on her tiptoes. "I love you watching me play, Layla. Though I bet Taite wishes you wouldn't come since I just nearly outscored his ass."

"Do you wish I wouldn't come?" she pouts at me. My head swims at how fast she can turn me on.

"If it's up to me, you'll always come. Come to every game. Then I promise to make you come *after* every game." I should be exhausted, but adrenaline is flooding through me, and my dick stands at attention. I lean down and kiss her softly. Something about brushing my lips against hers, that sweet promise of something much more intense to come, it just...does it for me.

Layla's small hands reach up and grasp my neck. I pull her to me, allowing her to back me up against the door. Her lips are wet and soft and taste like her milkshake. Fuck yeah, there's a to-go cup around here somewhere.

"Babe?" I murmur into her mouth.

Her shoulders tense and she pulls back. "Yeah?" Her eyes are wide and still burning from our kiss.

"Can I have a drink of your shake?"

Her forehead creases, and I barely manage to keep the smirk off my face. As she leans over to grab the Styrofoam cup from the edge of the desk, her shirt rides up and my mouth goes dry at the sight of her bare waist. I've got big plans for the rest of that milkshake.

When she hands me the cup, I lift the plastic lid from the edge and peer down at the three cherries resting in the dissolving cream. Thank the good Lord for extra cherries. Though thanking God for them considering how I'm about to use them, is probably sacrilegious.

Without a word, I take Layla's hand and pull her into the bedroom. She giggles at my urgency, but when we get to the bed and she looks up at my face, she falls silent. "Landen," she whispers.

And I know she's nervous even though we've been here before. She's still afraid, afraid I'll bail out again, or worse, just stop wanting her. I can see the uncertainty on her face, and it's ridiculous. I've never wanted anything more than this, more than her. Not even the Colonel's goddamn approval. Smoothing a hand down her cheek, I sink my gaze into hers.

"I love you, Layla Flaherty," I tell her because I can feel how badly she needs to hear it. "But you already know that, don't you?"

I watch as her pupils dilate and she licks her lips. "I do."

"So what are you going to do about it?" I lean back, despite my body's protest to throw her down and tear her clothes to shreds.

"I'm going to love you right back." And before I have time to respond, she thrusts her body into my arms, crushing her sweet mouth to mine. Firmly enough to let her know what I want, but gently enough to keep from hurting her feelings, I pull back, step closer to Corin's bed, and shake my head.

"Strip." The command comes out harsher than I mean for it to, but my brave girl grins up at me. Her slender arms cross in front of her body as she lifts the hem of her shirt up and over her head. Her black lacy bra suggests to me that she wants this, planned for it even before coming to my game. For a second, I'm back in the stadium, looking up at her as the field lights shine all around my glowing angel. And she gives me that look, the secret one that says I'm the only one who knows what she feels like from the inside, in my mouth, and tight around my dick.

I want to *always* be the only one.

"Slower," I command, hoping the damn milkshake doesn't melt too much.

Layla unbuttons her jeans and raises a brow at me. I nod, because yes, now she's going slowly enough. Once her jeans are down, she kicks them to the side, and I take in her matching lace panties. Every cell in my body screams at me to hit my knees, pull that tiny scrap of fabric aside, and plunge my tongue into her wetness.

"All of it, baby. I want to see all of you."

Layla's cheeks darken, and I keep my eyes on hers as she reaches back to unhook her bra. It falls to the floor, and my eyes fall to her perfectly supple breasts and the tight pink nipples protruding in my direction. Again, my tongue presses behind my teeth, aching to taste her.

"Panties," I practically growl at her.

My chest heaves hard because I'm running out of willpower here. Her skin begs to be touched, licked, bitten. I have the strangest urge to mark her. Claim her. Eying me with her wary gaze, as if she can read my crazed thoughts, Layla bends at the waist and slides her panties down her thighs, past her knees, and lets them drop to her ankles.

"Lie down. On your back." She blinks rapidly but does as I say.

My cock punches against the zipper of my jeans, and I'm done waiting. Setting the milkshake down on the night table, I undress quickly, leaving my boxer briefs on so I don't rush things. Climbing on top of Layla, I take a moment to stare down at her perfect body. Perfect face.

I'm dirtying up my angel and I know it, but dammit, how can I not?

The memory of her petite features scrunching in pain and ecstasy has precum dripping from my head, and I know I'm not going to make it as long as I planned. She drives me too insane with need. If she whimpers or moans my name like she did before, my intentions will be shot to hell. And I won't be able to wait two seconds before ramming myself inside of her and hitting that sweet, delicious center.

"Want some milkshake, baby?" I ask, lifting the cup from the table.

Layla's eyes widen. "Yes."

I grin. She's with me. Her chin dips to her chest. She nods and I allow myself a few seconds to imagine cupping those full breasts and sucking her into my mouth. "Say please."

"Please, Landen," she whimpers. My cock twitches against her thighs.

Filling the straw and closing the top with my finger, I pull it from the cup and place the tip against her lips. She opens without me having to ask, like the good girl she is. I watch her throat swallow and she shivers from the cold.

"More?"

"Yes. Yes, please." Her breath is coming harder and the swells of her breasts are pumping faster.

"Pretty please, with a cherry on top?" I prompt. She nods rapidly and repeats the plea obediently.

I fill the straw again, but this time, when she opens her mouth, I don't release. Instead I run it down her skin until those full swells rise to meet it. "For so long I couldn't even look at a goddamn milkshake. Couldn't even stand to hear one mentioned without picturing you drinking that first one on our first date. The way your eyes closed when you swallowed, and that little moan of pleasure you let out. Did you even know what you were doing to me?"

Layla shakes her head slowly, her eyes melting into mine. I release the cool liquid between her breasts and she twitches. "Cold," she whispers.

Smiling, I nod and lean down to remove the cold dessert with my warm tongue. When I swipe across her nipples, her back arches and she moans. "But you knew what you were doing tonight, didn't you?"

Layla licks her lips and nods her confirmation.

"Was my sweet girl teasing me?"

Her eyes darken and she shakes her head. "Not a tease, Landen. A promise."

"Well, I can promise you something," I say, leaning down and pressing my lips gently to the side of her neck just below her ear. "Next time you make me hard in public, I will fuck you in the nearest bathroom. Understood?" The thrill of panic that shoots through Layla's eyes says she understands perfectly. And that I give orders quite well. The Colonel would be so proud. "Hmm… or maybe I'll let my fingers fuck your sweet pussy under the table and we can see how well you can hide it when you come. *My* sweet pussy, I mean." I let my teeth graze her flesh just hard enough to let her know I'm serious. "You don't know it's mine, don't you?"

"Yes, yours. *Oh, God.*" Layla's breathing so hard and fast I'm almost worried for her.

"You okay, baby?"

She nods again, but I feel her twitching beneath me in an attempt to rub her thighs together. She must be aching, that deep ache that only I can soothe. "You need me to fuck you now, don't you?" I ask, releasing more shake across her stomach before lapping it up.

"Yes, *please.*" Her voice is so tight, as tight as I know her pussy is going to be. But I need her closer to the edge. Need her to come before I do.

"Pretty please…" I prompt, and because she knows what I want, she gives me the response I'm looking for.

"Pretty please with a cherry on top," she begs, still writhing.

"That can be arranged. Spread your legs for me," I command as I take the lid off the cup and sit it on the nightstand. Only one cherry still has its stem attached, so it's the lucky one I pull from the cup. Holding it between my fingers by the thin stem, I dip it into Layla's mouth. "Clean it off but don't bite." I watch as she licks the cream off. Now I'm the one groaning involuntarily.

After she's cleaned it, I drag the small red ball down her chin, between her breasts, and past her stomach, dipping it briefly into her belly button.

Just as I reach the small, closely trimmed landing strip at the juncture of her thighs, I stop. Layla rolls her hips in an attempt to get what she wants, but I don't move. "Now neither of us will be able to so much as *think* about a milkshake without remembering this," I tell her.

"Landen," she breathes, clutching the bed sheet beneath her.

"I need you open wider."

She complies, pulling her knees apart until her folds open and her already swollen clit is exposed to me. I suck the cherry into my own mouth, getting it nice and wet. Watching her face for any sign that she might not be into this, I lower my hand and run the cherry against her moist flesh.

"Oh my God," she cries out, tilting her head back so far I can't see her eyes. I glance down and watch her pink flesh throb against the little red orb. Damn, I planned a lot more slow torture involving her shake, but I'm about to lose the grip I have on controlling this situation.

Pulling the stem from the cherry, I toss it aside and put the tiny fruit in my mouth again. I bend down and use my tongue to roll it between her folds.

"Landen!" Everything else that comes out of her mouth is incomprehensible. Her cries have my entire body overheating, and I need to be inside her so fucking bad. Her thighs clench on either side of my head, and I want to make her come on my tongue. Her juices are even sweeter than the cherry in my mouth. I tell her so.

Her answering cry sounds pained, and I have to relieve that pain. For both of us. Biting into the cherry and swallowing it, I look up at her eyes staring down at me. A white-hot flash of possessiveness spreads through me, and I grab her hips hard. Too hard.

"Your cherry will always be mine. You will always be mine, Layla."

"I know, Landen. Y-yes, yours, always." She's panting, and it's so fucking hot it steals my own breath. Despite the way she shivered earlier, her skin is covered in a thin sheen of glistening sweat. Finally I give in to the urge to suck each of her full breasts into my mouth, giving each one their turn. Biting her nipples just enough to sting. My cock tenses in time with her moans.

Suddenly she sits up so fast, she almost headbutts me with a force that probably would've knocked us both out. For a second I have no clue what she's doing, until her hands reach the waistband of my boxer briefs and she starts tugging downward. I should stop her, maintain control, but my dick demands I let her do what she wants. Might as well get used to it. Probably what I'll be doing for the rest of my life, giving Layla what she wants, when she wants, however she wants.

"Baby, we need to use a condom this time," I mumble against the top of her head as she lowers herself along with my briefs. Her tongue lashes out against my bare chest and I flinch. Too much of that and it will be over before I get inside of her.

Lifting her from under her arms, I stand her upright. "You're all sticky from the milkshake. I think you need a shower." I retrieve the condom from my wallet and turn back to her.

Confusion softens to pleasure on her face when I pick her up bride-over-the-threshold style, turning sideways to make it through the two narrow doorways until we're in the bathroom. Lowering her gently to her feet, I glance in the mirror at our naked bodies. Part of me wants to press her against the sink, fuck her from behind, and watch her face in the mirror when she comes. But I saw the gleam in her eye when I mentioned the shower, and I'm betting we have a similar fantasy playing out in our heads.

I wink before tearing my mirrored gaze from her. *Another time.* We have time. All the time in the world. I don't care what her last EEG says. Cranking the knob to the red, I pull Layla close as we wait for the water to heat. Might as well make good use of the time. Wrapping my arms around her from behind, I press my erection against her smooth ass. One hand I leave splayed on her stomach, and the other I slip in between her legs.

My grip tightens as she widens her stance to let me in. "You're so wet. So fucking wet, baby," I say into her ear. I can't resist stealing a bite of her sweetness as I press my mouth to her neck. My teeth sink in hard enough to mark her.

"For you. Only for you," she murmurs, letting her head fall back onto my shoulder.

"Damn straight," I growl, pressing my fingers alongside her swollen clit. Her hips start to rock and I press harder, faster, until she's writhing in my arms. When she cries out, I sink my middle finger inside of her. Once, twice, leaving it in her the third time. Her walls clench my finger so tight my dick throbs with jealousy. "Fuck, Layla."

"Yes, please. *Fuck* me."

Holy mother. The tiny bathroom is filling with steam so I open the glass door and lift her inside. "You ready, baby?"

"Past ready," she breathes as I tear open the condom and roll it over my dick.

Lifting her against the wall, my arms strain and flex, adjusting to the weight. For a second I'm worried this might not work since she's so damn slippery. But then her warmth slides down, surrounds my cock, and I don't even have arms anymore. Rocking into her hard and fast, my mind screams at me to slow the hell down so we can enjoy this.

I pound into her until she's thudding against the shower wall, but her cries aren't painful. They're pure pleasure, and I want to make her come with everything I have. Her breasts lift and fall with each thrust, and it's too much. I won't be able to hold myself back for another second if we keep at it like this. I try to hold still, give myself a moment to slow things down, but she slides up and down my length of her own accord.

Who am I to deny the girl I love what she wants?

Lowering her to standing, I pull out and turn her in my arms. Sliding my cock over her ass, I apply the slightest pressure to a spot I know she probably won't let me enter.

Not yet, anyways.

"Landen?" she asks, sounding panicked.

"Shh." Chuckling like the evil villain that I am, I slide myself forward to the entrance that's already open for me and plunge in.

"Oh!" she cries out, because this is the deepest I've ever been.

Layla groans loudly, her voice echoing off the shower walls and adding to the urgency building inside of me.

"That's all of it, baby," I tell her, thrusting as gently as I can manage, reaching around to rub her clit as I sink myself into her as far as I can go. "Come hard for me, sweet girl."

Obeying my command almost instantly, she comes violently onto my dick. Her internal muscles squeeze me so tight I lose my breath. "*Fuck!*"

When I come, a whole list of words I never intended to say in front of her pour out of me along with my orgasm. Followed immediately by, "I love you, Layla. God, I love you so damn much."

Layla

Landen loves me. And I love him.

It's that simple. The realization hits me so hard it should make a sound. But the only sound I hear as he holds me in his arms is our breathing. Steady, in rhythm with one another. Just like us.

I'm sore from everything we've done to each other tonight, but Landen's warmth soothes my aching muscles. His heat is the balm I need for…everything. There were so many orgasms shared between the two of us tonight that I lost count. If his arms weren't firmly around me now, I'd probably be floating up near the ceiling somewhere. As it is I'm boneless and spent.

Tracing the hand he has resting over my breast and listening to his steady breathing, my mind wanders. What if he hadn't given up everything to come here? Would I be with someone else right now? Would he? What if things had ended the night he left Hope Springs? And if he knew what my last EEG had said, how short our time together might be, would he still be here with me now? It makes my stomach churn to think about, so I force myself to stop.

If I keep playing out all the ways things can go wrong, I'll miss out on the here and now. Which, for me, might not last that much longer. So I close my eyes and concentrate on every part of Landen that's pressing against my skin. The way his breath feels on me. The warm weight of his muscular arms. His masculine legs braided with mine.

Our bodies are so entwined that I can't imagine how we'll ever pull apart, which is fine by me because I don't want to. Ever.

As much as I try not to think, I can't stop. Rolling over in his arms so I can study him as he sleeps peacefully next to me, I reach out and trace the arch of his dark eyebrows, his smooth eyelids. What I wouldn't give to have eyelashes as thick as his. My finger glides down the perfect bridge of his nose and his firm, full lips. His face twitches, and I smile into the darkness.

Why would this beautiful creature give up everything for me? I have no idea. But he did. And just before I snuggle myself into his chest and doze off, I realize I'd do the same for him.

A crash of something slamming into the floor jerks me violently from the deep sleep I was in. "Sorry, shit. Sorry!" Corin's loud whisper rings out after another loud crash in the darkness.

I sit upright, pulling the covers over my naked body. My thoughts are still thick with sleep, and I barely register that Landen's next to me, sitting up and pulling me close.

"Dammit!" Corin hiss-whispers, and there's another thud as something hits the floor.

"Shh, you're okay, baby. It's okay," Landen murmurs into my hair.

And despite the fact that my heart is attempting to pound straight out of my chest, I am okay. I nod and let him squeeze me because I'm pretty sure he's trembling harder than I am. "I'm okay, Landen," I whisper.

He swallows hard and I feel him nodding against me as both of us go still. "What the hell, Ginger? Just turn the damn light on," he barks at her.

"Landen!" I don't want the lights on. We're naked for goodness sakes.

He shoves fabric into my hands and I pull it over my head as fast as I can manage. The lamp on the night table flickers on beside us, and Corin scrambles to grab her blanket and pillow from under the dozens of CD and the shelf that now lay on her bed. She bends down to collect the pieces of a shattered picture frame.

"Told you two push pins wouldn't be enough to hold all that," I tell her, stifling a laugh.

"Yeah, yeah," she mutters. "Sorry. I figured you had company so I was just going to grab my pillow and blanket and sleep on the futon."

Once again, I feel like the slutty roommate.

"We were just sleeping, Corin. You don't have to give up your bed. We can go sleep on the futon," Landen tells her before I can.

"It's fine, um, Skylar's here so…"

Raising an eyebrow, I look at her closely. Her clothes are a little disheveled and her curly mass of hair is a mess. "Oh, Corin, *no*," I say.

"Not what you think. *Shut up*," she commands under her breath, throwing a pointed look at Landen. Okay, guess we'll talk about it later then.

"Shutting."

"Night night, kids," Corin says, turning off the lamp on her way out.

After she slides the door closed, Landen huffs out a loud sigh and lies back down next to me. "Thank God for Topiramax," he mumbles.

Adrenaline shoots through my veins as I click the lamp back on. "What did you just say?"

"I said, thank God for Topir—oh God, oh shit. *Layla*."

I can feel the blood draining from my face. The room threatens to spin. No, it threatens to combust into flames. While spinning. Turning me, Landen, and the perfect bubble of happiness we've been in to nothing. Vapor.

He sits up and reaches out for me, but it's too late. I'm out of bed and standing in his gray T-shirt, barely feeling the sting as the tiny shards of glass Corin missed slice into the bottoms of my feet.

Dread washes over me, hard and cold. "How do you know what kind of medicine I'm taking?"

There's only one way he can know. And if he knows about Topiramax, he probably knows about the latest test results. Which would explain exactly why he'd give up everything to be here. Since it's temporary and all.

"I saw it on your nightstand," he says.

I know he's lying, but we both turn to the nightstand anyway. Corin's giant alarm clock, the lamp, and the now thoroughly melted shake are all that sit there. "No you didn't. Tell me how you know, Landen."

"Babe," he pleads but I don't want to hear any more bullshit.

How many lies has he told me now? I'm shaking, but not the kind I'm used to. "Tell me the truth. All of it. Starting now." The anger and pain vibrating my body are so intense it's distracting. My mind struggles to grab a coherent thought as Landen sits up and pulls on his underwear. Followed by his jeans. He still doesn't open his stupid mouth.

"Stop stalling." My voice breaks on the last word because deep down I know I probably don't want to hear what's coming. What I really want is to forget this ever happened and go back to the heavenly bliss that was lying in his arms.

Safe. Still. Loved.

He moves to the edge of the bed, resting his elbows on his knees. He rakes both hands through his hair.

"Look at me," I command, because I have the awful feeling that he's trying to come up with yet another lie to tell me. If I were smart, I'd let him so we could go back. But it turns out that I'm actually very stupid.

His eyes meet mine as he raises his head. "When you wouldn't answer my calls or texts, I started calling Kate."

"Kate, as in, my Aunt Kate?" He doesn't answer because it's a pointless question.

"She's the one who told me about you coming here. And about the new meds."

I wring my hands and try to think back. How did I not know this? "So what you said about Cam and DW was a lie? You really knew where I was going because you were talking to my aunt?"

Behind my back, I silently add.

He nods and clears his throat. Wrapping my arms around myself, I lower myself onto Corin's bed. "I asked you. I asked you point-blank what you were doing here." My voice is low and raw but I make sure it doesn't break.

"You did."

"And you lied. Why?"

Landen rubs the back of his neck and tries to pin my eyes with his. I won't even give him that. "Because I was afraid if you knew the truth, you'd send me away. I knew you'd be pissed that your aunt and I interfered with your fresh start. And I meant what I said Layla. I wanted a second fucking chance."

"So you thought a good way to get a second chance was to lie?" My voice breaks despite my best efforts not to let it. "What else have you lied about?"

Danni? Loving me?

"Seriously, Layla? You've got to be shitting me. So what if I didn't tell you how I knew you were here? So what if I kept up with you after I moved? I *love* you. I loved you then, too. Do you understand what that means?"

I'm not sure how to answer him so I just pull my knees up to my chest. "No. Tell me," I say sarcastically.

"It means that when I left Hope Springs, that wasn't the end for me. There's never been an end for us, as far as I'm concerned. Love changes. Yeah, sure. It twists and grows, and maybe for some people it evolves into something different. But for me, all I feel for you has only gotten stronger. More intense and overpowering. I love you, dammit. I never had a choice when it came to that. Did I do some stupid shit because I was afraid you might not love me back? Hell yeah. But I'm a fuck up like my dad says. So what did you expect?" He leans forward, closer. Waiting for my answer.

"I expected you to be honest with me," I say softly. But a nagging voice in the back of my mind wonders if he's right. I can only imagine how I would've acted towards him if I'd known my aunt sent him here to babysit me. Damn manipulative lawyers. The way his entire presence darkens tells me it was the wrong response. I was supposed to tell him that he isn't a fuck up, that his dad was wrong.

But it's too late.

Eyes blazing, he turns to face me. Hurt and fear are contorting his beautiful features. "You're one to talk. You don't even tell your goddamn roommate that you could seize out and drop dead any minute. That you have an inoperable hematoma the size of a golf ball pressing on your brain, and if it ruptures, she won't be able to call 911 fast enough."

I choke back a sob because of that word. I hate that word. Hate it coming out of his mouth even more.

Inoperable.

Broken. Beyond repair. Unfixable.

But he's right. And he knows. Of course he does. That's the only reason he would give up everything to be with me. Guilt and pity for the poor little dying girl.

"Were you ever going to tell me?" he asks quietly, looking away finally so I can breathe.

"It's no one else's business," I whisper.

But it's a lie and we both know it. They're a part of my life now. I've let them in. Made it their business.

"Bullshit." His gaze hardens and I just want to be alone.

"Get out," I say evenly.

"No."

"I want you to leave, I mean it. And I don't just mean this room."

Landen recoils like I've shoved him with all my might even though I haven't laid a finger on him. "What?"

"I want you to go on with your life, like you would be doing if you'd never met me. If my aunt hadn't convinced you to come here and babysit me. Go play soccer in Ecuador, or wherever. Just *go*."

"Jesus Christ, Layla. I'm sorry. I didn't mean to—"

"Get out!" I scream, and Corin and Skylar be damned. I need him to get away before I lose it.

"Layla, what the fu—"

"Landen?" Skylar's in the doorway looking tired and confused.

"Layla?" Corin appears behind him, and I feel instantly guilty.

This is why I don't let people in. This is why I kept to myself—it was so much better that way. I hate the way everyone is looking at me. Their faces are the identical masks of shock and confusion and repulsion everyone wears when I come out of a seizure.

"We're fine." Landen glowers at them and our roommates disappear from the doorway. "Don't do this. I know you're mad and I get it, I do. I'm sorry. Just please—"

"Just please go."

"Why?" His expression is so wounded that I almost crawl into his lap to comfort him.

But I don't. "Because it hurts to be around you. It hurts knowing that you came here because of what's wrong with me. What do you think you are? The one-man Make-A-Wish foundation? You're not. I was fine before you. I don't want you here." My heart winces in pain at the lie. He has to know I don't mean the last part.

I must be one hell of a liar because Landen stands up, and I can see his chest heaving from the deep breaths he's taking. We're ruining it. Or rather, I am. Just like I knew I would. But he shouldn't have to waste his life waiting for me to die so he can finally move on.

"You don't mean that," he says quietly. But I can hear the doubt in his voice.

I want to ease his doubt. I want to tell him I need him and can't stand the thought of being without him. But I don't. Somehow, I don't. "Yes I do."

Even I'm surprised at the conviction of my words. But part of me doesn't want him here. Part of me wants to go back to going through the motions so I don't have to constantly ache at the thought of not getting a long, happy life with him. With anyone. A small outdoor wedding in Georgia after graduation, a kid of our own, or two or three. A future. I didn't want one after my parents died. Until Landen. And knowing I won't have one is *killing* me. As is the hematoma on my brain. Maybe even more so.

But I won't take away his future, too. I won't leave him mourning me for the rest of his life, like the man who murdered my parents did to me. He deserves better than that. He deserves a healthy girlfriend, one he can make plans of a future with, plans that might actually happen. I never should have let things go this far.

"I'm going," he says quietly. "But just to my dorm. And just for tonight. You can push me away all you want, Layla, but I won't go without a fight."

"Then you're as selfish as your dad says you are."

Oh God. The look on his face stabs me so deep I can't move. What the hell is wrong with me? I just wanted him to leave. I didn't mean to break him. "Landen, I didn't mean—"

"No, you're right. I forced myself into your life before, and here I am doing it again." He punches the door on his way out and I flinch at the sound. But then he turns back to check that I'm okay, and seeing his pain makes me want to run into his arms and apologize a hundred times.

"I'm fine," I say, sounding overly defiant. Maybe because I know I'm not.

"For the record, I didn't come here just because of what your EEG said. Or even because you think you're going to die any minute. We're all dying. We could all die any minute now. I could get hit by a bus on my way back to the dorm."

"Don't say that," I whisper.

"Why not? It's true. I came back because I need you. And I thought you needed me. But I can see now that you don't, and that I was being stupid. And selfish, just like you said. Guess I should've been listening to the Colonel all along."

He snorts out a sarcastic breath and steps out of the room. "Let's go," I hear him say to Skylar just before the door to our room slams shut.

Chapter Twenty-Six

Landen

"She knows," I tell Layla's Aunt Kate's voicemail. "And she's pissed. And hurt." I almost add, "And she hates me like I said she would," but it's not like this is all her fault. I came willingly. I lied when given multiple opportunities to be honest. I'm the one who fucked up the most.

Naturally.

I don't say anything else, because what is there to say? That Layla wants me out of her life because I'm a lying piece of shit? That I deserve it because I fucked her, knowing we should've told each other everything first? That I should have let her decide if she really wanted me before taking it to that level?

What's the point in telling her all of that? It won't change anything.

After pounding myself into the concrete during the mind-numbing eight-mile run I took after practice, I shower and lie on my bed. There has to be a way to fix this. A way to make her see that I did what I did because I want her so badly. Because I love her more than I even knew I was capable of. I love my mom, yeah. Who doesn't? But how many times did she turn her back while the Colonel shouted about what a pathetic waste of human life I am? How many times did she keep quiet when he punched me, shoved me against the wall, or flat-out told me I'm nothing?

So many I lost count, that's how many.

Somehow, with her quiet intensity, her strength for dealing with all the shit life threw at her, Layla came out better. Stronger. Seeing her deal with her loss and her seizures made me realize I couldn't let the way my dad was rule my life. I wanted to be better than that. Better for her.

And now I'm right back in the hell that is life without Layla.

"Dude? You coming?" Skylar pokes his head into the dark room.

"No, I'm not." The bus is leaving for our game in Washington in less than an hour.

"Uh, I don't exactly think it's optional." I can feel his disgust that I'm acting like such a pussy but I couldn't care less. I'm used to disappointing people.

"I'm a walk-on. They can fuck themselves."

He pauses, hovering in the doorway. "All right, man. I'll tell coach you're sick or something."

"Whatever."

He shuts the door and leaves me alone in the darkness.

Two weeks go by, and Layla leaves me in silence. I've gone to Intro to Academics every day only to find Corin there, telling me to be patient and give her some space. I've been escorted out of Campbell Hall by her RA twice, and her voice mailbox is so full that no one else can leave a message now.

I'm out of ideas.

I've been running so much and working out so hard that I've outscored Taite at every practice. I've started over him in our last two games, even though I refuse to go to away games. I'm not leaving her, no matter what. Even Taite's gorilla, Blackburn, has backed off. The whole team, and probably the coaches too, know I'm losing my shit a little. And no one wants to be responsible for me flying off the damn hinges.

After team workouts, the trainer removes the stitches from my arm. It will scar, he says. No shit. I'm scarred, all right. Marked with physical evidence of the permanent damage losing Layla Flaherty has left on my life. I stay in the weight room after the trainer leaves and decide to max out on every damn machine in there. Physical pain tends to be the only thing to take my mind off the other kind.

"Killing yourself won't make her want you back," Skylar says from behind me.

I almost drop the damn weight I'm holding. "I thought I was alone."

"You will be if you don't get your shit together."

I snort. "Worry about your own shit, Martin. Isn't that what you always tell me to do?"

Skylar comes around to stand in front of me. *Bad idea, dude.* All this hurt is pissing me off and I don't know what to do with it. I kind of wish Blackburn would get all up in my face so I could let loose on him.

I am my father's son, after all.

"I would. But your shit's affecting my shit. Fuck, I shouldn't call her shit." Skylar rubs the back of his neck as I put my weights down. I slow my breathing so I can listen to the rest of what he's saying. "Corin's upset. More than upset. Layla's barely even speaking. Cor said she goes to class, she smiles like a goddamn robot, and then she just sleeps all the time."

I hurt her. Again. "*Cor* needs to get a fucking life of her own. Or wait, she doesn't have a *fucking life,* does she?"

It was the wrong thing to say on so many levels, and I know it. Skylar's in my face so fast I barely have time to blink. "I'm gonna give you a pass this once, because I know you're dealing with a…whatever the hell it is you're dealing with. But I won't comment about your freaky chick and you don't comment about mine."

If he'd called her anything other than "freaky," I would've been okay. Memories of them treating her like a leper in high school slam into me almost as fast as my fist slams into Skylar's face.

He bull-rushes me and something falls, clanking loud and hard. Somewhere in my mind it registers that a weight room is not the best place to get into a brawl. Too late now.

"Goddammit, O'Brien," he huffs as I sink my fist into his stomach.

We're rolling over top of one another when I hear the door open and a herd of footsteps pounding towards us.

Hands clutch me and pull me off of Skylar. Half the team watches as we face off with Coach Wicks between us.

"What the hell happened here?" Coach asks, looking back and forth between us.

"My fault, Coach," I say, because it's true.

"Girl problems," Skylar mumbles, looking away.

Coach probably thinks we're fucking the same one now, but I don't give a shit what anyone thinks. I need to go for a run. A long one. "Won't happen again," I say, feeling guilty because Skylar didn't deserve that and I know it.

"You're damn right it won't. O'Brien, you're off the team. Get your shit and go. Martin, get your ass in my office, *now*."

You're nothing and you'll never amount to a damn thing. How can any son of mine be such a goddamn waste? Oh fuck, are you going to cry? Get out of my sight. Go cry to your mommy.

"Yes, sir."

The Colonel's voice carries on in my head as I leave. It's still reminding me of what I already know about myself as I head upstairs and start packing my things in the dorm. Skylar comes in at some point and says something but I have no idea what. So I ignore him.

"Where are you going?" he asks as I carry my shit out.

It takes me a second to realize it's Skylar talking now and not my dad. Thank God I have my truck back. "What?"

"I asked where you were going, dude. It's not like you have to vacate the dorms tonight. Being off the team doesn't mean you have to leave school." He cocks his head towards my bag, and I know I should apologize. I just can't get the words to my mouth.

"It does for me. Back to Colorado, I guess. Till I figure something else out."

But first I'm going to go see Layla. Try one more time to say goodbye so we don't leave it like this.

"Shit, Landen, I'm sorry. Seriously. Why don't you stay at my friend's loft tonight? He's still out of town. Sleep on it. Then maybe we can go talk to Coach tomorrow together and work something out."

"Naw, no worries. It was probably time to go anyways. Shouldn't have come here to begin with." So I wouldn't have hurt her like I did. Fucked up like I knew I would.

"Dude, seriously. Here's the key to my friend's place. It's on 16th and Lane, above the pizza place. Unit D." He slides the key into my hand. I take it even though I don't want to use it. I don't deserve his kindness. Or anyone's. "Just go and get some rest and we'll grab some food in the morning or something."

I can tell he's not going to drop it, and I'm exhausted. I should probably get some sleep before seeing Layla one last time anyways.

After a shitty night of not really sleeping, I wake to someone rapping incessantly on the door. For a minute, I have no idea where the hell I am. There's art all over the exposed brick on the walls, and I'm shirtless in my soccer shorts on a black leather couch. Then I sit up, remembering the past twenty-four hours.

Oh yeah. Right. I'm off the team, out of the dorm, and out of Layla's life. I'm so fucking glad someone decided to wake me at the ass crack of dawn.

I stumble over to the door and consider checking the peephole, but it's probably just Skylar. Or maybe his friend's a drug dealer, which is likely, judging from this badass apartment, and someone's here to kick his ass.

Bring it.

Opening it without looking, my knees go weak at what, or rather *who,* is on the other side. It's Layla, and she looks as bad as I feel. "Baby?" I say, reaching for her, but she steps back.

Red-rimmed eyes look up at me. "I went by your dorm and Skylar said you were here."

"Okay..." Wonder if he told her *why* I'm here.

"I talked to my aunt," is all she says. Her face crumbles and tears are coming.

"Layla, baby, please. Please come in." The urge to grab her and hold her to me is so strong that it hurts not to give in to it.

"No." She shakes her head and takes a step back. "She told me about the money. I just wanted to ask if you got paid extra for screwing me." Her voice breaks on the last part and her pain pierces through my chest.

At that moment I want nothing more than to wring her Aunt Kate's goddamn neck. The money. Fuck. Closing my eyes, I count to ten in my head. Lying to Layla has made my life a living hell. Well, keeping things from her has. Time for the truth. Though somehow I doubt it will set me free now.

My voice comes out flat. I've lost this battle and I know it. "They'd already given my scholarship away. The Colonel's military benefits only pay a portion of tuition, and I had to come up with the rest, for the dorm fees and books, on my own. The signing deal for the Barcelona Club in Ecuador included a ten thousand dollar lump sum up front. My mom had already bought a small house, and I'd planned to give it to her to help out since I wouldn't be there. Your aunt matched it to get me here."

Now I can finally breathe without that pressing down on me. But Layla's retreating, and I can see that something I've said has broken her. "I'm sorry, I should've told you. I shouldn't have even taken the damn money, but my mom was so upset about me coming here instead of going pro, and she's struggling and..." And I am worthless at helping anyone with anything.

"But you were going to go pro."

"I was, because you wouldn't answer my calls. Wouldn't talk to me. Kate said the new meds were working. I thought you didn't need me or want me in your life anymore."

"So why didn't you go to Ecuador, Landen?" She's trembling, and my arms are aching to reach out to her because it's just the response I've always had.

I take a deep breath, trying to suck in enough courage to be completely honest. "When the test results came back about the hematoma and your aunt said you were coming here, I thought you needed me—even if you didn't realize it or want to admit it." Wrong answer. I can see it on her face. My tongue trips over my words as I try to fix it. "And I wanted to be here—with you."

Which is why I got my ass kicked off the team. Because I'm a damn idiot.

Layla shakes her head, and her mouth turns down as she steps farther away. "I don't need you. I want you to get on with your life. Go to Ecuador or wherever. We're done."

Before I can say anything, she runs. Literally turns and sprints down the stairs behind her.

"Fuck!" I pound my fist into the heavy door, probably breaking all my knuckles in the process.

CHAPTER Twenty-Seven

Layla

I have no idea how long I've been sitting and staring off into space. Obviously too long, because Corin comes in with that look on her face. Maybe I've been here for the entire week since my last encounter with Landen. I know I haven't moved since my aunt called back.

Latest test results are in. The mass on my brain is in too critical of a spot to even consider removing. Ever. There's not a surgeon in the world that will touch it. I've officially become the ticking time bomb everyone in high school seemed to know I was.

"Layla, can we talk?"

"Sure." Just not about me going to class. And not about my aunt. And sure as hell not about *him*.

She bites her lip and sits on her bed across from me. "It's about Landen."

"Then no, we can't."

For a moment she just stares at me. Her eyes are clear. I know mine aren't. They're so swollen from crying I can hardly see her. "Well, I'm going to talk. You can listen."

I shrug because nothing she says will change anything. I was always a charity case to him. One with a big fat monetary bonus if he babysat me well enough.

"What I'm going to say is harsh, and I'm sorry." She runs a hand through her hair. "But Landen handles you with kid gloves, and I can see how much you don't like it. So I'm going to treat you like a big girl."

I raise my eyebrows as she stands up, but I say nothing. Her forehead wrinkles, and I can tell she's worried about hurting my feelings. She shouldn't be. No one can hurt me as much as he has.

"You're scared of living," Corin announces.

Okay. Well, that was unexpected. "Excuse me?"

She stares me down. "I don't know why or what the hell happened to you exactly, but you're hiding from life."

Oh. Yeah. That. "My parents were gunned down in front of me when I was thirteen," I say dryly.

Her knees give out and she sits back down. "Oh." Her eyes widen as whatever else she was about to say appears to fly right out of her head.

"I was going to tell you eventually. And about the seizures. How I moved in with my Aunt Kate after the funeral and then had my very first seizure on my third day at my new school when something exploded in Chemistry class. Pissed myself in front of everyone. I had some other…problems. Ended up hospitalized for a long time. Was homeschooled by private tutors until my senior year, when I finally decided to suck it up and go back. But no one had forgotten. They avoided me. And then Landen came and…"

I can't keep going without crying. Landen saw me. He brought me back to life. And then he left. Then I brought *myself* back. And we got a second chance. But now I wish I'd just stayed numb, kept going through the motions, so I wouldn't hurt like this.

Corin nods, and her eyes are moist. "He told Skylar a little bit about how things happened back then. But Layla, I'm going to tell you how things are now."

"Please don't, Corin. Just…I can't do this anymore. Every time I think he wants me for me, it turns out everything he does is out of pity. He gave up his dream, for God's sakes, to babysit a grown woman. He even got *paid* to do it." God, I wish she'd just leave me alone so I can go back to wallowing in my pain.

She nods. "Yeah, I can see how it looks that way. But you're wrong." Corin's frowning at me and I can tell she's worried whatever she has to say is going to hurt.

"Fine. Spit it out. No more kid gloves, like you said."

She lets out a breath. "He and Skylar got into a fight in the weight room. Skylar said something stupid, because Skylar's stupid, but the coach cut Landen loose because he took the blame and he's just a walk-on."

Oh God. It takes everything I have not to let my pain leak out onto my face. "Well, maybe it's for the best. Now he can go play overseas like he always wanted."

Now Corin appears to be the one in pain. "Um, yeah. There's more. Skylar felt like shit about the whole thing, so he went and told the coach exactly what happened. Their coach made some calls and got Landen a tryout for a team based in Spain."

"Good," I choke out because I know what's coming. I know how amazing he is. How could anyone not want him?

"His flight leaves in two hours." She glances at her watch. "Um, an hour and a half."

Jesus. Something inside of me fists itself into a tight ball. My hand covers my heart and my eyes clench closed. I don't know what to say, how to get this pain out of me. But it doesn't matter, because Corin's pacing all around and apparently there's even more because she's still talking. "I checked with the international studies department last week when Skylar told me about the tryout. Since you're majoring in Special Education, you qualify for the study abroad program. You can go with him, learn several other languages, and help kids in Spain while you're at it. There's a shit-ton of paperwork we'll have to do to get you admitted by next fall, if you want to still do the whole college thing even though…"

I hear the words she doesn't say. *Even though you might not live long enough to graduate.* So all my secrets are out then.

"…but I can help with whatever needs to be done here. So, um, you have about fifteen seconds to get your stuff together."

My thoughts scatter in confusion. What the hell is she talking about? How did we get from Landen going to Spain to me going? "He's *leaving*, Corin. I'm letting him leave." *Just like I did before.*

"Okay, see this?" Corin holds up both of her hands and mimics pulling gloves off. "Kid gloves gone. Now get your ass up and Pack. Your. Shit. Skylar's going to drive like a maniac to get us to the airport in time. Kate says you already have a passport, thank goodness, but you still have to get a ticket, go through customs, and check your baggage. It's a twenty minute drive to the airport, but Skylar says we can make it in ten if we hurry."

She reaches down and yanks my suitcase out from under my bed. I gape at her as she starts emptying my drawers into it. "Corin, stop!"

She freezes and glares at me. "No, Layla. *You* stop. Stop hiding from your life. If someone told me right now that I had a blood-filled tumor pressing on my brain, and I could die at any second, I'd get my ass out there and live. I'd be skydiving and deep sea diving and whatever other kinds of dangerous-ass diving they have. And if some crazy-hot guy wanted to reroute his life to spend whatever of mine was left with me, then you can damn sure bet I'd let him. If I've only got a few more minutes to live, I'm tying that fine piece of ass up in my bed and making the most of it."

I cover my mouth to keep from laughing about the "ass diving" part. But she's right. "I'll hurt him," I say softly. "When I'm gone, he'll be hurting."

I know this for a fact. I've been there.

"We *all* will be, Layla. And he has us—we'll be there for each other. You can't push us away because you're scared that we'll be sad when you're gone. You doing that is as bad as your aunt trying to run your life. You don't get to decide for us whether we love you or not. I do. Your aunt does. Landen sure as hell does."

"W-what if he doesn't want me to come to Spain with him? And what about you? What will you do for a roommate?"

She rolls her eyes at me. "Layla, I can almost guarantee he does. But even if he doesn't, you need to risk it, like he risked everything coming here for you. To be honest, I'm not sure I can handle looking into your eyes for the rest of the year if you don't at least try to work things out with him. And as for me, I'll figure something out. Maybe get a small apartment or see if Skylar's friend wants to sublet his. I got the job at the diner, so it'd be close."

I bite my lip, shocked I'm even considering this. But I feel more alive than I have since the last time Landen and I made love. "My aunt is going to flip out."

"Yeah, I called her. She did. Serves her right." Corin goes back to packing, and I can't believe what I'm about to do. But my heart is beating hard and fast because I *am* alive. And I'm going to live this life. Dammit.

"Wait. Shit. I'm doing exactly what everyone else does. Telling you what to do." Corin freezes for a moment and stares at me. "What do *you* want to do, Layla? Where do you want to be when you wake up tomorrow? Here? Georgia? With Landen?"

The answers to her questions come easily. I don't even have to think about them. Because I already know where I want to be. Who I want to be with.

It's time I started living. For however long I have left. And tying Landen up in bed sounds like an excellent thing to add to my bucket list.

My life flashes before my eyes twice on the way to the airport. When Skylar drops me at the curb, my legs are shaking for a multitude of reasons. Corin hugs me tight, and I'm a little bit sad we didn't get more time together.

"I packed the Blu-ray copy of *Pitch Perfect* for you," she says.

"I love you."

She laughs. "Love you too, crazy girl. Now go get your fine piece of soccer ass." My eyes are watering but I snort out a laugh into her hug.

If Landen were standing next to me as I buy my ticket and check my bags, he'd be locking me in a death grip for how hard I'm trembling. I put the eleven-hundred-dollar ticket on the emergency credit card Aunt Kate gave me. I'll call her when I get there. I'm dying, so technically everything's an emergency.

I finally find gate C11, and they're already calling for people to board. Glancing down at my ticket, I see that it's not my group yet. Is he already on the plane? Panicked insecurity hits me hard and fast. What if he doesn't want me to come?

I'm about to turn around and try to go get a refund on my ticket when I see him. For a guy whose dreams are coming true, he looks pretty down. Slumped in the farthest seat from the gate, he stares out the wall of glass facing the hangars. An enormous plane sits in front of us. My stomach drops out at the sight of both. A little over an hour ago I was sulking alone in my room. Now I'm about to jet to a whole other country.

At least, I *hope* I am.

At first, each step towards him is like trudging through wet cement. But the closer I get, the lighter I feel until I'm practically running. "Landen?" I ask softly, even though I know it's him.

"Layla?" He turns in his seat and looks up at me. I lose my breath. Jesus. I thought I looked bad. His normally bright eyes are dark, sunken into his face and encircled by bruise-like rings. Either he hasn't slept in a week or someone punched him.

Repeatedly.

"Did you get into a fight? Other than the one with Skylar?"

"What? No." His brow creases. Oh. No sleep then.

"I, um, wanted to see you."

"You came to say goodbye?" he asks, and a lump rises in my throat. His voice is like a little boy's, hollow and lost. Suddenly, I have no idea why we've been doing this to each other. It's love. Plain and simple. You love someone, you show it. Every day, up until your last.

"No. I came to say I'm sorry."

His shoulders slump farther down at my words. "Oh. Well. Apology accepted. I'm sorry, too. I should've told you—"

"Landen. I didn't *just* come to apologize."

His shoulders lift slightly and a tiny glimmer of hope shines from behind his eyes. "Did you come to ask me not to go?"

For a second, that option makes so much more sense than flying off to Spain with him. But Corin was right. I've been hiding from life, afraid to live for fear of how it might affect everyone when I'm gone. He came to California to be a part of my dream. Now I'm going to be a part of his.

"No," I whisper, because I'm still nervous he won't want me to tag along.

"Then what?" His voice hardens and I'm hit with solid weight of his disappointment.

Because that's what he wants, for me to ask him to stay, like I should've done in Hope Springs. Any insecurity I was holding on to dissolves.

I step closer. "I came to say I love you. And to see if you have a window seat because there's no way I'm sitting in the aisle all the way to Spain."

Disbelief holds him back until I produce my ticket. He stands, taking it from me and staring at it as if it might self-destruct in his hand. "Layla, what are you…what about—"

"I was afraid," I say, working hard to speak loudly enough for him to hear. "Of us. Of needing someone. Of hurting you. All of it."

"Baby, you don't have to—"

"Please let me finish." I look up into those soulful eyes of his, the ones that have seen every single version of me. Lonely. Lost. Sad. Seizing out. Humiliated. Thrilled. Turned on. In love. "You came to California for me, to be a part of my dream. To keep me still, to keep safe if I needed you." I take a deep breath, hoping the tears will hold off long enough for me to say what I need to. "I need you, Landen. I need you so much. I need us. I don't know how much time I have. I don't know how much time any of us have. But I know that I want to spend whatever time I have left, every second of it, loving you. Being a part of your dream. Please let me."

The world around us disappears—the people, the planes, all of it, as his eyes widen and he sucks in a breath, taking in my confession. His gasp fills my ears. My heart thuds hard in my chest. I barely have time to blink before I'm lifted swiftly from the ground. Then I'm in his arms, where I belong. Where I'm still. And loved. And safe. I never want to move again. But I have to because they're paging my seating section to board. His mouth closes in on mine and I open for him, coming to life as he presses his tongue into me.

I'm clinging to him for all I'm worth; writhing so hard against him he chuckles against my mouth as he sets me down gently. "And you definitely want to go to Spain? You're positive?" he breathes against my forehead.

"I do and I am. Corin's going to help me work out the details with school and everything."

I can feel his grinning mouth against my skin. "I love you, Layla Flaherty. But if we're going to make this flight, I have to go get another ticket. Because I returned mine."

"Why?" I lean back and look up into his beautiful face. "Why would you do that?"

He tilts his head in the way that always gets me. "I couldn't go, couldn't leave you. Not again. Never again." He reaches out to stroke the left side of my face, near my scar, and my hand meets his.

He couldn't leave. Not everyone leaves. Now my tears do come, tears of happiness, hard and fast as I throw myself at him once more. I can taste the saltiness of my joy on our lips. "Wait," I say, forcing myself to break the kiss but not my grip on him as we make our way to the gate to see if he can get his ticket back. "Do you think they have milkshakes in Spain?"

HOLD
Us Close
a novella

For Lauren
Because I quoted your infinite wisdom without even realizing it.
And for anyone who loved and didn't give up.

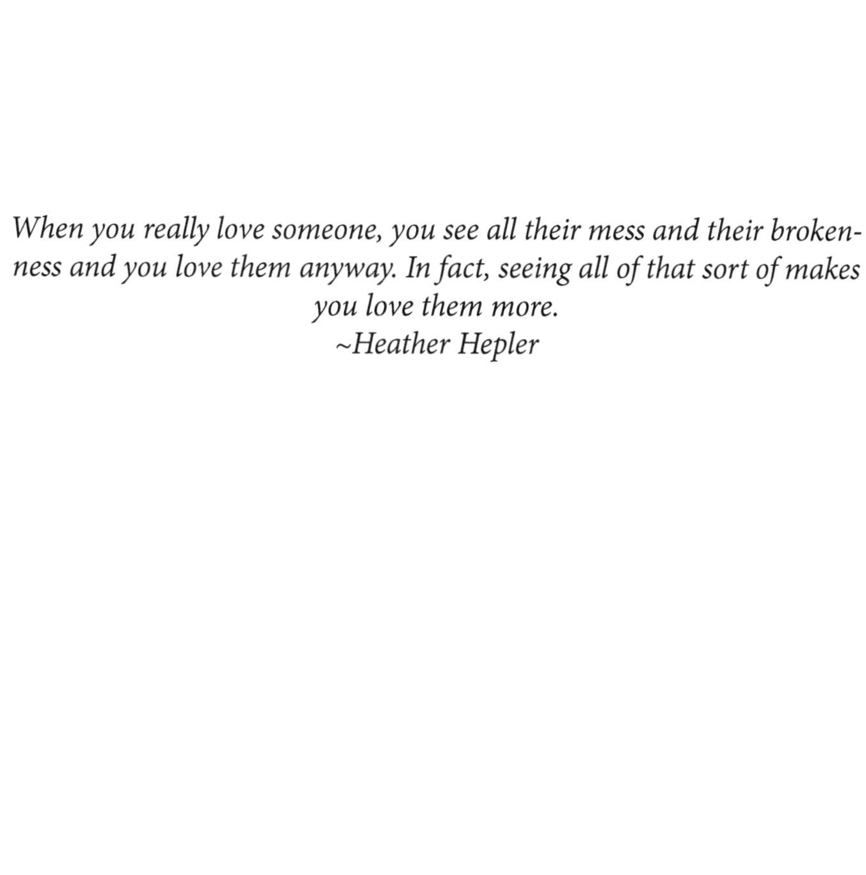

When you really love someone, you see all their mess and their brokenness and you love them anyway. In fact, seeing all of that sort of makes you love them more.

~Heather Hepler

"Layla! Put that down. Don't touch those."

My mother's urgent tone causes me to drop the twisted, silver seashell I just lifted into my small hand. "But I like this one. It's pretty, Mommy. Look." I bend to retrieve it but she grabs my hand before I reach my prize.

"Not those, baby." She points to the jagged edge of the shell next to the swirly interior that caught my attention. "Those are broken. They have sharp edges and will hurt you."

For the rest of the afternoon, she points out the smooth shells with perfectly rounded edges. The complete ones without flaws. They are the only ones allowed into my pink plastic bucket.

But when she isn't looking, I snatch up one I couldn't resist. It is dangerously twisted and curved, warped by water and whatever had torn it from the larger piece it was once a part of. It glints in the sunlight, and no matter how hard I try to resist, it catches my eye until I give in.

"Layla!"

At five years old, I'm not quite sly enough to get away with much. Nothing gets past her.

Just as I try to slip it into my pocket for safekeeping, my mother grips my wrist and forces my clenched hand open. The shell gleams proudly, giving me away.

"See? What did I tell you?" She lets the shell drop back into the sand, rejected, forgotten. She shakes my wrist gently, just enough to distract me from seeing where it fell.

Surprise and confusion crash over me like an ocean wave. My hand is bleeding. Not horribly, but enough to sting once I see it.

"Stay away from the broken ones, sweetie. They'll only hurt you."

She says it twice more as she cleans and bandages my cut back inside our small, rented bungalow.

Softly, too low for her to hear, I mumble under my breath once she's out of the room. "But I like the broken ones."

I wake up sweating. For a moment, I swear I can still hear the ocean. But Salobrena Beach is the closest one and there's no way I could hear it from here.

It's been years since I've dreamt of my mother. Of either of my parents. The night they were murdered in front of me still sneaks into my nightmares from time to time, but this one was different. It was a happy one, I think. Though for some reason I'm reminded of blood.

I struggle to hold on to the image of my mom in a floppy black hat and a polka-dot one-piece. I can still remember wanting to be just like her when I grew up. But the dream vanishes like a vapor dissipating into the darkness.

I realize I'm in bed alone, and for a second, I'm confused. But then I remember my boyfriend is out of town for work.

He'll be home tomorrow and I'll tell him. Even though I was thirteen when I lost her, I'm hoping I might get to be just like my mom after all.

~**FUTURE TENSE:** Used to mark an event not having happened yet, but expected to happen in the future. Or that tense feeling you get when you let yourself have hopes of a future in spite of everything.~

CHAPTER One

Layla

"Hey, do you want to have dinner at The Cantina or that new place we talked about trying out?" I ask my boyfriend as he enters our apartment and puts his gear down. "Or would you rather I cook something? I know you need a shower but I'm starving." And I have news. Important news I'm hoping won't freak him out. Or piss him off.

"Well, we can't have that, now can we?" He comes over and places a kiss on my forehead. "Hello, by the way. Missed you too."

He's been in Barcelona for two weeks with his job. It's only about eight hours from our apartment in Granada where I attend school, but I have a medical condition and don't drive so time apart is brutal. Landen is a professional soccer player. Hottest one on the team, in my opinion. In the league, if I'm being honest. And the fact that he agreed to live within walking distance of the School of Public Health I attend instead of closer to his job is just one of the many ways he's demonstrated his devotion to me, to us. I'm a lucky girl.

"Missed you back." I press my lips against his, the tightness in my stomach reminding me that I missed him even more than I realized. I've been so busy with classes and Bridging the Gap, the organization I volunteer with, that I haven't had time to think about it much. When we first moved to Spain, I missed him like crazy every time he went out of town. But somehow I've made a life for myself here. *We've* made a life for ourselves. And it's home. I glance around our apartment, proud of myself for the little touches I worked so hard on. Earthy colors are in the curtains, lamps, wall art, and picture frames that adorn our living room. I love it here, love the cozy space that is just so…us.

And now that Landen's here, wrapping his strong arms around me, I never want him to leave again.

"Wanna jump in the shower with me?" he asks, yanking his shirt over his head in one swift movement, leaving me speechless. No matter how many times I see the tight, tan muscles of his athletic body, I still get all hot and bothered.

I lick my lips and try to think straight. "Um, I do. But I've already showered. And I'm seriously hungry."

Pulling me to him, Landen growls in my ear. "I'm hungry too, babe. Starving, actually." His warm, wet tongue slides up my neck and I moan. "God, you taste so damn good."

His mouth meets mine in a kiss that's sweet temptation with a hint of something rougher. *Yes, please.*

Food can wait.

His hands grip my hips and lift me onto a stool at the breakfast bar. He spreads my knees and drops down on his. Every muscle in my body goes soft, and I can't help but moan as he slides my skirt up my thighs.

Raking my hands through his hair as he drops fiery kisses on my upper legs, I feel the smile spread across my face. "I love you so much."

He chuckles and his warm breath tickles me between my legs. As does the stubble he's sporting. "I love you too, baby."

Baby. The word echoes in my head. A reminder of the talk we need to have.

"Landen," I call out urgently, squirming as his tongue licks a path next to my panty line.

"Yeah, babe?"

"Um." He uses a finger to pull the soft scrap of lacy fabric to the side, grazing my wet center. "Mm."

Talking can wait.

The same instant that the tip of his tongue slicks up the most sensitive part of me, Landen's phone rings. We both ignore it as he brings me closer to ecstasy with his relentless strokes. I barely hear mine ringing over my own sounds of pleasure.

"What the fuck?" he grumbles, standing as I come down from a heaving orgasm.

Both of our phones are ringing in turn. His. Mine. His. Mine again.

He wraps me in his arms and I lean into him for support. No way I can get down off this stool right now with my legs still trembling like this.

Keeping one arm around me, he reaches for my phone on the counter. "It's your aunt," he says over my head.

"Okay," I pant, struggling to catch my breath.

"I'll give you one minute to call her back and see what the hell she wants. Then we are finishing what we started. In the shower. I promise to feed you after." He winks and I shake my head.

My hands are unsteady as I dial her back. "Hey, is everything—"

"Is Landen there? Put me on speaker," my aunt demands before I can even finish my sentence.

I do as I'm told while staring into the still heated, needful gaze of the most beautiful creature on Earth.

"Hi, Kate," Landen greets her through gritted teeth. "I just got home. Excellent timing."

If she detects the sarcasm, she doesn't mention it. "Good. I need you both to hear this. I have two words for you. Well, three. You ready for this?"

It isn't like her to be all dramatic, so we're both tense as we wait. "Hope so. What is it?" I ask, hoping to hurry things along so we can get back to what we were doing. Or about to do.

"Dr. Clayton Kirkowitz."

The name doesn't ring any bells. Judging from Landen's expression, it's unfamiliar to him as well.

"Oh-kay. What about him?" I ask.

"He's the one doing the procedure I told you about. The laser removal of hematomas like yours. He's had an astonishing success rate, Layla. I'm talking miracle status."

Right. She did mention this the last time we talked. But the procedure was still experimental and not covered by insurance. Plus the man had a waiting list ten years long. "I remember now. But—"

"You're next, Layla. I've been calling in favors and pulling strings and outright begging. His assistant said he had an unexpected opening. The insurance company is still giving me the runaround, but if you two can't afford it, I'll take out a second mortgage. Whatever I have to do. He's scheduled your surgery for next Monday at eight a.m. I've already booked our flights to Los Angeles. I just wanted to make sure Landen doesn't have a game and would be in town before I bought his."

No. No this is not happening right now. The room spins around me and every word out of her mouth is a ten-pound weight piling onto me until I can't breathe.

"Hell yes we can afford it," Landen practically shouts. "I'll do whatever it takes. Tell him we'll be there Monday. I can get my own ticket if you'll text me the flight informa—"

"No," I say evenly, interrupting them as they throw their Save the Layla Project party.

Landen turns to me, confusion contorting his handsome face. "Lay? I don't care about the money or whatever you're worried about. This is—"

"This is not happening. I'm not having surgery on Monday."

"Layla? What'd she say?" I hear my aunt's voice. It's coming through the phone speaker on the counter right next to me but it sounds a million miles away.

"I can't. I can't have surgery," I whisper. My eyes fill with tears because I already know from the look on Landen's face how angry he's going to be. "Not for the next eight months or so anyways."

"What?" they both ask at the same time.

This isn't how I wanted to tell him. I wanted it to be private. Special. But everything's ruined. Because of me and my stupid defective brain.

"I'm pregnant."

CHAPTER *Two*

Landen

I *have* no idea how much time passes as I stand there staring at my girlfriend. Thank God the human body will keep breathing and blinking and beating all on its own. Somewhere in the distance I hear Layla ending the phone call with her aunt. I struggle to listen as she promises the woman ten times that she will call her later.

I glance down to see if my body is vibrating. The steady hum of shock thrums through me and it seems like it must be.

"Still up for that shower?" Her lips are moving, so I know it's her talking. But I'm already underwater. I blink at her.

"Um."

"Yeah, I figured." She huffs out a breath and leans against the counter. "Landen, I was going to tell you tonight. At dinner. I went to the doctor at student health last week. I'm almost four weeks along."

Four weeks. The rewind button in my brain must've been pressed because I see the highlight reel of the last four weeks in reverse. Four weeks ago I was home for a few nights between games. The night before I left to go to Milan, she made spaghetti. Because it's my favorite. Cheesecake for dessert. We didn't make it. I ended up eating my piece off of her on the living room floor.

My mind searches for an alternate version of reality. One where I stop licking cherry glaze off her stomach and go grab a condom. Yeah. I didn't. My brain can't find the memory of that part because it isn't there. We made love over and over until we passed out on the floor. I almost missed my flight the next morning.

"Landen. Please. Say something." Layla's ocean-colored eyes sparkle up at me like fine gemstones. But my expression darkens them. "Or don't. But just know I'm not unhappy about this. I'm excited. And nothing you say is going to change that."

I take a deep breath and tell myself to reach out to her. Hold her. Reassure her that we'll figure this out together. My father's voice is loud and thunderous in my head, stopping all forward motion.

You ruin everything.

It's been so long since I heard it that I'd almost forgotten what it sounded like.

CHAPTER Three

Layla

"I need to go for a run," Landen says. His eyes are unfocused and his fists are clenched. My head is spinning from the sudden change. One minute everything was perfect and now it's a mess.

"You just got home," I say, unable to keep the soft sound of pleading out of my voice. "I thought we were going to dinner."

"Just order in. I'm not hungry."

My eyes widen in shock. I mean, we've had fights. We've yelled and slammed doors. He doesn't like me taking night classes, says that it's unsafe. When I signed up for one so I could volunteer with Bridging the Gap during the day, he nearly lost his mind. But this is different. It's not usually me causing the rage he tries so hard to outrun.

Until now.

I stand there, at the kitchen counter, in the spot where my life just went to crap in zero to fifteen seconds and watch him grab his T-shirt and walk out. I flinch at the sound of our door slamming shut.

For a minute, I'm overcome by loneliness. I was excited about telling him, nervous, but looking forward to it. Mostly. And now I can't swallow. Can't fight off the tears that well up so fast they're falling faster than I can wipe them.

He left. Left me alone. Except…I'm not alone. Glancing down, I realize I'm already cradling my stomach with my arm.

"Daddy will be back, baby. I promise."

It's after midnight when I hear him come in. I hold my breath and wait. Surely he'll come crawl into bed, apologize, and hold me. We'll talk about our fears, reassuring each other that we're in this together. By the time we fall asleep, everything will be okay. That's what I tell myself as I release the breath my lungs were holding hostage.

We'll keep each other still because that's what we've always done.

I listen to the sounds of doors opening and closing. Hear the shower turn on. And off a few minutes later. Straining, I can barely make out the sounds of him fumbling around our small apartment. But I never hear him come in the bedroom. I don't hear it because it doesn't happen. He doesn't even open the door to check on me. Which is so unlike him it makes my chest ache.

A lump rises in my throat as the apartment falls silent. We have a second bedroom with an old bed and a computer desk in it. The realization that he's decided to sleep in there hits hard and provokes a fresh wave of tears.

I let my arm out from under my pillow. My hand slides across the cold sheets where he should be.

In the darkness, my mind races to take stock of what my options are if Landen doesn't want this. If he only wants me and if pregnant me is a deal breaker. My heart refuses to accept that as a possibility. Landen loves me with a ferocity unlike anything I've ever known. But my mind…my mind is already a mother. Already trying to scheme and plan and make sure this child growing inside of me gets everything he or she will ever need or want. And that they never, ever have to feel this kind of sharp, stinging pain and rejection.

I lost my parents when I was thirteen and a stranger murdered them. I want this baby to be loved and hugged and have the kind of childhood I did before my parents were taken away. A hint of a smile tugs at the corners of my mouth as I let myself remember. My mom and dad used to dance in the kitchen. They used to sing embarrassingly loud in the car. Even if I had a friend with me. Hot tears burn down my face and leak into my ear. They kissed me—and each other—in public. They held my hands everywhere we went.

They would've been amazing grandparents. Manufactured memories of Christmases we'll never have together assault me and I cry harder. For what I've lost. For what my child will never have.

Something warm stirs inside of me and it takes a few seconds to realize what it is. I'm sad about Landen's reaction. I know this. I know I'm disappointed and hurt. But underneath that lies an emotion I'm not all that familiar with.

I'm angry.

How can he not want this? I know in the depths of my soul that he's afraid. Scared that something will happen to me if I don't have this surgery. I'm scared, too. But at some point, maybe the instant I realized I was responsible for the life growing inside of me, I stopped being afraid for myself.

I just want this child—my child, *our* child—to have the kind of life he or she deserves. And if Landen doesn't want this and something does happen to me, I don't know what kind of life my baby will get. My aunt is not the motherly type at all. She loves me and would do anything for me, but she's not the most affectionate human being on the planet. She's kind of cold actually and singularly focused on her career now that she isn't raising me anymore. I love her and am so grateful for everything she's done for me, but she's not someone I would want to raise my child. And Landen's parents…Oh God. *Oh God.* It makes so much sense that I could cry out in relief.

His mom is a decent person as far as I know, but his father is a nightmare. Literally. He's an awful man that I've only met a few times and each time he was horrible. He was violent and abusive, and how Landen turned out to be such an amazing man in spite of that is nothing short of amazing.

That man is never coming near my child. Ever. If this hematoma on my brain bursts and I die, I will come back from the grave and haunt him to death if he ever goes anywhere near my baby.

Understanding that this is most likely the cause of Landen's reaction earlier sinks in and allows me to breathe a little more easily. He never talks about his dad. He refuses to and shuts down completely if I ever dare to bring the man up in conversation. We don't discuss his childhood at all unless he's telling me about one of the many cities he lived in.

I tell myself that Landen probably just feels overwhelmed. Like he won't know how to be a good dad because he didn't have one. My stomach unclenches slightly and I focus on overcoming the sobs. Lord, this night did not go as I expected it to.

My friend Corin is the only person I've told I am pregnant.

"Are you worried about what Landen will say?" she asked when I told her. I told myself since she's in California she couldn't possibly understand what Landen and I have. How strong our connection is. I smiled and shook my head even though we were on the phone and she couldn't see me.

But now, lying here alone with tears slipping down my face and onto my pillow, I'm thinking maybe she understands a whole lot better than I do.

CHAPTER Four

Landen

I don't sleep. Despite nearly running a marathon, my mind won't give me rest. My body is exhausted and screaming at me to ice it or just never do that again. But I can barely hear it over the sound of my father telling me what a colossal fuck up I am.

I had a feeling it would be like this so I'm in the guest room. I don't know jack shit about pregnant women, but I'm pretty sure anyone growing a human being inside of them needs their sleep. The last thing she needs is for me to be tossing and turning and keeping her awake.

No, asshole. The last thing she needed was for you to just walk out.

I lose count of how many times I get up and cross the room towards the door, only to talk myself out of it and lie back down. I don't know how I feel yet, and I don't know what she needs to hear.

When the sun comes up, I'm still lying here, trying to figure out a way to save some semblance of the life Layla and I had together. *Have* together. Shit.

I rub my fists roughly into my eyes and wish that I could go back in time. Wish that I had been more insistent about using protection.

But I can't and I wasn't. So Layla gets to pay for my selfishness. For my wanting to feel nothing between us when we made love. And if this pregnancy means she can't have the surgery she needs—the surgery that could save her life—then I basically killed her.

The thought hits me at the exact same instant a clenching ache seizes my chest. My stomach pitches, and for a second, I'm positive I'm going to throw up.

A whistling noise from my phone pierces the air, indicating I have a new message. Probably Layla asking where the hell I am. Stretching my arm out, I grab it off the nightstand.

The screen lights up but it's not Layla.

It's another woman, one I'd rather not talk to at the moment. But I can see the eleven missed calls and my screen is filled with text messages. Look up *relentless* in the dictionary and there she'll be. For synonyms, see *pain in my ass.*

"Kate," I greet Layla's aunt.

She doesn't bother with a greeting. "You've got to talk to her, Landen. She'll listen to you."

I sigh and roll onto my back. *Now* I'm suddenly tired. Exhausted really. "Good morning to you, too."

She huffs a breath right back at me. "We don't have time for this. You want to make jokes? Fine. Make jokes. While you're busy laughing, I'll be on my way to the airport. And when I see you in California, I'm going to murder you. Lucky for me, I know enough people at the DA's office to make a convincing case for suicide."

My sleep-deprived brain can't even make sense of her words. Though it does register that my life was just threatened and it's not even eight in the morning. "Wait, California? Did you not hear what she said?" Layla's aunt is an extremely successful litigator and is generally pretty sharp. I don't want to insult her intelligence by stating the obvious, but clearly she's confused.

Trying to muster the courage to say the words out loud, I clear my throat. "Uh, not to be a dick because I know you're stressed and probably having as hard of a time dealing with this as I am, but Layla made herself pretty clear. She's pregnant, Kate. She can't have surgery on Monday."

Jesus. She's pregnant. I hear her soft, sweet voice, full of determination echoing in me head. *I'm pregnant.*

Since Kate has no trouble insulting my intelligence, she continues. "Yeah. Got that. Landen, listen to me. I know this is a delicate issue. But we don't exactly have the luxury of time on our side."

"I'm listening." I sit up and put my feet on the hardwood floor. "If you have some miracle solution to this, I'd love to hear it."

For a moment, she hesitates. I hear a small intake of breath and then the words I should've expected but didn't. "She can have an abortion. There are several clinics in LA. I could meet the two of you at one and she could get it handled this weekend. By Monday she'd be fine for surgery."

An intense throbbing begins to vibrate in my head. Fuck. How did it get like this? One minute I'm damn near bursting with excitement about coming home to my girlfriend after a huge win and the next…*Christ.* The next thing I know I'm discussing abortion clinics with Layla's aunt before I've even had breakfast. Once again, I'm strangled by the fierce urge to vomit. And overcome with the need to hit something. Hard.

My jaw clenches and I breathe through my nose. "Sure, Kate. I'll just tell her that we're heading out today and that we'll swing by an abortion clinic once we land. How well do you think that's going to go over?"

"Well then let me hear what you've got, Mr. Can't-Be-Bothered-To-Cover-His-Dick. Because I'm out of options over here. Dr. Kirkowitz doesn't reschedule. If she doesn't get the surgery now, then it could be five or ten years before he has another opening. If she even makes it that long. Do you get that, soccer boy? Has that ever really resonated with you?"

My fist closes so hard on the phone that it's a wonder I don't break the thing in half. "You're damn right it resonates with me. Every hour, every minute, every second, I'm painfully fucking aware that any one of them could be her last. Every time I walk out the door for practice or a game or camp or to go get a jug of milk down the damn street, I know. I know that it could be the last time I see her face, her smile. That I could come home to ambulances or her body lifeless on the floor. So I screwed up, okay? I get that and I'm sorry." Bone-deep regret settles over me and I sink to my knees, weighed down by desperation. Thank God she can't see me. "I'm so fucking sorry. Tell me what to do. Tell me how to fix her, how to fix this."

"I don't need fixing." I hear her voice, angelic and ten shades of pissed off, from behind me. Looking up at her, I see the burning determination in her eyes. And the tears.

"Baby," I say, reaching for her. But she steps out of my reach.

"Hang up the phone, Landen," is all she says.

"I have to go, Kate." Her aunt starts to say something, but I press end and she's gone. And it's just me and my girlfriend. Well, and someone else I can't bring myself to think about yet.

"Talk to me. Don't run. Don't go for a run. Don't shut me out and pretend this isn't happening. It is." A nearly imperceptible shudder passes through her and I want to hold her. To wrap her in my arms and protect her like I've always done. But I can't fix it this time. Can't fix us.

Rocking back on my heels, I slide myself down the side of the bed and sit on the floor. She sighs and leans against the wall. Waiting. Waiting for me to say whatever I'm supposed to say to make this right. Except...I don't know what that is.

CHAPTER Five

Layla

I've only seen him like this once before. When we first started dating in high school, his mom invited me to Thanksgiving. His dad was drinking. And awful. He hit Landen in the face right in front of me.

Later we sat alone in his basement and he was just like this. Broken. Closed off. Angry. Lost.

Somehow, I was enough back then. Our feelings for each other, his need for me, broke through the pain. But I can't reach him now.

Because now I'm the one causing his pain. And he's causing mine. This is unfamiliar territory for us.

I stare at him for what feels like an eternity. Our hurt feelings are swirling around us, pummeling him farther into the ground, and backing me up against the wall. He props an elbow on his knee and stares vacantly at nothing.

I lick my lips and take a step closer to him. Pulling in a lungful of air and hopefully all of my courage, I open my mouth to speak.

"Don't," he says before my words escape. "Don't say it will all be okay. Don't say we'll get through this together. If you…" He shakes his head and looks away once more. I hear the words he doesn't say. *If you die on me, then we won't be getting through anything together.*

His voice is dead and cold and it backs me up. "Why are you doing this? Why are you pushing me away?" My questions are barely a whisper, and he's so far gone I don't know if they even reach him. Until he looks up at me. His normally vibrant green eyes are dark and ringed by exhaustion.

"Because I'm afraid."

The tension holding me rigid eases up and I relax a little for the first time since yesterday. "I know. Me too. But that's part of it, right? I think we're supposed to be—"

"Not of that." He shakes his head. His eyes close briefly and I take step closer. "Well, not of *just* that."

"Of what then? Of…" I crouch down so we're face to face. "Of something happening to me? Of being left alone with a baby to raise? Of becoming your father?" Hearing all of it out loud makes my heart hurt for him. It's a lot for anyone to deal with. And they're perfectly rational, valid fears for him to have.

His eyes widen as they meet mine. The hardwood disappears from beneath me and I'm lost in his desperate, pleading gaze. "Of telling you the truth."

Confusion contorts my face and has me tilting my head. "I don't understand."

He rubs his hand across the back of his neck and brings it around to his face. His long fingers rest on his lips for a moment, as if he's trying to keep the words in—the ones he obviously doesn't want to tell me.

"Layla, I always knew I wanted to play soccer. And from the first time I saw you…" The hint of a smile plays on his lips. But I'm looking into his eyes and there's no trace of a smile in them. "The first time I saw you, my world stopped. Things I thought mattered—soccer, how much my dad hated me, the fact that I'd never really had anywhere to call home, all of it—it just ceased to mean anything. All I could see was you, and I had to know you, had to have you."

"You do have me," I tell him, hoping the reassurance will help him to say whatever he needs to so that we can move forward.

He nods, and the thick knot in his throat bobs as he swallows. There's a sudden shift in the air. I don't know how or why, but I feel it and it sets me on edge. My pulse speeds up, sending blood rushing in my ears. Whatever he's about to say is bad. I know it way down deep in my bones. He's going to say something awful and change everything. Ruin everything.

"Landen, maybe we should—"

"There's something else I know," he begins, silencing me with the cold calm in his voice. "Something I've always known. About myself."

I nod. "Okay. Whatever it is, I'm sure we can—"

"There's one thing I never want to be, Layla. Ever."

The icy hand of dread grips me by the back of the neck. I want to launch myself at him, stop him before he says it. But I'm frozen where I stand. "Landen—"

"A father." He closes his eyes and lowers his head. "I never want to be a father." It's a confession and an apology all in one. Barely spoken above a whisper and yet it feels like he just shouted it in my face. My body caves, crushing my insides.

Seven words. Seven awful words change my entire life. In that moment, the room might as well have split down the center, cracking wide and deep between us.

It wasn't "I'm nervous about becoming a father," or "I'm scared of not being a good father," or even "I didn't ever *plan* to become a father." His words are present tense. And final. *I never want to be a father.* They echo off the walls, slamming into me over and over. Seven sharp daggers carving into my heart.

His confession turns the chill of anticipation to the hot burn of anger. "Well, it's kind of late for that. Maybe you should've mentioned that one of the, oh, I don't know, twelve dozen times we had unprotected sex? Or just at any point in the three years we've been living together." I jerk upright and turn but he's longer, taller, and quicker than I am. He's on his feet and reaching for me in a split second.

Grabbing me by the arm and spinning me to face him, he pulls me closer in what feels like a hug and a goodbye all at once. My vision is blurry from the tears but I can see the intense anguish on his face.

"Layla, just…let's just talk for a second. Your aunt said…she mentioned—"

"No," I say, giving him a forceful push and managing to free myself from his grasp. "Don't. Don't say it. I can imagine what she said because she's the kind of person who sees something in the way of what she thinks is right or necessary and misses the big picture."

I'm shaking my head, but he continues. "It's just that, she has a point about—"

"Don't, please God, don't," I choke out. My tears fall and Landen pulls at me again, trying to hug me or hold me or…I don't even know what. I thrust my arms out in a pathetic attempt to push him away. "Don't say it."

"Dammit, Layla! Just think for a second. With your medical condition and my—"

"Stop!" I practically scream at him. "Listen to me, please. Just stop. Just stop talking," I beg. Reaching up, I place my fingertips against his lips. "Don't, Landen. Don't say those words out loud. Because once you do, then we're ruined. No matter what happens, you'll never be able to un-say those awful words. Promise me you won't say them. Promise me."

Understanding flashes in his eyes and he nods. I remove my hand from his mouth and back up a step, nearly slamming into the computer desk. His gaze flickers to the door and I want to slap him. He always does this. Runs. Bails when anything gets too intense. We're having a baby he doesn't want and his idea of dealing with it is going for a run. For the first time since we met almost five years ago, I realize I hate him. Oh, I still love him. But I hate him a little bit too. I didn't even know I was capable of hatred. The realization makes me feel sick.

I sigh and yank myself away from him.

This is a first. This time, I'm the one who walks out.

CHAPTER Six

Landen

The sound of the drywall giving way against my fist is only slightly satisfying. The pain distracts me but only momentarily. For all the years I wished to escape my father and his hatred, I've spent more time than I want to admit wishing he was still around to kick my ass. Apparently I'm sick and twisted and need it.

What a great parent I'm going to make.

You are worthless.

The burning heat of my rage flares inside of me. It's red, darkening to black, and then white-hot and blinding.

You ruin everything.

Glass shatters on the floor but I don't even know what I've hit. My fist connects again with something solid but I don't feel one iota of relief. So I hit it again and again with the soundtrack of my dad's voice telling me exactly what he thinks, what he knows, is true.

Her chance to have the ax of doom hanging over our heads removed finally came, and I fucked it up. Life as we knew it is ruined. Destroyed.

Much like our apartment.

When I come to, I'm sitting on our bathroom floor, propped against the doorframe. Surrounded by broken ceramic tiles, a cabinet door I must've torn from its hinges, and my own shame.

What the hell?

My left hand hurts like a son of a bitch. Glancing down, I see it's swollen and my knuckles are caked with dried blood. My right hand isn't much better. Looks like I clawed my way out of a wooden box.

Jesus.

Groaning, I use the sink to pull myself up. My bloodshot eyes widen in the shattered mirror.

Because it isn't my reflection staring back at me. It's my father's.

Before I have time to fully freak the fuck out, I hear the front door open. And there's a gasp. I turn in the doorway as quickly as I can manage, hoping I can somehow shield her from the destruction.

But I don't make it.

When I step over the pieces of busted lamp in the middle of the living room floor, she gapes at me. The horror and hurt shine from her face so brightly I can't look directly at her.

"Baby, I'm…" What am I? There's nothing I can say to make this any better. I watch her take in the evidence of my rage, watch her run her hand gently over the splintered glass covering the picture her friend Corin took of us when she and Skylar visited last summer.

"You're broken," she whispers, eying a vase of seashell pieces she adds to every time we go to the ocean. Miraculously, it's still intact.

Am I? Pain shoots up my arms as I attempt to clench my fists. Yes, yes I am.

My soul tears in two as I watch her grieve for every piece of damaged furniture. I'm two men now. One of them loves her so much he wants to drop to his knees, beg for forgiveness, and make a million promises—whatever it takes to keep her here. To keep her from saying to hell with this. With me.

The other one sees past the most recent destruction as the older evidence of my temper comes into view. Small cracks and dents I've made over the years. I don't deserve her forgiveness. I'm never going to change.

She needs to see.

She needs to understand.

I can't do this.

CHAPTER Seven

Layla

Everyone can leave. I learned at a young age that nothing is forever. No matter how pretty and shiny your life is, it can all change in an instant.

If you ignore the small incidents, turn a blind eye to the tiny fissures spreading through the foundation, the smallest thing, the lightest touch, can send your entire world crashing down around you.

Standing in my living room, the one I worked so hard to make feel like home, I grieve for the splintered shards of what was once my life.

Glancing up, I see Landen, his eyes warring with darkness and light, love and hatred, anger and kindness. Sometimes it's like he's two different people, and I can't help but wonder which version of him will finally win the battle for his soul.

"I'll get a garbage bag," I say softly, because someone has to say something.

"Wait."

His voice is scratchy, almost like he's been crying. Well that makes two of us. I turn on a sigh.

"I'm sorry. I'm sorry for this, Layla. For my temper. For the way I am." He pauses to rake a hand through his hair. "But you need to see. *This* is how I am. Who I am."

My throat constricts and I pull in my lips so my mouth doesn't do the turning-down-about-to-ugly-cry thing it does.

His shoulders slump and he steps towards me, something snapping beneath his foot as he does. "God, I love you so much. I swear I don't want to do this to you. To us. But…" He offers me a pleading attempt at a smile. "But I can't be a parent. You see that, right?"

My heart beats so hard it throbs throughout my entire body. I close my eyes for a second and listen to the sound of my own breathing before looking into his. "Landen, we had a fight. You've been under a lot of pressure and this isn't an ideal situation. I get that. You lost your temper and—"

"And you're making excuses for me. Like you always do." He's so close his scent surrounds me, permeates my skin. It's sharp and clean, cologne and soap, and just…him. Familiar. It takes every single ounce of self-control I have not to pull him to me and let him make everything better. But somehow I manage. Maybe because I know it won't be enough this time.

"So what, Landen?" I choke out over the sob rising in my throat. "My aunt wants me to have surgery on Monday whether I like it or not and you can't control your temper? So I have to have an abortion because the two of you don't want me to have a baby? You must be out of your fucking minds."

I rarely curse so I'm not surprised when Landen's eyes go wide.

I take two steps, planning to brush past him to get to the kitchen and grab a garbage bag, but his arm strikes out to stop me. Strong hands grip my shoulders and spin me so I'm facing away from him. When he speaks, low into my ear from behind me, his angry, even tone sends chills up my spine. "Look. Look around you. What do you see?"

Shaking my head, I jerk and twist in an attempt to free myself. His fingers dig in deeper—not enough to hurt but rougher than he's ever handled me. "I see a mess, okay? One that needs to be cleaned up."

"Look closer. Look at the walls, Layla. Look at the cabinet doors. Think. Why doesn't the refrigerator door open unless you lift while you pull? Why do we have so much fucking art on the wall? Are we opening a museum?" His voice is thick with pain, and it cuts into me even more than seeing our home destroyed.

The answers to his questions rush to the forefront of my mind, drowning me. Two of our cabinet doors are broken because he slammed them too hard when he was angry about something that had happened at practice. The refrigerator door has been jacked up since the night I told him I was taking night classes. He was getting something to drink and nearly ripped the thing off its hinges.

I can't even count the number of holes in the walls or recall exactly where each came from. He always apologized and I would just buy another picture to cover them.

He's right. No child should have to grow up in a home like this.

"It's my fault, too," I say, turning in his arms to face him. "You're right. I made excuses. I covered it up. Pretended it was normal." There's nothing I can do to stop the warm, wet tears that fall. "But we can get you some help. Maybe the team—"

But he's already shaking his head. "It's who I am. No amount of therapy or whatever can change that."

"Landen—"

"I'm my father's son." He reaches a hand out to wipe away my tears and I see moisture gathering in his eyes. "And I won't do that to a kid. I won't."

My heart breaks for him. I feel every tiny splinter as it happens. "I know you won't. Landen, it'll be different. You're not—"

"I'm not doing this, Layla."

"Not doing what?" I whisper, cringing at the thought of hearing his answer.

"Not risking being an abusive asshole that makes another human being feel worthless. I won't cause that kind of pain."

"You won't. I wouldn't let you. I'll—"

"I used to wish I was dead."

The depth of his sadness, the hollow echo of his voice sets off a bone-deep ache in my core. A sob escapes, making me sound like a wounded animal.

Landen huffs out a sarcastic breath and swipes his hand quickly across his eyes. "Actually, I used to wish he was dead. And then I realized that was never going to happen. So I just wished that I was."

My knees go weak, and Landen sinks to the floor right along with me. We just sit there, holding one another. Smack in the middle of our mess. One that neither of us knows how to clean up this time.

Landen

A week has passed since I practically tore down our apartment with my bare hands. We cleaned up the best we could, but it's a pretty safe bet we won't be getting our security deposit back. I walk through the door and see Layla standing in the middle of the living room.

"What are you doing here? Why aren't you in Barcelona?"

I take a deep breath and answer, skipping the formalities of greeting her just as she did. "I'm suspended."

Indefinitely, but I don't tell her that part.

"What happened?" she asks, but I see the accusation in her eyes. She really means *What did you do?*

I lay my car keys on the table by the door and set my bag on the one remaining barstool in the kitchen. How it survived my rampage is beyond me. Clearing my throat, I turn to face her. "Got into a disagreement with Vasquez." More like my fist got into a disagreement with his face. Without me even meaning to, my right hand covers my left.

"And?" she prompts.

"And Coach said I needed to relax. I told him we were having some… issues. He said to take some time and get it handled."

Her forehead wrinkles and she glares at me. "Get it handled? Landen, I told you I'm not—"

"Coach's words, Layla. Not mine."

She drops herself onto the couch and I do the same. We're not touching, but the ever-present current of electricity warms the space between us. We've been sleeping in separate beds. Making small talk and avoiding any mention of anything that could set me off. Which is part of why I lost it on Vasquez today.

So low I have to lean in to hear her, she speaks without looking at me. "I talked to Corin last night about…about everything."

There's probably a sniper rifle trained on my forehead right about now. Her college roommate from New York has made it clear to me on multiple occasions that if I hurt Layla my balls will be pureed.

"By everything you mean…"

"All of it," she says softly. "The baby, the surgery, you…you not wanting this."

"Ah. And what did Ginger have to say?"

Finally she turns her beautiful ocean water eyes to mine. "She invited me to come stay with her for a while. She doesn't think it's good for me to be home alone so much. And you and I…"

You and I are done. I hear it even though she doesn't say it.

"You're leaving me?" Fuck. My voice comes out weak and pathetic. My father's two favorite nicknames for me.

"No! God, Landen, it's just…I don't know where we are right now. We pretend like…like there's nothing to say, like not talking about it makes it not real. But how are you going to feel when I look like I swallowed a soccer ball? I don't want you flying into a rage at the sight of me, and honestly…"

At some point, my head dropped into my hands. My elbows dig into my knees and I lift my eyes and turn to her. "Honestly what?" Her perfect mouth is doing that heartbreakingly adorable thing it does when she's about to cry. I can't help myself. I reach out with my thumb and brush it tenderly against her lips. "Honestly what, baby?"

Her eyelids flicker and she shakes her head before pulling back out of my reach. "Honestly, I don't want to spend this entire pregnancy feeling guilty… and…and afraid." The last word isn't even loud enough to call a whisper, but it cuts me the deepest.

I stand, pulling my hand from her mouth as if she bit me. "Jesus, Layla. The last thing I want is for you to be afraid of me." I'm pacing, and already I know I need to settle down, but she's leaving and she's afraid of me and everything is all screwed up. "You know I would never hurt you. Christ almighty, I'd rather peel off my own skin than hurt you."

"I know that. That's not what I meant. Not exactly."

"Not exactly?" I stop pacing and examine her face. She still looks like an angel. Just a sad, tired angel. The stress of our situation is taking its toll on her. Like it or not, I'm hurting her.

"I know you're unhappy," she confesses. "When you hurt, I hurt."

In that moment, the one when she utters those words, I am consumed utterly and entirely with inescapable self-hatred. I open my mouth to speak, but she's not finished.

"I'm not afraid for me, Landen. I'm afraid for you. Afraid you'll lose yourself. Sometimes, when you're angry…" She closes her eyes for a few seconds, and I need her words like I need air to breathe. Except it feels like both are going to choke me to death. "Sometimes it's like you're someone else, and it's like I don't know you, or know how to help you."

I kneel in front of her, pulling her to me until our foreheads touch. "Baby, you do help me. I don't even want to think about the man I'd be if it weren't for you." Bile rises in my throat at the mention of me without her. The reflection of my father staring back at me thrusts itself into my head.

"I love you so much," she whispers into my hair. "So much."

I let my weight press against her. "I love you, too. God I love you so damn much it hurts. I swear we'll get through this. Somehow. We will." It's then that I see the small, black suitcase peeking out from beside the couch. Fuck. "Please don't leave me," I plead. It doesn't escape me that I'm literally on my knees begging.

"I won't," she reassures me. "I could never really leave you, Landen. You know that." But I pull back and look up into her eyes. They're shining with the promise of more tears. More pain.

You ruin everything, my father reminds me.

"I know."

CHAPTER Nine

Layla

I've been on the phone with Corin for over an hour explaining why I'm not coming to visit her after all. I'm freaking exhausted.

"He needs me," I tell her on a sigh. "And he's always been there for me when I needed him." That's what love is, I want to tell her. Being there. Keeping each other balanced. Not that we've been doing such a great job at it lately.

"Until now," she snaps back, still as heated as she was when this conversation began. "You're the one who's pregnant, Georgia. He needs to get his shit together and man up. You can't baby him anymore. You're growing a human being inside of you for fuck's sake."

I huff out a breath and lie down on the bed. Landen left for his run as soon as I picked up the phone. Glancing at the alarm clock, I see it's going on two hours since he's been gone. The more upset he is, the longer he runs. "I know. I think I'm going to take a nap, Cor. It's all just been…" A nightmare, I want to say, but I don't because then she'll launch into her ninety-nine reasons why I should just come stay with her. And this isn't what I want to remember. I don't want to look at my child one day and think, *Being pregnant with you was the worst nine months of my life.* Going over it all again seems like a surefire way to burn the pain into my memory.

"Okay," she says, finally relenting. "Get some rest. But if he so much as raises his voice at you, I swear—"

"I know. And I love you for looking out for me. I know it sounds bad, but he really doesn't direct his anger at me. Even at his worst. He just holds everything in and then he breaks. He can't help it. I can't imagine what it was like being raised by a man like his father."

"You always make excuses for him," she says softly. I almost nod, even though she can't see me. Because she's right. I do. But how can I not? It's not his fault he's like this. "Layla, if I'd known he had such an insane temper, I might not have encouraged you to—"

"Corin, stop. I'm a big girl and I make my own decisions. I moved here with him because I love him. Because this is my life and I want to spend it living and loving and hurting and feeling everything there is to feel. It's just a crazy time right now, and we're both adjusting to…the news."

"Mmhm," she mumbles. "If you say so. But seriously, if you need me, for anything, call. Or if you want Skylar to talk to him or whatever."

"I will," I tell her as my heavy eyelids start to drift shut. It's not even all the way dark yet but I'm struggling to stay awake. "Promise."

We say our goodbyes just as I lose consciousness.

The music pulls me suddenly from the depths of sleep. I might've been dreaming of the ocean again. But it isn't waves I'm hearing crashing on the shore. Instruments, brass and wood fill the room so fully that I'm certain there's a mariachi band outside my window. Looking at the clock on the nightstand, I see it's just after ten. My bed is depressingly empty. The sheets on Landen's side are cool when I brush my arms across them. Loneliness twists in my stomach as I sit up and listen for a few more minutes, wondering briefly if our neighbors are having a party.

My bare feet land on the hardwood and I step over to the window. A small festival is taking place on the street below. I vaguely remember seeing signs about it earlier this week. For a few minutes, I watch the people dancing as the sounds of their laughter float up to me. They look so happy. Carefree.

When Landen and I first moved here, we went to every festival held anywhere near us. We danced in the streets until we could barely stand. He'd twirl me around and around until I lost my balance and crashed into his arms. An unwelcome tear traces a path down my cheek with another close on its trail. Opening my window, I rest my head on the sill to listen. I gaze longingly at the scene in the street, wishing there was a way we could get back to that place. To happiness and dancing and being so consumed by love that seizures, angry rages, or dead or abusive parents couldn't even hurt us anymore.

"Babe?" Landen's voice startles me, and I rush to wipe the evidence of my sadness away.

"Hey, sorry. Did I wake you?" I close the window before turning to face him. The glow from the hallway lamp illuminates the outline of his tall, dark figure.

"No, I was up." He steps closer, and I'm aching to reach out to him. The sleeping apart has wedged something solid between us that I don't know how to remove. "Guess they're partying pretty hard out there, huh?" Landen tilts his head towards the window.

"Remember that first night we moved in?" I ask him, stepping closer so we're nearly touching. "We were nearly dead from the flight and still had a ton of boxes to unpack, but they had that Saints Day thing going on and we ended up dancing until almost sunrise." I smile at the memory. Landen takes the final step to close the space between us, and I'm ready to beg him to put his arms around me. My need for contact, for his touch, is so strong it's palpable.

"I remember," he says.

"Remember after?" I breathe. My body trembles at the memory. After we drank and danced and had been welcomed by everyone and their brother, we stumbled half drunk up to the apartment and made love.

"Like I could forget," he says, finally using both hands to pull me towards him.

"I've missed you," I whisper, tilting my face up to his.

He nods and I watch the muscles move in his neck as he swallows hard. "I'm here now," he answers just before claiming my mouth with his.

He backs us up to the bed and we fall into it together. The down comforter tangles around us as we pull at each other's clothing.

"I need you. I need you so much," I tell him between kisses. The emptiness inside me begins to wane as he pulls me higher so my head reaches a pillow. Our mouths separate only long enough for him to pull off the practice jersey of his that I sleep in.

"I know, baby. I need you too. I'm here. I'm not going anywhere."

"Promise?" I suck his full bottom lip into my mouth before he can answer. His answering kisses are full of a fervor I can't even match without hurting one or both of us.

"Swear. Cross my heart." Landen sits up and pulls my white lace panties down my legs. I watch him toss them over the edge of the bed. Even in the darkness I can see the light shining in his eyes as he stares down at my naked body.

The force of his stare is so intense that he pins me to the mattress without even touching me. "Mine," he says low into the room as he trails a finger between my breasts towards my naval.

"Yes, always," I breathe, arching up in a plea for him to touch me where I need it most. Every night I've spent alone in our bed has filled me with a bone-chilling cold that made me ache. It dissipates inch by inch as he warms me with his touch until I'm burning up.

His hand stops, palm down on my stomach. I'm only about five weeks along so there's no bump, but there's something. A fullness. Maybe it's in my head because I know I'm pregnant. I go completely still and wait for him to freak out and run. To leave me aching and alone. But he doesn't. Instead, he leans down and presses his lips to my stomach.

"Mine," he says again, and his voice is so possessive, so absolute, I want to cry. But I don't. I rise and grab his face, pulling his mouth to mine. His tongue dances inside of me, and I'm dizzy from lack of oxygen as I try to get enough.

"Make love to me, Landen. Please. I need you. *Now*," I mumble into his mouth.

He tears his mouth from mine long enough to strip off his black boxer briefs. Once he springs free, I reach down and stroke his hard length. He groans and leans over me once again. "Easy, baby," he murmurs against my mouth. "I've missed you too. A lot." His lips smile against my cheek and I pull him closer, lining him up with my already wet entrance.

"I've hated this bed without you. Don't ever leave me again. You promised you'd never leave," I whisper without even meaning to. I'm lost, mindless with emotions as my need for him overtakes all reason.

His eyes meet mine, pain and anger and regret flashing in them. "I'm so sorry, baby. I never meant to hurt you."

My dreams come back to me, flooding me with memories I finally understand. The broken seashells. The ones I've always collected, even though my mom and my aunt both tried to push the perfect ones on me. Landen is my broken shell; he's beautiful and dangerously jagged and sharp. He can cut me and hurt me and make me bleed tears. But maybe, just maybe, I can be the water that washes over him and smoothes those rough edges.

He says something else, but I'm drowning in memories of the ocean, deafened by music from outside and waves crashing in my mind.

I kiss him fiercely, plunging my tongue into his mouth as deep as I can. Reaching up, I press firmly against his shoulders until he gets the message and rolls onto his back. He stares up at me in wonderment as I ease myself down onto him. My head lolls back at the fullness.

I slide up and down, whimpering and moaning at how good he feels inside. How right we are together. We fit. Perfectly. Nothing that comes from this could ever be bad. No matter what anyone says.

"Layla, slow down." His hands tighten on my hips. His tone is urgent. He's pleading with me but I'm so close. I stroke myself against him as slowly as I can manage before slamming back down, impaling myself on his thick erection. A loud groan escapes his throat and it propels me forward. Digging my fingers into his shoulders hard enough to leave bruises, I pause for a moment to enjoy the sensation of my walls constricting around him. Finally succumbing to the pressure building in my center I ride him harder. Faster.

"Come inside me, Landen. Come now."

"I…fuck," he bites out.

"I can't get any *more* pregnant. Come in me. Please come in me. I want to feel you." My words come out rushed and I'm breathless but he understands.

He fills me with rapid, scorching bursts and I cry out. The current inside of me shifts suddenly and I'm thrown headfirst into a violent orgasm of epic proportions. I collapse on top of him as my body becomes boneless.

The veins in his neck are straining as he finishes, and I lick his throat. He grunts a sigh of relief, and I place several more open-mouthed kisses on his neck and chest.

"I love you. God, I love you so damn much," he says, kissing me on top of my head.

Resting my cheek against his bare chest, I try to form a coherent thought. "I know. Just…don't ever stop."

CHAPTER *Ten*

Landen

I *wake* up Monday morning with a sickening realization in the pit of my stomach.

Today is the day Layla would be in California having surgery that could save her life if not for me.

Using all the strength I can muster, I push against the guilt as the weight of it hovers above my chest.

She's still in bed beside me, beautifully naked and peaceful. She's facing away from me. I lean over and kiss her on her cheek. Her temple. Her jaw.

"Good morning," she mumbles, her voice still thick with sleep.

"Shh. Sleep, baby. I've got some phone calls to make then I'll make you breakfast. Omelet okay?"

"More than okay," she says, turning over to kiss me back.

I stroke a blonde strand of hair out of her eyes and she blinks up at me. "I love you, you know that? I'd do anything for you, Layla Flaherty." *Even become the one thing I never wanted to be.*

Her gaze widens with understanding and she nods.

Placing one more chaste kiss on her mouth, I sigh. Time to face the firing squad.

After I've pulled my jeans on, I head into the guest room and retrieve my phone. Eighteen missed calls. One number. One voicemail.

"I hope you're happy," Kate hisses into my ear. Thank God it's just her recorded fury and not the real thing. Still, it raises my blood pressure. We're about six or seven hours ahead of her. Apparently she spent her evening calling me. I don't even want to think about the kind of messages she's left for Layla.

"If anything happens to her, Landen, I swear to God, I'm holding you personally responsible." Tension ripples across my shoulders and my chest constricts. She *should* hold me responsible. I am responsible. Closing my eyes, I picture what Layla's life would've been like without me. She would still be in California, rooming with Corin probably. Graduating on time.

I can see her. Sunlight glinting off her beautiful hair, carrying an armful of books, smiling at something some asshole said. Walking to class with Corin. Happy. Alive.

If not for me, she'd be having surgery today that would give her the fair shot at the long, happy life she deserves.

After I've listened to her aunt's angry words enough times to memorize them, I close my eyes and let the darkness come. Until it covers me. And then a small light flickers in my mind's eye. I'm standing there. A small child holding my hand. In a cemetery. At a headstone.

I don't know how to deal with the fury from a situation I caused. There's no one to blame, no one to shout at, no fingers to point. It's me. All me.

I dragged her into my life, pulled her into this hell she doesn't deserve. I practically stalked her to college, telling myself she needed me. When the truth was, the truth *is,* I'm the broken one. I'm the one who needs her the most.

And the worst part? I'm hurting her, hurting us. And I need help. From the last person on Earth I ever want to speak to again. The one I swore I was done with.

I open my eyes and stare down at my phone.

His number is still in there. I deleted him from my life but never could bring myself to erase him from my phone. Bet the team shrink would have some overly analytical thoughts on that. My heart pounds as I scroll to his name. *Colonel* is all it says. The violent throbbing in my temples causes my vision to blur as I stare at it.

A buzzing in my hand startles me and I almost drop the damn thing on the floor.

Coach, the screen tells me. My nerves rattle at the thought of what this might be about. Shit. Maybe I'm not just suspended—maybe I'm fired. I swallow hard and answer.

"Hey Coach," I say, trying to speak over the fear that's strangling me.

"O'Brien," he answers. "We need to talk, son." His voice is strained, weary. More guilt piles on top of the mountain that's already smothering me.

"Yes, sir."

"This a good time?"

No. "Yes, sir. I'm suspended—I got nothing but time, right?" I try to force out a laugh but it sounds more like I'm choking than anything else.

"Yeah, about that. Look, O'Brien, I did some checking. I know about your arrest a few years ago and I know you've been in altercations that I probably don't even want to know the details of. I accepted you to this club because a friend gave you a high recommendation. The same friend who mentioned he was cutting you loose because you lost your temper on a teammate."

He pauses to clear his throat. I press my fingers into my eyes with my free hand. This is not good.

"You're the best damn striker I've come across in my entire career. And maybe because of that, I've been too lenient. The club's been lenient. But you have more red cards than the entire team combined, and frankly, I'm seeing a pattern of behavior that has apparently been going on for some time."

I open my mouth to defend myself, but there's really nothing I can say. Everything he's said is true.

"You there?"

"Yes, sir. I'm here."

He lets out an audible breath and I sit up straighter, bracing myself for what he's about to say. I can already hear him firing me in my head.

"So I've met with the staff and we've been making some hard decisions. I know you've got a situation with your girlfriend and I don't need to know the details. Truth is, there's a dozen guys lined up right behind you, ready to take your spot."

"Coach, please. I know I'm not—"

"I'm just going to cut to the chase. They want to let you go, O'Brien. We have enough to deal with without our first team striker being a liability. You hit a teammate at *practice.* I don't even want to think about what might happen the next time a ref makes a call during a game you don't agree with."

I want to tell him that I would never do anything like that. But I'd be lying. Because when I lose my temper, I lose myself. I lose that voice in my head that reminds me I don't want to be like *him*.

For as long as I can remember, soccer has been the only thing that has helped me to channel my rage. It's been the outlet for all the pent-up emotion and aggression, not that it's even been enough. And now it's slipping away. What will I be like without it?

"Is there anything I can do?" Working hard to keep my voice even, I try to focus on my breathing. Uncurling my clenched fists, I glance around the room. There's a lot of breakable shit in here and I've done enough damage already. "Or has the decision already been made?"

Standing, I walk out into the living room, thankful Layla's still asleep.

"It's like this, O'Brien. You're a hell of an athlete. We don't want to lose you, but if you spend your career sidelined by back-to-back suspensions, you're no good to us anyways. You get what I'm saying?"

You're no good.

You're worthless.

I can't even hear my own voice over the Colonel's. I think I mumble out yet another "Yes, sir," but I can't be sure.

"So here's my proposition. Take some time off. We'll extend the indefinite suspension to January. Get some help and a letter from a doctor saying you've attended an anger management program. How's that sound?"

"Do I really have any other choice?"

"Life is full of choices, O'Brien. You want this? Come back in January a new man. That's the only way I can keep you on. Otherwise, you should just walk away."

My jaw clenches and I breathe through my nose.

"Understood. I'll clear my gear out this weekend." My finger hovers above the disconnect button.

"Son? For what it's worth, I hope you get it together. Whatever's eating you up inside, the club could get you some help. Say the word and I'll make the calls."

"Thank you, sir. I'll keep that in mind."

We hang up, and I step into the bedroom. Layla's back on her side, her hands folded underneath her face. The sun lights her up like the angel she is. My eyes roam over her naked, slender arms and shoulders. I know exactly how good her skin feels under my hands. How I feel inside of her. She looks so fragile. Breakable.

She's fine china, and I'm the bull.

Her aunt's words mingle with Coach's in my head. *I'm holding you personally responsible. Life is full of choices. Walk away.*

Casting one last longing glance at the goddess sleeping peacefully in our bed, I step out onto the balcony.

I need to know why I'm like this so I can figure out how to stop.

And there's only one person who can answer that for me.

He picks up on the third ring. "Hello?"

"Colonel?"

"Landen." He doesn't even sound surprised. My name isn't a question.

"Yeah," I say shortly. "We need to talk."

I wait for the "The fuck we do," "Go to hell," or "I don't have time for your sissy bullshit," but it doesn't come.

A deep sigh passes from wherever he is, half a world away, to my ear. "I've been expecting your call," he says evenly.

He has?

"You have?" I haven't spoken to this man in three years. His voice still sends a shiver down my spine. He terrified me, angered me, and made me feel dead inside. Residual tinges of those emotions swirl inside of me.

"Surprised it took this long actually."

Blissful numbness covers me as I speak. Thank fuck. "Yeah. Well, to be honest, I never planned to speak to you again if I could help it."

"That right? Makes sense I guess."

I pull in damp, humid air and try to put some type of priority rank on the crazed parade of thoughts trampling through my head. "I have some questions. I need answers. Think you can give me that?"

"Landen, listen. A lot has happened since—"

"You know what, I don't give two shits about what you're about to say. If you've got excuses or whatever, save your breath. I don't want or need them."

"Son, I understand that you're angry. I deserve it."

My blood pressure ramps up right along with my pulse. It's a wonder I don't drop dead of a fucking heart attack right now. "Don't fucking *son* me. Don't apologize or even *think* about spouting some bullshit about how or why or try and tell me what either of us deserves."

Somehow, over the sound of blood rushing in my ears, I hear him clear his throat again. "Okay. You said you had questions. Say whatever you need to."

Condescending prick. I pull the phone from my ear for a second and close my eyes. Taking deep breaths until my vision clears, I remind myself why I have to do this. *Layla. Our child. My job.* My family's life pretty much depends on me getting my shit together. Doesn't mean I have to be cordial.

"Listen to me. Do not think for one goddamn second that I *need* anything from you. I don't. Truth is, I want some answers for why..." Dammit. Stupid lump in my throat makes it hard to talk.

"I know. I know you don't. You've done well for yourself despite...me. I owe you answers, son—er, Landen. Ask away."

He's placating me with this passive aggressive tone that makes me want to murder him with my bare hands. This is why I need him to tell me. Because I can't keep turning into him every time I get upset.

I suck in another lungful of air and fire my questions at him. "Why? Just tell me why you hated me so much. Why everything I did, everything I said, everything I was, made you so fucking angry all the time."

I hate how weak my voice sounds. Red rage looms on the horizon. I hold it off as long as I can.

"I didn't hate you," he says quietly. "I hated what you represented. What you reminded me of."

His words confuse me. I don't know what I expected to hear, but that wasn't it. "I was a fucking kid. What the hell could I have possibly *represented*?"

Another deep sigh from his end. "It's been a tough few years for me. Your girlfriend's aunt almost had me decommissioned. Things with your mother are finally—"

"What the hell are you talking about? I don't give a damn how hard the past few years have been for you." I have no idea what he's talking about with Layla's aunt, but I can't bring myself to ask. I don't want to know about his life. "Please tell me you're not looking for my sympathy. My whole life was hard because of you."

"Your mother is just now speaking to me again. If I tell you this…if I tell you the truth, a truth that isn't mine to tell, she might never forgive me."

Screw this. He wasn't worried about her forgiving him for the way he treated me my entire life. But now it's suddenly of monumental consequence. "Whatever. You know what? Never mind. I should've known better than to expect anything from you." Tears of rage well in my eyes, and I'm just about to hang up or pitch my phone off the balcony when he speaks up.

"Landen, wait. You're right. I can't erase the past, but this…this I can do."

"Do what?"

"Tell you the truth."

I don't say anything because I'm pretty sure it's just going to be bullshit. But I wait for whatever it is, everything inside of me boiling to the surface as I do.

"The truth is," he begins, pausing just enough to piss me off further. "The truth is you aren't my son."

CHAPTER Eleven

Layla

I wake to sunlight streaming in through the blinds. Memories of the night before come back slowly and I savor them. Landen's sharp, clean scent stirs as I rouse the blankets around me. Smiling, I disentangle myself from the sheets and make my way to the bathroom.

I smile at my reflection in the mirror. Things aren't perfect, but I feel like we made real progress. Landen and I are "us" again. For the first time in a week, I feel like I can breathe. No secrets, no more separate beds.

My still sleep-heavy brain vaguely recalls a mentioning of omelets. After debating showering for five minutes, I decide omelets come first. Wrapping my robe around me, I head into the living room. Muffled shouts are coming from somewhere but I don't see Landen. Until I do.

He's on the phone on the balcony, waving his arms wildly. Panic sends all of my physiological responses into overdrive. Oh God. Something's happened and it's bad.

My heart thrums hard against my ribs, sending blood rushing to my head. If he got let go from the team and he's screaming at his coach like that, his entire career will be over. Without thinking, my body propels itself forward and slides the glass door to the side. I step out onto the warm concrete and reach for him.

"Landen," I say softly, approaching him from the back and reaching for him. Either I startled him or he's just heard something awful because his arm flies up and the back of his hand connects with my mouth.

For a moment, I'm confused. A far away ringing sound grows louder and I blink until I can see straight.

"Oh God. Shit. Layla." Landen whirls around and takes me in with wild eyes. He was already angry and now he's panicking. His phone clatters to the ground as he reaches for me. "Baby, I'm so sorry. You're bleeding."

"I'm okay," I reassure him. But I might not be. My upper lip feels five inches thicker and the faint metallic taste of blood touches my tongue.

"The hell you are," he says, lifting me in his arms and carrying me into the kitchen. He sets me down on the counter like I'm made of glass. I watch helplessly as he grabs a dishtowel and runs it under the sink faucet.

Wincing in pain as he presses the damp towel to my mouth, I try again to mumble that I'm fine. But Landen is a man on fire. Once I've taken the wet rag in my hands, he practically leaps over the breakfast bar to get to the freezer. In a blink, he's tucking ice into the dishtowel and placing it gently against my lips.

"Who were you talking to?"

"No one," he says evenly, avoiding my eyes by staring at my wounded lip. "No one important," he finishes. So much for no more secrets.

"I'm really okay. Promise," I tell him. But with the ice on my mouth, it comes out more like, "I'm ribby okay. Probbise." Tilting my head upwards with the intention of reassuring him, my eyes meet his and I'm terrified of what I see in them. Pure, unaltered self-loathing. His expression resembles one of actual physical pain. I wrap my legs around him and pull him closer to me. "Hey, look at me. I'm okay."

I put my hand over his and tug until he lowers the makeshift ice pack. Immediately I wish I hadn't. His already turbulent gaze widens and clouds over.

"I hurt you," he whispers. "All I do is hurt you."

"Landen, don't. Don't get like this. It was an accident." Reaching my hand up, I stroke the rough stubble on his jaw.

His pain breaks over both of us and I'm trembling from the sheer force of it. Placing his hands on either side of me on the counter, Landen braces me in his arms. Resting his forehead on mine, he sighs. "I don't know what to do anymore. I can't stop hurting you. Literally. Everything I do hurts you in one way or another."

My heart aches for him. He does hurt me, but not in the way he thinks. He hurts me by not seeing what I see when I look at him. Sliding both of my hands around the back of his neck, I whisper, "I'm tougher than you think, Landen." I'll never tire of the way his name feels on my lips. Even when they're swollen and hurting.

"Tell me what to do, baby. Tell me how not to hurt you." He stares down at me with pleading eyes. All I want is to make him understand. I love him, anger and all.

"Kiss it better," I say, pouting my injured lip at him.

His brows dip in confusion. He's the broken shell, and I'm the water. Need pulsates within me. The need to wash over him and ease his pain, smooth the jagged edges he uses to hurt us both.

The warmth of his breath teases against my skin. Stretching to kiss him, I'm startled when he grips my chin in his large hand. A small whimper escapes as I stare into his tortured gaze. For a split second, I'm terrified. Swallowed whole by the fear that he's about to tell me he can't do this—or just doesn't want to. But then he sighs and places his lips within a centimeter of mine. "Do you remember our first kiss?"

I nod. How could I forget? It was only a few years ago, in California, in an alley outside a nightclub. It nearly crushed me, my need for him. "Of course I do," I whisper, my lips barely brushing against his.

He peppers my jawline with whispered kisses, causing me to shiver. "It was the first time I ever controlled myself. Held back. Didn't give in to the inferno burning me up inside."

"Oh yeah?" I breathe, my chest rising against him as I do.

His nose traces the trail left by his hot mouth. "I'd never really been able to control myself before. Before you."

My head lolls back as the muscles in my neck give out. "Glad I could help you with that." I feel the curvature of his mouth as he smiles against my neck.

He groans as I pull the string that holds my robe closed. "Layla."

"Sometimes losing control is a good thing, Landen. Sometimes I want you to. I know you're careful with me, and I appreciate that. I do. But sometimes..."

His strong hands stroke up my inner thighs and I gasp as he spreads my knees apart. "Sometimes what, baby?"

"Sometimes I want you to lose control. Want you to take me however you want. Wherever. Whenever. As hard or fast or rough as you need to."

"Jesus, Layla." His eyes are wide as his lust and fear mingle in his stare.

"I'm serious. Let me be what you need, Landen. You've always kept me still when I needed you, when I was falling apart." I brush my nose against his. "Let me be that for you Don't run. Don't break anything." I lean up so that my mouth is next to his ear. "When all that aggression builds up, just...give it to me. However you need to."

He bolts upright as if I've literally shocked him with a live wire. "Baby, I'd...I'd hurt you." Shaking his head, he stares at me like I've lost my mind. He takes a step back as if I've become dangerous to him somehow.

Reaching out, I use the waistband of his jeans to pull him back to me. Licking my lips, I gather all my courage and look up at him. His gaze penetrates mine and I tug the hair at the nape of his neck. "You wouldn't. I promise. Fuck me, Landen. Just let go. Give me your anger. I can take it. I want it."

Turmoil burns in his expression. We've made love countless times. He's always gentle. Always thorough and attentive. But I've watched him play soccer, watched him lose his temper. I know what's inside of him. He needs more than slow, sensual love-making, and I want so badly to give him what he needs. Just like he's always done for me.

If fucking me will siphon off some of his excess rage, I'm ready to take whatever he can give. Maybe I need it too.

Crashing my mouth to his, I ignore the scream of pain from my injured lip. When he tries to pull back, I yank his hair even harder. My heels dig into the denim covering his ass as he presses against me.

His teeth scrape my bottom lip, causing me to moan out loud. He lifts me from the counter top and I let my robe slip all the way open. Wrapping my legs around his waist and hanging on for dear life, I tear at his flesh with my hands and mouth.

Air whooshes from my lungs when he slams my back against the refrigerator door. Something that must've been on top of it crashes to the floor. Bottles clank together inside but we don't stop.

"Dammit," Landen bites out when we run out of breath.

"Don't stop," I pant, struggling to suck oxygen into my lungs.

He shakes his head, and I can see him warring with himself. What he wants is battling it out with what he thinks I can handle. "What about the…" He clears his throat and lowers me to standing. "What about the baby? I don't want to hurt the—"

"You won't. I checked. Unless you have a baseball bat in your pants, I think we're fine."

He grins and pins me against the fridge. "Well, I have been told it's pretty impressive."

Rolling my eyes, I lean up and kiss him softly. "That it is."

"You really want this?" he asks hesitantly, tilting his head in this sweet way he has.

Instead of answering, I pull him to me roughly once more. I let my hands explore his bare chest, the muscles in his stomach, his sexy hip bones that jut out just above the dark trail of hair that leads to his erection. And then I lean in and bite him. Hard. Just below his rib cage.

"Ow, Layla. Fuck," he calls out. Good. I surprised him.

I smile sweetly up at him, giving my best innocent expression. "My bad, babe." I lower my head and place my lips over the spot I just sank my teeth into. Running my tongue over to the other side causes him to suck in a breath. And then I bite him again. Harder this time.

"What the hell?" He grips me by the shoulders and hauls me upright. "Fucking quit."

"What are you going to do about it?"

His eyes gleam. He's turned on and confused. But mostly turned on. He breathes in and out deeply enough for his chest to press against mine as we stand there facing off.

"About our first kiss," I say, trailing a finger down his heaving chest. "What exactly did you want then?"

He eyes me curiously for a moment before placing a hand flat against my chest, backing me up against the fridge once more. "This. I wanted this." Before I have time to blink, he thrusts two fingers deep inside me.

I cry out, lost in sensation as he plunges in and out.

"And this," he says, lowering his mouth to my neck and sucking hard enough to hurt.

"Oh god, oh god, don't stop." His fingers find that spot inside of me, and my legs give out.

"I wanted to fuck you right there in that alley. Wanted to bury myself in your tight wetness. I wanted to claim you, make you come so hard you'd never push me away again." He pulls his fingers out, causing me to cry out in protest. "Don't say you want me to fuck you, Layla, unless you really do. Because you know better than anyone, there's a lot of shit built up inside of me. You know I can hurt you. I will hurt you. Even if I don't mean to."

"Sometimes hurting is good. It makes me feel alive. You want to know something?" I breathe out as he slips his fingers back inside of me.

"I do."

"I would've let you. I would've let you take me in that alley. I would've let you put your fingers inside of me in high school, would've let you lick me, finger me, fuck me, whatever you wanted that first night. I want you every way there is. All of you. Always have. Always will."

I can see in his eyes as he stares at me, his breath sharp pants, the desire radiating off of him—my confession sets him on fire. Landen grips me under my butt and lifts me onto him. Before I know what's happening, I'm flat on my back on our breakfast bar. I watch as he tears his jeans off and yanks my legs apart.

"Hold tight, baby. It's going to be rough."

CHAPTER *Twelve*

Layla

When I come to, the room is bathed in orangish-blue light. I rub my eyes and glance around. Sunset. Stretching, I see that Landen is sprawled across me, both of us naked as the day we were born. And we're on the kitchen floor. I stretch and my back aches in protest. My stomach growls, reminding me that I haven't eaten.

My head hurts and everything is blurry. I smile as my memory returns. I have a sex hangover. Landen fucked me. *Really* fucked me. Not just hard and fast sex like we've had before. Head-banging-into-the-wall, glass-shattering-on-the-floor, screaming-orgasms-of-epic-proportions *fucked me.*

And now he's asleep in my arms, looking like an innocent little boy. Kissing him on top of the head, I ease out from under him. After a quick search, I find my robe slung over the breakfast bar. Pulling it on, I glance outside and see that it's sprinkling. Something breaks through my sex-sluggish brain and I remember that Landen left his phone on the balcony. I step out to retrieve it, hoping it's not too late.

When I tap the button to activate the screen, nothing happens. Hopefully it's just dead. Stepping quietly back inside, I take it into the bedroom and attach it to my charger. The screen comes to life instantly and I'm relieved it's not ruined. I start to set it down on the nightstand, but nagging curiosity gets the best of me. Whoever he was talking to really upset him. And if he's been fired, I deserve to know. I enter his password, knowing it's the day we met, and pull up his recent calls.

Holy shit. Shock hits me so hard I almost drop the sleek black phone.

Two calls. One missed from The Colonel and one where it appears Landen called him. I check the time. Eight minutes. They spoke for eight minutes.

Disappointment makes my chest ache. What in the world would he be calling his dad for? And why wouldn't he have told me?

I can't help it. I know I shouldn't, but I peek at his text messages. There are several from his coach.

Here is the link to the place I emailed you about. They're worth checking out.

Landen didn't respond but his coach kept texting.

The club would handle the cost. It's covered by your insurance.

I hope that you'll at least consider it.

Let me know something soon.

I have no idea what he's talking about. Glancing in the living room to make sure Landen's still sleeping, I click on the link. Oh my.

If his coach is sending him info about a place like this, he must be in serious trouble. I read the description of the place. It's in California. Then I click on the frequently asked questions. Several of the services mentioned sound a lot like the kind of help Landen could use.

"What are you doing?"

His gruff voice scares the crap out of me. I drop the phone as if it's on fire.

"Um—"

"What the fuck, Layla? We go through each other's phones now?" His broad frame blocks the light in the doorway.

"Sorry. It's just, you left it outside and I wanted to make sure it wasn't messed up from the rain."

"Oh yeah?" Landen takes two steps, closing the distance between us, and snatches his phone up off the bed. "You had to read my texts and open my web browser to be sure?"

Swallowing hard, I stand up to face him. We have plenty of issues, like any other relationship, but we don't lie to each other. "No. I wanted to see what upset you. I checked your recent calls. The text notifications popped up and I was curious."

"Whatever," he snaps. "Here. Knock yourself out." He pitches his phone at me and stalks out of the room.

I let his phone bounce off the bed and hit the floor. "Hey. Talk to me," I demand, following him out of the room, which is never a good idea when he's pissed. But he's overreacting this time. More so than usual. If anyone should be upset, it's me. We live together. I tell him everything. If he has so many secrets he's going to flip out over me looking at his phone, then we have bigger problems than I realized. Which is saying something.

"Why?" he asks, whirling around to face me. "Nothing you can't figure out by snooping in my phone."

"Don't be an ass. I was worried about you. I do that sometimes."

He snorts and turns from me again. "I'm going for a run."

"Oh good. That'll help. It always solves all of our problems."

"What's that supposed to mean?" He glares at me as he pulls on a T-shirt.

"It means, you've been talking to your dad, your suspension is obviously more serious than you let on, and my aunt has called you a million times. None of which you've even bothered to try and talk to me about. So yeah, good idea. A run should take care of everything." I huff out an exasperated breath.

"I'm pissed off. Looks like you are too. It's better for me to run off my anger than lose control of it here." He laces up his running shoes as I stand there seething.

"Landen, we talked about this. You can't run every time you're mad." I move in front of the door in a pathetic attempt to keep him from leaving. *It didn't work.* I thought maybe I could help somehow; take some of his anger away. But the look in his eyes tells me I was wrong.

"Like hell I can't. If I fucked you right now, I'd fuck one or both of us right into the emergency room."

"Please don't do this." Angry tears burn my eyes. "I want to know what you and your dad talked about. I want to know what he said."

"Tough shit." He steps towards the door. "I don't want to talk about it right now. Move."

But I don't move. I fold my arms and will him to stop being this way with everything I'm worth.

He looks at me as if I'm an unknown species he can't understand or communicate with. His eyes are intense and desperate. "I'm trying to keep myself from hurting you. Christ. What do you want from me?"

"I want you to stay," I say, knowing I sound like a petulant child. "I want you to grow up and stop running and stop acting like the incredible hulk. Don't rip your shirt off and beat on your chest and blow up every time something doesn't go your way. I'm pregnant. We're both scared. We had messed up childhoods and we might both suck at being parents. You're keeping things from me and I looked at your stupid phone. Let's deal with it."

Both sides of his jaw tick as he gives me a slight shake of his head. "Fine. You want me to stay? Here, I'll stay."

My shoulders sag forward with relief. We're finally going to talk things out. For once. But before I can apologize for my hateful words, Landen grabs the vase off the end table, the one that holds the shells my mother and I collected every summer in Gulf Shores before she died. Before she was taken from me. It's the one thing I have left that really reminds me of her.

"Don't, please don't—"

I wince when it hits the wall, shattering apart just like the vase does.

"Get out," I sob, running over to where glass and sand and my memories are scattered all over the floor. "Just go."

I don't even look up when the door slams.

After I've cleaned up the mess the best I can, I find my cell phone in my purse and dial the only person I feel like I can really count on.

"I need help," I choke out as soon as she answers. "How soon can you be here?"

CHAPTER *Thirteen*

Landen

I wish I'd never been born. I wish I'd never met Layla Flaherty. I wish that I hadn't called my dad. Because all of that, being born, having a childhood where I was afraid to breathe the wrong way, bottling everything up inside, meeting Layla, hearing what my dad had to say, it all led to this.

To me being the sorriest motherfucker on the face of the planet.

I take a breather about five miles into my run. I've practically been sprinting and I've sprinted my stupid ass into a bad part of town.

My side pinches and burns so I lift my arms above my head. Fuck it. I lower them and let the pain come. Leaning over, I place my hands on my knees. A few guys stand lined up on the other side of the street. One of them steps towards me and I straighten up and meet his gaze. If he thinks he's getting anything from me, he has another thing coming. For one, I don't even have my wallet on me. And for two, if he and his friends plan to beat the shit out of me, I'd welcome it. I deserve it. Crave it.

Bet he's not expecting a sick, twisted fucker to laugh when he produces a knife from his back pocket. But I do. This is just perfect.

You're not my son.

That's just perfect too.

I was deployed. Your mother had an affair.

It's like someone just shined high beams on my black soul. My dad isn't my dad. Just a man who had to look at the reminder of his wife's infidelity every day for eighteen years.

And I'm not blood related to that piece of shit. So in a way, it's a relief. But

I'm still me. Still angry all the time and fucked up and unable to control the hatred for him that burns inside of me.

When two of the other guys step forward, I see how dangerous the man in front of me really is. He's big, armed, and looks like he just busted out of prison. The reality of my situation hits me hard enough to hurt. Her parents were gunned down in front of her, and her boyfriend is about to be gutted on a back road in Spain.

"Hey, sorry. I was just passing through, man." I hold my hands up in a gesture of what I hope is innocence.

He says something in Catalan, which I know enough to recognize as not Spanish but not enough to decipher meaning from it. His voice is a growl and makes my blood run cold.

"Amigo," I say, because it's the word I know means friend and I've lost the bloodlust desire to fight, to hurt and be hurt. My pulse races and I just want to get home and apologize. Beg my girl to forgive me. Whatever it takes.

One of the other guys mutters something and I recognize the word for money.

"No dinero. Por favor," I say, hoping they understand. "Lo siento."

"Demasiado malo para usted," the guy with the knife sneers at me. My brain struggles to translate his words just as he comes close enough for me to smell the alcohol on him.

He cocks his fist and Layla's beautiful face flashes behind my eyes. I hurt her. Again. Whatever's coming, I deserve it. That's the last thought I have before everything goes black.

"¡Oh. Dios mío! Somebody help! Llamar a la policía!"

I'm in a tunnel. I don't know how I got here. A woman's voice comes from far away. It's a pretty voice. Not as pretty as Layla's, but nice.

I want to tell her it's going to be okay, whatever she's freaking out about. But I can't. I'm disconnected from my body.

"¿Cuánto tiempo ha sido?

"Una hora o así."

Florescent lights greet me, shooting lightning bolts to my brain as I open my eyes.

"Where am I?" I hear myself ask.

"Está en el hospital. San Juan de Dios," a woman says. Different woman from before. Not Layla either. Shit, my head hurts. "Do you know your name?" she asks in Spanish.

"My name?"

I sit up and glance around me. Heavy dread presses down on me as I realize I really am in the hospital like she said. An attractive dark-haired woman holds a clipboard and stares at me with interest.

"Um, it's Landen. Landen O'Brien."

"Ah. Well, Señor O'Brien, it seems you were jumped. A young lady found you in the street, beaten and barefoot."

"Jesus." Fuck me. "How long have I been here?" Layla's probably worried sick.

"A little over an hour."

"Okay, can I go home now?"

"Perdón?? You have two dozen stitches, a busted face, and possible internal bleeding. You just now came to, the police are waiting for your statement, and it's a wonder you were even left alive. And you ask when can you go home?" Her face twists in confusion.

"Yes, ma'am," I croak out. "My girlfriend, I need to call her. Can I do that at least?" My ribs stab me in protest as I sit all the way up.

"I don't know. Can you?"

Bile rises in my throat and my head swims in response to the overwhelming pain. "I'd like to try."

"Speak with the Policía first. Then make your call."

I thank her and nod at the two uniformed officers who push the curtain around my bed aside and enter.

I give them a brief statement about what happened, trying to rush it along so I can call Layla.

"Hell of a place to go for a run," one of them tells me. At least I think that's what he says. After three years, I can hold a decent conversation in Spanish, but my head is pounding so I'm struggling to translate as quickly as they're speaking.

"Yes, sir. I won't be revisiting that part of town anytime soon."

"Let's hope not," the taller of the two says, putting his notepad away. "You were lucky this time. You probably wouldn't be again. Call us if you think of anything else."

I assure them that I will and breathe a sigh of relief when they finally leave. Pretty sure one of them mumbles the Spanish word for "fucking idiot" on the their way out. Agreed.

Being careful not to disturb my battered ribs, I reach for the phone on my bedside table.

She answers on the first ring.

"Hey, baby."

"Landen? Where are you? Are you okay? Whose number is this?"

The panic in her voice, the concern weighing her questions down, kills me. Hurts a hundred times worse than any of my injuries. I treated her like dirt. Worse than dirt. I fucked her like a man possessed and then blew up over something stupid and walked out. And here she is, worried about me. Still loving me more than I deserve.

"Calm down. I'm okay. I'm so sorry, Layla. So damn sorry." Tears well in my eyes. I hate myself. How can I love her like *she* deserves when I hate myself so damn much?

"Please come home," she pleads. My chest tightens, squeezing my heart so hard I can't breathe.

"Um, I would. Listen, don't freak out. I'm okay. I'm just…kind of in the hospital."

"What? Oh my God, what happened?"

I can picture her beautiful face, those gorgeous eyes widening in panic. "Breathe, angel. I swear I'm fine. Can you grab my ID and the insurance card and meet me at San Juan de Dios? There's cash for a cab in my wallet."

"I'll be right there."

We say goodbye and I lie here waiting. Swearing to myself that I won't ever do this to her again.

But if I'm being honest with myself? That might be a promise I can't keep.

CHAPTER *Fourteen*

Layla

God I hate hospitals. But I don't even take the time to weigh just how much I hate them as I barrel out of the cab, tossing money at the driver.

The smell hits me as soon as I walk through the doors to the emergency room. Sterile with undertones of human waste. Voices surround me, speaking Spanish and what I think might be Portuguese.

I spot a desk with a heavyset dark-skinned woman behind it. "I'm looking for Landen O'Brien. Can you tell me where I can find him?" She looks at me like I'm nuts and I repeat the question in my broken Spanish.

"Señor O'Brien?" an attractive woman says from beside me. "You must be his girlfriend."

I don't know who she is, but I take a second to thank God for her. "I am. Where can I find him?"

"Come with me," she says, so of course I do. She's not walking nearly as fast as I'd like for her to, but I'm grateful for any help I can get.

"W-what happened to him?" I ask, deathly afraid of the answer.

She stops and turns to face me. "He was beaten. Probably by gang members. He'll be residing with us overnight."

My heart drops to my toes. Fighting to remain upright, I swallow the contents of my stomach as they push their way north. "Is he okay?"

"See for yourself," she says, pulling the curtain beside us back.

In all of my twenty-two years, I've never seen anything like what I see when I look at him. His eyes are closed. His face is black and blue and a sickly shade of yellow.

I know from the memory of my parents' murders that blood isn't crayon red like in the movies. It's darker and spreads quickly. It stains the bandages covering Landen's chest. My hand flies to my mouth in an attempt to keep my horror from escaping. But it doesn't work. A sound like that of a wounded animal breaks free and I have to fight not to drop to my knees.

The air has been stolen from my lungs, and hot, wet tears flow freely down my face. "Oh God."

My words have his eyes fluttering open until they lock on mine. "Come here, baby. I'm fine." Landen opens his arms to me and I launch myself at him, careful not to land on his bandages. "Shh," he murmurs into my hair. "I'm sorry, angel. So sorry."

A violent sob racks my body as he wraps his arms around me. He's the broken one, comforting me. But I can't help it. His pain is my pain. It seeps into me, weighing me down until I can't move.

"Landen," I whisper against his bandaged chest.

"It's not as bad as it looks," he promises. I raise my tear-stained face to his and he frowns.

I wince as he rubs his thumb across my upper lip. I already forgot about it. I checked the mirror after he left earlier. It's bruised and swollen. But nothing compared to what he looks like right now. "It's not as bad as it looks," I say right back to him. But it is. I don't know how everything got so messed up. But it is.

"Take it easy," I tell Landen as I help him up the stairs. His arm is draped over my shoulders but I know he's only got about half his weight actually on me. "One more step."

My stomach tightens at what awaits us inside our apartment. Or rather, what his reaction to it will be. But I was out of options.

I pull out my key and unlock the door. But before I push it open, I lose my nerve. "Babe, I need to tell you something. I'm sorry, please don't be mad."

He turns to me with an arched brow.

I take a deep breath, trying to steel my nerves with oxygen. It helps a little. Not much, but enough. "I didn't know what to do. I still don't. But you need help. *We* need help."

"What are you talking about?"

I push the door open, hating myself for feeling grateful that he's not in any shape to run out.

Four pairs of eyes regard us warily as we walk in.

"Fucking hell," Landen mumbles under his breath. "Seriously?" he turns to me with betrayal in his eyes.

"I'm sorry," I say as tears pool in my own. I tug him forward gently.

"Well isn't this a nice welcome home." His tone is sharp and wounded all at once. I take a few deep breaths. I knew this wouldn't be easy, but what other option did I have?

Skylar, Corin, Landen's mom, and the manager of the soccer club he works for all stand to greet us.

"I'm guessing you weren't expecting us," Sean McBride says. The Barcelona Club manager is short and stocky but has an air of authority that makes him seem ten feet tall. He also has a Scottish accent that makes *us* sound like *oos*.

"No, sir, I wasn't," Landen says through gritted teeth.

"Well, I'm sorry to hear that. Your girl here, she's worried about ya," he answers, coming forward to shake Landen's hand. "Truthfully, we all are."

I watch Landen's green eyes darken as they skitter over his mother. But they lighten again as he nods to Skylar. "Skylar, you worried about me?"

Skylar jerks his chin upward. "Yeah, man. Shit keeps me up at night." He grins as if they share a private joke.

"Well I'm not fucking worried about you. Even if you do look like you were hit by a truck," Corin chimes in. "I'm worried about my best friend. And if her lip looks like that because of you, you're going to look a whole lot worse."

Oh crap. I forgot about that. "Corin—"

"No, she's right. Call your boys, Ginger. Give them my address. I deserve it."

Corin glares at him and I step between them. "Stop. Just stop."

"Landen," his mother breaks in from beside us. "Baby, I—"

"Don't you baby me," he snarls at her. "In fact, don't even fucking talk to me."

This is going well.

"Sit down. All of you," I command. "Now."

They all do as I say, which nearly shocks me into silence. I spoke with the lady at Allied about how to handle this. Her advice was to stay calm and in control. Not to let anyone's emotions escalate too high. Obviously she's never met Landen. She might as well have told me to relocate Mt. Kilimanjaro while I was at it.

I take a deep breath and stand. "I've asked each of you here because I don't know what else to do. You all know that Landen and I keep our personal lives personal, maybe too personal. So personal that when things started to spiral out of control, I felt like I had no one to turn to."

My mouth turns down and tears threaten but I swallow them back. "I called Corin yesterday before Landen got attacked. After we talked, I decided to call a professional for help. Her name is Megan Sanderson and she's a doctor at the Allied Center—a place in California that Landen's coach recommended he visit for help with his anger. As some of you already know, he's currently on his second suspension for losing his temper."

I keep my eyes on Landen as I speak. His hands grip his knees, and I want to drop to mine and apologize. Tell everyone to leave and forget it. But I know it's now or never. Making excuses for him won't help him. "Dr. Sanderson suggested we each tell him how we feel about him. How his anger affects us and why we would like for him to seek help." My hands shake as I pull the first picture off the wall. "I'll go first."

His expression is pained when I turn back to face him. "Why are you doing this?"

I shake my head and give up on holding back my tears. My vision blurs as I look at him. "Because I love you," I whisper. "But I can't love our problems away."

After I've taken all the pictures off the wall, revealed all of the damage he's done, I walk over to him. "I'm as guilty as you are. I covered it up. Made excuses. Saw what I wanted to see. I'm sorry, Landen." After pausing to pull in a rattled breath, I continue. "I want you to get help because I want to spend my life with you. I want to raise our child together in a happy home without being afraid that you'll destroy it."

His mom reaches over and clasps my hand. My tears fall as I meet her questioning gaze and nod. She didn't know I was pregnant. The knowledge that Landen hasn't told his own mother stings, but I try to convince myself that it's a reflection of their relationship and not ours.

His mom stands and I take her spot on the couch. Regret and longing pour from her words as she speaks. "I want you to get help because I love you. Because you spent your life paying for my choices. Because I wasn't strong enough to admit the truth. I want you to have the life you deserve because you are a wonderful man that I'm proud to call my son."

I think she's talking about his father but I'm not sure. The truth about what? I give Landen a sidelong questioning glance but he just shakes his head. His back is ramrod straight, his shoulders rigid, as if he's braced for an attack. In a way, I feel like that's exactly what we're doing to him.

Mr. McBride clears his throat and locks eyes with Landen. "Son, I think you already know how the club feels. You're the best striker we've had in years. The kind of player that changes the game, reminds me why I love it so much. Be a shame for you to throw away such a bright future over your pride. It's easy to run from our problems. Takes a man to face them head-on."

I slip my hand into Landen's, praying silently that one day he'll forgive me for this. He gives me a gentle squeeze in return and I tell myself there's hope.

Skylar is next. Running his hand through his curly hair, he sighs. "Look, I can't tell you how to live your life. I fuck mine up at least once a day. But I can tell you this: what you and Layla have…it's not something you find around every corner, you know?"

Glancing over, I see Landen nod at his friend.

"I mean, shit. Corin would have me taken out if I'd so much as raised my voice on the wrong day of the week."

"Truth," Corin says with a shrug.

"So if you love her, if you really want to make it work, I'd do whatever she wants if I were you. Go into anger management rehab or whatever the hell. And then there's bank to be made playing professional soccer. And you're having a kid. So money's kind of an issue." Skylar looks over at me. "Is that good? Did I do okay?"

I can't help but smile as I nod. He sighs with relief and sits back down. Corin probably threatened to give him an at-home vasectomy if he screwed this up.

My stomach flips as Corin stands. Holy heck. Here we go.

"Honestly? I kind of want to just toss your stupid ass over that balcony and save everyone the trouble."

"Corin—"

"Everyone else got their turn. Now I get mine, Layla."

She points a manicured finger at Landen. "I talked her into coming here with you because I thought it would be a good thing. I rooted for you. Thought the reason you acted like such a fucking psycho was because you needed her. Loved her. But you've got her and obviously you're still a mess. So…everyone else thinks you're great and wonderful and wants you to get help. Well, I think you're lucky Layla gives you the time of day and I don't want to have to take out a loan to have you murdered. Since she obviously sees some redeemable quality in you that I don't, you should live up to that."

"Okay," I say, trying to cut her off once more.

"I'm not done."

"Might as well let her finish," Skylar informs me with a knowing look. "You know she's going to one way or another."

"Look at her," Corin says to Landen. He raises a cocky eyebrow at her. She cuts her eyes to me. "Fucking look at her, asshole. How does that make you feel? Her tears? Her busted lip? Is that what she deserves? That's the best you can do?"

His jaw ticks as he clenches it shut. Corin's pushing his buttons as hard as she can. I feel helpless. I want to ease his pain and shut her up, but it kind of seems like…like she's the one actually getting through to him.

"Answer me, O'Brien."

"No," he croaks out, his voice gravelly as he turns to me. "No it's not. And it makes me feel like shit."

I stare into his eyes, searching for forgiveness, trying to comfort and love him with my gaze.

"I'm so sorry, baby," he mouths at me and I nod.

"Me too," I mouth back.

Something shifts in his demeanor and he rests his forehead on mine.

I don't how I know for sure, because things look pretty bleak right this second. But somehow, I think everything might be okay.

CHAPTER *Fifteen*

Landen

"Here at Allied, we give you the tools to cope, teach you realistic strategies to manage your anger by controlling your reactions and responses to everyday stressors." The woman giving the introduction speech in what I refer to as the white room reminds me so much of Layla that it causes a pang in my chest. Her eyes are a crystal clear shade of blue behind her glasses, and she wears her sleek blonde hair in a ponytail. This is going to be the longest six weeks of my entire dammed life.

I sigh and settle in to listen. I'm still jet-lagged from the flight, and I didn't sleep well last night for fear Corin was going to stab me in the middle of the night. She's the only person who hates me as much or maybe even more than I do. Not that I blame her.

After the thirty minute "you're all kinds of fucked up but we're here to help" speech, I'm shown to a small room.

"No roommate?" I ask the stocky dark-skinned guy who hands me a stack of towels and bed sheets.

"Not for those of you in here for anger disorders." He eyes me like this should be obvious.

Yeah, angry dudes living in close quarters. Probably not the best idea.

I set my stuff on a chair and lie down on the bare mattress. The words *anger disorders* flash behind my eyes.

I am officially a complete fuck-up of a human being. I'd laugh at myself if it weren't so pathetic. I had everything I ever thought I wanted. A career I'd thought was a pipe dream. The beautiful woman I love loves me back and is risking her life to have my kid. But something in me—something uncontrollable that thirsted for pain and destruction—obliterated everything good in my life.

Which led me here. Rehab for out-of-control assholes.

I turn on my side and stare out the window at the ocean. I always liked the ocean. Its raw power is able to destroy, but mostly it stays calm, pushing and pulling with the current. Closing my eyes, I imagine that I can hear it. An image of Layla splashing me in the water and laughing on one of our many trips to the beach washes over me. It's been so damn long since I've seen her truly happy. Since I've made her laugh.

I just want to make her happy. I'll do anything. Everything.

I open my eyes and look around the small room. God I hope this works.

As my first session with Dr. Sanderson is ending, I make the request I've been wanting to make since I walked through the door to her office. "Can I ask you something? Something kind of off-topic?"

"Sure, I guess so."

I pull the folded envelope from my back pocket. "Do you know a Dr. Clayton Kirkowitz? He's a neurosurgeon."

Dr. Sanderson nods. "I've heard of him. All good things. Why?"

"Um, I have something for him." My hands are shaking, rattling the envelope that holds the words that poured straight from my soul onto paper. "I was wondering if you could pass it along."

The doctor looks apprehensive as she takes it. "It's not a death threat or anything, is it?"

I can't help but smile. Shaking my head, I raise an eyebrow at her. "Do I really come off as *that* out of control?"

Relief hits me when she smiles back. "Permission to read what's in here to be sure?"

I swallow hard and nod. "Sure."

"Okay. I'll see what I can do."

"That's all I can ask."

Because apparently these types of places enjoy torturing their patients, every Sunday is Family Day. Odds are most of us are in here because of our families. So yeah, let's please take a day to celebrate that.

I don't tell Layla about it because she doesn't need the stress of a trip here. Her medical condition and pregnancy are enough to deal with. And because she's the only person I actually consider my family, I'm shocked on my second to last Sunday when there's a knock at my door.

"You have a visitor, O'Brien," a male voice calls out from the other side.

Shaking my head, because I should've known she'd find out and show up, I pull the door open. "You didn't have to—"

"Landen," my mom greets me. "I know you weren't expecting me."

I clear my throat and stare at her. Her dark hair is cut shorter than I ever remember her wearing it, and there are flecks of gray in it. "No. No, I wasn't." My lungs seem to want to breathe a little harder and my heart pounds into my ribs with a vengeance. "What are you doing here?"

"It's Family Day," she says, as if that makes everything perfectly okay.

"Right. But since our family was pretty much based on bullshit, and I'm a grown man now, I was hoping we could stop pretending."

She doesn't even flinch at my words. "I knew you'd be angry. And I get that. But your doctor said we could use a conference room and there's someone I want you to talk to."

From the way she says *someone*, I know exactly who she means. "No. Hell no. I've heard everything I need to hear. From both of you."

Instead of yelling, the preferred method of disagreement for The Colonel and I, my mom stares me down with folded arms. "You're here to get help, right? So you won't end up being the kind of father he was? I can't imagine a better person to give you advice about how not to be like him than him. Can you?"

"I don't want his fucking advice."

She sighs and lowers her arms. "Landen, you're still angry. And you're angry because of him. Or because of me. Or both. But either way, we're all a part of this. You can face the source of your anger head on or I can take a cab back to the airport and you can go it alone. But I would really like—"

Shit. Her voice breaks and she's crying. I clench my jaw in an attempt to remain unaffected.

"—a chance to know my grandchild. Please," she finishes.

"If either one of you lies to me, about anything, I'm done." I step out into the hall beside her. "And I'm not making any promises."

"Good," she says, sniffling out the last of her tears. "Then neither will I."

The conference room is small and plain. A square table with four chairs and a phone. Dr. Sanderson sits at the head of the table and I notice a red light flashing on the phone.

"Landen. Your mother surprised you with this visit. How does that make you feel?"

"Just jump right in with the psychoanalysis, Doc. It makes me feel sad. Hold me," I answer, pulling out a seat for my mother and then one for myself.

She forces a tight smile but her eyes meet mine and amusement sparkles in them. "Sarcasm won't help you. It's not one of the suggested tools for dealing with anger. You know that."

"That I do." I sit while she and my mother say brief hellos.

"Okay," Dr. Sanderson begins, taking a deep breath and pushing her wavy red hair behind her ear. "It's up to you two if you want me here or not. I can stay and mediate, or you can have this conversation in private. Which would you prefer?"

"Private," I say at the exact same moment my mother says, "Stay."

We glance at each other and I shrug. "Whatever."

"How about I give you a few minutes alone and then I check back in a bit?" Dr. Sanderson stands and places a hand firmly on my shoulder as she moves past me. "You can do this," she says softly.

"Is that him?" I ask my mom once the doctor closes the door behind her. Jerking my eyes toward the flashing light on the phone, I try to ignore the tension building inside of me, the tightening of my chest.

"It is," my mom answers, obviously not needing clarification. She takes a deep breath and locks her eyes onto mine. "Landen, I know this isn't easy. None of it. What you and Layla are going through, dealing with a truth that was hidden from you, paying for the mistakes of others. But before we hash this whole thing out, I just wanted to say that no matter how you feel about all of this once we're finished here today or how you feel about me, I love you." Her eyes begin to fill with tears and I look down. No matter what she's done or hasn't done over the years, I hate seeing my mom cry. "And I'm proud of you."

I close my eyes and I see myself destroying the apartment in Spain. Layla's heartbroken expression when I threw her vase of seashells against the wall.

There's nothing about me that anyone should be proud of.

When I glance up my mom reaches a hand out and places it on my cheek. I don't lean into her touch but I don't flinch away either.

"Ready?" she whispers.

No. "Guess so," I say instead.

I watch as she presses the red button below the flashing light. "Jack?"

"Annie." The Colonel's voice still causes my organs to seize up. "Is he…did he agree to—"

"I'm here," I say, wishing his goddamn voice didn't make me feel five fucking years old. "Let's hear it. Whatever bullshit story you two want to tell me. I'm listening."

"Landen, your mother and I—" The Colonel begins, but mom cuts him off.

"I was nineteen. I had no idea what I wanted to do with my life. There was no money for college and I had no skills, no real ones anyway, to get a job. But they hired me as a receptionist in the Army enlistment office at the community college." Her body is still and her eyes are glazed over as if she's actually somewhere much further from me. "Your father signed up on my first day. He also asked me to dinner."

"I still remember that red sweater you had on," The Colonel says from the speaker. "I was nervous as hell about enlisting, but it was the family business so I didn't have much of a choice. And then I walked in and you smiled at me and I couldn't wait to sign those damn papers and get back out there to ask you out."

My teeth are on edge as I listen to them reminisce. I don't like it. Because it tells me they were happy once. And then I came along and wrecked everything.

"We dated for six months and then, much to both of our families dismay, we were married." My mom gives me a small smile that I don't return. I always wondered why my grandparents didn't stay in touch. As a kid I blamed it on the fact that we moved so much. Guess there was more to it than that.

"Right after our honeymoon, I was sent on three back-to-back deployments. Leaving my beautiful, young wife home alone. Alone in our house, alone in our marriage." Regret thickens The Colonel's voice. My stomach clenches at hearing him like this. He sounds so…human.

"It was lonely. *I* was lonely." My mom reaches out to touch my arm, or maybe my hand, I'm not sure. I pull back because I can't stand the thought of being touched right now. Not by anyone involved in this conversation anyways. The one person I want to be here isn't. Her eyes reflect the hurt my action causes, but I just can't right now. "It's still no excuse," she says so low I barely hear her.

The Colonel clears his throat. "It was a long time ago, Annie."

"Don't make excuses for me, Jack. He deserves to know." Squaring her shoulders as she sits up straight, my mom pulls in a ragged breath. "Some of the girls from my office were going to a soccer game. A tournament of some type. I went along for lack of anything better to do. That's where I met Javier Guzman. He was part Italian and completely over the top when it came to getting my attention."

I always thought the expression "you could hear a pin drop" was an exaggeration. It isn't. I'm holding my breath and I'm betting The Colonel is too.

My biological father was part Italian. A professional soccer player, like me. And now I know his name.

Watching my mom smile at a memory I'm not sure I want to know about makes my head pound. "He was amazing on the field. Full of energy and aggressive…like you," she tells me. "His team won the tournament that weekend, and my friends and I agreed to go out and celebrate with them. It was…" She bites her lip and her expression clouds over. "It was not the decision that I should've made as a married woman."

She phrases it carefully. But I hear what she doesn't say. *It was a mistake. You were a mistake.*

"That's enough," I say, because I can't take anymore.

"Landen—"

"No. I got it. You had an affair. You made a mistake and then you got to pay for it for eighteen years."

"Son, give her a chance—"

I huff out a harsh laugh, interrupting whatever The Colonel was about to say. "Did you miss the point of the story, Colonel? I'm not your son. But wait, you knew that already." Shoving my chair back, I stand to leave.

"Sit down. Now," my mother commands in a voice I don't recall ever hearing her use. "You are a grown man as you so helpfully pointed out. You're about to be a father yourself. So sit your ass back in that chair and listen. You can be pissed and storm out when we're finished."

Where was this woman all those years when I needed her to be strong for me?

I wait a beat but then I sit. Might as well let them get it all out there so they'll leave me alone.

"I came home two months later and your mother told me the truth. She didn't lie or try to hide it. She was ready to sign divorce papers and walk away the day I returned." The Colonel's voice fills the room. My mom and I both look at the phone as if it's actually him sitting there. "And I told her the truth as well. I hadn't been the picture perfect husband while I was away either. Plus I was up for a promotion, and the Army likes family men. Men with wives and kids. So we talked and we decided to do what we could to make it work."

"Except it didn't work. Because you hated me," I choke out, startled by the sound of my own voice.

"I never hated you, Landen," he says evenly. "Never. But every time you did or said something that reminded me that you were another man's son, I…I lost control. I'm sorry. God, there aren't words to say how sorry I am."

Squeezing my eyes shut, I take deep breaths and think of Layla. Of our child, the one who—so help me God—will have a better life than I did. If I have to live at the fucking Center, or in a whole other country, whatever it takes, I will not ever put my child through what I went through.

"I blamed myself. I blamed Jack. I blamed Javier. I even blamed the Army," my mother says quietly. "I let my own shame keep me quiet in the corner when I should have stood up for you. Your father…The Colonel was powerful and had government connections. I knew my options were risk having to share custody with him, or letting my secret affair come to light. Looking back it was all such a—"

"Such a what, mom? A huge fucking mistake? Go ahead and say it. I'm a walking, talking, living, breathing mistake."

"No," she says, her shoulders shaking with sobs. "Never. I regretted stepping out on my marriage, betraying my husband, but I never regretted you. Not once after I found out I was pregnant did I regret what happened because I loved you the moment I knew you existed."

"Hell of a way to show it," I mumble under my breath.

"The only person who should be regretting anything is me," The Colonel breaks in. "I said I could step up, could be a father. But I only half-ass committed. And I let you both down."

"Don't expect me to fucking forgive you," I practically yell at the phone. "You treated me like a dog. Hell, worse than a dog. You know what the really screwed up part is?" My voice cracks under the strain of emotion, but I don't care. "The really sick, twisted, fucked up part is that I preferred it when you hit me. Preferred when you yelled and threatened and punished me. Because that was better than the alternative. Better than being completely ignored. At least when you were screaming and swinging I knew you knew I existed." A hard sob breaks its way to the surface and I want to smash everything in the fucking room.

"Landen," my mother says softly, her voice sounding so much like Layla's it hurts to hear.

"I was a kid. An innocent fucking kid who never asked to be born. Nothing I did was ever good enough because neither one of you wanted me to exist. Like I could fucking help that."

"Son, please. Please give me a chance to explain. It wasn't you I was angry with. It wasn't you who wasn't good enough or did anything wrong. It was me. I hated me. And that spilled over onto both of you."

"Oh yeah? What's with the epiphany, Colonel? Army make you go to sensitivity training or some shit?"

I'm up and pacing, trying to regain control of myself when he speaks again. "As a matter of fact, they did. After I hit you on Thanksgiving, your girlfriend's aunt reported my behavior to anyone who would listen. And she has some serious connections. Thanks to her, I got some mandatory help. But it did help, and even though I'm still the same hard ass son of a bitch I've always been, I see the error of my ways, son. And I'm man enough to be sorry. To admit that to you. And to your mother. I can only hope that one day you both will be willing to give an old man another chance."

"You can go to hell," I say through gritted teeth. Leaning forward to glare at the phone, I brace both of my hands on the table and try not to tear the damn thing in two. "You should've walked away. You don't say you'll be a father and then spend eighteen years taking out the fact that you don't want to be on a kid that had nothing to do with anything. If you were man enough to say you'd make it work then you damn well should have."

The irony of the situation hits me so hard I nearly stagger backwards.

I've been doing the exact same thing to Layla. Telling her we'll figure something out and then losing my shit over and over. We're having a kid. A kid I know without a doubt is mine, and I've been a complete and utter asshole. She's willing to risk her life to have my baby. *My baby.*

My airway constricts and I can't breathe. Vision blurring from the tears welling in my eyes, I interrupt whatever my mom and The Colonel are saying to soothe me. "I'm done here. I have to go."

CHAPTER Sixteen

Layla

"Thanks for letting me stay, Corin. It's been kind of nice being here. In Spain, with Landen always out of town for work, I was alone a lot."

"Um, he was obviously *in town* at some point," Corin says nodding to my belly. "And you're welcome."

I laugh and roll my eyes. "So, any chance you're going to give me some details about you and Skylar? Has he been *in town* yet?"

"God, pregnancy makes you such a perv." She swats me with a napkin.

"Uh huh. Three years, Corin. You've been *I don't like labels but we're together* for three years." I drag out the last word to make my point.

"I'm focusing on school. It's not easy getting into law school, you know? Skylar knows that. We have an understanding."

"Uh, *you* probably have an understanding. Skylar probably has an on-going relationship with blue balls."

"Layla Flaherty! I cannot believe you just said that. What the hell are they doing to you in Spain? Where did my sweet little Georgia go?" She gapes at me and I laugh, but a sharp pang in my mid-section stops my laughter in my throat.

"Oh, ouch." I rub one hand across my stomach and the other on my lower back until it subsides.

"Are you okay?" Her green eyes are wide and filled with fear. "Do I need to call someone?"

I snort. "No. Just growing pains. I'm fine."

"Hey, um, Lay? I know you don't want to hear this, but have you thought about alternate living arrangements? I mean, it's something you should probably consider."

"You're right," I tell Corin as we set the table for dinner in her small apartment. "I don't want to hear that."

"Layla," she huffs out my name on an exasperated sigh. "I know you love him and I know we all want to believe that this place is going to be the answer to our prayers. But—"

"But what?" I ask, folding my arms over the small bump that's begun to jut out between my hips.

"But what if it's not? What if it would be better for you and for the baby to stay here?"

"Here as in…"

"Well of course you're welcome to stay here as in right here in this apartment for as long as you like. But I mean here as in California. You're all caught up on your correspondence classes, right? So why not just finish up the rest of them here and walk at graduation? Maybe get an apartment in this building. We could be neighbors. I could babysit." The hopeful expression she wears makes it impossible to be irritated by her suggestion.

Thankfully the doorbell rings and the Chinese food we ordered is here. Sitting at the kitchen table as she pays the deliveryman, I imagine what it would be like. Me, on my own. Raising my child, mine and Landen's child, alone. As much as I hate to admit it to myself, if Landen can't get control of his anger and his temper, then Corin might be right. But he can do this. I know he can. Just the fact that he went to the Allied Center proves he's a better man than his father could ever be. Because he wants to be more than anything.

Corin brings the food in and we're quiet throughout dinner, which is unusual for us. The light jovial mood from earlier has been replaced with tension that thickens the air between us. Finally Skylar stops by to drop off some notes from a class Corin missed, and I excuse myself to go lie down.

The sound of a baby crying startles me and I jolt upright. I'm in bed. Something beside me is ringing. But there's no baby. For a few seconds, I'm disoriented. Sitting up and noticing the plum-colored walls, I realize I'm in Corin's guest room. The light from beside me catches my attention. My phone.

Glancing over I see Landen's smiling face.

"Hey," I greet him, knowing he'll hear the heavy sound of sleep in my voice.

"Did I wake you?"

"Not really. I just woke up from a nap." Cradling the phone to my ear, I prop myself up on my pillows. Well, Corin's pillows. "How was today?"

He's quiet and I can tell something's wrong.

"Landen?"

"Fine, babe. It was fine. Just long is all."

"Same here. You want to talk about it?" I trace the ivy pattern of Corin's comforter with my free hand.

"Nah. I just needed to hear your voice." He's quiet for a moment. "Layla?"

I stifle a yawn to answer him. "Yeah?"

"I love you. And I'm trying to be ready for this, trying to be the kind of man worthy of being a father. I'm sorry if I haven't acted like it lately." The apologetic regret weighs down his voice.

I lie back all the way and stare at the ceiling. "I love you, too. And I know you're trying. It means a lot to me that you're trying so hard."

A muffled sound, almost like a sniffle or possibly static comes through the line.

"Landen?"

"Yeah," he says, his voice rougher than before. "Yeah, I just..." Through our less than stellar connection I hear him sigh. "I just don't want to be like him. God I don't want to be anything like he was."

The full weight of his words presses me down deeper into the mattress. "I know, baby. You won't. You aren't anything like him."

"I've been acting just like him, Layla. I've been treating you like you dumped this kid on me instead of seeing it for the miracle it is. Instead of being grateful to have someone strong enough and capable of loving our baby for the both of us while I grew the hell up."

Tears well in my eyes at his confession. He's right, and it hurts to accept, but it's true. "I know it's a lot to deal with. I didn't expect you to—"

"He isn't my dad, Layla. The Colonel, he isn't my biological father."

If I weren't already lying down, I'd fall over. "What? Landen, what are you—"

"My mom had an affair. I've been this constant reminder of her infidelity. Not to say that makes it okay, but...that's what he told me the day everything went to shit. I'm sorry that I didn't tell you sooner."

I'm so surprised I don't know what to say. He rushes on. "I've been trying to tell you every day since I found out but I...I just couldn't...deal. And I didn't want that to be another excuse for the way I am. It's not one. It's just something I have to accept and learn to handle. Like my anger issues."

My arms ache to wrap around him. The urge to ease the pain I hear in his voice is visceral. "God, Landen. I'm so sorry, baby. I wish I were there. I wish I could hold you and kiss you and just...make it better somehow."

"It's okay. Honestly, I'm glad to know the truth. I feel like...like it makes some kind of sense now. But it's still no excuse. I'm done making excuses and letting anyone else make excuses for me. I left you alone in this. I won't do that again, angel. I promise."

Nodding, even though he can't see me, I wipe my tears away. "I know. I knew you would get there. Eventually."

"Sorry, I took so long," he says softly.

"You were worth the wait."

CHAPTER Seventeen

Landen

Five weeks of the same routine is enough to make a man *need* therapy. Wake. Shower. Eat. Therapy. Exercise. Eat. Therapy. Read. Eat. Therapy. Sleep.

Wash. Rinse. Repeat.

Fuck me, I'm going insane.

And speaking of fucking, if I don't get to see my girl soon, I might die. Seriously. I get to talk to her on the phone every night before bed, so that helps. Though it's in a common room, and privacy is pretty much a foreign concept in this place.

But if I'm being completely honest? It was worth it. Coming here. Talking my shit out. For the first time in forever, I feel hopeful. I'm looking forward to getting back to Layla, back to Spain, and back to the team. Back to my life, which feels like it's been suspended in limbo for five long weeks. It feels good to feel hopeful.

That is, I felt hopeful. Right up until my final evaluation with Dr. Sanderson.

"So, Landen. This is your last week here. How do you feel about that?" She leans back in her chair and eyes me passively. Like she couldn't care less about my answer.

"Well, no offense, Doc, but I'm ready to get the hell out of here."

A small smile teases at her lips. "That so?"

I shrug. "I mean, no disrespect or anything. It's a nice place and I appreciate the fact that I'm not the only one with issues. I actually enjoyed group therapy a lot more than I thought I would. But yeah, I have a life to get back to."

"Understood," she says, leaning forward. "Let's talk about that life for a moment."

"Okay." I fold my arms because I feel like I've done nothing but talk about my life for the past thirty-five days. What the hell else is there to say?

"Tell me a little about what you're going back to."

I frown, unsure of what her game is. She already knows all of this. "You know. My job, my team, my girlfriend."

She nods. "Your pregnant girlfriend, right? The one with the brain tumor?"

"Hematoma," I correct her through clenched teeth. "Your point?"

She sighs and leans back in her chair. "My point is," she begins, aiming the pen she holds at my hands gripping the arms of my chair, "that your life still contains difficult situations that remain out of your control. True or false?"

"True," I relent.

"So I've got good news and bad news, Landen. Which would you like to hear first?"

"Whichever."

She stares at me for a moment. "Landen, your father…he was abusive. You've come to terms with that somewhat in the past few weeks. Yes?"

Fucking hell, I am over rehashing this shit. "Yeah. My mom had an affair when he was deployed. With a soccer player on a traveling team. Guy died of cancer a few years ago. It's all out in the open now. Why my dad hated me so much."

"Right. Well, can I be honest?"

"Please do," I answer.

"I think there's more to it than that. More to why you are the way you are and why he is the way he is. Would you like to hear my theory?"

"Isn't that what I'm paying you for?" Well, what the club is paying her for, but no need to split hairs at this point.

"I suppose. Okay, well…bear with me for a second." I don't say anything so she continues. "Landen, did you ever hear about the road rage guy a few years ago? He got out of his car and had a confrontation with a woman in which he grabbed the small dog from her car and flung it into oncoming traffic."

"Yeah, I guess. Sounds vaguely familiar. You think I have road rage?"

"No. And I don't think he did either. I think that what he had was actually something called Intermittent Explosive Disorder. He didn't have a criminal record or a history of violence. He did have a sudden outburst, which caused him to do something hurtful that most people wouldn't have done."

"I'm guessing this is the bad news portion of our session?"

She folds her hands in her lap. "It is. This is the part where I tell you that I'm pretty certain your father, or the man who raised you, has IED. And I'm fairly certain you have it as well. Childhood abuse is one of the leading causes."

"IED." I test it out in my mouth. It tastes like shit.

"Yes. Intermittent Explosive Disorder. I can give you some pamphlets or you can google it. Up to you."

I feel like a neon sign flashing the bright red words FUCKED UP is hanging over my head. "Okay. So how do we cure it? I mean, how do I make it go away before I toss Fido into traffic?"

She tilts her head and gives me an apologetic smile. The full weight of what she's saying settles onto my chest.

Shit. "There's no cure, is there? I'm stuck like this for life?" A lump constricts my airway. I try to think about the strategies I've learned these past few weeks. Deep breathing. Taking stock of the good things in my life. Layla. Soccer. Finally knowing the truth.

"Tell me what happens, Landen. When you first feel yourself getting angry. What happens?" The doctor sits right across from me but her voice is far away.

You are worthless.

"I hear him. My—The Colonel. Telling me I'm worthless. Pathetic. That I ruin everything." My voice sounds strange in my own ears.

"Breathe, Landen. Take a few deep breaths."

I do as she says.

"Focus. Stay with me, okay? There's more, Landen. Remember, I have good news too, okay?"

I open my eyes. I don't even remember closing them. "Right. Okay."

"Listen, lots of people go through things and come out better for it. I just watched you tamp down your anger all on your own. So that tells me you have been paying attention these past few weeks."

I nod, realizing she's right.

"Here," she says, handing me two squares of paper. "One of these is for your blood pressure. As expected, yours is pretty high."

"And the other?" I ask, glancing down at the unrecognizable scrawl on the pages.

She gives me a tense smile. "It's an antipsychotic."

"Holy shit. You think I'm psychotic?" Well this just went from bad to worse.

"Relax. No. You're far from it. But it also functions as a mood-stabilizer. At first it will make you sleepy. But once your body adjusts to it, which usually takes about two weeks, it will keep your physiological responses from sky-rocketing when you get upset."

"Do you think it will work? Keep me from having rages when I get angry?"

"That would be the hope. But if it doesn't, we can try Clonazepam, also known as Klonopin. It's been used from everything from seizures to anxiety."

"I'm actually familiar with that one. My girlfriend took it for a while. She has seizures. Or she used to have them. New medication seems to be working extremely well." Thank God. Another thing to be thankful for. My mouth goes dry at the thought of anything happening to my girl. Or the baby she's carrying.

"Ah. Well, here's the thing. And as a doctor, it might sound strange coming from me."

That gets my attention. "I'm listening."

"Ultimately, I don't want you to be on medication. I want you to be in therapy on a regular basis. I want you to use what you've learned here to keep yourself in check when things get out of control. So if it's up to me, meaning if I'm the doctor who oversees your care, we'll start with the heavy hitter, the antipsychotic, then we'll wean you down to a mild anti-depressant, and then hopefully, one day, we'll stop the meds altogether."

"When I'm cured."

"Um, no." She pins me with another sympathetic head tilt. They must teach it in med school. "The thing is, the *truth* is, there's no cure for IED. It's not something that goes away, Landen. It's something you learn to live with. To deal with in more appropriate ways than flying into a rage and breaking every stick of furniture you own every time you get upset."

She says something else. Actually, she rambles on for what seems like forever. But I don't hear her. All I hear are the words that ruin my life, shattering the picture of my family I have in my head. The one where Layla and I raise our kid in a safe, happy home like she wants.

I have IED. And there's no cure for it.

That past five and a half weeks have been a complete waste.

CHAPTER Eighteen

Layla

"He's here," Corin says. "Skylar just pulled up."

I barely refrain from squealing. I haven't seen Landen in six long weeks. I pull the striped shirt I'm wearing over the bulge protruding from my midsection, noticing how prominent it is for the first time. Suddenly I'm self-conscious about it.

"Keep your clothes on, Georgia. No doing it until after dinner at least."

I roll my eyes. But then panic sends my pulse into overdrive. "I'm nervous," I whisper to her.

"Aw. Sweetie. Don't be. I'm not exactly your baby daddy's biggest fan, but he went to that place for you. I can at least admit that that's a start. He obviously loves you very much."

I'm about to tell her that Skylar obviously loves her very much and press for details about how serious they are when he walks in.

"Hey. Landen's waiting for you outside, Layla."

My heart is racing but I'm grinning like an idiot. "Okay."

"He's down by the water."

"Thanks." I start to step out the back door when I realize I have more to say. "And um, thank you both. For hopping on a flight to Spain when I needed you. For letting me stay here, and just…for everything. Y'all know I don't have much in the way of family. In my head, y'all are my family."

"Dammit, Georgia. You're going to make me cry." Corin sniffles and wipes her hand roughly under her eyes. "Go get your fine piece of soccer ass already."

"Hey, I'm a fine piece of soccer ass, thank you very much," Skylar pipes up, pulling her to him.

She answers him with a kiss and I smile at the both of them. "I love y'all. Very much."

"We love you, too," Corin says, swatting Skylar on the arm as he says something into her ear I don't catch. "If he steps out of line out there, let us know. It's a big ocean. We can make him disappear."

I laugh, knowing she's only half kidding. Taking a deep breath, I step outside and make my way down the wooden steps to the deserted beach. Just as my feet hit the sand, Landen turns.

The sunlight glares off the water, sending light glinting all around him. It takes all the self-control I have not to break into a headlong sprint and launch myself into his arms.

Squinting up at him as I get closer, I bite my lip to keep from grinning maniacally. "Hey, stranger."

His navy polo shirt is tight on his chest and arms. He's been working out. His hair is a little longer than before, but other than that, he's the same. Still my Landen. My fine piece of soccer ass.

"Hi there, beautiful." He smiles but it doesn't reach his eyes.

"I've missed you," I say, reaching up to touch his face. It was only six weeks, but it was the most time we've ever spent apart. And it sucked.

"Me too, baby." His eyes drop to my stomach and widen. "Whoa."

"Easy. Make any mean jokes about my huge belly and I'll sic Corin on you."

He laughs as he puts his arms around me. "Pretty soon I probably won't be able to get my arms around you."

"Watch your mouth, O'Brien."

"Yes, ma'am. Hmm, speaking of mouths worth watching..." His mouth lands on mine and I open to him, moaning as his tongue sweeps inside. Suddenly I'm hyperaware of how long it's been since we've made love. Being turned on while pregnant seems to be a bit more intense than what I'm used to. Or maybe it's the time apart. Or both. I press myself against him, feeling the evidence of just how much he's missed me as well.

"Landen," I breathe, pulling him as close as humanly possible.

"I know, baby." His hands drop to my bottom and he gives me a firm squeeze. "But we need to talk, okay?" Placing a disappointingly chaste kiss against my lips, he sighs and pulls back.

"Okay. Want to tell me about it? I'm kind of dying to know and also unsure of what's okay to ask."

Landen takes my hand and helps me lower into the soft sand and sea grass. "You can ask anything you want."

"Was it awful?" I whisper into the wind. *Do you hate me*? I want to add but don't.

His eyes scan the ocean as he answers. "No, not awful. It was...enlightening,

I guess. I learned some things. A lot of things. It was awful being away from you though."

"Agreed. God I missed you." We both prop back on our arms, letting the ones closest to one another intertwine as we do. Leaning my head on his shoulder, I watch the waves. I wish I could freeze time. Put this perfect moment on pause and hold onto the serenity. "Do you think it helped?"

"I think…I think I don't know yet. Listen, Layla, I have to tell you some things. Some things that are going to be hard to hear."

Oh God. My world pitches and rolls right along with the ocean. "Oh-kay. Such as?"

He turns his head and our gazes collide. "Such as I have a diagnosis. And not a great one."

"A diagnosis?"

"Yeah. Apparently I have something called Intermittent Explosive Disorder. It's why I fly off the hinges. Why I get into fights, why I break shit, and why I still don't think it's a good idea for me to be a father."

"Landen, no, I don't—"

"Please just listen. Just hear me out, okay?"

Holding my breath in an attempt to hold back the tears, I nod for him to continue.

"What I have, an anger disorder caused by my—by The Colonel's particular brand of child rearing, it doesn't have a cure. I can't take a pill or see a doctor or whatever and make it go away. It's part of who I am."

"I love who you are," I say softly.

"I know you do. And God, Layla. I love you so damn much it doesn't even make sense. I grew up not even knowing what love was exactly. But you…you are the most amazing girl. Woman, I mean. You lost your parents, or they were taken from you, brutally and right in front of you. As a result, you end up with the kind of medical issues that soldiers who spend years in combat have. Plus a hematoma pressing on your brain. And you don't complain. You don't get angry. You just deal with everything head-on as it comes. I wouldn't even know how not to love you."

His words break my heart and make me smile all at once. But there's more. And from his expression, it doesn't look like it's a good kind of more. "I sense there's a but coming."

"But…you deserve better. The kid growing inside of you deserves better. And honestly, knowing what I know about myself, knowing there isn't a cure for this, I don't know if I can be better."

"You are exactly what we deserve, Landen."

He clears his throat and glances out at the water again. "I'm not, baby. I'm a fucked-up mess of a man who probably shouldn't be trusted with a goldfish, much less a kid."

"What are you saying?" I hold my breath as I wait for his answer.

"I'm saying I love you, and I want you and our child to have everything. The best of everything. Dr. Sanderson wants me to stick around a while and continue therapy. Next month I'll go back to Spain and move into team housing. I'm going to set it up with Coach so that my paycheck goes directly into your account. The one I think you should set up at a bank here. Where you should stay. We can talk to Corin about staying with her until we find a place," he says with a small attempt at a smile.

"No," I say evenly, heat building inside of me. "Who do you think you are, just making decisions for us?"

"Layla, calm down. I just want what's—"

"No. No I will not calm down. If you say one more word, I'm going to show you what an anger disorder really looks like." I'd jump up, but my little bump has made me less agile. "You listen to me, Landen O'Brien. You think you can just pawn us off on Corin and tell yourself it's for the best? Well I've got news for you. Big news. Ready? Brace yourself. This may come as a shock."

I wait until I have his full attention to continue.

"I'm pregnant. The baby is yours. No, it's ours. And we will raise it together and you will spend every day for the rest of your life trying your hardest to be the kind of man, the kind of father, I know you can be. To tell you the truth, I'm two seconds from asking Corin to make a call to her New York connections and having a hit put on The Colonel. I hate him for what he's done to you. For how he's made you feel. But let me tell you how you've made me feel. Do you have any idea what my life was like before you?"

"If it weren't for me, you'd have had surgery two months ago that would've saved your life, Layla." His voice is flat. Even. But his entire being is consumed with disgust. At himself.

I struggle for the words to help him understand. To make him see himself as I do instead of how his dad did. "Or I could've had a stroke and died on the table during that surgery, Landen. There's no way to know for sure. But here's what I do know. You taught me how to live. I was a walking corpse, going through the motions, getting through my life as if it were a prison sentence. In a lot of ways it was after my parents were killed."

He opens his mouth to interrupt me, but I place a finger over his lips. "I wallowed in self-pity, in self-doubt, and in the unfairness of it all. I was invisible, mostly because I wanted to be. And then you came along. And you blew my mind. You live. You live every second of your life one hundred and ten percent. Watching you on the field made my heart race—it still does. Being on the receiving end of one of your excited grins after you score a goal makes my life worth living.

"I love the kids I work with. I love Bridging the Gap and the fact that I look forward to each day I get in this life. I have a life in Spain, too, Landen. But more than anything, I want to be where you are. Because like it or not, we're family. You are my heart and my soul, and your passion for life inspires me to live mine." I pause to pull in more air so I can finish. My head swims as the truth overwhelms me.

"I will never, ever give up on you. I refuse to believe that you can't get control of this disorder, regardless of what anyone says. I've seen you in action. You're the most intense man I've ever known. You give everything you have to everything you do. You love me more than anyone has ever loved me. And yes, you hurt me more than anyone has ever hurt me. But I know you don't want to. You went into that place to get help because you want to be better, because you want to be a good father. I have no doubt in my mind that you will be. So stop doubting yourself. I have enough faith in you for the both of us." I stop to pull his face to mine with both hands. "You will never be like your father. You have something he never did."

"What's that?" he chokes out, searching for the answer in my eyes.

"Me," I whisper.

His eyes fill and he shakes his head. "I don't deserve you, Layla Flaherty. I never did."

"But you have me—always," I promise, resting my forehead on his. "And you knocked me up, so there's no getting rid of me now."

"I want you to know what you're getting, Layla. There's no cure for this. If at any time you wanted out, I would understand."

I stare straight into his eyes as I speak. "I will never want out. Never. Do you understand that?"

Fear fills his beautiful green eyes. "What if I lose it? What if I can't control myself and I lose your faith?"

"Then you will work your ass off to get it back. Same thing you do when you miss a goal, Landen. You get it back."

"What if you get tired of giving me second chances?"

I sigh, leaning in and wrapping my arms around him. "Love isn't measured in chances, Landen. When you love someone, there isn't a limit. As long as you keep trying, I will keep loving you. I don't even know if I could stop. Not that I'd ever want to."

His tears are slipping down his beautiful face and onto me. "Tell me what you want me to do, baby. I'll do whatever you want."

Pressing my back against his front, I take his hands and wrap his arms around me. His palms rest on my belly. A flutter under my skin startles us both. "Just hold me—us. Just hold us close. And don't let go. Ever."

For a few minutes we just sit there, wrapped up in each other. Until he breaks the peaceful silence. "I got you something," he says barely loud enough for me to hear. Despite my request for him not to let go, he removes one hand from my belly. I try to twist in his arms to protest but I'm not quick enough. A tiny black and white scrap of fabric lands on my stomach. I touch it gingerly and then glance up at his face. "Perfect fit," he says softly.

I smile at the tiny soccer ball beanie on my midsection and settle back in to his embrace. "Just like us."

CHAPTER Nineteen

Landen

SIX MONTHS LATER

"Dude, the bulge in your pants is distracting."

"Shut up, you jackass. I'm recording." The digital image of Layla on the screen as she gives her graduation speech doesn't do her justice, so I lift my head to see the real thing.

"You know everyone can see it. Hell, she probably already knows what's coming—I know she knows your dick isn't that big." Skylar laughs at his own joke.

"Can you two knock it off for five minutes, please?" Corin glares at us and snatches the camera from me so she can record the next part. The part that's going to change everything.

As soon as Layla finishes her speech about the children she worked with in Spain and steps down from the podium, I stand and walk up on stage. My damn hands are shaking so hard that they're racking my entire body. Everything that's ever happened to me, even the really shitty stuff, led me here. And even if she says no, I wouldn't change a thing.

Every cell in my body is singeing as if my blood has become electrically charged to the point of pain. "Layla Flaherty," I say as I meet her in the middle of the stage and sink down onto one knee.

Whoops and hollers and squeals reverberate all through the auditorium so loudly it's deafening, but I can't take my eyes off her. Off my beautiful girl. Still glowing like the angel she's always been. My angel.

"Landen?" she asks, her brow furrowed and her eyes wide. "What are you doing?"

My face breaks into a grin. "Would you please, pretty please with a cherry on top, do me the honor of being my wife, for as long as we both shall live?" Which I intend to be a very long time—for both of us.

It takes all my powers of concentration to hold the black velvet box steady as I present her with the ring I bought nearly a year ago in Spain. Before I knew we were going to be a family of three. Those gorgeous eyes shine down over her round belly at me as they fill with tears. "Yes, God yes, Landen. Yes, yes, yes!"

I jump up and grab her as one of the Administrators shouts, "She said yes!" into the microphone on stage.

Layla's very pregnant midsection is the only thing keeping me from crushing her to me. Our child. The one due in two weeks—just enough time to get back to Georgia so we can get married in a small ceremony her aunt's already got planned. Thank fuck she said yes.

I'm holding her tightly, and it's our moment. Even though I knew a long time ago that Layla was my forever. And that I was hers, if she would have me. But it's short lived. Because as soon as I let go and turn to escort my fiancée back towards her seat to the soundtrack of wild applause, she flashes her ring at Corin and Kate in the audience and her body stiffens and jerks away from me. I almost don't catch her before she goes down.

CHAPTER Twenty

Layla

The moment Landen drops to his knee in front of me is the happiest moment of my entire life. I'm acutely aware of every single smiling face in the auditorium as they clap and smile. The light catches the ring as I hold it out for everyone to see.

Time slows and I hear my own breathing.

In. Out. Blink.

"Oh, God. Layla," I hear his tortured voice say from far away.

And then…silence.

Chapter Twenty-One

Landen

I climb in the ambulance, answering the paramedics' questions as rapidly as they fire them off at me. How far along is she? Is she on medication?

I tell them everything I know, choking out the words over the lump of panic rising in my throat. Once they go to work on inserting Layla's IV, I yank my phone from my pocket and call the number Dr. Sanderson was able to get me for Dr. Kirkowitz's office.

A nurse promises to page him. I'm practically screaming at her that it's an emergency when she hangs up.

It might be seconds, or minutes later, when my phone buzzes in my hand.

"Dr. Kirkowitz?"

"Mr. O'Brien. My nurse said it was an emergency. I'm guessing Layla is going into labor."

"I don't know. She had a seizure. She's unconscious. We're on our way to the hospital right now. Can you meet us?"

He clears his throat. "Landen, I want you to know that I got your letter. I was once an underserving jerk myself and my wife, God rest her soul, was an angel as well. But without prior knowledge of Layla's—"

"Can you meet us or not? Look, please, just come to University Hospital as soon as possible. Please, I'm begging."

I hear him sigh on the other end. I'm a millisecond from losing control of myself when he finally speaks. "I'll be right there."

The ambulance jerks to a stop as I disconnect the call. I owe Dr. Sanderson my life for talking us to staying in California.

"Her doctor is on his way," I call out after them as they whisk her into the doors to the ER.

Now all I can do is wait.

Layla

There's a faint beeping sound in the distance. A bright light above me. People talking. But I can't make out what they're saying.

I want to ask them something but I can't remember what it is.

And then…darkness.

Chapter Twenty-Three

Landen

Sixteen. It's how old you have to be to drive a car in most states. And it's also the number of hours I spend in the deepest, darkest pit of hell wondering if the two most important women in my life are going to make it.

Wondering if I'm going to have to live in a world where Layla doesn't exist. Where the tiny creature with Layla's chin, according to the ultrasound picture, has been taken from me before she's even had a chance to wrap me around her tiny little finger.

Kate, Corin, Skylar, and my mom surround me in the private waiting room. But I don't want them here. I don't want anyone here. I don't want to have ever existed.

"She's so strong, Landen. She's the strongest girl I know," is all Corin can say. Over and fucking over as I clench my hands in my hair and stare at the floor. They've all developed these little chants of reassurance. What none of them say is, "It's going to be okay."

Because no one knows if it really is.

I'm being punished, is all I can think to myself. Punished for forcing myself into her life. For taking her to Spain with me instead of letting her live her own life. Punished for taking her virginity, for getting her pregnant before we were married. For the way I reacted when she first told me the news. For being the colossal fuck-up my dad always said I was. For not being able to get a handle on my own anger. I ruined my angel. And now she's paying for my weaknesses.

"Waiting is the hardest part," my mom says softly from somewhere beside me.

But she's wrong. If some doctor comes out here and tells me they didn't make it, or that one of them did but the other didn't, that will be the hardest part. Getting out of bed tomorrow with the world going on like everything good in it didn't cease to exist will be the hardest part. Looking at myself in the mirror and wishing I could go with them but knowing Layla would never forgive me for taking my own life will be the hardest part.

"Family of Layla Flaherty?" a voice says into the dimly lit room.

I literally propel myself out of the seat and towards the voice. And then I freeze where I'm standing. Because if the news is bad, I don't want it. I want one more minute, one more hour, where I can believe she can still be okay. If she'd left this world, wouldn't I have felt it somehow?

"I'm her husb—fiancé," I tell the man. *Please God, please give me a chance to be her husband. Please.* "Are they okay?" My voice breaks, and the doctor makes a face I can't decipher.

The man in scrubs—*fuck,* blood-covered scrubs—is a head shorter than me, but he holds my whole damned life in his hands. "Dr. Kirkowitz is coming to speak with you shortly." He must see my wild I'm-about-to-grab-you-and-shake-you-senseless expression because he rushes on. "They're okay," he informs us with a nod. "Mom just came out of surgery and is sedated, but baby is in the nursery and is healthy."

"Thank you. Oh God. Thank you, thank you, thank you." It takes everything I have to keep from dropping to my knees then and there.

"Can we see them?" Corin asks from within the huddle that's gathered behind me.

"Of course."

I don't wait to hear anything else before tearing out of the room and through the double doors. "Flaherty?" I bark at a nurse walking past, who points a dry erase board on the wall.

Rec Rm 1, it says next to her name.

"Where is Recovery Room one?" I bark again, barely resisting the urge to grab the tiny woman and shake her.

"Far end, last on the left," the same nurse tells me, eying me cautiously.

Of course. Layla's always made me work for it.

I sprint to the room, damn near ripping the door off the hinges as I yank it open. The soft white curtain is pulled closed, so I step around it. "Layla? Baby?"

Her head is bandaged and her eyes are closed. She's so pale her skin is nearly translucent, and her blonde hair fades into the pale yellow bed sheets. Why isn't she moving?

"She's sedated," the nurse, who must've followed me in, says quietly. "But she's okay. Surgery was successful."

"I n-need…" *Dammit, breathe, O'Brien.* "I need to see her. I need her to open her eyes and tell me she's okay herself."

"She'll come around. Just be patient."

Story of my life, lady.

Stroking what I can reach of Layla's hair, I lean down and place a gentle kiss on her bandage, then on each of her eyelids, then on her nose before pressing my lips to hers.

"I hope your name is Landen. Otherwise my fiancé's going to be super pissed," she murmurs against my lips.

Startled shock shoves a noise from my throat and I step back. "Oh God, oh dear God. I have never been so scared in my entire life. You can never, ever, ever leave me. Ever."

Everything that's been holding me rigid loosens, and I bend, letting my head fall to her chest so I can hear the beautiful music of her heartbeat. Tears burn fiery trails down my face, but wiping them would require moving.

"I won't. Well, I'll try not to. Landen, I don't understand. What happened?" Her small hand reaches up and fingers the bandage on her head. And then her eyes widen in panic as she reaches for her stomach.

The monitors around us begin beeping like crazy. "Shh, babe, it's fine. Everything's fine. Breathe."

"H-how is she, Landen? Is she okay?" I can see in her eyes she's doing the same thing I was. Stalling for a few more minutes of hope. "Can I see her?"

I grin. "She's healthy. The doctor told me just before I came in. Want me to have them bring her in?"

"Yes, more than anything." She's breathing so heavily that I'm worried, but I know it's excitement more than anything.

"Baby, you have to take it easy. As soon as the C-section was over, Dr. Kirkowitz performed the laser removal of your hematoma."

"He did? Wait, how—"

"Hey now, your aunt isn't the only one that can pull strings. I'm a pretty big deal, you know." I wink at her and she smiles.

"Did they say how the surgery went? Am I, I mean is it…gone?" Her voice is strained. I would get her some water if I could stand to be more than five inches away from her.

"The doctor said it went well. He removed the hematoma but I didn't wait around for details. I needed to see you."

As much as I don't want to tear myself from Layla's side, I'm as anxious to meet our daughter as she is. And I'm terrified. I'm thrilled that we're meeting her together, that she's healthy and has two living parents who love her. I could probably combust at any second. So I step into the hall and ask a different nurse, since the previous one has seemingly vanished, to bring in our daughter. From down the hall, I see my mom and Kate and the others heading our way.

"Can she have visitors?" Corin asks as they approach.

"Yeah, but she's been through a lot so just…you know..."

We've all barely squeezed quietly back into the room when a male nurse wheels a clear plastic cart in. Skylar claps me hard on the back. A pink bundle with a tiny soccer ball beanie on her head is wrapped inside. And then it hits me. I'm somebody's dad.

Please, please don't let me fuck this up.

Just as I wait for The Colonel's voice to remind me that of course I'll fuck it up, someone clears his throat in the doorway. I'm holding our daughter as Layla smiles sleepily at us with tears in her eyes. And he's here. The Colonel—in all his fully uniformed glory.

"How about we let Layla hold her?" my mom suggests, nodding to The Colonel and silently telling me to go speak with him.

Other than a phone call while I was at Allied, it's been years since we've spoken. Placing a kiss on Layla's and then my daughter's head, I hand Roxanne Hope O'Brien over to my mom.

"Be right back, baby," I promise Layla before I walk over to The Colonel. "Didn't expect to see you here, sir," I say, shaking my father's hand stiffly.

"Your mother called, and I just—"

I wait as patiently as I can while he clears his throat, but I'm practically twitching to get back to my family. *My family.* Jesus, what did I ever do right to deserve this? "Yeah?"

"I just wanted to say congratulations," he finishes.

He came all the way from Georgia to California to say congratulations?

"Okay. Thank you, sir."

I glance over to see Corin assisting Layla so she can hold Hope. We've decided she's going by her middle name—like her father. My career will have us moving around a lot and I don't want guys using 80's music lyrics as a way to charm their way into the new girl's pants. Suddenly I hate every single person with a dick on the planet. Layla's propped up and looking more alert than I expected while Kate and my mom take pictures.

God she's so damn beautiful.

"Well, I'll let you get back," The Colonel tells me, gesturing towards my daughter and soon-to-be wife. "Good seeing you…son." He nods, and so do I. "Yeah. Thanks."

He looks so…sad. Looking at him, I see a version of myself. The one I likely would have become if not for Layla. I feel bereft, but what else is there to say?

"Landen." I hear Layla call my name softly, but firmly, from across the room. She tilts her head towards The Colonel's retreating figure, and I know what she's reminding me of. You don't measure love in the number of chances you're willing to give someone. Love doesn't run out of chances.

God knows she's given me more than I deserve.

"Colonel? Um, dad?" I call out.

"Yes?" He turns back around to face me with his brows raised.

I shift on my feet. "Do you maybe want to hold her? Get a picture for the baby book? Since you came all this way, I mean."

A smile transforms my father's face into a version of him I can't remember ever seeing before. "I would like that, very much, yes."

And somehow, some way, Layla has given me everything I've ever wanted and didn't know I needed. That girl, that beautiful girl who floated through the halls like an unseen angel, who suffered such a devastating loss before I met her, has touched my life, brightened it, formed it. Made it worth living and helped me to focus on living it instead of punishing myself.

She gave me the strength to forgive. Kept me still when I was weak and stupid, when I lost my temper, when I got scared and ran and nearly made the biggest mistake of my life. And I vow, here and now, watching everyone fall in love with my perfect daughter before my very eyes, to never take a single second for granted. If Layla's surgery went as well as they say, she won't need me to keep her still anymore.

But it doesn't matter. I'm still keeping her forever.

EPILOGUE

"Daddy! Daddy! Did you see me? That's five! I beat my record!"

I watch my daughter run off the field to her father, her dark ponytail flying behind her. My husband drops his clipboard and lifts her into his arms. My heart swells with happiness as the love between them cocoons them in a private celebration.

"Mommy, did you see? Did you get it?"

I press the pause button and lower the video camera. "I got it, sweetie. Way to go, superstar!" I high-five her and stand on my tippy-toes for a kiss. She's a head above me in her father's arms.

"No kiss for the coach?" my husband asks, his green eyes gleaming with mischief.

"Hmm…okay. You're a superstar too, honey." I wink and make a kissy face just before his lips graze mine. Even after five years of marriage, a tingling sensation from his touch still overwhelms me.

"I'll show you superstar," he murmurs into my ear. For a moment, I'm lightheaded from his words.

"Landen! This is a family place!" I slap his arm playfully and reach up to tickle Hope. He grins as our daughter giggles before launching into her play-by-play recap of the soccer game we just watched.

"Can we go get ice cream now? I get extra sprinkles, Daddy. You promised!" Hope forces him to meet her gaze as he confirms he's going to follow through.

"Yes, ma'am. Extra sprinkles it is. And if Mommy is a good girl, she can have extra cherries."

I almost drop the video camera. And Hope's soccer bag. I clear my throat as we walk to the car. "Behave yourself, Coach."

"Never," he mouths, waggling his eyebrows at me.

I roll my eyes, even though anticipation coils tightly in my belly. Watching him fasten our daughter in her booster seat, I can't help but ogle his muscular backside. Later, when Hope's been bathed, and stories have been read, and she's asleep and the house is still and quiet, I know he'll make good on his promise to me as well.

He stands and closes her door. "Speaking of behaving yourself, I think you've got some drool there, Mrs. O'Brien." He grins, and I shake my head and step around to my side of our SUV. It's been almost five years since I've had an episode. As far as we know my surgery was a success, but I still don't drive—just in case.

We pull out of the parking lot and I glance around at the other families leaving. I can't help but wonder if everyone is as lucky as us. If they realize what a gift life is. How fortunate they are to be alive and healthy and able to come watch their able-bodied children play a game they enjoy.

"Grandma and Grandpa were there. I saw them. Grandpa waved to me," our daughter chirps from the backseat.

Landen's hands clench on the steering wheel as he pulls out of our parking space. I reach over and place my hand on his knee.

"They were, sweetie. They had some errands to run but said they'd be at the tournament next week for sure."

"Can they come have ice cream with us? Grandpa likes sprinkles, too!"

Rubbing what I hope are soothing circles on my husband's knee, I twist in my seat and crane my neck towards Hope. "Tell you what, how about they join us for dinner next week after the game? We can have ice cream for dessert."

Landen's muscles tighten under my hand. His parents reconciled after Hope was born. When The Colonel announced he was retiring to California so they could be near their granddaughter, no one was more surprised than us. Landen's relationship with his father is still strained. They're like warring countries that have declared a temporary truce. But I've seen the power my daughter has over The Colonel. Over everyone, really. But she owns him more so than anyone else, heart and soul.

Not that it erases Landen's memory of what his childhood was like. I don't expect it to. After his injury last year, I feared he'd destroy our family with his darkness once and for all.

Glancing at the smiling man next to me as my daughter agrees and chatters on about how she wants pink striped socks to cover her shin guards like so-and-so has, it's almost hard to picture the man he was a year ago.

In last year's playoffs, the opposing team's striker missed the ball and nailed Landen with a kick hard enough to tear three separate ligaments in his knee. We prayed it was just a sprain, something temporary. But when the final results came in, he knew. We both did. His career was over.

For weeks, he marinated in his own anger, sitting alone in silence, barely responding to Hope or to me as he struggled to recover from his injury. Thick clouds of disappointment shrouded him in a place I thought I'd never be able to reach him.

And I wasn't. It was Hope. Day after day, she'd climb into his lap, lay her head on his chest, and just sit quietly with him. This alone was a feat in and of itself, as Hope rarely sits quietly. Even when the physical therapist came to force him through his exercise routine, she stayed glued to his side.

Watching my beautiful full-of-light daughter even go near Landen when he was in such an awful place was difficult. He didn't yell or hit things or break anything, but I could feel the force of his pain and frustration radiating from him. My instincts said to grab our daughter and keep her as far from him as I could until after he'd self-destructed. I even considered taking her back to Georgia and staying with my aunt for a while.

I was standing in the kitchen making dinner and contemplating this when she began to pull him back to us.

"Why are you sad, daddy?" I barely heard her small voice from the next room. I stepped into the doorway to see his response.

Landen blinked a few times, as if he hadn't even realized she was there. He forced a smile and stared into her face. Again, I wanted to snatch her up so his pain couldn't spill out onto her. But I waited.

"I'm not sad, sweet girl. Just trying to figure some stuff out is all." He kissed her on the head and went to remove her from his lap.

But she wasn't done. Thank God for the tenacity of four-year-olds. "Do you still love me?" she asked, her voice quivering enough to shatter my heart.

He recoiled like she'd slapped him across the face. "Of course I do, baby. So much." He gave her a small squeeze and she frowned at him.

"Do you still love Mommy?"

I held my breath. I knew he still loved me. We'd been through worse than this. But I also knew his anger was a very dangerous part of him that could overshadow the loving man I knew if he let it.

"More than life itself, angel. I love you and Mommy more than anything. Always."

"More than soccer?" Hope shot back at him.

Landen nodded. "More than soccer, more than air, more than chocolate ice cream cones with extra sprinkles." She scrunched her face in disbelief and Landen rubbed his nose alongside hers.

Hope sighed in the dramatic way she has, placed a hand on her hip, and pinned him with her most serious expression. "Then what do you still have to figure out?"

Sometimes it really is that simple.

Later, we talked a lot about that day. About that entire year. About how Hope would ask him frequently if his boo-boo hurt and how he realized that she wanted him to get better because his behavior was hurting her.

This year he began coaching the men's soccer team at the state university just outside of our home in Sacramento. And of course he coaches Hope's pink-shin-guard, sock-wearing team on the weekends. He coaches both teams with equal enthusiasm—one of the many things I love about him. He never does anything halfway.

He's even remained passionately committed to controlling his anger disorder. He takes his medication religiously and still attends therapy twice a week. The guys he coaches would probably love to see him doing yoga with me in our living room every morning.

If you glanced at us right now, you'd probably be envious. We look like the perfect all-American family. I'm hugely pregnant, Hope's healthy and bright and beautiful, and my husband is handsome and successful. But if you look close, you might see our scars. We don't hide them. Like the broken seashells I once loved to collect, what marks us is what makes us who we are.

We wear our scars proudly, the one's we got on our way here. But we are here now. Walking into an ice cream shop as a family. Smiling, teasing, laughing. This is our happily ever after, where we keep each other still in smaller ways that don't involve seizures or angry rages—ways that need only a kiss, a hand on the knee, a hug. And this is where we will stay. Together. Loving each other with everything we have. Forever.

LANDEN'S *Letter*

Dear Dr. Kirkowitz,

You don't know me, but my girlfriend was scheduled to have laser removal surgery of a hematoma that's pressing on her brain several weeks ago. I'm writing to explain why she didn't.

I'm sure you get tons of letters like this one. Letters asking you to make an exception, to find time in your already slammed schedule for someone's loved one. I don't know that my letter will be any different or that it will stand out enough to make you take it seriously. But my hope is that it will. Because Layla—that's my girlfriend—is the most amazing girl, and she deserves a shot at a long, happy life more than anyone I know.

When we were in high school, Layla taught me about patience. She taught me to overlook the unkindness of others and find value in life beyond the day-to-day hassles that we tend to focus on. I grew up with an abusive father, who, as it turns out, isn't my father at all. Layla grew up without parents, because hers were shot by a mugger in front of her when she was just a kid. She was injured in the attack and her medical condition is a result of that injury. Most people would hold on to that, use it as an excuse or a place to lay blame for their problems. That's what I did. Not Layla. She uses it as a way to remind herself to appreciate the fleeting happiness that life has to offer. She sees the good in people—even people like me.

As I write this, I'm in a treatment center. I have a serious problem with anger. Most women would have cut me loose long ago, but Layla has stayed by my side, even when I've become the worst version of myself.

During the past few years, Layla's strength and dedication have taught me about love. I grew up unsure as to what that word meant. My mom said it often, but when I needed her to stand up to my dad for me, she didn't. So most of my life I questioned whether or not that word had value. If it existed in the truly unconditional form so many people claimed to feel. Until I received an opportunity to live my dream—to play professional soccer in Spain. No one was more surprised than me when the girl I loved showed up at the airport, uprooted her life, and moved to Spain with me. And I learned yet another valuable lesson. A dream is worthless unless the person you love is a part of it.

And this is the part where I make my desperate plea. Layla couldn't have surgery a few weeks ago when she was scheduled to because she is pregnant. As I write this, she is somewhere around eight weeks along. As much as I'm ashamed to admit it, I didn't take the news that we were expecting very well. The procedure you perform would have most likely saved her life, and if something happens to her now, then by getting her pregnant, essentially I am killing the one person I love more than life itself. The fact that she is willing to risk her own life to protect the life of our child is typical Layla. She's kind, selfless, and beautiful inside and out. I wish that you could meet her so you could see for yourself what my words can't do justice.

Layla is due in May, and it's my hope that you can arrange to be on standby so that as soon as the baby is born she can have the procedure. I realize that this is a lot to ask, and I know that my chances of getting this request granted are slim. But what were the odds that an Army brat like myself, an undeserving jerk with a temper, would get even a small amount of time with an angel?

I've already taken up enough of your time, but I have one last plea for mercy. You see, I have nightmares. In them, I'm taking my child to visit his or her mother in the cemetery. Because all they know of her is a cold marble stone instead of the warm, compassionate woman that she is. I'm not just asking this enormous favor for me. I'm asking for the unborn child that deserves to know what a wonderful mother they have. I'm asking for my girl. I'm asking that you give her a chance to be the kind of mother everyone should be fortunate enough to have.

I'm asking for my family. The one that I may or may not ever get a chance to have. I don't deserve it. But Layla does. I'm in this treatment facility so that I can be the very best father that I can. So that I can give our child what I never got. A happy home full of love and laughter. And patience. And acceptance. And hope.

You are my only hope right now. You're literally all I've got. Please consider my request. I can't offer you much except maybe World Cup tickets, but whatever I've got, it's yours.

I've included both my and Layla's contact information below.

Thank you for your time.

Sincerely,

Landen O'Brien

ACKNOWLEDGEMENTS

This book is so very special to me. It's the very first one I wrote from start to finish way back in July of 2012.

Special thank you to my wonderful critique partners and writing pals, namely Diane Alberts, who also writes as Jen McLaughlin, and who read the very first draft last March. You gave me so much valuable feedback that not only improved this book but all the ones I've written since. Without Emily Tippetts, I wouldn't have had the courage or the know-how to self-publish and my books probably never would've seen the light of day. She is truly a special and wonderful human being who I am beyond blessed to know.

I am extremely grateful to the super talented Sarah Hansen for all of her hard work and patience with me on this cover. Jessica Estep and Kelly Simmon are two people I owe huge thank yous to for their support and for taking me on as a client. Thank you both for all the wonderful things you do, not just for me but also for the entire book community. Love y'all very much! I feel truly blessed to be a part of the InkSlinger family!

Big appreciative hugs to Elizabeth Lee, Anna Cruise, Rachel Harris, Rahab Mugwanja, and Mickey Reed for all of your much-needed support. Thank you EL for promising me this story wasn't sucky crap. And Anna, you were dead on about the Thanksgiving scene. I hope I got it right! Rachel, you are so sweet and precious to me. Even in the midst of your own blog tours and book releases, you make time to help make my stories better. I can't tell you what that means to me. Mickey, you are my angel and without you, people probably wouldn't believe I was once an English teacher. Rahab, as always, your eyes miss nothing and I love you for it.

To those of you who take the time to read and review my books, you are all so very special to me. Thank you for your time, your support, and your honesty.

Of course I have to thank my wonderful family for always putting up with me when I'm stressed and losing my mind over fictional situations. Thank you for giving me the support and unconditional acceptance I need to live my dream.

So many people inspired me to write these characters and helped this book to become what it is, but the very first moment I knew I would write this story, this way, with this ending, was when I read *Bonds of Justice* by Nalini Singh. There was this line: **"We fit, you and I," he whispered looking into that haunting gaze. "Two broken pieces making a whole,"** that did something to my heart, to my soul, the moment I read those words. Thus Layla and Landen were born. I would be remiss not to mention it and thank that author for writing it.

Last, but certainly not least, thank you Parachute for recording the song *Kiss Me Slowly* that inspired Layla and Landen's first kiss.

ABOUT the Author

Caisey Quinn is the bestselling author of the several New Adult Romance novels featuring country girls finding love in unexpected places. She lives with her husband, daughter, and other assorted animals in Birmingham, Alabama. She wears cowgirl boots most of the time, even to church. You can find her online at www.caiseyquinnwrites.com or as @CaiseyQuinn on Twitter, where she spends entirely too much time chatting with readers, authors, and anyone who's willing.

AUTHOR'S *Note*

Seizure Disorders are extremely complex, and many of the causes are still unknown. My niece, the dedicatee of *Let You Leave*, suffers from grand mal seizures. In real life, wrapping your arms around someone having a seizure is not recommended. Please know that this story is fictional and is in no way representative of actual medical symptoms, medications, or procedures involved with seizures, PTSD, or hematomas. For more information on seizure disorders, I encourage you to visit the webpage of The Cleveland Clinic (my source when I had questions) or contact a health professional or specialist.

Intermittent Explosive Disorder (IED) is not something I made up. It's a very real medical disorder, though I took creative liberties in Landen's case, as this is a fictional story. The Axis Residential Treatment Facility in California is also a real place. I owe a huge thank you to the staff members who were kind enough to respond to my endless questions.

For more information about Anger Disorders such as IED, as well as the Axis Center, you can visit http://www.axisresidentialtreatment.com or http://www.axisresidentialtreatment.com/anger-management/intermittent-explosive-disorder/.

This paperback interior was designed and formatted by

www.emtippettsbookdesigns.blogspot.com

Artisan interiors for discerning authors and publishers.

Made in the USA
Lexington, KY
10 February 2014